CRASH INTO YOU

**His hands go to my waist—my waist!
And they feel so right. I like this
closeness.**

Maybe I like it too much. A guy has never been this close
to me. Never. And I can't believe it is happening, even if
it is to keep from being arrested.

My heart beats frantically in my chest. Isaiah is hot and
scary and hot. Why on earth would a guy like him want
to be anywhere near a girl like me?

It's the adrenaline rush. That's what it is. His arm shifts
and I love how that movement causes his muscles to flex.

Stop it, Rachel. It's the adrenaline rush. Focus.

'Kiss me,' he whispers. "'If you kiss me we'll blend in.'

My mouth drops open as if to make a sound, but nothing
comes out. How do I say the words…I don't know how
to kiss.

CRASH INTO YOU

Katie McGarry

MIRA Ink is a registered trademark of Harlequin Enterprises Limited, used under licence.

First published in Great Britain 2013.
MIRA Ink, an imprint of Harlequin (UK) Limited,
Eton House, 18-24 Paradise Road,
Richmond, Surrey, TW9 1SR

© Katie McGarry 2013

ISBN 978 1 848 45254 1
eBook ISBN: 978 1 472 01071 1

47-1213

MIRA Ink's policy is to use papers that are natural, renewable and recyclable products and made from wood grown in sustainable forests. The logging and manufacturing processes conform to the legal environmental regulations of the country of origin.

Printed and bound by
CPI Group (UK) Ltd, Croydon, CR0 4YY

Katie McGarry

was a teenager during the age of grunge and boy bands and remembers those years as the best and worst of her life. She is a lover of music, happy endings and reality television, and is a secret University of Kentucky basketball fan. She is also the author of *Pushing the Limits*, *Dare You To* and the novella *Crossing the Line*.

Katie would love to hear from her readers. Contact her via her website, katielmcgarry.com, follow her on Twitter @KatieMcGarry, or become a fan on Facebook and Goodreads.

CRASH INTO YOU

Isaiah

ELEVEN YEARS, TWO MONTHS, SEVEN days.

The last time I had physical contact with a blood relative.

The fingers of my left hand drum against the steering wheel and my right hand grips the stick shift. The urge to shift into First, slam the gas and hightail it out of the dismal gray parking lot pulses through my veins.

I force my stiff fingers to release the gear stick. Music could take the edge off, but the bass from the speakers vibrates in a way that could draw attention to my car hiding in the employee-only lot. From here, I can watch the visitors enter and exit the social services building.

Ninety minutes ago, my mother walked in. Now I need to see her walk out. With each intake of cold air, the itch to leave grows. So does the itch to meet her.

The heater died a half hour ago, and the engine stalled twice. A few more things to fix on the growing list. In need of a new resistor, the heater will be a cheap fix.

My cell rings. Without checking the caller ID, I know who it is, yet I answer anyway. "Yeah."

"I see you." Annoyance thickens my social worker's Southern accent. "She's waiting."

My eyes flicker to the corner windows close to her cubicle and six feet from my car. Courtney draws the shades and places a hand on her hip. Her ponytail swings from side to side like she's a pissed-off racehorse. Fresh out of college, she was assigned my case back in June. I guess her boss figured she couldn't jack me up more than I already am.

"I told you not to schedule a visitation." I stare at her as if we were in the same room. What I like about Courtney? She stares back. She's one of three people who have the guts to hold eye contact with an inked seventeen-year-old with a shaved head and earrings. The second one is my best friend. The third...well, the third was the girl I loved.

Courtney sighs and the ponytail stills. "It's Christmas Eve, Isaiah. She showed early *and* brought you presents. She's waited patiently for a thirty-minute visitation that should have ended forty minutes ago."

Waited. Patiently. My neck tightens and I roll it from side to side to keep from blowing steam at the wrong person. "Ten years."

I throw those two words at her every time she mentions my mother. Courtney drops her chin to her throat. "Don't do this. She had her reasons, and she wants to talk to you."

I raise my voice and pound my hand against the steering wheel. "Ten years!"

"It could have been fifteen, but she was a model prisoner," she says, as if that was a concession on Mom's part. "She wrote you once a week."

I glare at Courtney through the windshield. "Then be *her* social worker if you're up her damn ass so much. She's been out for over a year and she's just now coming to visit."

"Isaiah," she says with defeat. "Come in. Give her a chance."

I place one foot on the clutch and the other on the gas. My engine roars with anger and the car's frame vibrates with the need to run. Third Street ends at the social services building and my parking spot gives me a straight shot to the clear strip of road. Give Mom a chance? Why should I? When have I been given one?

"You have no idea what she did," I say.

"I do." Courtney softens her voice.

"I'm not talking about why she went to prison." I shake my head as if the action can dispel the memory playing in my mind. "You have no idea what she did to me."

"Yes, I do." A pause. "Come in. We can work this out."

No. It can never be worked out. "Did you know that the lights on Third Street are on a timer?" I ask her. "And that if you hit the sweet spot speed you can cruise the entire strip without hitting a red?"

Courtney bangs her fist against the glass. "Don't you dare!"

I rev the engine again. "Ever hit a quarter mile in ten seconds, Courtney?"

"Isaiah! You'd better—"

I hit End and toss the phone onto the passenger seat. Focusing on the red light, I shift into First as my foot hovers over the gas. Speed. It's what I crave. I can race the emotions away. The light turns, I release the clutch and my body slams into the seat as my foot crashes down on the gas.

Is it possible to outrun memories?

Rachel

WAITERS IN WHITE FRANTICALLY STEP out of my way as I race down the hall. The expensive art on the wall becomes a colored blur the faster I go. My breath comes out in a rush and my dress ruffles and crinkles against itself. I'm creating too much noise and garnering too much attention. None of that is good when I'm trying to make a quick getaway.

My heels dangle in my right hand and I lift the hem of my shimmering blue-gray ball gown with the other. Cinderella ran away because her coach was going to turn back into a pumpkin. I'm running away because I'd rather be knee-deep in axle grease.

Rounding another corner, I enter the desolate hallway near the country club's kitchen. The sound of the crowd laughing and the rhythmic beats of the jazz band become muffled the farther I run. A few more steps and I'll be home free in my sweet, sweet Mustang.

"Gotcha!" Fingers slide onto my arm and I experience whiplash. My hair stings my face as it flies forward, then back. One hand-curled spiral strand of blond bounces near my eye when it breaks loose from the jeweled clip holding the sides of my hair.

My twin brother turns me to face him. A hint of laughter plays on his lips. "Where are you going, sis?"

"Bathroom." To the parking lot and as far as possible from the ballroom.

Ethan points back toward the long hallway. "The girls' bathroom is that direction."

I lean into my brother. My eyes widen and I wonder if I look crazy, because I feel a little crazy. "Mom wants me to give a speech. A speech! I can't give a speech. I can't! Do you remember the last time Mom put me on display? Two years ago when she threw us that horrid 'surprise' fabulous fifteenth birthday party. I vomited. *Everywhere*."

"Yeah, I was there. It even grossed me out." His face twists in mock disgust. Ethan is laughing at me and I cannot be laughed at—at least not now.

I grab hold of his white button-down dress shirt and shake him. Or try to. The boy doesn't budge. "It took me months to find the nerve to talk at school again. Everyone there has long memories, Ethan, and they've just now forgotten. I would like to be kissed before I graduate from high school. Boys will not kiss girls who keep vomiting."

"Have you ever noticed you talk a lot when you're on the verge of a panic attack?" Ethan's kidding, but my panic is real. I'm close to an attack—very close. And if I don't get out of here soon, he'll discover my secret.

"Besides," he continues, "that was two years ago. So you hate public speaking. You'll sweat a lot, stutter a little and move on."

I swallow. If only that was my worst fear.

Ethan's my opposite. He resembles Dad with black hair and dark eyes, he's a good foot taller than me and he's brave. His eyes narrow and he tilts his head as the last word of my outburst registers. "You said *vomit*. Which means an actual panic attack. I thought you were over that."

My fingers curl tighter into the material of his shirt. I messed up. How could I make such a careless mistake? For two years I've kept this secret from my family: that I still suffer from panic attacks. That when I'm the center of attention or too anxious or stressed, I become paralyzed and lose the ability to breathe. Nausea will coil in my stomach, bile will rise in my throat and the pressure will continually build until I throw up.

Life has been hard on my parents and two oldest brothers. I made the decision after the horrendous birthday party that they would never have to worry about me—the child who won't die from her illness.

"I am over it," I say. "But I don't want to make a fool of myself. I...I..." Can't think of anything good enough to get myself out of this. "I forgot my speech and I left my notes at home and I'm going to sound like an idiot." Wow—fantastic save. "Look, I'm calling twin amnesty on this."

His eyes search my face, I'm sure assessing my level of near-crazy. Years ago, we agreed to cover each other ten times in a year, regardless of repercussions. Ethan burned through his amnesty cards weeks ago and knows I usually use mine for midnight drives so I can push the speedometer on my Mustang.

"You've got one amnesty card left this year," he says as a blatant reminder that in a few days, when the new year rushes in to greet us, we'll be starting with a clean slate and I'll be covering for him again.

"Are you sure this is the hand you want to play the card on?" he continues. "Do the speech and then I'll cover your ass when you sneak out to drive the Mustang later. Driving always makes you feel better, and this ride should be relatively guilt-free. It'll be your first legal midnight run."

My brother enjoys reminding me that my infatuation with driving late at night was illegal on my intermediate license. Ethan's right—I love to drive and I have a full license now. The only way I'll get caught for breaking curfew is if Ethan blows my cover or if I leave before the speech. Either one of those options will mean a grounding for life.

All of this should be taken into consideration, and I should be thinking it through logically, but I abandoned logic back in the ballroom. My pulse begins to throb in my ears. "Yes." Definitely. "Yes, I'm playing the card now."

He lets go of my arm and glances down to where my fingers are still clutching his shirt. "I didn't see you. Do you understand? You slipped out the entrance and we never talked. I'm not taking heat from Gavin for this, twin amnesty or not."

"Not taking heat for what?" Gavin's deep voice calls from down the hallway. My hope disintegrates and falls to the floor. Crap. I'm never getting out of here.

I force myself to release Ethan and fake the smile on my face even though my heart thuds against my rib cage. My brothers are used to my disposition, what Ethan annoyingly refers to as sunshine and rainbows. I'm *so* going to be sun-

shine and rainbows if it kills me. "Hi, Gavin. I saw you dancing with Jeannie Riley. She's nice."

Gavin's the oldest of my parents' brood of five children.
We're a close family, even though a huge age gap extends between the siblings. Gavin was eight and Jack was seven when
Ethan and I were born. Jack stands beside Gavin and they
both fold their arms over their chests when they see me and
Ethan. Guess this time I didn't feign sunshine and rainbows
well enough.

"Mom's looking for you," says Jack. "It's time for your
speech." Jack's quiet and that may be his longest monologue
for the night. Which makes it rough for me to say no to him.

"Come on, Rach," Gavin says. "You're the one that ap-
proached Mom and Dad about speaking at this event. Not
the other way around. You need to get over this fear of being
in the spotlight. It's in your head. It was one thing when you
were seven, but it's gotten old. You're a junior in high school,
for God's sake."

Gavin's right. I offered to speak at the leukemia event. A
couple of weeks ago, I stumbled upon Mom crying over a picture she'd found of her oldest daughter, Colleen, and I hated
the pain in her eyes. I had overheard Mom mention a few days
before to a friend that she'd always dreamed of me talking
on Colleen's behalf. When her friend suggested Mom should
ask me to participate at this fundraiser, Mom declined, telling her she'd never put me in a situation that made me uncomfortable.

Mom's been in hell for over twenty-one years and the sole
reason for my birth was to make her feel better. She still cries,
so I guess that means I haven't done a very good job.

My stomach cramps and my hands begin to sweat. It's coming—the attack. I try to remember what the therapist in middle school said about breathing, but I can't breathe when my lungs won't expand.

"I changed my mind," I whisper. "I can't do the speech." I need to get out of here fast or everyone will know that I've been lying. They'll know I still have the attacks.

"Are you really going to let us down?" asks Gavin.

The squeak of the back door announces the arrival of my last brother. In one easy stride, West lopes into our private circle. The two of us favor Mom with our blond hair and eyes so blue they almost appear purple. Along with his white tux shirt and undone bow tie, West wears a baseball cap backward. "Not sure what's going on, but you should leave my little sister alone."

"Get that hat off, West," says Gavin. "Mom told you she didn't want to see a thing on your head until tomorrow morning."

Gavin leads us. He always has. But just because the four of us have always followed doesn't mean we think Gavin's awesome. In fact, Ethan, West and I find Gavin annoying. Jack is Gavin's best friend.

West pulls the cap off his head and flashes the smile that says he's playing the field...again. "There was a girl and she likes hats."

I roll my eyes as my brothers chuckle. There's always a girl. Less than a year older than me and Ethan, West is our high school's version of the guys from an MTV reality series that sleep with a new girl each night. And lucky us, Ethan and I have front row seats to watch West's show. "You're a pig."

West waggles his eyebrows at me. "Oink."

Gavin points at West. "No hat." West shoves it in the back pocket of his dress pants.

Then Gavin turns on Ethan. "She's not getting out of this, so stop trying to snatch her keys."

My head jerks to the small matching purse attached to my wrist and I catch Ethan dropping his hand, my keys in his fist. Gavin motions with his fingers for Ethan to relinquish them. With a huff, Ethan tosses to my oldest brother my only chance at escape.

Gavin raises his arms at his sides as he nears us. It's a gesture that makes me feel part of this inclusive family, yet the action also makes Gavin, who is already massively built, larger. His frame so encompasses the small hallway that I draw my arms and legs into my body in order to give him more room. Each of us responds to Gavin in our own way, but I always withdraw because I am the youngest, the lowest and the weakest.

"This is important to Mom and Dad," says Gavin. "And if you don't get in there and say a few words, you're going to disappoint both of them. Think of how upset you'll be later tonight when the guilt eats at you."

A lump forms in my throat and my lungs tighten. Gavin's right. I hate disappointing Mom and Dad, and I don't handle guilt well. But at least if I choose to bolt, I won't run the risk of humiliating myself in public.

"Rach," Gavin pleads. "This is important to them."

"To us," adds Jack.

I inhale deeply to keep from dry heaving. Mom and Dad have thrown this event during the week between Christmas and New Year's for the past sixteen years. It means the world not only to them, but also to Gavin and Jack. My strongest allies, Ethan and West, both lower their heads. For the three of us, this night reminds us why we're alive, why Mom had more kids. She longed for another girl.

West shuffles his feet. "Breathe through it, okay. Look at me or Ethan while you talk."

Ethan shrugs one shoulder. "Or look at Gavin and pretend he's grown antlers to match that obnoxiously large snout of his."

Gavin flips Ethan off and soon my brothers toss insults like athletes toss balls. I don't want to give a speech. My brothers see me as weak, and maybe I am, but how do I make them understand I have no control over the panic that consumes me? "Why me? Why not one of you?"

My questions stop the flurry of insults. The four of them exchange long glances. I know the answer, but if I have to do this, then someone has to admit it out loud.

"Because," says Gavin. "You're the one Mom wanted."

No, I'm not, but I'm the best replacement Dad could give her. I close my eyes and try to find some sort of center. I'll do it. I'll give the speech. If I'm lucky, the worst thing that will happen is that I'll stutter and shake my way through the performance. Why did Mom and Dad have to invite West and Ethan's friends this year? Just why? "I'm never going to be kissed."

I open my eyes to see my brothers gaping at me like I've lost my mind.

"You don't kiss boys," says West. "Boys shouldn't be anywhere near you. Guys only want one thing, Rach, and it ain't conversation. I should know." He waves off the subject in frustration, then shakes his head as he speaks again. "Why are we even talking about this? You aren't seeing anyone."

"Ah, hell," mumbles Jack. "We're having the sex talk with my baby sister."

"Is she dating?" Gavin demands of West and Ethan. "She can't be dating. Now we have to beat the snot out of some horny teenager. You should have told me this was going on."

"Make them stop," I whisper to Ethan. Along with the dread of speeches and vomiting, I'm also dying of embarrassment.

"She's not dating!" West shudders as if spiders cover him. "That's just sick, Rach. Don't talk like that. Ever. Again."

Gavin sends me a glare clearly meant to warn me off from kissing and dating boys before he heads for the main ballroom. The look is lost on me as either of those things happening would require a guy first showing interest in my general direction.

Jack and West follow Gavin, both mumbling about having to beat up boys. Ethan locks an arm around my neck and pushes me forward. "Two sentences. Three tops."

Easy for him to say. He's not the one that has to stand in front of hundreds of people. Each of them hanging on my every said and unsaid word. The adults' eyes judging my shaking hands and quavering voice. Anyone age eighteen or below will giggle as they remember my past failure involving a crowd.

With each step, my knees tremble as if they're going to buckle and a cold sweat breaks out along the nape of my neck. My stomach lurches and I clap a hand over my mouth. As I fall back against the wall, Ethan's eyes widen with concern.

My gaze flickers to our brothers and he jumps in front of me, blocking their view.

"Give me a sec with her," he calls out. "I promise she won't run."

"Ethan," I warn, the moment I hear the doors to the ballroom click shut.

Ethan presses his hand into my back, edges me into the women's bathroom and locks the door behind him. I drop my shoes and they clatter against the floor of the empty restroom. I stumble and trip over my big, fluffy dress and barely catch the toilet. Water runs in the sink behind me and Ethan approaches when I'm able to breathe for thirty seconds without retching.

He hands me a cold, wet paper towel. "Was there blood?"

I wipe my face gingerly. "No. Don't tell Mom or Dad, okay? Or anyone else."

"What the hell? I thought you hadn't had an episode since freshman year." I wince from the mixture of anger and reprimand in his tone.

I hate this illness. I hate it in ways that make my blood run cold and my muscles heavy with rage. I hate the way my family has always looked at me as if I'm breakable. I hate how I've been a constant disappointment when each of my brothers has excelled at so many public things like sports or debate teams.

I'm always off in the shadows and after my disastrous fifteenth birthday, I decided to suck it up and force a happy public front even if I'm dying inside. My facade must be working if Mom and Dad permitted me to make the speech when I offered. They'd never do anything to purposely upset me.

"Have you been throwing up this entire time?" Ethan persists.

"Leave it alone."

He rubs his eyes. "Mom and Dad want to know when you have a panic attack. I want to know. This isn't a game."

My temples throb. I'm the weakest member of this family. I always have been. "If I tell them, they'll send me home and Mom will hover. You guys are right. I'm a wuss and I can get through this. Tonight isn't about me. It's about Mom and Dad. This is their night to remember Colleen, and I can't stand in the way of that, okay?"

Ethan slides down the wall and sits beside me. "I'll cover you tonight. Get through the speech, then go for a drive. I'll make sure you aren't missed." He sighs. "I'll do anything to keep you from getting sick again."

Isaiah

I ENTER THE OLD TWO-STORY house converted into apartments and I'm greeted by the sound of Elvis Presley's "Blue Christmas" still carrying through the first-floor apartment's door. Skipping the third and sixth steps because of dry rot, I climb the stairs and slip into the door on the right.

I've been here since August, even though Courtney believes I live in a foster home. What she doesn't know doesn't hurt me. My assigned foster family agreed to let me move out as long as I stay clear of trouble and they keep receiving their checks from the state.

Plaster flakes from the walls when a train rolls by, the wood smells like old men when it rains and rats the size of rabbits call it home, but this place beats the hell out of foster care.

Noah walks out of the bedroom with a smug smile and no shirt. "Hey, baby, Isaiah's back."

"Hi, Isaiah!" Echo pops her head around the halfway-open door to the bedroom. Her red curls flow over her shoulder.

"Hey, Echo," I say in return as she closes the door. A trail of shoes, Noah's shirt and Echo's sweater make a path from the couch to the bedroom. Looks like the two enjoyed my belated Christmas present to them: time alone.

Noah picks their clothes up off the floor. He knocks on the bedroom door, opens it and mumbles something as he hands her the sweater. Noah has tried to play it off for a couple of weeks, but he's worried about her. To be honest, so am I. Echo began covering her arms again last week.

He touches her face as he talks to her. It's a simple touch, but one she responds to by hugging him. I once thought I had found what Noah and Echo share: love. But I was mistaken, or maybe I was too late. Either way, I fucked up.

Noah shuts the door, giving Echo privacy, and clears his throat. "Thanks, bro."

"No, problem. Is she, ah...okay?"

He shrugs his shirt on. "Her mom's been screwing with her, using the excuse of the anniversary of Echo's brother's death in order to do it. I don't understand why Echo gives her the time of day. Her mother is a worthless pile of shit."

Noah pauses, waiting for me to agree, but I'm not interested in being a hypocrite. I spent two hours last week stalking my mother in a parking lot. Evidently, Noah is a magnet for people with mom issues. Not that he would know it. The only person I told about my mother's release from prison was Beth, and I haven't talked to Beth in over two months.

"Everything all right?" asks Noah when I say nothing.

I think about it—telling him that my mom was released from prison over a year ago and has just now requested a visit. Noah and Echo are the closest thing I have to a family and it would be nice not to carry the burden of the secret around by myself. To have someone empathize with what it's like to have been thrown away as a child.

I could even tell them why she went to jail and how I was part of it.

As I start to answer, my eyes rest on Noah's new stack of college textbooks. Noah wouldn't get it. Technically, he wasn't a throwaway. "I'm good."

I open the door to the refrigerator and find the same scene as this morning: two beers and nothing else. "Guess we should have hung a stocking in the fridge, man."

"Fuck that," says Noah. "We need to put a stocking in a savings account."

He sits on the only piece of furniture in the living room besides the television: the couch we bought for thirty dollars at Goodwill. Noah and I live simply. We have a closet called a bedroom, two mattresses with box springs, one bathroom, and one larger space that contains our living room and a kitchen. *Kitchen* is a loose term. It consists of one sink, the refrigerator, two cabinets and a microwave.

Noah holds his hands between his knees and bends his head as if he's lost in prayer. My best friend isn't a heavy guy and this load he's shouldering—it's weighing down the room.

"Your student loan didn't come through, did it?" I ask.

Noah kneads his eyes. "I need a 'responsible' adult to co-sign."

"That's bullshit." It's like the world wants people like me and Noah to fail.

"Is what it is."

"Did you ask anyone to help?" Noah's got some nutcase therapist he's been close to since last spring, and he's been working things out with his younger brothers' adoptive parents.

"Cosigning a loan isn't asking for gas money."

He gives no indication of whether he let pride get in the way or whether he sought help and people said no. Because of that I let the subject drop. Me digging would only be shoving the stake in further.

"I hate to ask," says Noah, "but how much can you contribute to bills this month?"

Not much. Business at the auto shop where I work has been slow and what little work they do have is completed while I'm in school. Plus what money I have scraped up after bills, I've given to Echo to pay off a debt I owe her.

A debt I took on because of Beth. When the familiar ache flashes through my chest, I immediately deflect all thought to the subject at hand. "How much do we need?"

Noah cracks his crazy-ass grin. "All of it. I used my last paycheck to buy the books I need for next semester and that jar of peanut butter we've been eating from this week."

His smile wanes and the heaviness returns. "When we agreed to move out of foster care together I thought I'd be taking on more hours at the Malt and Burger instead of dropping them, but you know..."

Noah looks away. His grades took a nosedive in the first semester of his freshman year. My best friend is a smart son-of-a-bitch, but the transition from high school to college kicked his ass. In order to raise his GPA, the hours at work went down. That student loan was his last-ditch effort to find a way to exist.

"Ask Echo to move in," I suggest. "You spend all of your

free time together. A third body could help with bills. You two can have the bedroom and I'll crash on the couch."

He cocks his head as he contemplates, then shakes it. "Her scholarship covers everything and she's too focused on school and her art to make decent money." A rat scurries from one corner and disappears into another. "Besides, visiting is one thing. Living here is another."

True. His depression becomes contagious and I lean against the refrigerator. "Say what you gotta say, man."

"The one advantage of graduating from foster care is that the state pays for my college tuition. They'll also pay for me to stay in the dorms."

My stomach sinks like I'm falling down a damn well. He's looking to take advantage of the deal he gets for being a system kid and he wants me to return to the foster home we shared before he turned eighteen and graduated. "I can't go back to foster care."

"You have five more months until you graduate," Noah says. "Shirley and Dale weren't that bad. They were the best foster home I had."

"And they're Beth's family," I snap. At my side, my fists open and close. I gave the girl everything inside of me and she still walked. There's no way I can crawl back to her aunt and uncle and beg for them to take me in again, and I'd rather die than go into another home. "There's got to be another way." There has to be.

"I get it," Noah says. "I was there in hell right along with you, but we're drowning here."

"What if I find a way to make it work? What if I raise the money?"

"How?" Noah's mouth tightens.

"Just let me fix this." 'Cause I can, but in ways Noah doesn't want to know about.

Neither one of us blink as we stare at each other. Yes—we've both experienced hell, and Noah promised me when he graduated from the system that he wouldn't leave me behind.

Noah nods right as Echo opens the door to the bedroom. She stretches her long sleeves over her fingertips. I swear under my breath. She's definitely hiding her scars again. The girl has had a messed-up life and last year she finally found the courage to not give a shit what people thought of her. Leave it to a mom to reappear in her kid's life and jack everything up. Echo and I would have been better off raised by wolves.

Noah pulls her into the shelter of his body. "Ready to roll?"

Right, dinner with Noah's younger brothers' adoptive parents. Noah and I—we're brothers despite not sharing blood, and Echo became my sister the day she put a smile on his face. They're my family and I'm going to fight to keep what's mine. "I think I'll miss this one. I got business to take care of."

Rachel

THE DRIVER'S SEAT OF MY Mustang is one of the few places where I find peace. I guess I could go on some tangent about how my older brothers influenced my love of cars, but I won't, because it's not true.

I get cars. I like the feel of them. The sound of them. My mind clears when I'm behind the wheel and there's something about the sound of an engine dropping into gear as I press on the gas that makes me feel...powerful.

No fear. No nausea. No brothers to boss me around. No parents to impress. Just me, the gas pedal and the open road. And a big, fat, fluffy dress that reminds me of a flower. Shifting in this getup was a nightmare.

The fluff from the ball gown pops out of Ethan's old gym bag, and I try to shove the overflowing lace back in as I exit the gas station bathroom. No matter how I try, the fluff won't fit. I wind through the aisles and out the automatic doors into the cold winter night. My parents would kill me if they knew I was on the south side of Louisville, but this isn't my destination. Just a pit stop. The county south of here contains backcountry roads that are flat for several miles. Perfect for maxing out the speedometer.

Two college-age guys in jeans and nice winter coats chat as one pumps gas into a 2011 Corvette Coupe. She's impressive. Four hundred and thirty horses are compacted into that precious V-8 engine, but she's not as pretty as the older models. Most cars aren't.

On the opposite side of the pump, I insert my credit card and unscrew the gas cap. My baby only receives the best fuel. It may be more expensive, but it treats her engine right.

I suck in a breath, and the cold air feels good in my lungs. My stomach had settled when I left the country club and the nausea rolled away when I turned over the engine. I'd made it through the speech with shaking hands and a trembling voice. Only a few people from school laughed.

When it was over, my mother cried and my father hugged me. That alone was worth the trips to the bathroom.

The guys stop talking and I glance over to see them staring at my baby.

"Hey." The driver nods at me.

Did he just talk to me? "Hi."

"What's going on?"

Uh...yep, he just talked to me. "Nothing." This is called conversation. Normal people do it all the time. Open your mouth and try to continue. "You?"

"Same as any other day."

"I like your 'Vette," I say and decide to test them. "V-8?" Of course it has a V-8. It's the standard engine for the 2011 'Vette, but some guys have no idea what sweet cargo they own under the hood.

The owner nods. "3LT. Got her last week. Nice Mustang. Is it your boyfriend's?"

Loaded question. "She's mine."

"Nice," he says again. "Have you ever raced her?"

I shake my head. It feels strange to talk to guys. I'm the girl who hangs on the periphery. The other girls who attend the most expensive private school in the state don't want to discuss cars, and most guys get intimidated when I know more about their car than they do. When it comes to any other type of conversation, my tongue often grows paralyzed.

"Would you like to race?" the guy asks.

Our gas nozzles clink off at the same exact time and my heart flutters in my chest with a mixture of anxiety and adrenaline. I'm not sure if I want to faint or laugh. "Where?"

He inclines his head away from the safety of the freeway and down the four-lane road—deeper into the south end. I've heard rumors of illegal drag races, but I thought they were just that—rumors. Stuff like that only happens in movies. "Are you for real?"

"It doesn't get any more real than where I'd be taking you. Stick with us and we'll help you get a nice race."

I have four brothers, and one is the type that mothers warn their daughters against. In other words, I'm not that naive, but to be honest, his proposal intrigues me. But I'm also sure this is how horror movies begin.

Or the best action flicks on the face of the planet.

I lift the nozzle, place it back on the pump and scan the guy's car out of the corner of my eye. A University of Louisville student parking tag hangs on the rearview mirror along with a maroon-and-gold tassel. Only my school has those god-awful colors.

But to be safe... "Where did you go to high school?" I ask.

"Worthington Private," he says with the arrogance most guys from my school use when saying the word *private.*

"I go there." And I don't bother hiding my grin.

Neither do they. The car owner continues to be the spokesman for his duo. "What year are you?"

"A junior."

"We graduated last year."

"Cool," I say. Very cool. My brother would be a year behind him, but West has made it his business for people to love him. "Do you know West Young?"

"Yeah." He brightens. I've seen that look before with guys as they talk to other girls at school. 'Vette boy thinks he's so close to scoring. It's hysterical that he has that expression with me. "He's a hell of a guy. Do you two party together?"

I laugh and I can't stop myself. "No. He's my brother."

Their smiles melt quicker than a snow cone on a summer's afternoon. "You're his baby sister?"

"I prefer to be called Rachel. And you are?"

He runs a hand over his face. "Going to get my ass kicked by your brothers. I saw the last guy that pissed off West Young and I'm not interested in a nose job. Forget I said anything about racing, or that we even saw each other."

As he inches to his car, I spring over the small concrete barrier. I only meant to make sure the guy would keep his distance, not sprint for Alaska. "Wait. I want to race."

"Your brothers don't play around when it comes to you, and aren't you supposed to be sickly or something?"

Stupid, stupid brothers and stupid, stupid rumors and stupid, stupid hospital visits when I stupid, stupidly was so panicked my freshman year I had to stay overnight twice. "Obviously the whole sick thing is wrong and if you don't take me to the drag race, I'll tell West about tonight." No, I won't, but I'll try bluffing.

Owner Guy looks over at his friend hovering near the passenger door. His friend shrugs. "I bet she'll keep her mouth shut."

"I will," I blurt. "Keep my mouth shut."

Owner Guy curses under his breath. "One race."

Isaiah

I LEAN AGAINST MY CAR door and assess the group illegally loitering in the parking lot of the abandoned strip mall. Green, blue and red neon lights frame the bottom of different makes and models. A few of us puritans remain on the streets, refusing to decorate our cars like Christmas trees. The bass line of rap rattles frames and a couple drivers are brave enough to blare the screeching electric guitar of heavy metal.

Clouds cover the sky, leaving all of us in a dark pit. Close to a week after Christmas, the presents have been opened, the turkey dinners have been demolished, and mommies and daddies are either tucked in bed or sucked into a bottle of Jack. Time for the rats to hit the streets.

"Isaiah!" Eric Hall abandons two girls in short skirts and faux fur jackets to head for me. Most people underestimate the bleached-blond, skinny son of a bitch, but that mistake could prove lethal for your billfold and your health. On the streets of the south side, this nineteen-year-old is king. "Merry belated Christmas, my brother. Did Santa bring you some good shit?"

"Don't know if I'd call it good." I accept his outstretched hand and the half hug.

Eric is who I came to see, and if I don't watch myself, I'll end up indebted to him. My goal in life is to be free of everyone—foster care, school, social workers. Eric Hall may not be official, but he's an organization all his own with the street business he created. He even has "employees": guys with bats and tire irons that willingly beat the hell out of anyone who doesn't pay.

He motions to the two giggling girls. "Santa brought me twins, and in the spirit of the season, I'm willing to share. That is, if you drive for me tonight."

This is the reason why I'm here. Noah and I need cash, and Eric can make that happen. If I play this right, I'll rake in money and stay free.

While sucking on a lollipop, the twin with black hair stares at me longer than her sister. "Ho, ho, ho," mumbles Eric.

My thoughts exactly and I turn my back to them. I have a bad track record with girls with black hair. "You know I don't street race."

Typically, I don't. Street racing can put my ass in jail and cost me the setup I have with Noah. I have no intention of being placed in juvie—or worse, a group home. I race legally at The Motor Yard, but The Motor Yard is closed for the holidays. Tonight will be a onetime deal.

He leans in close as if what he's about to say is a secret. "I'll give you twenty percent of what I make on top of the Christmas cheer. I'm giving my other boys ten."

I consider twenty percent. Eric has never offered anyone

such a commission, but if he's starting off high, maybe he'll go even higher. "Twenty percent isn't going to cover my bail if I get arrested."

"I know you, my brother," says Eric. "You need speed, and I have the need for green. Say yes and you can race my recently acquired suped-up Honda Civic with two full tanks of nitro."

I cross my arms over my chest. "Recently acquired" means some messed-up kid got in over his head on a bet and lost the papers to his car. He possibly also spent a couple nights in the hospital.

"Nitro and Honda," I slur as a curse. "Give me American-made with a real live engine pushing horsepower."

Eric shakes his head. "FYI—James Dean died over sixty years ago." He pauses as realization snakes onto his face. "You aren't saying no."

"I'm looking for a onetime race, Eric. That is, if we can come to an understanding."

The sweet purring of an engine grabs not only my attention, but that of every hot-blooded, car-worshipping male in the lot. Jesus—that's a 2005 Mustang GT. And unlike the other muscle cars parked on the strip, not a piece of her looks like it's seen the inside of a body shop.

A flood of male bodies surround the beautiful pony. I drop back and let the wolves have first crack. A car like this is here for one reason—to race—and any new piece of machinery has to pass Eric's inspection. Someone is going to have to approve the engine and I have no doubt I'll be the one caressing that soft underbelly.

The driver shuts down the engine, opens the door and a

halo of sunshine slides out of the car and into the light of the only working streetlamp. Fuck me. God does exist and he sent an angel in a white Mustang to prove it.

Angels are small—at least this one is. She stands barely a foot taller than the top of her car. Her long golden hair curls at the ends and she has a slender frame. Her leather-gloved hand grips the top of her door and she uses that door as a shield between herself and the street rats.

"Nice car." Like a vulture, Eric slowly circles her.

"Thanks." She glances at two guys exiting a Corvette. Those college boys belong here even less than she does. All three of them are easy prey.

Eric knows how to play people. He told me once he was voted most likely to succeed in high school. If bleeding people dry of their money and manipulating them into deals that only benefit him is a measure of success, then Eric met his high school buddies' expectations.

The angel tucks her hair behind her ear. "Is this where I can drag race?"

I wince internally at her words. Asking for anything on the streets is a cardinal sin. Asking nicely is basically serving your soul to the devil. God didn't send this angel to save me. He sent her as a sacrifice.

Several people laugh, and her eyes flicker over the crowd to pinpoint danger. I watch the two guys cowering near the Corvette. *Come on, boys. Now's the time to step up and protect your girl.*

Eric's eyes wander the length of her body. I agree, she's something to look at in the black fabric coat tailored to her curves, but everything about her screams high-priced and high-maintenance. Only the conceited girls at school wear clothes that nice. Eric gestures to the Corvette with his chin. "Are those your boys?"

Answer yes, angel. Tell him those rich boys are cocky serial killers with jealousy issues and will happily take down anyone who messes with their girl.

She clears her throat. "No. They told me about the race."

Dammit. A muscle in my jaw jerks. It's like the girl wants to be taken advantage of. If this were any other night, I'd shove my way through the crowd, toss the girl back in her car and tell her to go home. But this isn't a normal night, and I need money. I can't do it. I can't get involved. My neck tightens, and I pop it to the side to release the pressure.

A sly smile spreads across Eric's face. "Good. Then we'll work out a deal. Open the hood and we'll get started. Isaiah, I need a little help."

Because no one messes with me, the crowd parts without my having to say a word. The angel's eyes widen and travel over my arms. What is she concerned about? That it's forty degrees and I'm not wearing a coat? Or is she unnerved by the tattoos?

It doesn't matter. In less than ten minutes, this girl will be out of my life.

I raise the hood and a rush of adrenaline hits me when I see the pure power and beauty before me. My eyes snap to hers. "Do you have any idea what you've got in this?"

Of course she doesn't. She's some stupid rich girl who got her Daddy's leftovers for Christmas. She bites her lower lip before answering, "Four point six-liter V-8."

"The girl knows her shit," says Eric with a hint of respect. Too bad her knowledge of engines won't save her from him.

I place my hands on the frame of the car and bend over to get a closer view. "It's the goddamned original engine." Untouched as if it just rolled off the line. The engine's aluminum has a shine that only comes with reverence. Someone has taken care of this beauty.

The girl abandons her safe shield of the door and flitters to my side, waving me away. "I'd really rather that you not touch it."

Yeah, because I'm trash that knows nothing about cars and my one stroke will destroy the engine. "Scared Daddy will know you lifted his car if he finds fingerprints?"

She takes a possessive step, wedges herself between me and the car and looks me square in the eye. Her chin lifts in a kittenish cute-pissed way. "No one but me touches that engine."

A chorus of "Ohs" and "Damns" rises from the crowd. One of my eyebrows slowly pushes toward my hairline. She called me out. If she were a guy, my fist would have already made impact, but girls deserve respect. She holds my stare for a record-breaking five seconds before losing her short burst of courage and lowering her head.

"Please don't touch my car," she says softly. "Okay?"

Her eyes dart to mine for assurance, and I incline my head a centimeter. If this was my car, I wouldn't want anyone else touching it, either. "Go home," I mutter so only she can hear.

Lines wrinkle her perfect forehead, and Eric claps a hand on my back. "What's the verdict?"

The angel and I glance at each other. *Come on, don't make me get involved more than I already am.*

"Isaiah?" prompts Eric.

Damn. "The car has speed," I say loud enough for everyone to hear. Eric can make plenty off the unsuspecting owner, but he cashes in on side bets. "But it's the original engine. No modifications. No nitro."

"How much?" Eric asks her.

"How much what?" Holding her elbows, she folds into herself, as if becoming smaller will help the situation. *Go home, angel. Take your beautiful pony and park her back in a safe garage in an upscale neighborhood where you both belong.*

Eric chuckles deeply and his fingers flick the air. The movement reminds me of the way the legs of a spider gracefully work as it spins a web. "How much money are you putting down to race your car?"

"Can't I just race someone?"

"Excuse me." The driver of the Corvette approaches us at a strange, hesitant yet eager pace. As if his feet are afraid to move, but the top half of his body gravitates toward us. "Did you mention that she needs to make a bet?"

The angel closes her eyes as she visibly relaxes and mumbles, "Finally."

"Yes," says Eric, mimicking the asshole's more formal tone. "Are you willing to place that bet on her behalf?"

"Are you the person that holds the bets?" he asks.

Eric eyeballs Corvette Guy. "Yes."

The guy becomes eager as he reaches for his back pocket. No. Not happening. I've seen that front hundreds of times on guys at races—the attitude that says he gets a hard-on from betting. This girl will lose the slip to her car by the end of the night if he gets involved.

Fuck. Just fuck. "Do you have money?" I glare at the angel.

"Yes," says asshole Corvette owner.

"Not you, dickhead." I size him up and stare him down to keep him from opening his mouth again, then snap my gaze to her. "You. Do you have money?"

Her golden eyebrows furrow together. Worry isn't an expression angels should wear. "I have twenty dollars."

The crowd laughs and so does Eric. I pull out my wallet and slam my last twenty onto the hood of Eric's car. The laughter stops and the only sound filling the night is a pounding bass line and an electric guitar.

Eric slides a hand over his drawn face. "Whatcha doing, my brother?"

"Calling my race."

Eric glances at the crowd that's completely absorbed in us. I'm costing Eric money, and everyone here knows it. Assessing me, Eric takes a tripped-out gangster stride in my direction and leans in close. "Fill me in on what I'm missing here."

I match his low tone. "You asked me to race for you. This is me accepting."

"Racing for me means I pick the races you drive and I negotiate the racing fees."

I know that. Hell, everyone here except the angel and her fucked-up friends knows that, but I claim ignorance. "My bad. We never got to the negotiating part."

"True that," he says slowly. "Are you trying to play me?"

I assess the Corvette owner. Two feet distances him from

the angel. He's either the worst boyfriend ever or she meant what she said earlier—he just informed her about the races. Still, she shouldn't be in this position.

Regardless, this girl ruined whatever negotiating room I had. "She's got an '05 Mustang GT. Original engine. I'm curious if my pieced-together Mustang can take hers. You get better betting when the cars are evenly matched. Let me do my shit and you do yours."

Eric stares at the angel before replying. "Fine, but the next time you decide you want a personal race, you talk to me first. Did you get a good look at that college boy? I could have made a couple grand off of him."

The boy wears slacks and a watch that costs more than I make in a year working at the auto shop. Eric shakes his head, clearly disgusted at the lost opportunity. "Your commission is twenty percent tonight as a signing bonus, but because I like you, I'll give you fifteen every night after this. You'll drive my cars, not your own. American-made can't beat nitro."

"Tonight is a onetime deal."

Eric snorts. "Sure it is."

He turns, and I remember the question I should have asked before I accepted the deal. That damn angel shot this whole night to hell. "What happens if I lose?"

From over his shoulder, Eric cracks his maniac smile. "My brother, I suggest you don't lose." He glances over to the GT and winks at me as if we're friends. "You should get over Beth and make a move on that chick. Mustang Girl owes you for saving her car."

Rachel

I GIVE THE GUY WHO introduced himself as Eric twenty dollars, and my legs hit the front bumper when I step back to keep a safe distance between us. He seriously creeps me out in a need-to-take-a-shower type of way.

The other one, the guy they call Isaiah, doesn't freak me out, though he should. Tattoos decorate his arms and two silver hoops hang in each ear. He turns from a black Mustang and pins me with his gaze. He reminds me of a high school version of Gavin's friend Kyle, an Army Ranger. Well, minus the piercings. Isaiah shares the same rugged, strong build, dark hair buzzed close to his scalp and a five o'clock shadow lining his jaw. He's a muscular thick. Like a jaguar.

What I like about him is his eyes. They're serious. Too serious. And they're gray. Gray and mesmerizing.

Not that I should be looking straight into his eyes, because when I do, he has no problem staring back. I don't like people focusing on me, and I especially hate it when people I don't know stare at me.

Isaiah moves to my side and my heart skips a beat. Guys don't stand this close to me. Ever. With a touch more gentle than I could have imagined coming from a guy like him, he shuts the hood of my car with a simple snap. His eyes rove from me to the street leading to the freeway.

"You're not safe here," he says. His deep voice is like water running over a creek bed of smooth rocks. "You need to leave."

I glance at the different groups of people talking and laughing and betting. The way some of the guys ogle me propels me to cross my arms over my chest. Even with that small barrier of protection, I feel as if they still see parts of me no one has seen before.

"I'll leave after the race," I say, not sure if following West's friends to this place was officially the worst decision of my life or the best. My blood hums with anticipation. I want this race. I want to know what it feels like to push my car against another.

"Last bets!" calls Eric as he eyes me and Isaiah. "Mount up!"

Isaiah inclines his head to his shoulder as if trying to release tension. "Do you see the side street running parallel to the abandoned warehouse?"

The two opposing parts of my personality, the girl who panics and the girl who loves speed, declare war and the result is a head rush. "Yes."

"Pull up to the first line of the white crosswalk. We'll race a quarter mile to the stop sign. Then you leave and never come back."

He pivots on his heel and returns to the black Mustang. Excitement ripples through me when I notice the body. That's a '94 GT. I'm racing against a '94 GT! "What if I win?" I call.

"You won't," he replies. I snort and his shoulders stiffly roll back. Like a '94 Mustang GT could beat my baby.

The crowd moves. Some hop into their cars and drive toward the abandoned road. Others travel by foot. I slide behind the wheel and shut the door. As I turn the key, my lips curl up at the familiar rumble of the engine.

I love this car. I really, really do.

I shift into First and maneuver to the starting line. The moment I ease into place, the battle for control over my body kicks into gear. Surrounding the edges of the street, people my age shout and smoke and laugh and drink. I rub my hands onto my jeans. My car may be where I belong, but I don't belong here.

My throat tightens and I ignore the sensation. Nausea is not welcomed in my car. Nor are shallow breaths and sweaty palms and disoriented thoughts. This is my car—my world.

Announcing its presence with an angry growl, the black Mustang joins me at the line. Isaiah and I glance over at the same time, and I immediately look away, busying myself with knobs and buttons. I take a deep breath and try to suppress the panic.

Logic. I need to focus on logic. Turn off the heater fan, the radio, the nonessentials. Don't rob the engine of power.

West's friends park their car next to Eric and hand him money. I wonder if they're betting on me or Isaiah. Losing confidence in myself, I think fatalistically that I'd place my money on Isaiah.

Eric and West's friends stare at me.

In fact, they're all staring at me.

Every single person standing along the road has their eyes fixed on me.

My heart beats twice and I wait for the familiar heat to explode upon my face, but nothing happens. I grip the steering wheel tighter as one single thought blankets my brain: this is my car and this is my race.

Two thumps on the hood and my eyes narrow at a boy with blond dreads motioning for me to inch closer to the line. What the hell? Why do people think they can manhandle my baby? With the press of a button, I lower both of my windows. "Don't touch my car!"

He rolls his eyes. "Did you hear that, Isaiah? The rich bitch doesn't want me touching her car."

With a grumble, Isaiah's Mustang lurches forward then stops just short of hitting the guy. In front of Isaiah's fender, he holds his hands in the air toward Isaiah. "You need to smoke something to chill."

I move my car to mirror Isaiah's. My right hand strangles the stick shift as I place my foot on the clutch. Isaiah's car roars next to me as he stays in Neutral and hits the gas. My 300 horsepower with 320 pounds of torque against his 215 horsepower and 285 pounds of torque.

This race is mine.

Adrenaline hammers my bloodstream as I feel the power of my car begging to be unleashed. The guy with dreads throws both of his arms into the air. I've never done anything like this before. I've only built up to fast speeds, never taken off from them, but it can't be that difficult. Lift the clutch at the exact same time I press the gas while shoving the car into gear.

This is what my Mustang was made to do.

Isaiah's engine roars again and the sound vibrates between the layers of my skin and muscle. The guy with dreads looks at me once. Then at Isaiah. In a heartbeat, his arms rush down to the ground.

My right foot hits the gas, the other slips off the clutch. Isaiah's Mustang's front end rises into the air as I shift into First. His car lunges forward and I'm preparing for the whiplash of speed when my car shudders once and stalls out into silence.

No.

This isn't happening.

No.

I took my foot off the clutch too quickly.

No.

I didn't gun the engine in time.

Hell.

I never had a shot.

Isaiah's already past the halfway point. I turn over the engine, ignore my instincts for a full-on start and focus on getting the car into gear. I'm finishing this race, even though it's obvious who won.

Isaiah

IN MY REARVIEW MIRROR, I watch as the angel restarts her car and floors it. Seconds ago, I had my doubts about whether I'd win, but my instincts were right on—she didn't have the reaction needed to pull off a start at the flag. I won a whopping twenty dollars from the straight bet on this race, but I'm hoping for at least a grand once Eric gives me my take from his winnings.

My lips turn up as I pass the stop sign. My piece of crap beat an '05 GT. That feat alone deserves a trip to the tattoo parlor. That is if I had money.

I ease off the gas and check the angel's status. Damn, that car's fast. I slow to a stop and wait for her to join me. The crowd gathered at the quarter mile calls out smack. A huge part of me wants her to cruise past and head straight home. Girls like her shouldn't hear the words being tossed into the night. A small part of me wants her to stop so I can see her cute-pissed expression when she realizes that a street punk beat her *and* her expensive car.

The angel finally catches up and I lose the smirk as I examine her. The streetlamp above us creates a glow around the mess of hair angling her face. She shouldn't be here. In fact, there's nothing right about this situation.

My throat moves as I swallow and, suddenly, my skin feels too tight on my body. Instinct? A sixth sense? I learned early in life to never discount the sensation. The noise of the on-lookers becomes a shallow buzz as I glance at my side mir-rors for the oncoming danger.

That's when I see it—a faint strobe of light. I ignore all other sounds and strain to hear the one that can ruin my world: a distant wail.

"Cops!" I yell.

Blue and red lights blaze in the distance. Chaos erupts as the bystanders scurry to their cars. Doors slam shut and anxious motors rumble to life. Feet pound against pavement as voices call for others to head into the dark alleys between the warehouses.

I shift my car into First and stomp on the gas. My tires squeal as I peel out. A curse leaves my mouth when I throw the car into Second. Eric has my money and collecting what I fully earned will be a lot more difficult without a crowd to verify the bets made.

No matter how fucking hard I try, I always come out on the bottom.

I check my mirrors to see the direction of the invasion. There're three ways out of this labyrinth of warehouses and the cops know one, maybe two, but the third will be a hell of a drive.

A solitary white barrier in the middle of the street causes me to hit the brakes. "Fuck!"

She's still sitting there—the angel—like a damn sacrifice

nailed to the ground. I yank on the steering wheel and one-eighty it back to where I started seconds before. What the hell is wrong with her?

My driver's side mirror barely misses hers as I stop next to her open window. "Get out of here."

"I don't know where to go." Red flushes brightly on her cheeks, in stark contrast to the pale white skin surrounding her eyes. Eyes that are wide and wild with fear.

My grip on the steering wheel tightens. Fuck. Just fuck. Losing the cops in one car is hard enough. Having a tail will only complicate things, but I can't leave her. "Follow me."

Rachel

ISAIAH CIRCLES MY CAR AND speeds off the way he originally came. I chase after him and do my best to shift with arms and legs that no longer want to accept orders. The speedometer climbs in my race to not fall behind.

The police.

Air catches in my lungs and throat, causing me to choke. My brothers are going to murder me. Kill me. Crucify me. And never let this screwup go. My hand slips off the gearshift to press against the nausea eating at my stomach.

My father will take away my car. My baby. He never would have bought it for me if he knew I had an addiction to speed.

And my mother...

How do I explain any of this? Why I'm out past curfew? Why I'm on the south side? Why I'm drag racing? Even worse, how do I explain why I wanted to be drag racing?

Isaiah turns sharply to the left. His brake lights never appear. I reach for the gearshift and switch pedals in order to make the turn. My back wheels slide out from under me and both hands struggle with the wheel as I fight to keep the car from spinning into a Dumpster.

Claustrophobia consumes me as the buildings gradually close in, making the road narrower and almost impossible to navigate. Garbage covers the roadway, and my stomach sinks as I realize there's no way to avoid the debris. Isaiah runs over it and so must I.

Isaiah's lights flash off and I follow his lead. The glow of the full moon is the only pathetic light leading us. His Mustang pulls farther away from mine, and I shift into Fourth. We're going too fast. Too fast on a too-narrow road. I shudder as the wheels roll over trash and a clink from under my car makes me cringe. Did something hit the gas tank? The transmission?

My heart pounds out of my chest when my car becomes airborne through an intersection. From the corner of my eye, I spot police cars running parallel to us on a street much wider than ours. Sirens scream into the night and as my car hammers back into the ground, I wait for that sound to shriek from right behind me.

Darkness envelops me again and I drop gear as Isaiah takes a last-second right. He's too fast, which is impossible because my car is better than his. I shake my head as I understand the difference: he's a better driver. It's not hard to imagine. I'm not good at anything.

Isaiah's car fishtails and I slam on my brakes to keep from crashing into his rear end. My breath leaves my body in a hiss. On either side of my car, metal warehouse walls threaten to scratch my side mirrors. He slows, and thanks to the dim security light hanging over a bay door, I see the reason for the reduced speed: shredded rubber spikes out from his front driver-side wheel. Isaiah destroyed the tire.

Crap. I'm going to jail and my mother is going to freak.

She'll cry and then she'll know I'm nothing like the daughter she really loves—that I'm nothing like Colleen.

Isaiah's arm extends from his window, waving me on as he eases his car into a space between Dumpsters. I pull alongside of him and he hops out. "Two rights. One left. Then hit the freeway. Watch the cops. They're running on the streets to the left and right of us."

My throat tightens. To the left *and* the right? "Come with me."

Isaiah places his hands on the top of my car and leans over so that his head is level with mine. The strong scent of dark spices tickles my nose and I inhale deeply. A brief calm washes through me and somehow I know Isaiah will get me out of this.

"They're pressing hard to find the racers, meaning us. If they pull you over—" his eyes trail over my hair then over my clothes "—they'll probably let you go, but not if you're with me. Especially if you're with me. Go. Now."

I nod and stare at the road in front of me. Two rights. One left. And if I get caught, they'll probably let me go. I glance at Isaiah. He's touching my car and I don't even care. Which tells me I'm either beyond freaked or I like him. I flex my hands, which are sweating on the steering wheel. I pick the first option. I'm definitely freaking. "What will you do?" I ask.

"Walk." His silver hoops glint in the moonlight as he performs a half shrug. "Go. I can take care of myself." Isaiah steps away from the car, taking the dark scent of calm with him.

I put the car into First, and a fresh wave of adrenaline floods my bloodstream when a cop car speeds across an intersection two warehouses ahead. Isaiah falls into the shadows with his back against the warehouse wall. His eyes travel back and forth down the alleyway. An hour ago, I never would have thought that someone like him would be my savior, but he is. What type of person would I be if I left my savior behind? "I'm not leaving without you."

"Dammit." He rubs a hand over his shaved head. "Just leave."

"Promise you won't get caught. Promise you'll be okay."

He freezes midrub and shoots me a chilling look. "I won't rat you out."

Rat me out? My forehead scrunches. To who? A siren wails, the sound much closer than I'd prefer. I blink rapidly as the answer dawns along with a sinking feeling. The police. Isaiah knows he's going to be caught. "I'm...I'm not worried about that. I'm worried about you."

He mumbles a word that begins with *F* and stalks toward me. "I'm driving."

Driving? No way. No one drives my car. "I don't think..."

Isaiah opens the door and stares me down with his hard gray eyes. "Passenger side. Now."

Passenger side. Right now. On it. I slide over the console and grasp the side of the seat when Isaiah simultaneously shuts his door and guns the engine. I click my seat belt in place as he takes a sharp left. The speedometer continues to climb.

"I thought you said two rights."

His restless eyes check the rearview mirror. "The cop we saw took that route. I'm not interested in chasing him. Are you?"

I shake my head, but I doubt he sees it. He keeps his eyes trained on the ever-constricting slender space. It's like we're not even on a road anymore, but a sidewalk. My stomach cramps. Holy freaking crap. This is a walkway. The deep sound of the engine pushing out revolutions increases until Isaiah shifts into Fourth. Oh, hell, I'm gonna puke. We're doing sixty. "Slow down."

"Slow down?" He smiles. I'm seconds away from a full-on panic attack and the guy actually smiles. "Your car can do over double what I'm asking it. In fact, it was built to be let loose. You should try it sometime."

"I do let it loose. Garbage can!" I close my eyes and bite back a scream when the car swerves to the left. *Breathe, Rachel, breathe.* Going mental is not going to help this situation. "I mean, slow down." I reopen my eyes only to wish I hadn't. Dumpster. Big Dumpster. Big freaking, going-to-wreck-my-car Dumpster. "You can't make it. You can't, you can't, you can't...."

And he swings the car to the right and into an actual alleyway. "Don't hurt her. Just don't hurt her. Okay?" Tears prick my eyes and the breathing thing isn't working and everything feels out of control. "She's mine. This is mine. I don't have much that's mine. So you can't destroy her, okay?"

"What's your name?" he asks in the calmest, deepest tone I've ever heard.

"What?"

"Your name. I want your name."

"Rachel," I squeak.

"Rachel," he says with a long drawl. I glance over at him when he says nothing else. His eyes flicker between me and the road. "I'm Isaiah, and I swear I'll take care of you and your car."

Breathing becomes a little easier. "Okay."

I smell it again, his scent. The calming aroma. The one that's become my new favorite. I take a deeper breath.

Isaiah drops gears and for the first time hits the brake. "As soon as I stop, get out."

I don't have time to ask what he means. Isaiah slams the car into Park, hops out and punches buttons on a security keypad. I do what he said and rub my arms as he eases my car into the garage, turns her off and relocks the garage door.

"What are you doing?" I ask.

We both jerk our heads to the right when a siren cries on the other side of the warehouse. Flashing blue lights reflect against the wall. Isaiah grabs my hand and leads me away from the police. "I can't get busted here."

My heart stutters. He's holding my hand. A guy is holding my hand. Touching it. Like his fingers entwined with mine. I've never held a guy's hand before and it feels good. So good. Warm. Strong. Awesome. And it would only be a million times better if the guy holding my hand liked me.

Or if I liked him.

Isaiah and I step out onto a bustling sidewalk. Fear slams into my body, and if it weren't for his sturdy hand wrapped around mine, urging me forward, I would have stopped dead.

Oh, hell.

Holy hell.

Oh, holy hell with lettuce on top.

I'm on the strip. This isn't the place you go when you're seventeen. No. This is the place you go when you're twenty-one. Or the place you go when you're pretending you're twenty-one. And in college. And want to get drunk. Or pretending to

be in college. And want to get drunk. Or you own a motorcy-
cle. And want to get drunk. Or you're a prostitute. And want
to get drunk. Or you're a slimy guy. And want to get drunk.

My brother West comes here.

But me? I don't.

Neon lights hang over bars and burly men guard the en-
trances. Long lines weave along the sidewalk as people wait
for admittance. Guys loom over barely clothed girls. Most of
the people on the sidewalks laugh. Some of them make out.
All of them are sloshed.

Isaiah tugs on my hand, guiding me closer to him. Our
arms touch and I shiver as if I was zapped by lightning.

"We're not out of the woods yet," he says. "Cop cars are everywhere."

I turn my head to the street and stop when Isaiah squeezes
my hand. "Don't look. We've got to blend in."

"I don't understand," I say in a hushed voice. "We're not in
our cars. How would they know?"

Isaiah keeps his eyes straight ahead. "I only said I wouldn't
rat. I didn't say anything about anyone else."

My mouth dries out—West's friends. Did they escape or are
they telling the cops my phone number and address? Can
this get any worse?

Isaiah lets go of my hand and in a blur, pushes my back
against a cold brick wall. His body becomes a hot, thick blanket over mine. The fine hair on my neck stands on end and
my eyes close at the sensation of his warm breath on the skin
behind my ear.

I'm absolutely terrified, but at the same time my body tingles with a weird anticipation.

"There's two cops walking the street," he whispers.

Peeking beyond his biceps, I see the two blue uniforms stalking in our direction. "What do we do?" I barely breathe out.

His hands go to my waist—my waist! And they feel so right. I like this closeness. Maybe I like it too much. A guy has never been this close to me. Never. And I can't believe it's happening, even if it is to keep from being arrested.

My heart beats frantically. Isaiah is hot and scary and hot. Why on earth would a guy like him want to be anywhere near a girl like me?

It's the adrenaline rush. That's what it is. I like how he feels because I'm still experiencing the adrenaline rush from Isaiah's NASCAR driving skills. His arm shifts, and I love how that movement causes his muscles to flex.

Stop it, Rachel. It's not real. Focus.

"Kiss me," he whispers. "If you kiss me we'll blend in."

My mouth drops open as if to make a sound, but nothing comes out. How do I say the words…I don't know how to kiss.

Isaiah

RACHEL'S BODY STIFFENS AGAINST MINE. I've scared her. Of course I have. I've thrown an angel against a wall, into darkness, and asked her to do something unthinkable.

The area between my shoulder blades itches as if I've got a bull's-eye painted on my back. The cops must be scanning us.

She places her soft hands on my bare forearms and whispers my name with an edge of panic. "Isaiah, they're looking at us."

Girls like her never notice guys like me and damn me to hell for enjoying her touch and the sound of my name on her lips. I may be a lot of things, but naive isn't one of them. Her dependence on me is because she's terrified of the cops. "Tell me how close they are," I demand.

"Very," she breathes out.

"Are they still looking at us?"

She nods. Fuck.

Kissing would be better, but I won't drag her further into hell by forcing her to be physical with me. I lower my head away from hers and hover my lips near her neck. Rachel's chest moves as she sucks in air. God forgive me for scaring her. "Angle your head to mine to hide your face," I whisper. "It'll just appear like we're hooking up."

She does, and her forehead brushes against my cheek. "I'm sorry," she says.

My eyebrows furrow. "For what?"

"For...for...messing this up. You would be safe if it wasn't for me."

"No, I wouldn't." I turn my head in her direction. Her face is centimeters from mine, and she looks up at me with wide, beautiful blue eyes. Above us, a security light flickers on, then off. I'm wrong. They aren't blue. Those eyes are so dark they're violet. "You could have left me behind."

I'll never forget that. Never. Only one other person in my life would risk everything for me. That's Noah. Our bond is one forged through the blood of battles won and lost in the system. We understand each other. Get each other. Have each other's backs. We're surviving warriors.

But this girl...she owed me nothing. Yeah, I turned back for her, but when I did, I knew I would still make it out. Her scenario was different. When I blew a tire, Satan was breathing down our necks and she stood against the flame. Hell, without batting an eyelash, she's still standing in the inferno.

I owe her.

She lets out an unsteady breath. Her eyes fixate on the Brothers of the Arrow Knot tattooed on my left forearm then follow the flaming tail of the dragon that winds up my biceps and disappears from view at my short sleeve. I know what she sees: a punk.

Without moving her head, Rachel glances to the right and

sucks in her lower lip. I've seen roses the color of her lips. "They've gone across the street."

The tension eases from my muscles. I slide my fingers through hers again and pull her in the opposite direction of the cops. We need to get inside so I don't have to keep tossing the girl against buildings. She deserves better than that. My apartment is close, but not close enough. Rachel and I need walls between us and the streets.

Rachel obviously said a prayer to her God, because a few feet down the sidewalk, beneath a neon sign, is our answer: a guy who owes me for fixing his car. The line into the club stretches beyond the plastic ropes and wraps around the building, but we won't have to wait.

Jerry lifts his chin in acknowledgment the moment he sees me. "Isaiah, what's doing?"

"I got problems."

"I'm not twenty-one," Rachel whispers. Neither am I, but we can hide here.

The rolls on the fat son of a bitch shake as he eyes me then Rachel. She fastens her other hand securely on my wrist and moves so that she's behind me. *Good job, angel. Let him know that I'm your man. At least you're a fast learner.*

I rub my thumb over her smooth skin in approval, then stop. She doesn't need my approval. I'm not her man, but, for now, I am her protector.

Two guys in the middle of the line shout, asking what the holdup is, and Jerry informs them where to shove their complaints. He lights a cigarette and inclines his head to the police scanner sitting on the small table next to the door. "Someone called in a street race and the cops are all over it.

First solid tip they've had in months. They're pulling people in left and right. Not part of that action, are you?"

"Would it matter?"

Jerry grins with the cigarette still dangling from his bottom lip. "No." He lifts the rope and takes a step to create a path. "Impressed you got out."

With Rachel on my heels, we brush past Jerry. I pause in the door frame, half of me heated from the warmth of the club, the other half freezing from the night air. Jerry said the cops had a tip, not a report. A dangerous anger curls up my spine. "Did you say someone informed?"

He draws in smoke, then releases it. "Yeah. Tell Eric he's got a snitch."

A snitch. Fuck. Not what anyone needs. Eric's a mean asshole already, and he'll go insane if he thinks someone turned his business over to the police. A gentle tug on my hand coaxes my attention back to Rachel. "Isaiah, let's get inside."

Yeah. Inside.

The door closes behind me and I wait for Rachel to drop her hand. Instead, she inches closer to me when she surveys the narrow room. The chipped, worn wooden bar stretches the length of the left wall and in a nook on the opposite wall sits a stage.

The throb of an electric guitar playing Southern rock pulses against my skin. I place a hand on the nape of Rachel's neck and guide her through the thick crowd so we can find a booth in the back. Even if the cops come in, they'll give up before they maneuver past the groupies.

"Maybe you should go first," she yells as I push her forward.

I lean down to say in her ear, "And take a chance on some drunk asshole grabbing your ass? I'm not interested in getting into a fight."

Her head whips back to see if I mean what I say. I nod for her to keep moving. A crowd this packed? They'd also try to cop a second-base feel, but no need to tell her that. The music becomes muffled as we continue toward the back. She pauses to take a seat at a table in the wide-open. I shake my head and point to the corner booth. "That one."

Preferring a view of the room, I motion for her to claim the space across from me as I settle on the bench against the wall. Rachel takes off her coat, sags in her seat and hides her face in her hands. "My parents are going to kill me."

I don't know why her statement hits me the way it does, yet it happens. For the first time in months, I laugh.

Rachel

I SPLIT MY FINGERS APART and peek at Isaiah between the gaps. He's laughing at me. It's not loud or boisterous. At first his eyes hold a bit of humor, but slowly the humor dies and his laughter becomes bitter.

"What?" I ask.

"You," he says while scanning the crowd.

Feeling very self-conscious, I sit straighter and shove a hand through my hair. I'm probably a mess. "What about me?"

"There's an entire task force against street racing hunting us and you're concerned about getting grounded." Isaiah leans forward. His arms cover most of his side of the table, plus a little of mine. I place my hands in my lap and move my feet as he sprawls his legs underneath. The funny thing is, he appears relaxed, but his eyes keep searching the crowd.

"What are you looking for?" I ask.

"Trouble," he says without glancing at me.

I swallow and grab a paper napkin out of the dispenser on the table. My heart beats faster as I let the events of the past hour register. "Are the police here?"

He says nothing and my hands start to sweat. I smooth the

napkin flat, then begin to fold. "Should we leave? Or stay?" Panic stabs my chest. My car. Oh, crap, my baby. "What about my car? Is it safe? Will they find it? Will someone else take it? And your car? What do we do?"

"Rachel," Isaiah says in a low, calm tone that makes me meet his eyes. "We're good. We lost the police. Your car's in the garage where I work. And someone has to be damn desperate to jack my piece of shit."

My muscles still, including my heart. Did he just say... "Your car is *not* a piece of shit." I flinch at using the word *shit* and the right side of his mouth turns up in response. I stare at the napkin my hands continually fold and refold. I don't like that he reads me so clearly.

"She's...she's gorgeous," I stammer. "Your car, I mean. My favorite is the '04 Cobra."

My parents bought me and my siblings the car of our choice for our sixteenth birthday. I asked for a 2004 Mustang Cobra, the last year that model was made, but Dad didn't think I'd notice the difference and got me my baby. I love my baby, but I knew the difference, even though I pretended I didn't.

"I've never seen a '94 GT up close before," I continue, hoping for a spark of conversation.

No response. His eyes become restless again even as his body stays completely motionless. Fold. Refold. Fold until the napkin's so thick I can't fold anymore. My fingers release the napkin and the folds tumble out. I smooth out the paper and begin again.

I don't know this guy and he doesn't know me. He hates me. He has to. I'm weighing him down, and I've noticed how he's looked at my clothes, my diamond earrings, the gold bracelets on my wrist, my car. He can tell I'm not from this part of town—that I don't belong. Not that I belong at home, either. But he told me before the race to leave. I didn't. And now I'm a burden he's dragging around.

My lower lip trembles and I suck it in. First that horrid speech. Now this. I'm scared, I'm seconds from a panic attack and I want to go home.

I try to breathe deeply. It's what my middle school therapist told me to do. That and to think of other things. "You shouldn't talk about your car that way." And I don't know why I can't stop talking, but his car is a gem, he should know it, and cars are the only things that don't make me cry. "It won *Motor Trend*'s car of the year in '94."

"Yeah," he responds in a bored voice.

"That was the year they put the pony emblem back on the car's grill."

"Mmm-hmm."

"It has a V-8." And I've run out of good things to say about the car. "But what I don't get is how Ford was okay with producing the thirtieth anniversary car using the same engine as the '93 and losing 10 horses off the power." And I'm rambling. I press my mouth shut and sigh heavily. Not that he's listening anyhow. As I said before, guys don't like girls who talk cars.

He surprises me by answering. "I don't have the original motor in my car."

My eyes snap to his. "For real? I know it probably sounds like I'm talking bad about your car, but really, the engine rocked. I mean, add a different air filter, or pulleys, or, I don't know, some other mods and bam, your pony's flying."

Lines bunch between his eyebrows as they move closer

together. He opens his mouth. Closes it. Tugs on the bottom loop of his right ear and relaxes back into his seat. "How do you know so much about cars?"

I shrug. "I read."

His eyes mock me with amusement. "You read."

"I read," I repeat. A moment of silence stretches between us, and the band begins to play Jason Aldean. "Thank you for coming back for me."

It's his turn to shrug. "It's nothing. Thanks for not leaving me back at the warehouses. I owe you."

I owe you.

A tiny whisper of wings tickles the inside of my chest as he says those last three words. Or maybe it's the way his gray eyes become charcoal as if he's swearing a pact. Either way, the moment is heavy, and I can't help but look away in response. "Anyone would have done it."

"No, they wouldn't have," he says. "You could have gotten away clean without me. I can't be arrested, Rachel, and I owe you big."

The cuticles on my fingernails have never been so interesting. "So I'm assuming I also owe you, since you came back for me."

"No," he says automatically. "You sacrificed a hell of a lot more for me."

I bite the inside of my lip to conceal the smile forming. All right, so this is cool. Very cool. I'm well aware that I'm barely seventeen and in a bar because I'm hiding from the police, and the guy across from me is my opposite in more ways than I can calculate, but I can't help but feel like a princess who has a knight pledging his loyalty.

And because this moment is so intense, and there's no way it's as powerful for him as it is for me, I clear my throat and force a change of subject. "So, does that make us friends?"

Okay, last-minute game changer. I know, I know, any self-respecting girl would have let the subject drop, but I need to know. I don't have that many friends, and I like the idea of having a friend who isn't one of my brothers.

"Yeah." He taps his finger against the table. "I guess it does."

Cool. I release the napkin and turn my head toward the stage. The drummer wraps up "My Kinda Party" and the guitar player rips right into "Sweet Home Alabama." "I like this song."

The people crowded near the stage throw their arms in the air and sway with the beat that vibrates not only the floor beneath me, but also the table and my seat. So much so that my entire body trembles with the sound. There's an energy surrounding the stage that illuminates the once-dark bar. What was moments ago brooding and overwhelming now appears light and hypnotic.

"Do you dance?" I ask, with a smile on my face that even surprises me.

Isaiah stares at me for a second, appearing as still as a statue. "No."

"Why not?"

"Not a fan of crowds."

No one would call me a crowd enthusiast, yet I glance over my shoulder again at the swarm of bodies rocking their fists in time with the lead singer as everyone belts out the chorus. "It looks like fun. As long as you're not onstage no one would be watching you."

"Too many variables in a crowd that size."

I'm lost. "What do you mean by variables?"

As if searching for patience, he releases a small frustrated breath. "Drunk assholes looking for a fight. Sober assholes looking for a fight. Pickpockets. I can't control what goes on out there."

"I don't think anyone would mess with you." And my stomach automatically sinks. That was a crappy thing to say. "Not that you're scary or anything."

He raises an eyebrow. "I'm not?"

"No," I say quickly, and grow hesitant as I spy a playful spark in his eyes. Even though every sane part of me screams to drop the conversation, I decide to follow the small amount of amusement in his face. "Now if you drove a Camaro, I'd have to reevaluate the situation."

And he laughs. Not the heavy laughter from before. It's a great laugh. A deep laugh. One that makes my lips lift. Isaiah, the guy who an hour ago carried himself like a jungle predator, now has the content aura of a lazy cat bathing in the sun.

"How old are you?" he asks.

"Just turned seventeen."

"Senior?"

I shake my head. "I'm a junior at Worthington Private."

Reminding me he's still lethal, a hint of the panther reappears when he pops his neck to the right. Guess he's heard of my school.

"How old are you?" I ask.

"Seventeen."

Air catches in my throat and I choke, coughing into my hand like I'm dying of the plague. Not that I thought he was ancient, but how he acts, talks and moves...I thought he had to be older than... "You're seventeen?"

"Yeah."

For a brief, startling few seconds, his forever-roaming gray eyes meet mine and I see it—seventeen. Within them is a small shred of the same vulnerability that consumes and strangles me. Just as fast as it appears, it's gone, and he's searching once again for some unseen threat.

I like that we're the same age, at least physically. Something tells me his soul is much older.

The lack of conversation creates awkwardness so I force us forward. "And?"

"And what?"

"You are a..." Is he going to make me draw every answer out of him? I motion with my hand in the air for him to continue. "This is where you fill in the blank with your year in high school."

"Senior," he finishes. "And I don't go to Worthington Private."

"You don't say." I let the sarcasm flow. "I thought for sure you had run for student body president last year."

He scratches the stubble on his jaw and I swear he's covering a grin. "You're too brave for your own good."

My eyes widen. Did he call me brave?

Isaiah leans in my direction, laces his hands together on the table and does that thing again where he stares straight into my eyes. I want to break the hypnotic trance, but it's honestly as if his gaze imprisons me. "Was one of those college boys with you your boyfriend?"

A slight bit of heat creeps onto my cheeks. Not from panic this time, but from...from... "No, I don't have a boyfriend."

And the answer makes me shy, and the shyness gives me the power to look away. To think he called me brave. I wish I was brave. I wish that every person I'd meet would think of me that way. Not as the coward I really am.

"Good. Those guys were losers. Stay clear of them."

"You're sort of bossy." I'm teasing. Isaiah's way too serious to find time to be bossy. But the main point is that he's totally unlike my brothers, who demand everything from me by plain bullying.

"I'm not bossy," he says and I get a little thrill that he's playing along.

This isn't me. In my day-to-day life, I could never find the courage to talk to guys, much less tease them, yet here I am. "No, I have four older brothers. Technically three older brothers and a twin, but Ethan claims he's older by a minute. The point is I know what bossy is—and you're it."

"Think of it as strongly encouraged tips for survival."

I laugh, and the dark shadow on his face moves as he cracks a grin. Even though this isn't his first smile tonight, it's the first one to touch his eyes, and from the wary way the smile flickers on and off his face, it appears to surprise him. Maybe he's out of practice, which is a shame. He has a drop-dead stunning smile.

I don't want the game to end. I don't want this rush to end. I want to stay right here in this booth for as long as possible. "So, my first tip is to stay away from my brother's friends?"

"No. Your first tip is to stay the hell away from street racing."

"And my second?"

"To become better aware of your surroundings. You focus too much on what's in front of you and not what's lurking on the sides. Avoiding your brother's friends is the third. And if your brother's anything like them, avoid him, too."

"We're up to four tips. Any more?"

"A ton."

"Lay them on me."

It's only then that I realize that we're both angled across the table. We're mirrors of each other and we are shockingly close. So close our foreheads almost touch and I can feel the heat radiating from his body. Our heads tilt in the same direction and, in the center of the table, our hands are a breath's distance from a caress.

The energy and the warmth surrounding us...butterflies swarm in my stomach and take flight. This isn't me. None of it. I'm not the girl who hangs in a bar. I'm not the girl who is comfortable talking to guys. And I'm sure not the girl who leans over the table to be close to anyone.

Yet I'm doing all those things and I'm loving every freaking second.

Isaiah

A LOCK OF HER LONG golden bangs falls forward and highlights the sexy curve of her chin and her thick eyelashes. I'll do anything to keep her talking as the sound of her voice creates a contact high. Rachel's this brilliant flame blazing in the darkness. I don't know what the hell is going on, but I've always been the kind of guy that likes a fire.

She asked for another tip for survival. Like at the end of any good buzz, I experience the first drop into reality. If I were honest with her, I'd inform her the next tip is to stay clear of me. A punk who could never fit into the world of a girl who wears the type of jewelry she does, drives her car or goes to her school. A punk raised by the system, by the streets.

"Isaiah," she says with a dazzling smile, "are you going to tell me the next tip, or what?"

Be a man. Tell her you're bad news.

Or take her home and enjoy the night.

I could, but maybe I shouldn't. While I have undressed her several times in my head, each time slowly and methodically, and imagined that blond hair sprawled out over the pillow in my bed, the girl's naive.

But naive about the streets doesn't mean naive about the world. Beautiful girl, confident enough to tease me...she's probably played her share of games. After all, she was the one looking for the drag race—a thrill.

"I don't get you," I say.

"What do you mean, don't get?" Rachel cocks her head to the side like a puppy and she's so damn cute that I have to fight the urge not to smile at her again. This playful thing going on between us, it's new, and I'm not a fan of new.

"Why were you out on the streets tonight?" I ignore her question by asking one of my own.

"The race tonight was a fluke. I typically just drive around." Rachel fiddles with one of the solid gold bracelets on her wrist. I could probably pay rent for a year if I pawned that. A shadow descends onto her face and steals some of her light, which is a fucking shame. "Being in my car, letting her run...it's one of the few moments I feel like me."

Rachel withdraws onto the bench, looking a little lost. I don't care for how her outside reflects my inside. It's too much of a reminder of the things I try to shove away.

"Anyhow." Rachel mock-rolls her eyes, downplaying her statement. "I drive for fun. I know it sounds stupid, but driving my car—it's just me being me."

"It doesn't sound stupid." It's how I feel when I'm behind the wheel of my Mustang.

"Really? You really don't think it's stupid?"

"No."

A shy smile tugs at Rachel's lips and while she keeps her

focus on the bracelet, she flips it around with a renewed energy. I kick back and rest against the seat. What the fuck is wrong with me that I like that I made a rich girl feel better? Damn, I need a beer.

A crash of glass rips my attention away from Rachel and jolts me to my feet. A mad flurry of arms and fists beating the hell out of each other causes my instincts to flare. The two college guys going at it collapse onto a nearby table. In fight-or-flight mode, I gear up to fight. Rachel, on the other hand, does neither—she freezes.

"Stand up on the bench!" I yell at her. "Get against the wall."

The guys roll to their feet and before Rachel can process my words, the asshole with blond hair rams into the dark-haired guy struggling to stay upright. Jumping onto her bench, I haul Rachel to her feet, press her against the wall and shield her with my body.

Wrapped in a fighting hug, the two guys slam into our table. It flips and the edge breezes against my arm and leg. I lean to the right to keep it from tearing into my thigh. The table completes a one-eighty and lands where I sat moments before.

"Oh, my God," she whispers. In the same exact instant, wetness spreads down my T-shirt and a drop of liquid trickles along my arm.

"Sorry." Standing on the bench beside us, a man taller than Rachel holds an empty beer bottle tipped in our direction. "Got caught watching the fight."

He moves to touch her, possibly to wipe off the beer, but the ice forming in my eyes must have stopped the son of a bitch. *That's right, place your hand back at your side. Touch her and die.*

The sounds of the scuffle disappear.

"Fight's over!" The easily two-hundred-and-fifty-pound bouncer dares anyone to tell him differently as he straightens and clenches his fists. Two other bouncers return from the front. They've already thrown the troublemakers outside.

The bitter scent of alcohol burns my nose and as I glance at Rachel, I close my eyes. Beer soaks her hair and shirt. Shit. "Rachel..."

"I can't get into a car like this." The edge of panic is clear in her voice. "If I get pulled over, the police will think that I drink and I don't drink. Ever."

I take a step back as she shakes her arms like a kitten coming in from a rainstorm. A few drops of beer cascade off her onto the bench. I run my hand over my head. If this were any other girl, I'd give her a hard time for being overly dramatic, but the way the color drains from her face and how her body begins to tremble tells me she's not being dramatic. She's terrified.

"And what if I make it home? What am I going to do?" She shakes her arms again. Her voice rises higher in pitch and the words tumble out on top of each other. "I can't go home like this. I can't!"

"Rachel." I need her to focus. "Are you hurt?"

Her body goes still as her eyes immediately dart over me. "Are you okay? They were closer to you. Oh, my God, Isaiah. Do you need to go to the hospital? Oh, hell, you're bleeding.

You're bleeding! Oh, my God!" Her hand flutters near her mouth.

I follow her intense gaze to my elbow. Fuck me, I am bleeding. The edge of the table must have struck me. I turn my elbow up and use the hem of my T-shirt to remove the small pool of blood. "It's barely a scrape."

Soft fingers grip my wrist and forearm. My eyes shoot to hers, but she's too busy fussing over the noncut to notice how her caress is turning me inside out. In a good way. In a strange way. In a way I haven't felt since...Beth.

"But there's blood." Her chest expands and deflates faster than it should, and she sucks in too much air. "You're hurt. We need to make sure you're okay. Can you move your arm? Is it broken? Oh, crap, what if you broke your arm?"

A bead of liquid appears at her hairline and slides down her face. When it hits her cheek, I can't tell if the drop is from the beer or from her eyes. My hand moves, the need to touch her more powerful than thought. Before I know what I'm doing, I wipe away the wetness.

Aw, dammit, no. I don't want to be the fucking guy that wipes anything away. I tried this merry-go-round with Beth once, and the moment she saw a life other than what she had known with me, she threw me into the gears of the ride. *Pull back, man. Pull back.*

"What you've done for me already tonight," Rachel continues, "and what you just did for me, and you're bleeding!"

Take the hand away. Take the fucking hand away from her face.

But I don't. Instead, my thumb moves again to capture one more drop. It's as if she doesn't notice my touch, which is annoying because my fingers are memorizing every curve of her face.

In one long, run-on sentence, she continues, "It could be a hairline fracture or a sprain and you're bleeding and I don't know how deep a cut should be in order to need stitches. Oh, hell, oh, hell. Staples. What if you need…"

"Rachel?"

"Staples! That can be serious!"

The honest to God worry she feels is over me. Something solid in my chest shifts, and it shoots a warning tremor though my system. Whatever the fuck is going on inside me has to stop. "Rachel!"

Her violet eyes, full of hysteria, finally meet mine. Since entering the system, I've never met anyone who cared enough about me to freak out over a cut. She's not just worried. She's panicked.

"I'm okay. Take a deep breath before you pass out." I'm kidding, and I'm not.

She nods as if I'm dispensing quality advice, and she does exactly what I said. Her small amount of cleavage moves up with the inhale, then slowly down. Rachel performs the exercise one more time, her hands tightening around my arm as if she's leaning on me for support.

"I'm good now. I am. Sorry about that."

Because I want to, I keep my hand against her face. Rachel's cheek is warm and smooth. I like touching her and, even more, I like her touching me. This angel has blown my every idea of what a rich, private school girl should be. No drinking, no boyfriend, likes fast cars—hell, *knows* fast cars—and is concerned over me.

"Who are you?" I mumble. Another drop of beer descends from her hairline and I move my thumb against her skin a third time in order to catch it.

She blinks. "What did you say?"

"Nothing." I lower my hand and snag her fingers. I should take her straight to the garage and send her home, but, because I'm a bad son of a bitch, I won't. The dickhead who spilled his beer has given me an excuse to enjoy her for a little while longer. "Let's get you cleaned up."

I jump off the bench and keep her hand to "steady" her as she also hops to the floor. The bar's employees hastily pick up the broken tables and chairs. The bouncer with the dustpan and broom looks at us. "You two okay?"

"Yeah, can we go out the alley entrance?"

Giving me the green light, he tilts his head toward the back door. Knowing I no longer have a reason to hold Rachel's hand, I let her go and snatch her jacket off the broken table. But I do place my hand on the small of her back to lead her out into the alley.

As we step outside, I regretfully remove my hand, then lift her jacket to my nose. The jacket has a sweet scent that reminds me of the ocean. It's a bittersweet smell for me. I shove the memories away and focus. I can't detect the scent of beer, but then again, we're covered in it. "I know it's cold, but if you can keep your jacket off, it would be better. It'll keep the smell of beer off of it."

From behind us, a garbage can clanks against the asphalt. I quicken my pace and Rachel has to double her steps in order to match my stride. I should slow, but I don't like the idea of being in dark alleys with her. Too many things there go bump and jackass crazy in the night.

"What about the police?" she asks. "Won't they still be looking for us?"

"I live a few blocks over. They've probably caught everyone they think they can catch, but I still want to stay off the main streets."

"We're going to your house?" I hear the hint of relief.

"Apartment." She probably lives in a huge house full of nice shit. I lower my head. Damn. Suddenly, this no longer seems like a good idea. She'll be shocked when she sees my place. "We don't have much."

"That's okay. Are you sure you want to take me there? It's late."

Noah won't care. "What time is your curfew?" Because girls like her have those.

The only sound besides the honking coming from the main street behind us is of our shoes hitting the pavement. She's silent, which, from the short time I've known her, strikes me as odd.

We turn into another alley and I breathe easier when I spot the fire escape to my unit. Home sweet fucking home. Hopefully before Noah left, he emptied the rat traps.

Rachel's arm brushes against mine, and I flinch from how cold it is. "We're almost there. You can take a shower if you want to wash off the beer."

"Ten," she says in a small voice. "My curfew is ten."

I hike one eyebrow, and when I glance at her she quickly looks away.

"Little late, aren't you?" By two and a half hours.

She twists a strand of her hair around her finger. "My twin brother and I have an agreement. We cover for each other when—well, when we want to be out past curfew."

I don't get her. Not at all. "So you don't drink?"

"No." She releases her hair and raises her chin. Guess I should keep my mouth shut about how I do drink and how I've been known to get high.

"And you don't have a boyfriend."

The chin drops. "No."

The answer may bother her, but it's the best news I've heard in days. Though it shouldn't matter, I don't like the idea of another guy kissing her. My stomach twists with the thought of the hundreds of guys that must be following her around, waiting for her to take notice.

I rub at my neck. What the hell is wrong with my thought process tonight? She's not my problem. What's between us is just for tonight. "And you like to drag race."

Becoming more thoughtful, her forehead relaxes. "Not really. That sort of sucked. Drag racing is a lot different than when I push my car to see how fast it can go. I do like to let her loose. She can hit sixty in five seconds."

Her excited eyes seek validation. She hesitates, and I nod for her to continue. As if my approval rocks her world, an extra spring appears in her step.

"It was cool, though. I had this huge adrenaline rush when I heard your car take off. But I got sort of frazzled. Like my arms and my legs started working separately. And by the time I got my act together, you were done."

We reach the old Victorian house my landlord left to rot

once he converted it into four separate apartments. I hold the front door open for her, then lead the way up the stairs.

"Watch the third and sixth steps."

"This is where you live?" Rachel wraps her hands around her stomach and peers over the railing to the floor below. The light over the stairwell flickers.

"Yep." I unlock the dead bolt then switch keys to unlock the actual knob. "It's not much, but it's home." The hint of pride in my voice surprises me.

I open the door, switch on the light and motion for Rachel to enter. With her arms still clinging to her sides, she slowly shuffles into the apartment. As soon as she's in, I shut the door, rebolt and head to the bathroom. She'll want to clean up and the water takes at least five minutes before it'll be lukewarm.

The water pipes groan as I spin the knobs. "I'll put a towel out for you. You'll need to crouch to use the shower—or maybe not. You're shorter than me," I say over the water pouring into the old claw-foot tub. "I'll give you one of my shirts to change into. Your jeans should be fine."

I walk out and go for the bedroom to find her a T-shirt, but stop short. Rachel stares at the dead bolt on the door with one hand still clutching her stomach, the other pressed to her throat.

"Rachel? Are you okay?"

"Where are...where are your parents?"

The air rushes out of my lungs, and I scratch the stubble on my chin to hide the horror. I'm so used to people knowing...or assuming...or flat out accepting that people where I come from don't have them...or if they did have them, that they weren't any good. "I'm a foster kid."

"Okay," she says slowly, obviously not okay. "So what about them? Your foster parents. Where are they?"

I shift my footing and clear my throat as I come to terms with the situation I've put her in without knowing. All right, I knew. Fifteen minutes ago I contemplated bringing her home for the night. But that was before I realized how pure she was. Still, I brought her here, even if my intentions changed.

I force out the words. "I moved out of my foster parents' home a couple of months ago with my best friend, Noah."

She glances quickly around the room, searching for the threat. "And he is—"

I cut her off. "A good guy who's probably staying the night with his girl. He goes to college and so does Echo. She came from a real good neighborhood, like you. Middleheights, I think."

"I live in Summitview," she says softly while staring at the empty rat trap in the middle of the kitchen floor.

Of course she does. That's the damn Beverly Hills of Louisville. It's gated. With guards. And she's probably wondering if I've got body parts in the freezer.

The shower continues to pound against the porcelain tub and the damn insomniac old lady downstairs begins to play Elvis. Except this time, it's one of his depressing songs.

"Rachel, I swear, my intentions are good. I won't touch you. I'll stay on the other side of the room from you at all times." And why the fuck should she believe me? "You looked so damned scared at the thought of going home smelling like beer. I don't know what shit you've got going down in your house, but I've been around enough to understand. Look, honestly, I'm just trying to help."

She nibbles on a fingernail. "So you still go to high school?"

"Yeah. Eastwick."

Silence. Her leather boots squeak as she adjusts her weight. The water still crashes against the tub. Elvis sings about rain.

"Eastwick's a good school." She drops her hand and peeks at me from below her eyelashes.

Finally, I'm getting someplace. "Yeah, it is." No need to mention that my foster parents live right on the line between Eastwick, a good high school, and the one school in the county that is a step above a detention center. "I'm in the Automotive Accelerated Program. I've been the highest-ranking student in the program for the past two years."

Past four actually, but I never tell people that I received that honor, let alone how many years I've earned it.

"I've heard about that program. I read the brochures when I was in eighth grade, but..." Rachel puts a hand over her mouth as if to prevent herself from saying anymore. "Anyhow, do you like it?"

"Yeah, I do." I did it, I talked her down. The relief running through me is like a chaser after a shot. I push away the instincts that I'm playing with an unpinned grenade. People like her, nights like this, they don't come around, and I just want to hold on to this flame for a little longer. Guys like me, we don't make girls like her smile. "It's where I learned to rebuild the engine in my Mustang."

A spark ignites in her violet eyes. "You rebuilt your own engine? That's sweet. I've played with the idea of adding some modifications to mine to increase the horsepower."

I flinch at the thought. "Why? Your car is a perfect virgin. Never touched and in great shape."

"Which is why I haven't, but between you and me—" Rachel leans her body in my direction as if she's revealing a highly guarded secret "—I really wanted an '04 Cobra."

That damn smile she's already brought out in me once tonight crosses my face again. "An '04 Cobra. That would be..." And I steal one of her words. "Sweet."

"Yeah. It would, wouldn't it?" Rachel rocks onto her toes and slides her long, beer-drenched hair behind her ear. "So, do you have a hair dryer?"

Rachel

I PLACE THE DRYER ON the sink and run my fingers through my hair again. There—dry and officially beer-free. The edge of Isaiah's dark blue T-shirt ends an inch short of my knees and I catch my silly smile in the blurry mirror. I'm wearing a guy's shirt. Too freaking awesome.

I lower my chin to smell the shirt again. I want to wear this forever, without washing it. His dark, spicy aroma consumes the material. I peek at him from the corner of my eye, wondering if he spots me catching a whiff or if he knows how addicting his scent is to girls.

A knot forms in my throat. Does he have many girls?

As promised, Isaiah sits on the kitchen counter on the other side of the room from me. He leans forward, his legs lazily stretched apart with his joined hands resting between them as he watches me.

He's observant. Overly so. I think he could tell me more about my actions than I could. A huge part of me doesn't like it. In order for me to fit in at home, people can't notice me. It's harder to pull off being someone else when you're the center of attention. But I'm not home. I'm miles from there.

And here, in this room, I like how Isaiah looks at me as if I'm the only girl in the world.

Or like an antelope he's going to pounce on.

My heart patters faster at the thought of him pouncing on me.

I fiddle with my hair for a few more seconds to buy time. What do you say to a totally hot guy when you're alone with him in his apartment?

Alone.

A thrill of tickles moves in the center of my chest, and I think of the way his strong hand caressed my face at the bar. The tickles explode into my bloodstream as an adrenaline rush and I release a long steady breath to keep myself calm.

I really, really want him to touch me again.

One more tuck behind the ear, and I step out of the bathroom. "Thanks for the shirt." I fuss with the ends again.

"It looks good on you," he says as his eyes settle on the curve of my hips. Holy hell, it got hot in here.

My jacket lies over the arm of the couch. I walk over to it and fish my cell phone out of the pocket. One a.m. and one text from Ethan: where r u?

Isaiah shifts uneasily as I text Ethan back. I glance at him while typing a reply. He changed while I was in the shower, switching a black T-shirt with wording for another with different wording. Isaiah keeps surveying the apartment, and I finally get it. He's wondering how to keep a safe distance from me.

"You don't have to stay so far from me," I say. "I trust you."

"You shouldn't."

Lying by typing still driving, I push Send and put the phone back in my coat pocket. "If you were going to hurt me you wouldn't have saved me from that fight or brought me home to use your shower. You also wouldn't be standing all the way over there, so I trust you."

"And that's just bad for both of us," he mumbles and then speaks to me in a normal tone. "Are you in trouble at home?"

I shake my head. "Not yet. My brother is good at distracting my parents."

"That's not what I mean," he says. "You were seriously trippin' when you thought you had to go home with beer on you. Your parents—how hard-core are they?"

I swipe at my forehead as if there's a stray hair to be restyled and feel naked when I don't find one. "I don't understand."

Isaiah hops off the counter, and I'm mesmerized by the fluid way he walks: a sleek predator on the move. "It's okay. I get it. Sometimes things are..." And he's near me. Close enough that I have to lift my head to see his face. "Rough."

"It's...ah...it's..." I love his eyes, and my skin tingles with the thought of his hands on me again. "Ah..." What were we discussing? Parents. Right. My parents. "It's complicated."

Complicated as in I've been failing miserably at replacing my mother's dead daughter. My parents and oldest brothers have told me enough Colleen stories for me to be well aware that she would never have broken curfew, participated in a drag race or been alone with a guy.

"Right," he says so slowly that the word sounds unbelievably sexy. "Complicated. So." He pauses. "Are you ready for me to take you back to your car?"

Yes. No. Yes. Maybe not. Oh, crap. It's ending too soon and I don't want it to. I'm not good at this. I'm not smooth or good

with words or good with guys or good with people. I'm silent.
I blend in. How do I make this not go away?

"I like you," I whisper and immediately stare at my shoes.
Of all the things I could have said, that shouldn't have been
it. I. Am. An. Idiot.

A gentle tug on my hair sends goose bumps raining down
my arms. I close my eyes and relish the sweet brush of his
knuckles against my neck as he flips my hair over my shoulder. "Rachel?"

"Yes?" I say so softly he may not have heard me.

His hand caresses the sensitive spot right below my chin,
and with a gentle pressure, Isaiah raises my head until I look
into those warm silver eyes. "I like you, too."

The right side of my mouth quirks and a spring of hope
bubbles up inside me. He likes me. A really hot, really awesome guy likes me.

"Good," I say a little breathlessly. "That's good." More than
good. It's great.

Isaiah

I GLANCE DOWN AT RACHEL'S mouth and feel the urge to press my lips to hers. *I'm a fucking jackass.* I suck in a breath through my mouth to avoid her scent and step back, dropping my arm to my side. I did not bring her back here to have sex.

Hell yes, she's hot and my mind won't stop replaying the twelve different ways I could possibly do her, but she's not that type of girl.

I rub my eyes. I haven't touched anyone since Beth, but that doesn't mean I have the right to come on to a girl that's too good for me. I slump onto the couch and notice how Rachel shifts uncomfortably. Dammit, she shouldn't have to put up with my mood swings.

"I do like you," I repeat. "There's only one other person who'd stick their neck out for me. If there's anything I can do for you, name it and it's yours."

The chaos in my mind begins to clear as I start to understand why I'm acting like a maniac. Beth's been the only girl to mean something to me, and I generally don't give a shit about people. I'm confusing lust and friendship and creating crap that's not there. Fuck yeah, I'm attracted to Rachel, but the emotions going on...it's because I owe her.

"Will you let me clean up your cut?" she asks.

I check out the small hunk of skin missing from my forearm, having forgotten about the wound. "It's all good. I've had worse."

"No, you said that if you could do something for me, you would, so let me do this."

"Yeah. If I can do something for *you*. Not have you do something for me."

Rachel clasps her hands behind her back like she doesn't know what else to do with them. "I want to do this, and I'd like you to let me."

Keeping my hands off her and being respectful are going to be hard as hell if she continues to put herself within arm's reach. "Fine."

I stand and spend more time than needed rifling through the cabinet beneath the sink to find Band-Aids, rubbing alcohol and a towel. Echo bought this stuff for us when we first moved in, and neither Noah nor I have touched it since. As I set it all on the floor in front of the couch, Rachel motions for me to sit and when I do, she joins me with her knee grazing my thigh.

Fuck me, she's warm.

Rachel opens the box of Band-Aids and searches through it as if she's an actual doctor picking a scalpel. The scent of the ocean enters my nose and my jeans tighten. "If you're serious about modifying your car, I'll do it if you get the parts. No cost."

That can be the way I repay this debt and stop thinking

about letting my fingers drift up her shirt to caress what would probably be the softest skin on the planet.

She peels back the paper to reveal the Band-Aid and balances it on her knee. "If I do make modifications, I think I'd like to do them myself. I don't get to work with cars that often, and I sort of get a rush when I do."

Jesus, it's like I've met my twin. One glance at her slim figure and I erase that thought. I wouldn't be attracted to someone I was related to. "Then think about what you want and I'll score you the parts." I've got favors I'd call in for her.

"Hold out your arm," she instructs and though it makes me feel like a damn fool, I obey.

Rachel pours alcohol onto the towel and begins to dab it on the cut. "Maybe I'll take you up on that, but I'm not sure I want to mess with her. My real dream is to find an old Mustang and supe her up. Kind of like what you're doing with yours. That would be awesome."

Ignoring the slight sting on my arm, I turn my head to survey her. This girl is too good to be true. "Then I'll help you with that."

Rachel holds the towel to my skin. "You don't have to."

"I owe you."

Her nose wrinkles as if she's thinking something she believes is not worth saying. I have to keep myself from asking what.

"Does it hurt?" she asks. "Because sometimes I blow on my cuts when I put alcohol on them."

"I'm good."

"Then I guess I'm a wuss. I would have thought the alcohol would sting. You're missing the top layer of skin."

Without another word, she places the towel on the floor, takes the plastic off the Band-Aid and presses it to my skin. I haven't worn one of these since I was five. Earlier tonight, everything felt hopeless after I talked to Noah, but being around her erases bad thoughts.

Rachel raises her head and her forehead scrunches. "What?"

Under the dim lighting, parts of her hair shine and I crave to run my fingers through it. Fuck it. Once she goes home, she'll never come back. If Beth taught me anything, it's to grab hold of what's in front of me while I can. "What would you do if I kissed you?"

Rachel

MY MOUTH FALLS OPEN, AND only when it starts to get dry do I close it. What would I do if he kissed me? Go into shock? Have multiple seizures? Jump up and down? I take in a shaky breath. Isaiah called me brave so I rush out the words. "Kiss you back?"

His gray eyes soften as if I gave an acceptable answer, but then he studies my face with a sober expression. "How many boyfriends have you had?"

My entire body sags, and I lace my fingers together, unlace them and lace them again. "Why?"

"Because." His hand covers mine to halt my serial lacing. "I've never met anyone like you. I'm...trying to understand you."

I don't want to answer. I like the idea of him thinking of me as brave, as the girl who teases him in a bar. I don't want him to see me as I really am—the tongue-twisted 'fraidy cat who's never dated a guy.

"I don't care what the answer is," he prods. "But I need to know."

There is no way I can admit this and meet his eyes, so I focus on our combined hands. "I've never had a boyfriend."

I take a quick peek and Isaiah nods once, as if he already knew what I would say. He raises his hand to my face again and I allow the touch. His fingers slide along my jawline and the warmth of his caresses radiates past my skin and into my bloodstream. Pleasing goose bumps rise on my neck.

"Do you think you'll come back sometime?" he asks. "And let me help you with your car?"

My ears ring with the staccato thrum, thrum, thrum of my heart. Holy crap, I can't believe this is happening to me.

"I'll make it work. I swear." The words tumble out of my mouth without thought. That's not true. Actually, they tumble out with a lot of thought of how my parents won't approve, of how my brothers will kill Isaiah, then possibly kill me. But in this moment, I don't care what any of them think.

"I want to kiss you," Isaiah says.

A rush of terror and excitement floods my body. "Isaiah, I've never..."

"It's okay." Oh, God, his voice is dark and smooth and hypnotic.

I suck in air and sort of clumsily move my head so he knows this is what I want. "What do I do? I mean, how do I..."

And he doesn't let me finish. Isaiah lazily yet deliberately tilts his head as he stares into my eyes. My entire body hums and a fuzzy sensation fills my head, making it hard to focus. My mouth opens then closes. And as he slowly bends down, my tongue quickly licks my dry lips.

I hope I'm doing this right. I want to do this right.

Isaiah slips his hand from my chin to cradle my head. His

fingers tunnel through my hair, making the back of my neck tingle with anticipation as the pad of his thumb whispers gently against my cheek. His lips hover right next to mine and his warm breath heats my face.

The blood pounds so wildly in my veins that he has to sense the vibration. There's a magnetic pull taking over the small distance between our lips. An energy I can't resist. My head inclines opposite his and the moment I close my eyes, his mouth brushes mine.

Soft. Warm. Gentle. His lips move slowly, exerting pressure. And I feel like I can't breathe, yet like I'm flying. The pressure ends, but his mouth stays near mine. His hand grips my waist and my spine gives at the shockingly right pleasure of his touch.

Isaiah senses my weakness and his hand snakes its way around my waist, his strong arm holds me up. And he explores again. A little pressure on my lower lip. A little pressure on the top. And then I remember that I'm supposed to kiss him back.

Nerves send small shock waves through my chest, and my hand trembles as I raise it to his shoulders. I press both my lips into his lower one right as my fingers caress the side of his neck. Isaiah shivers. In a good way, I think.

I open my mouth to ask when his lips move fast against mine, sucking in my lower one, causing warmth and excitement to explode in my body, the aftermath of that divine encounter melting every piece of me.

I moan, and Isaiah's arm tightens, bringing my body closer to his. My lips maneuver against his in response. A *yes* to his pulling me closer. A *yes* to his lips taking in mine. A *yes* to the fact that he allows me to perform the same succulent kiss on him.

I can't help it. I permit the tip of my tongue to barely brush his lower lip. Isaiah curls my hair into his fist and I love how my touch affects him, affects me. Wrapping my other arm around his neck, I lose all sense of independence with his sweet taste.

I like this. I like this a lot.

Isaiah takes over again and kisses me gently once more. Twice. The third time a little longer. And then his lips let me go.

Isaiah

RACHEL SMILES.

It's a beautiful smile. One that brightens the rat-infested attic room. No one has ever smiled like that at me. No one. Everything inside me twists with the need to keep her close.

I should be pissed. Who knows if I'll ever see the money from Eric. Who knows if Noah and I will lose the lease, sending me back into the system. Right now, I don't fucking care. I'm touching an angel.

My spine prickles as the window near the fire escape groans. My grip on Rachel tightens, and I bring her up with me as I stand. A leg pokes through the widening gap, and I shove Rachel behind me. Every instinct screams to protect her, to fight. I automatically widen my stance and hold my arms out at my sides, willing to take whatever bullet is coming our way, willing to run right into the bastard the moment he's through.

With half of his body in, Noah halts in the window frame. His muscles tense as he warily sizes me up. "Rough night, bro?"

I lower my arms. "We've got a fucking door, man."

Noah shuts the window and attempts to lock it, only to curse as he remembers that the latch is still broken. "Forgot my key at Echo's. Your car's not out there so I assumed you weren't home."

He walks to the bedroom and stops as his gaze shifts to what I'm assuming is Rachel. "My bad." Noah pivots on his heel and heads for the door.

"Noah, wait." Locking my arm around her shoulder, I bring Rachel to my side. "Don't go."

"It's good." He reaches for the doorknob with one hand and rubs his eyes with the other. "I forgot something in my car."

"Stay." I glance at the clock. It's after one. He's been pulling morning shifts at his job and will need to be awake in a few hours. The guy's wiped with black circles under his eyes, but has my back because he thinks I'm trying to score. "I was going to walk Rachel to her car."

"You sure?" He jacks his thumb in the direction of the stairwell.

"Yeah. Don't sweat it. Rachel—Noah. Noah, this is Rachel."

His eyebrows slowly rise so that they disappear beneath his hair. He and I, we don't introduce each other to the girls we bring home. In the past, sometimes the one-nighters became clingy and neither one of us wanted the other dealing with that situation. Of course, Noah's not like that anymore. Now that he has Echo.

Noah's eyes sway between me and her. "S'up, Rachel."

"Nothing," she says as if wondering if her response is correct. Rachel leans closer to me and I stroke her shoulder in an act of comfort and in the hopes Noah sees that Rachel is more than a fuck.

"I think I left my bracelets in the bathroom." Like a small bird in flight, Rachel flits across the room and abruptly closes the bathroom door behind her. Drywall drops from the ceiling and scatters across the kitchen floor.

Noah's mouth tugs up. "Guess that means we're losing our security deposit."

I spread my arms out and half whisper, half yell, "What the hell? She's not a whore."

"Never said she was." He crosses the room and opens the fridge. "Want a beer?"

Sure. Why don't I go ahead and light a joint while I'm at it? I follow him and place my hand on the open door of the fridge to get his attention while still whispering. "I'm serious. She's not like that. Treat her with some respect."

Noah twists off the top of an MGD and surveys me while he swallows. "I thought I was treating you both with respect." He also lowers his voice when I gesture at the bathroom to indicate I don't need her overhearing this conversation. "I tried to leave."

"You made her think she was a one-night stand." I slam the refrigerator door shut.

"Excuse the shit out of me. I thought she was." He points his beer at me. "You're not dating. The last girl you touched was Beth."

My fists ball at the mention of her name, and Noah waves me off. "And don't start on that shit. She's gone, she's happy and she ain't coming back. And, yeah, I still talk to her because she's the closest thing I've got to a sister, so I can say her damned name if I want to."

"Noah," I say as a warning.

"Beth," he tauntingly whispers. "Beth, Beth, Beth, Beth, Beth. If you're going to take a swing at me, bro, do it, because I'm damn tired of walking on eggshells because of that girl."

My heart rips open again with every acknowledgment of her existence. He needs to stop and he needs to stop now. Especially with Rachel here. I like her and I don't need Noah ruining it with her by reminding me of a past that will never change. "You're a cranky son of a bitch when you're tired."

The tension between us drains when Noah chuckles and swigs the beer. I'm not good at much, but I'm good at deflecting. He kneads his eyes with his fists again and releases a long breath. "Look, I walk in at 1:00 a.m. to find you holding a pretty girl wearing your shirt."

He's right. I overreacted. "Noah," I interrupt.

"Do I sound like I'm done talking? It looked like you were hooking up so I assumed you were hooking up. My apologies. I'm sorry. I'm the asshole. It's done so get the fuck over it. As for making her feel like a one-night stand, last time I checked, saying 's'up' doesn't translate to 'thanks for banging my best friend.' And do you want to tell me why the hell I'm whispering in my own apartment?"

"Because I like her."

Noah blinks because words like that don't come easily from me. He tilts up the bottle, finishes the rest and places the empty container on the counter. "That changes things."

"As a friend," I add quickly but then realize friends don't kiss. Shit, I've messed this up.

The door to the bathroom opens and we both stare at Rachel. She plays with the gold bracelets on her wrist. "Sorry it took so long. My bracelets fell and rolled behind the sink and...it took a bit to get them out."

Even Noah visibly cringes at the thought of anyone putting their hand in the two-inch gap behind the sink. "You should have called me," I say. "I would have gotten them."

Her gaze switches between me and Noah. "It's all right. I got them. So—" she rocks on her toes "—are you ready to go?"

"Yeah. Let's roll."

Rachel gathers her coat from the couch and pauses when Noah says her name. *Damn, Noah, don't screw this up.*

"Rachel," he repeats, obviously searching for something good to say. "It was nice to meet you. You should come back. Meet my girl, Echo. We'll hang out or some shit like that."

Or some shit like that. I want to slam his head and my own into the wall.

"Okay." She has that what-the-hell look people get when they watch reality TV. "It was nice to meet you, too."

When her back's to us both, I mouth at Noah, *Or some shit like that?*

He mouths back, *I'm trying.*

I unbolt the door and when she steps into the hallway, I whisper to him, "Real elegant, man. And the girls thought you were fucking smooth."

Noah laughs. "I am smooth, bro. But now I'm only smooth with Echo."

Right before I shut the door, I flip Noah off. His laughter rings through the hallway.

At the bottom of the stairs, Rachel waits for me to open

the door. I've never seen a girl wait like that before or known a girl who'd make the assumption that a guy would open it for her. Rachel was probably raised to expect guys to open doors, and she's probably around enough guys who were taught to do it.

I like that she waits, and I like opening it for her. When I was a kid, I preferred the guys my mom dated who did crazy stuff like that.

The cold air clings to my bare arms as we walk out onto the sidewalk. The temperature has dropped dramatically since we first met at the drag race. A moment that feels like lifetimes ago.

Rachel shivers and places her hands in her coat pockets, leaving me unsure of what to do. Is she cold and I should put my arm around her shoulder, or is she telling me to stay clear? The muscles tighten in my neck and I shake my head to clear the chaos. *Get a grip, man.* How can I be confused over a girl?

"Your roommate seems nice," she says with forced lightness.

Her attempt to make us okay rattles me—in a good way. I can't think of many people who have ever tried to make things work with me. "Noah's great, but he was off tonight."

"It's okay. I'm sure it was weird to see a girl in his apartment."

I pull at my bottom earring. I've been with other girls. The ones who were interested in being with the guy with the tattoos and earrings for a night. I've never minded being used. But with Rachel, there's a softness that hits her eyes when she looks in my direction, and it's messing with me.

"Tell him I'm sorry I was there so late," she continues. "I don't want him to think badly of me."

"You...ah..." *Didn't pick up that he thought you were a one-night stand?* "Weren't scared of Noah?"

Rachel sort of laughs, "No." She pauses. "Should I be? He seemed friendly."

"No, he's cool. You bolted into the bathroom and..."

She dips her head, and as we pass a streetlight, I catch the red invading her cheeks. "Sorry about that. I *did* forget my bracelets and I *did* drop them, but it was weird, you know, meeting someone at 1:00 a.m."

"Yeah." Weirder than that? She was there at one in the morning and I hadn't slept with her. I shove my hands into my jeans pockets and silently curse myself.

I glance at Rachel, and she quickly averts her eyes when I spot her spying on me. What the fuck does she see when she looks at me? If she saw what was inside, she'd be screaming. The outside is modest projection.

Rachel can't like me because she doesn't know me. The real me. For Rachel, life is still sunshine, rainbows and pink fucking fuzzy unicorns. I'm nothing but darkness, clouds and rats.

I should never have kissed her or brought her home. She deserves better than the brokenness inside me. I'll hold on to tonight. Burn the memory of the way she's looked at me into my mind because that's as close as I'll ever get to something like this again. Besides, if she saw me in daylight, away from the filth that I live in, she'd change her mind.

Just like Beth did the moment she left town.

Faster than I would have preferred, we reach the parking lot of the auto shop.

"What about your car?" she asks as I enter the security code.

The motor whines as the garage door lifts. "I'll head over and fix the tire now."

"Do you want help? I'm pretty crafty with a jack and a tire iron."

I turn to tell her no and stop when I see her face. I swear, she glows. Her eyes shine like stars, and her smile radiates with a light all its own. My throat swells. I don't want to give her up. "No. I don't want you getting into trouble at home."

"See, you *are* bossy." She finally takes her hands out of her pockets and nudges my biceps with one delicate finger.

My heart stutters with her caress, and as she drops her arm, I quickly reach out and snake my fingers through hers. So close to letting her go, I shouldn't touch her, but in my defense, she touched me first. "Not bossy. Concerned. Truth, Rachel, I want to know if you feel safe going home."

"It's fine. Ethan would have texted me if there were problems. Mom and Dad probably haven't even come home for the night."

Yeah. I knew all about guardians who stayed out late to party. I guess having money changes nothing in the realm of shitty parenting. "Tell me your brothers protect you." Because if not, I'd have to meet them in a dark alley sometime and school them on how to treat their sister.

"More like they're overprotective."

I savor the feel of the smooth skin of her hand. No girl

I have ever touched has had hands this soft. "That's not a bad thing."

Rachel releases a frustrated sigh. "You know, I'm starting to think I misjudged you. You sound annoyingly like my brothers."

She's right on one thing: she has misjudged me, but not in the way she thinks. "Good. I'm all for overprotection."

"Bossy."

I chuckle, and the sound makes her smile. I'm going to miss that smile. *Tell her it's over, asshole.* Tell her that you come from two different worlds and that it would never work. Tell her that kiss meant more to you than she could ever imagine. Tell her that you'll dream about her and think about her, but that's where it ends.

The color drains from her face and her hand goes limp in mine. Did she figure out I'm bad news on her own? She heads for her car. "Do you have my keys?"

I fish them out of my pocket and toss them to her. With the click of a button, the car unlocks and she opens the passenger door. She keeps her back to me for a second then turns with a piece of paper in her hand. "Here's my number. I almost forgot to give it to you."

I swallow as I stare at the number. *Tell her. Just fucking tell her.* "Rachel..."

"You'll call, right?" And the small amount of hurt in her voice stabs my heart.

I envelop Rachel in my arms and cup her head to my chest. She smells good. Like the ocean. Like her jacket. I try to memorize the feel of her body against mine: all soft and warm and curves. The paper in her hand crinkles as she links one arm, then another around my waist. Leaning into me, she lets out a contented sigh and I close my eyes with the sound.

Ten seconds. I'll keep her for ten more seconds.

I want to keep her.

Two.

I shouldn't.

Four.

Maybe she can see past what I am. We don't have to be more. We can be friends.

Seven.

I can fix this.

Nine.

I can make anything work.

Ten.

"I'll call."

With bright eyes, she shoves the number into my hand. "Okay. I'll talk to you soon."

I nod, and without another word, Rachel slips into the driver's seat, turns over the engine and glides her Mustang out of the auto shop. Grasping my lifeline to her, I watch as her red taillights fade into the distance.

I smile, then groan as I inhale.

I can recognize three girls by their scent. Tonight I learned that Rachel smells like the ocean. Beth reminded me of crushed roses. And this girl—wild honey. I may not see her, but she's there. Every ounce of happiness flees with the realization that my life can't be changed. "What do you want, Abby?"

The shadow of a slim figure ghosts its way toward me

from the side of the shop. "I hadn't heard that you found a new plaything."

I cross my arms over my chest. "I haven't."

She steps into the streetlight, brushing her long, dark brown hair over the shoulder of her tightly fitted hoodie. "Why so testy, Isaiah? She seemed cute. Spunky. I like cute and spunky. I had a bunny like that once, one of those large fluffy ones."

"You don't seem like the bunny type."

"I'm not." Her dark eyes wickedly flash over me. "Hence the word *once*."

"What do you want?" I repeat, glancing at the nonexistent watch on my arm. "It's late."

Abby and I have a weird friendship, which is odd since Abby doesn't do relationships. The sarcastic curve of her lips indicates that, in this moment, she's temporarily placed our friendship on the back burner. "My, my. We are emotional tonight. But to answer your question, I was on my way to your apartment because we have business to take care of, and I decided to stall our plans when I saw cute and spunky."

She pauses, waiting for me to fill her in on Rachel. The only answer she receives is the buzzing from the overhead streetlight. "So does this mean you're finally over Beth?"

If Abby were acting as my friend, I might tell her. But life for Abby, especially here recently, is all about business. Even though she's only on the verge of turning seventeen. "Cut to the chase."

"You are no fun," she says as she reaches into the back pocket of her practically painted-on jeans and pulls out a wad of cash. "I saw Eric tonight. Well, I hid Eric tonight."

That catches my attention. "You hate Eric." And Eric hates her. Their "businesses" often collide on the streets.

"I like the idea of Eric owing me a favor." Figures. Abby is always working an angle.

"What's this have to do with me?"

Like a five-year-old on a playground, Abby grabs on to the metal utility pole with her outstretched hand and walks in a slow circle. "We had time to kill so we chatted."

"You chatted?"

"Yes." She sticks her tongue out at me. "I'm capable of conversation at times. You know, will U of K make it to the final four this year, will the original Guns N' Roses ever get back together, will I graduate from high school, and what people we know in common. Guess who came up in our chat?"

I shrug and fake an innocent expression. "Me?"

She scrunches her pixie face. "Smart guys make me so hot, but unfortunately, you do nothing for me. I've known you too long."

"Abby," I say with a bit of impatience. "Are we gonna wrap this up or not?"

"Eric said he owed you, so I volunteered to play mule."

"That was extremely generous of you." My instincts flare. She wants something.

"Yes, it is. But that is beside the point because now, sir, you owe me."

I shake my head before she finishes talking. "Wrong. You volunteered to mule my money. I don't owe you shit."

Abby laughs and my mouth dries out. Where the hell is she heading? "We didn't only talk about you, silly. Eric had a lot to say about two college kids who tipped off the police in order to create chaos so they could pull a gun on Eric and jack him."

I focus on keeping my expression from changing. Abby doesn't give info because she likes to talk. She's fishing.

"How much did he lose?"

"Five thousand dollars, and let me tell you, Eric is not happy."

I'm sure he's not. Jacked in his own territory and he lost money. I'm sure Eric is on the warpath. "So if Eric got jacked then why is he willing to pay me?"

"You know Eric—he doesn't believe in banks or investing, which is a shame with the amount of money he brings in. One of these days someone's going to shoot him in the head and find his secret cubbyhole full of cash."

Part of me wonders if Abby will be the one to do it. I let out a sigh. I took it too far. Abby's all business with selling drugs, but she's not a killer. At least not yet.

Abby continues, "You saved some of his guys tonight by spotting the cops. He wanted to make sure he paid his debt to you."

"Not that I don't find you interesting, but give me my money."

"I like you better when you're around cars. You're less tense then. Anyhow." She rubs the wad of cash between her fingers. "I think I'm going to hold on to this cash as a reward for keeping my mouth shut."

"Give me my fucking money, Abby." I'm tired of her games.

"All right, but you should know that Eric was not only interested in the whereabouts of those two college boys, but also in a particular blonde we both just saw leave. You looked cute together—you and the blonde. I'm sure Eric would pay royally to know you were up on the girl."

A roar fills my ears as every muscle tenses. No one is going anywhere near Rachel.

No one.

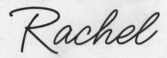
Rachel

HE NEVER CALLED. I WAITED. And he still never called. What I have a hard time comprehending is why I grieve for something that obviously was never mine to begin with.

A few tables away, my brothers laugh. Each of them holds a bottled beer. In order to hide our youngest brothers' involvement in underage drinking, Gavin and Jack stand in front of West and Ethan. Cold air drifts into the bottom of the large white tent housing the hundreds of guests and chills my ankles. The overhead heaters keep me warm, but the alcohol keeps my brothers warmer.

A votive candle floats in a crystal bowl full of water and translucent rocks. My hand hovers over the single flickering flame. Every white-cloth-covered table contains one of these centerpieces. I'd bet I'm the only guest wondering how close I can place my hand to the flame before I get burned.

Seated at the table farthest from the couples slow-dancing in front of the stage, I cross one leg over the other. It's a continual fidget meant to keep my limbs from falling asleep, and each time I move, I smooth out the material of my golden gown as if wrinkles will be the death of me. I think I look kinda pretty tonight, which is why every time I glimpse my reflection in the mirror my eyes water. I wanted Isaiah to see me this way.

"Would you like to dance?"

My heart beats twice and I glance up, hoping and praying that somehow Isaiah has found me, even though I'm at an exclusive New Year's Eve party at the Lieutenant Mayor's house. I mean, it's possible. At least it's possible in the daydreams I've had since I sat at this corner table over an hour ago. I force a wannabe smile when I find Brian Toddsworth staring down at me. A month ago, I would have loved for him to ask me to dance. Today... Why didn't Isaiah call?

I shrug my bare shoulders while shaking my head. Heat flushes my face when I realize I have yet to answer and that I'm conveying so many different body language signs that it probably appears I'm having a seizure. "No, thank you," I barely whisper.

Brian belongs in a different realm of popular than me, and the thought of saying the wrong thing and becoming a laughingstock makes my insides squirm. As if he's shocked by the response, Brian's head rears back. "Are you sure?"

"Nice party, Brian." My twin, Ethan, moseys over from his seat with my brothers. All of whom are watching Brian and me closely. Sort of like how vultures watch the last twitch of roadkill.

Brian extends his fist to Ethan and they knuckle bump. They've been friends since kindergarten. Brian and I've been friends since never.

"The party's awful," says Brian. "Everyone from school is

at Sarah's. Spending New Year's schmoozing for my parents blows. Part of me hopes Dad loses the primary next spring."

Ethan jerks his head in my direction as if I'm a five-year-old who can't follow a conversation. "Whatcha doing with Rachel?"

Brian's cheeks redden. "Your mom mentioned to my mom that no one was talking to Rachel, and you know what happened last weekend, so I'm not in a position to disagree."

Wow, Brian didn't even try to pretend I wasn't a pity dance. When my heels click on the temporary wooden floor of the tent, the pair evidently remembers my existence.

Ethan gestures at Brian then to me with his beer. "Can you try to have some tact when it comes to Rach? She is my sister."

Twin. I prefer the word *twin.* Gavin, Jack and West are my brothers. I feel a special connection with Ethan. Brian acknowledges me with a glance. "I meant no disrespect. My parents grounded me when they found my pot, and if I do what Mom wants she'll back off."

I stare at my hands laced in my lap. I've always wanted to be told that dancing with me is a punishment reserved for the severest of offenders. Brian, I guess, rethinks his words and backtracks. "It's not that you aren't pretty or anything. You are."

"What did you say?" asks Ethan. I bite my lower lip. *Shut up, Ethan.* Because my twin and I can't speak telepathically, Ethan continues, "Are you into Rachel?"

"Hell no."

Awesome. What girl doesn't want to hear that?

"You said she's pretty," Ethan spits out as if that comment is an insult.

"She is," says Brian. "But I'm not into her."

Ethan's shoulders sag with relief. "Good."

Great. I think I'm going to drive a fork into my brother's abdomen.

"Look." Brian turns to face me. "You're nice, but you're Rachel, you know?"

Yes, I'm well aware of who I am: the obsessively shy and anxious girl who stumbles over her own name. The one with the ridiculously protective brothers. "It's all right."

It's not. But what am I going to do? The only guy who has ever shown the least bit of interest in me never called, so why should anything else in my life be different?

"Apologize to my sister," says Ethan.

Brian's forehead furrows. "For what?"

"For existing."

Brian laughs and bumps Ethan's fist again. "Sorry I exist, Rachel. And Ethan, I'll catch you at Sarah's party later."

Later? With the self-proclaimed pot smoker? I tilt my head while Ethan briefly closes his eyes. I straighten my back, tap the seat next to me, then fold my hands daintily over my knees. "Sooo? How are you doing?"

Ethan collapses in the seat and rests his beer on the table. "It's nothing. Let it go."

I bat my eyelashes and smile like a stupid Southern belle because he must think I'm a moron if he believes I'm buying that. "It didn't sound like nothing."

"Brian experimented with pot. It's no big deal."

"Does that mean you experimented with pot?"

He stretches out his legs and remains silent. I drop the Southern belle act and lean into him. "If that conversation took place between West and any of his friends, I'd let it go.

West does stupid things. It's what West was born to do. But you—you don't do stupid things."

Ethan turns his head toward me, and all I see is dark eyes and dark hair—a reminder that he's my opposite. "I was with him, but I didn't do it, okay?" He holds out his pinkie. "I swear."

I press his pinkie down and pat his knee. The offer of a pinkie has always been enough for the two of us. If he swears it, I believe it.

Ethan regards my cell on the table. "Are you expecting a call?"

The disbelief in his voice stings. "No." Unfortunately. "I'm not."

Yet it doesn't stop me from looking at the wretched device. Because staring at it for ten hours straight will magically remind Isaiah that I gave him my number.

"I've been thinking," says Ethan.

"Which is never a good thing," I cut him off. "It will only strain the brain cells that actually function and those two deserve a break."

He smirks. "You know, if you'd crawl out of your shell and be yourself around everyone else, then that phone would be ringing nonstop, you might attend an occasional nonadult party and you wouldn't have to rely on Brian for a pity dance."

Once more, I focus on my lap and again smooth out my dress. I was myself with Isaiah, and look where that got me. "This *is* me."

"You hate attention...I get it. But I hate how everyone sees you. If it bothers me then I know it's got to bother you."

The back of my neck bristles and my spine straightens.

Ethan's never been so blunt and I don't care for it. "Sorry I can't be perfect like you." Lead scorer on the lacrosse team, voted onto the student council, popular...not me. Just like the rest of my fabulous brothers.

"Come on," he says. "Don't be like that. I'm only pointing out what you already know. Everyone thinks you're quiet, shy, a little off because of your anxiety attacks in middle school and..." He trails off and picks at the label on his beer. "And they think you're sick."

My gaze jumps to his. "I am not sick." I am not Colleen.

There's an anger building in his eyes that I'm unfamiliar with. "I thought you weren't either, but then I was the one holding your hair back a few days ago when you vomited in a toilet. So if you weren't sick, what were you?"

"I wasn't sick."

"And yet you claim you're over the panic attacks. So which rumor is true? Are you the girl who spent time in the hospital our freshman year because you're sickly, or are you the girl who spent time in the hospital because you had panic attacks?"

I hate that word: *sick*. I also hate the words *panic*, *fear* and *coward*. A lump forms in my throat, and I can't decide if I'm angry or hurt or both. "That is low."

"Lying to me is low."

My mouth pops open and no words come out. Part of me is dying to tell him. To let someone into my personal nightmare, but I've gone this long hiding my secret and if he knows, will he tell Mom? "One panic attack. That's it."

"You're lying, Rachel."

"I'm not."

CRASH INTO YOU   119

He leans forward. "You are."

Because of our relationship, he can read my poker face like no one else. What's surprising is that, after two years, he's just catching on to the lie.

"You can convince Mom that you aren't the girl who obsesses over Cobras, reads *Motor Trend,* sneaks out after dinner to bathe in axle grease and skips curfew so she can drive her car. If you can do that, I think you're capable of lying to me about being over the panic attacks."

I slam my hand on the table and people at a nearby table gawk. Ethan waves at them while I lower my head, embarrassed.

"You really want the truth?" I whisper.

"I'm sorry, Rachel. I never knew the two of us stopped telling each other the truth."

Hypocrite. "What do you do on twin amnesty night?"

A muscle near his eye flinches. "Lying and withholding information are different."

"Fine. Truth? You and I both know that I can't be me. She isn't who Mom wants."

"This isn't about Mom," he harshly whispers back. "This is about you and me."

My lower lip trembles. I made my brother, my best friend, my only friend, mad at me. Ethan squeezes my hand, then lets me and the subject go. "Don't cry. I hate it when you cry."

He finishes his beer in two gulps. "Do you ever wonder what it would have been like if we'd been born to anyone else?"

My stomach aches from the raw truth of his question. "All the time."

"Rachel!" my mother calls. When she's sure she's caught my attention, she motions for me to join her.

I force my practiced smile on my lips. "This is why I can't be me. Can you imagine how her friends would react if I discussed air shifters and turbochargers? These events...this is why she had another daughter. This is why I'm alive."

Gathering my gown, I stand. Ethan pulls on my hand and I know he wants me to look at him, but I refuse. "You make her happy, Rach. And we thank you for that. No one likes it when Mom's sad."

I release a breath, searching for my nonexistent happy place. "I get tired of playing the role."

"I know." He tugs on my hand again, and this time I give in. He flashes his playful smile. "Even I don't know what an air shifter is."

I smack his arm, and my smile becomes relaxed as I hear his laughter.

My mother is gorgeous in her slim-fitting red sequined dress and slicked-back blond hair. Like always, Mom is the center of a group. People are naturally drawn to her, and she naturally loves the attention.

The band has progressed onto jazz, and my mother's movements seem to flow with the beat. I need to go to the bathroom, and I've waited too long in the hopes Mom would maneuver her social networking away from the front of the tent. It never happened, so here I am—standing with a full bladder, in a golden gown, being gawked at by a group of aging women. The smile becomes harder to hold.

"Hi, Mom," I half whisper, half choke. There are way too many eyes on me.

"These are the ladies from the Leukemia Foundation. Ladies, you remember my youngest daughter, Rachel." My mother graces me with a smile I thought was reserved only for my brothers: one of pride.

They all comment on how it's nice to see me and how beautiful I look and ask Mom where we bought my dress. I move like a bobblehead while my clammy fingers twist behind my back.

"I loved the speech you gave the other night," says an elderly woman to my right. Her pungent perfume hits me wrong, and I concentrate on not gagging. I nod, and the gesture only encourages her to speak more.

To the left and a bit across from me, I catch sight of a lady my mother's age touching Mom's arm. Mom introduced us earlier—Meg is her name, I think. She was Colleen's private nurse. They both stare at me, and my heart sinks with the knowledge that I must be their topic of conversation.

"You're right," Meg says to Mom. "She does resemble Colleen."

The woman to my right continues to talk about the speech I made at Colleen's event. I make fleeting eye contact because I'm more interested in overhearing my mother.

"She's not as outgoing as Colleen," Meg adds.

"No," Mom responds with a hint of sadness. "Rachel's a little quieter." A very dramatic pause. "But her father and I are helping her with that. She's made huge improvements over the last two years. All on her own." I hear the pride. "All without therapy."

I miss therapy. I miss having someone to talk to, someone who can empathize with what it feels like to walk into a room and have fear and anxiety consume you to the point that you can't breathe. But what I don't miss about therapy is how my family regarded me as if I was breakable, as if I was weak.

"With each day, she reminds me a little more of her sister," Mom says.

I remind her of Colleen. I should be happy. I'm becoming what my mother wants. But right now, I want to cry.

"I'm sorry," I interrupt the older woman, who's still droning on. "I need to excuse myself."

Isaiah

I STAND ON THE EDGE of the crumbling brick wall built to protect people from the thirty-foot drop. In the distance, high-rises glimmer and thousands of white twinkling lights circle the city. Each light represents a neighborhood, a house, a home, a family, a person—people who are wanted. It's the last night of December and it's fifty degrees. Great for a guy who doesn't own a jacket.

Forty-eight hours have officially passed since I met Rachel. I've thought about her; her beauty, her laughter, that shy smile, our kiss. She discovered a deep hole in my chest and somehow filled it with her existence. Now she's gone, leaving me alone, leaving me hollow.

Glancing around the panoramic scene, I know I would have brought her here. This place has been abandoned for decades, and few care that you can still drive up the steep hill as long as you move the flimsy wooden barricades.

Sixty years ago, teenagers made out here. Legend says the braver ones drag raced the winding mile road and played chicken at the top where no wall exists. When I teeter on this ledge, I wonder if the drivers who flew over the drop tried to stop or if they were begging for an excuse to end it all.

I would have loved to see Rachel's expression when she saw the city like this. But Eric and his crew are watching everyone closely as they search for her and the two college boys. I refuse to be the link between Eric and Rachel. She's safer without me. She's better off without me. Besides, it's not like anything would have happened between us.

Movement in the brush catches my attention, and I turn to see a shadow emerge.

"You are so damn predictable," says Abby. I finally discern her features as she joins me on the wall. Like always, she wears a fitted blue hoodie and even tighter blue jeans.

I have a million questions, but stick with the important one. "What are you doing here?"

"Tradition, jackass." Not caring that thirty feet below is nothing but sharp rocks, she sits on the wall and dangles her legs over the edge. "I have a gift for you."

Still mad over losing my rent money, I angle my body away from her. "Leave, Abby."

"Cut the attitude. That was business. This is friends. Do you want your gift or not?"

The two of us have an odd relationship. We met when we were ten. My then foster father used to take me to the auto shop I work at now, and she used to play in the alley behind the garage. We struck up a friendship that never went away and never stopped being odd. Abby is the longest steady relationship I've had with one person, which makes her special.

Special means I'll put up with her shit. With a sigh, I sit, leaving several feet between us. "How did you get here?"

She reaches into her hoodie. "Asked a client to drop me off and then hiked."

A client, meaning a buyer, because she's a seller. "You shouldn't get in cars with them."

"Don't worry, Dad. I typically don't. But this guy is clean-cut."

"Which means you should definitely watch your back. Image means nothing." What people project to the world never shows what's lurking on the inside.

"You liked her, didn't you?" she asks, ignoring what I said. "The cute, fuzzy bunny?"

I say nothing and survey the northeast side of town. She's over there somewhere. Is Rachel happy I never called, or did I break her heart? As much as I hate the idea of it, I hope she's relieved. She deserved better than me.

"You know what I find interesting?" she asks.

"What?"

"That you still lie to Noah about where you go for New Year's Eve."

"My business. Not his."

"I also find it curious that Fuzzy Bunny isn't here with you if you liked her so much."

"I never brought Beth here," I say in defense.

"You never smiled at Beth like I saw you smile at her."

I shift, uncomfortable that Abby saw something so intimate between me and Rachel. "You said you had a gift."

I hear plastic rubbing together in her hand and, because Abby carries very little on her, it has to be a baggy. "Patience, Grasshopper. If I'm giving this type of gift then I want to know it's for a good cause. Answer me about the girl."

Flooded with the urge to tell someone, I pull on my bottom earring. "Yeah. I liked her." Because saying it makes it real, and it was real. "But we would have only been friends."

She's silent except for the sound of her heel occasionally hitting the brick wall. "I liked this guy last year, but I blew him off after a couple of days. He came from a good home and was a good guy. Sometimes it's better that we let the good catches go, you know?"

Her feet continue to kick against the wall. Abby's not one to share, so that statement had to take a lot out of her. "Yeah. I do know."

"I hear you need money," she says.

That grabs my attention. "Says who?"

"No one." Abby smirks. "You don't street race and you did. The only reason I could come up with is that you're low on funds."

"Wanna give me my money back?"

"Hell no."

Gotta respect her for that.

"I know someone that's interested in your skills with cars, Isaiah. He's been watching you for a while and he'll pay well."

"Does your friend give out W-2 forms?"

Abby chuckles. "One thousand in cash for every car you jack. All you need is a lot full of empty cars and your hot-wiring capabilities."

"Not interested."

"If you change your mind..."

"I won't." I'm not interested in becoming a criminal. Once you enter the land of illegal, someone, somewhere owns you.

She withdraws a joint from the baggie. "This is the last of my supply. Once this is gone, I swear not to sell again for the rest of this year."

Easy promise, since there are only minutes left until the new year begins. Abby's not a fan of what she does, but she's good at business and at selling. If she could ever get the hell off the streets she'd probably become someone. "You don't have to sell," I say.

"You didn't have to street race."

Point taken.

Abby stares out over the blinking lights of the city. "I saw my dad today." I hear the hurt in her voice.

My heart aches for her. Before I can think of something to say to help her feel better, she continues, "I was going to share this with you, but now I don't think I want to." Abby extends the joint to me. "You can have it."

I roll the joint in my hand: two inches long and thin. I first smoked up in eighth grade and hated the loss of control. But hanging with the people I knew, surviving in the homes I lived in, I learned quick how to blend in and conform. It's amazing what you can convince people of just by touching a joint to your lips. "Are you sure you don't want it?"

She shakes her head. I place the joint between my thumb and forefinger and snap it over the thirty-foot drop. Abby claps. "Well played." She hoots, then yells, "Happy fucking New Year, nature. You can have your shit back."

Abby lapses into silence. Somewhere in the distance below, glass shatters. Most likely a home invasion. The sad part is, neither one of us flinch.

"I knew you'd gone straight," Abby says. "I take that back—

not gone straight, but that you weren't as hard-core as everyone thinks."

"I know," I respond. Abby is the one person who has always known. When everyone else was higher than kites, she'd look over and realize that I was sober—because she was, too.

"If I had asked, you would have smoked it with me," she says.

I nod. Because she wouldn't have wanted to do it alone, and because the only reason she would have done it is because it hurt her so much to see her dad. "I would have taken a hit." One. Because that's the most I'd ever take with anyone.

Her phone beeps. "One minute to the New Year."

I stare at her in shock. "You set your alarm?"

Abby raises her face to the sky. "Maybe next year will be better." She's been saying that forever. I reach into my jacket and extract a lighter. Abby smiles because she knows what I'm about to do. "Do you want me to count it down?" she asks.

"Up to you."

Abby watches her phone and counts from ten to two. The moment she says one I flick my lighter and hold the single flame into the night.

That's right, world: one more year has passed and I'm still fucking here.

Rachel

I OVERSLEPT. LAST NIGHT, I had a hard time falling asleep as my mind replayed the events of winter break. I worried over Isaiah and Ethan and school and Mom and lies and... Isaiah. Like always, sleep eventually came, but not without consequences.

I'm late. Not really late as in school-will-start-soon late. But late as in I-have-a-routine-and-I'm-not-keeping-it late. West calls it superstition. I call him an idiot. My days, they go better if I follow the tradition: an apple and one slice of toast for breakfast, watch the first few minutes of the morning news, double-check my backpack, drive the long way to school and sit in my car for five minutes before walking into the school building.

Mom stopped me yesterday and I missed breakfast. That one deviation created a snowball effect that ended with me having to read a poem aloud in class. I barely hid the panic overtaking me, and I hated how Ethan's now-observant eyes noted the way the heat flushed up my neck.

Pulling a sweater over my school uniform, I bolt out of my bathroom, gather my scattered books off my bed and try to stuff them into my backpack as I race down the winding staircase.

Loud voices echoing from my father's office cause me to skid to a halt halfway down the stairs.

"Again?" my father yells, and my stomach drops. It's West. Dad only shouts like this at West. "Four fights alone since the school year began. When is it going to end?"

The fights. The chink in my brother's perfect armor. Honestly, West has gotten into more than four fights at school this year, but those were the ones broken up by some authority figure. God only knows how many he's been in outside of school walls. West is an easygoing enough guy, but when someone pushes him too far, West always pushes back. Part of me envies him that fearlessness.

"The fight happened last week," West replies in a low tone. "Did your secretary just now get around to telling you about it or was this the first time you could fit me into your schedule?" Mom must be gone if they're arguing so openly.

One of the books I had been shoving into my pack slips out of my hand and in slow motion, it bobbles on my fingertips. Instead of falling in the direction of the bag, it inclines away from me, drops and begins its rapid descent down the stairs, one loud thud at a time, until the book announces its grand entrance onto the foyer with a resounding BAM!

My spine straightens with the unusually still silence, and I know I've undoubtedly gained my father and West's attention.

"Rach?" Dad calls from his office at the bottom of the stairs. "Are you okay?"

I suck in a breath to steady myself. He doesn't even have to look to know it's me. No one else in this family would ever make such an awkward mistake. I rush down the stairs and pause in the large entryway of his office. "Just clumsy."

My father's lips quiver as if he wants to laugh like I'm a clown in a show. How he turns his emotions around so quickly, I'll never know, and I enviously wish he would share his secret. It's probably why he's never understood why I couldn't control the panic attacks.

When I fidget, the quivering stops. He remembers I hate being laughed at—and I hate that he remembers.

I steal a glance at West, who shoves his hands in his pockets and stares at the floor. Mom doesn't know about the times West's temper has gotten the best of him. West can fake perfection, where I always fall excruciatingly short.

"Maybe I should try out for the circus," I say to lighten the mood. "I'd be a whiz at juggling china."

And it works. Dad laughs...at me. "Good thing Grace isn't your middle name."

With a glare between West and Dad, West leaves the room and I watch him go.

Dad pushes away from the massive oak desk, stands to his full six feet and gestures for me to join him. This is what Ethan will look like someday: tall, dark chestnut hair, even darker brown eyes and full of confidence. Mom said she fell in love with Dad the moment she saw him at college orientation.

Dad sits in one of the two chairs in front of his desk and indicates that I should take the other. I rotate the gold bracelet on my wrist one time. I have a routine and he's ruining it.

"The guy provoked West." It had to be said. "I heard about it at school and—"

"I don't want to talk about West."

One more rotation of the bracelet. West and my impending lateness are warring for attention in my mind. "Mom's gone?"

"She left early this morning for a breakfast."

I should be eating breakfast. Why can't he let me continue with my routine?

"I wanted to tell you that I'm proud of you," he says.

Despite the tension of the morning, everything inside of me explodes with joy.

"What you did last week at the charity event was mind-blowing. If you had told me two years ago that you would make a speech in public, I wouldn't have believed you. You surprised me, Rachel, and you made me proud."

I'll be wearing this smile for a week. "Thank you."

Dad leans forward, rests his arms on his knees and combines his hands. "You know how hard it was for your mother and me to lose Colleen."

My joy drains, leaving me feeling cold. How could I expect anything different? I'm here so he can recite the same January speech. I glance over at the framed pictures on the table behind his desk. There are more of Colleen than of anyone else. I should know. I've counted them since I was six. "Yes."

"And you know how hard this time of year is on your mother."

I nod. Colleen's birthday was the twenty-eighth of December. The charity ball and assorted holiday parties keep Mom afloat, but after the Christmas decorations are boxed away and the donations are counted, she spirals into a month-long depression.

"After Colleen passed, I had no idea how your mother was going to continue, but then she found out she was having you—a girl. The day of your ultrasound was the first time I had seen your mother smile in months. You've always given your mom that extra push."

I blink twice so my father won't see tears. Does he have any idea how much I hate this lecture and the role I play in the family? I'm so sick of being Colleen's replacement.

Dad flashes a surprise smirk. "You remind me a lot of your mother."

I tilt my head, shocked by this new twist on the old speech. "Really?" I'd give anything to be like her. She's beautiful and poised and brave. My heart stalls with a twinge of pain. Isaiah called me brave.

"Yes," he says as his smile grows. "And Colleen, too."

I rub my forehead so he doesn't see the hurt clawing at my face. What will happen if they ever find out I'm nothing like Colleen?

"All girl from head to toe. I couldn't keep Colleen away from makeup, and your mother enjoys being a woman more than anyone I know."

And Dad loves treating Mom like a princess. My eyes drift to the picture of Colleen at the age of eight, dressed as Cinderella and posing near the castle in Disney World. When I was eight, I brought tears to Mom's eyes when I yearned to go with my brothers to Space Mountain instead of pretending to be a stupid princess. To this day, I hate the happiest place on earth.

Dad continues, "Despite it being your sister's birthday, your mom had a wonderful day last week. She enjoyed spending time with you."

He's referring to the hours we spent at the spa in preparation for the charity ball. This isn't a new twist to the story after all, just a new way of saying the same old thing. To help Mom through her upcoming slump, Dad will excuse me from school, like he's done every January since I was ten, and send me and Mom on a week-long, all expenses paid shopping and spa spree in New York City.

I'm not a fan of shopping. I'd rather have spikes embedded in my head than have anyone file my toenails. I could care less what designer made what outfit. Faking that I'm having a fabulous time in an environment that feels as foreign to me as living on Mars is exhausting, but our time together always cheers up Mom. That alone is worth the trip and sometimes there's a perk for me. Last year, I got to touch a Ferrari.

"Okay," I say, taking the preemptive strike. "When do we leave?"

Dad winks. "Sorry, no trip to the Big Apple this year."

Yes! "What about Mom?"

"I think I've been handling your mother wrong. The charity ball keeps her busy in December, but she needs that feeling year-round. At the New Year's Eve party, I talked to the head of the Leukemia Foundation and they agreed to offer your mom a fundraising position."

It's like someone shoved a hundred-pound weight off my chest. "That's great."

"It is." He points at me. "But your mother will only take the position if you do it with her. You opened a lot of checkbooks with your speech last week. She wants to raise more money to fund research for the illness that took your sister, and she wants you to give the speeches."

The weight returns with a crushing blow to my head. This is an excellent example of why I should never deviate from routine.

Isaiah

AS I WAIT IN THE school parking lot, my fingers glide over the pony embossed on the steering wheel and my thoughts return to Rachel. Three hours—the time I spent with her. It wasn't much, but there was something about her, a spark that made her...unforgettable.

I don't understand why I still think about her. Three hours with someone isn't enough to know them, but she didn't fit into any cliché or box. It's like she was a mystery I was in the middle of solving and then I was yanked from the case.

The damn sun hasn't even risen, and school starts soon. Seven hours of torture lie ahead of me. I'd rather be in the garage working on the Chevelle some guy brought in last night. Hell, I'd rather work on a Ford Focus. I'd rather be with Rachel.

My eyes drift to her number, which rests in the drink holder. She writes exactly like I'd expect from a girl like her: feminine with loops and pink ink. I shake my head. Who the fuck keeps a pink pen nearby? Rachel. She did. She would, and I liked that about her.

A muscle in my jaw tics and my left hand grips the steering wheel. Everyone on the street is aware that Eric's looking for her and those two loser college boys. No one but Abby knows that I left the race with Rachel, and the money I gave Abby bought her silence. As long as I stay clear of Rachel, she'll never be found.

My car door groans as I open it, and I make a mental note to oil the son of a bitch when I get to work later.

"Isaiah!"

A nervous adrenaline rush flows into my veins when I hear Echo's voice. Sliding out of the passenger side of Noah's car, Echo calls to me again. I immediately walk in their direction. Screw school. Echo and Noah—they're my family.

With her arms wrapped around her stomach and red curls blowing across her face, Echo places one foot in front of the other in a hesitant motion toward me. Noah stays next to his car. I glance at him, hoping for a clue as to what the hell is going on, but he gives me nothing as he leans against the fender. His gaze flickers to Echo and, for a second, concern flashes on his face.

"Echo," I say as soon as she's close. "What's wrong?"

My mind races through the possibilities. She mentioned her baby brother showed some signs of allergies. Is he sick? Is it her fucked-up mom? Did she try to hurt Echo again?

Echo brushes her hair away and exposes bloodshot eyes. "I've been trying to reach you since last night. Why didn't you go home?"

I look at Noah again. My staying out all night has never been an issue. Noah's my best friend, not my babysitter. "I worked late then crashed at the garage." All in a vain effort to drain Rachel from my mind.

Echo's foot taps the blacktop as she runs her hands over her arms. "I tried your cell."

"It's dead." Because I wanted to kill the temptation of calling Rachel.

Echo's head falls back and she sucks in a deep breath. "I screwed up and I'm sorry. So sorry. But she can't tell anyone. I made sure of it. I slipped during my session yesterday, and what's said during a session is privileged. I threatened her—if she tells anyone I'll turn her in."

My stomach begins a downward spiral. I hate where this is heading. "Told who what?"

"I accidently told Mrs. Collins that you're living with Noah. I'm so sorry, Isaiah."

The slap of her words makes me take a step back. Fuck. Echo told her therapist, a guidance counselor at my school, that I don't live with my assigned foster family. Every muscle I possess seizes with anger.

Her voice breaks and she wipes a hand over her eyes. "I'm so sorry. I swear to God I'll turn her in if she says one word. I swear it."

Another tear rolls down her face. Echo means what she says even though Mrs. Collins is the one person who can help her deal with her issues. I'm pissed. No doubt. But families have each other's backs.

"It'll work out," I tell her, though I have no idea if that statement is true. Forgiving her doesn't erase the fact that she may have ruined my life. "And if it doesn't, then I'll fix it."

Because Echo is a touchy-feely girl, she hugs me. I hug her back while meeting Noah's stare. He gets that his girl and I love each other in a brother-sister type of way. Noah nods his appreciation and I nod back. How the hell am I going to get out of this?

Rachel

"YOU KNOW WHAT I NEED?" I lean away from the hood of West's SUV and wipe my greasy fingers on a rag, careful not to touch my clothing. West snuck me out here to the massive "children's" garage after dinner, claiming a near-death emergency.

"A life?" West, my older brother by less than a year, slouches against my Mustang. With his baggy jeans and designer black T-shirt, he fits suburban ghetto wannabe to a T.

"Get off my baby."

"It's a car, Freak-a-sauraus. You realize most dudes aren't as obsessed as you are." Because he knows I'm serious, West moves away from her.

I drop the rag and slam his hood. "I didn't come out here to be insulted. Go inside, crawl to Dad, and tell him you forgot to change your oil again and let's see how this plays out."

West pulls his baseball cap off his head and pounds it against his leg. "Shit. The oil. I forgot to change the oil. That's why the light came on."

I snatch my jacket and am reaching to open the door when

West steps in my path. "I was playing. You know it. I tease, you take it. It's the game we play."

I slide to the right. "I'm done playing."

He mirrors me. "No, you can't leave. Dad will be pissed if he finds out I didn't change the oil again. You've seen how he is with me. Come on, Rach. Have a heart. You know you're my favorite sister."

"I'm your only sister." Well, the only one alive, that is.

"Gavin's a little girly."

I laugh. "No, he's not."

West releases a sly grin. I laughed, therefore he knows he's winning. "Come on, have you seen the dude's eyebrows? Un-natural for a guy. I'll bet you ten dollars he has them waxed."

Not quite willing to bend, I sigh and cross my arms over my chest.

West drops to one knee. "Please, Rach. Please. I'm begging here."

"Fine."

"Great." He hops up, steals my coat from me and slips his hat on his head backward.

"On one condition," I say.

"Name it."

"Change the oil. Regularly. You don't wait until a light flashes on your console and you don't wait until you're near bone-dry. It's not that complicated. Every three thousand miles or every three months. They put a reminder sticker at the top of your windshield."

"Yeah, sure. Whatever." And we're both aware we'll be hav-ing this same conversation again in a couple of months.

I open the cabinet and shuffle through some boxes to find

the extra oil filters I bought for West's SUV. "If I had a diagnostic code scanner I could tell you if there's another reason why the maintenance light came on."

West seats himself on the hood of my car and I throw a rag at him. "For the love of God, get off my car. Touch it again and I'll crack the head of your engine."

"Sorry." Repentant, West heads to the other side of the garage Mom and Dad built to house my brothers' and my cars. Our parents are the only ones allowed to use the garage actually connected to the house. "I thought you said I just need oil."

"Yes, you need oil, but you could have seriously damaged other things because the car needed oil a long time ago."

West slumps against the wall, and I throw him a bone. "Don't worry. It'll be okay."

Hope creeps along his face. "You can fix it?"

"Yeah, I can fix it." With new filter in hand, I repop the hood and begin the task of salvaging West's SUV. "But the scanner would be nice for when it's something more than a missed oil change."

West's cell phone chimes, and he pulls it out to read a text message. "You should have asked for it for your birthday or Christmas."

"I did," I mutter, but West is too caught up in whatever he's texting to hear. I asked for the scanner along with a few "girly" things, hoping my parents wouldn't notice and would just check the item off the list as they went on their shopping spree, but that didn't happen. They bought me a new ebook reader and jewelry. No scanner.

The tick, tick, tick of West tapping on his cell continues to my right. "Heard Dad asked you to work with Mom and the Leukemia Foundation."

Is anything in my life not a topic for discussion in this family? "Yep."

"You know she'll only accept the position if you agree to speak."

"Yes," I say more softly. I hate the guilt festering on my insides.

"And you also know," he says in a way-too-happy voice, "if she takes on the position, she'll have that I'm-planning-something manic high all the time."

And I'll constantly be on the verge of a panic attack and I'll have to constantly hide it. With those types of attacks, I vomit. Vomiting is what once led me to the hospital.

When I say nothing, West continues, "She'll be happy." He pauses. "Just saying."

I inhale deeply. Why does my mother's happiness always depend on me?

"Have you given Dad an answer yet?"

"No, I haven't." I wanted to say no, but I couldn't bring myself to do it. I couldn't say yes, either. Like a coward, I escaped when Dad's phone unexpectedly rang. Dad mentioned later that he was okay with giving me until Friday to think it over. It's Wednesday night, so I have one more day before the answer is due. Both Gavin and Jack hunted me down to tell me their opinion on the subject, which is to get over my fear of public speaking and work with Mom.

"You should do it, Rach," West says with his fingers still moving on his phone.

I lift my head and toss my hair to clear my ear. "What? What was that? Did I hear Dad calling for you?"

"Fine. Consider me backed off." West shoves his cell into his jeans pocket. "Will my car be ready by Saturday? I have a date."

When doesn't West have a date? "With who?"

My brother picks up one of my ratchets and spins it so that it makes the winding noise. "Some girl I met in French."

Surely he knows her name. I mean, he did ask her out, and I assume that was her he was just texting. I place the strap wrench on the filter and hesitate. "Do the girls you date ever mean something?"

"Mean something?" He stares into space for a moment. "I don't know. I guess. Some I like more than others."

My cheeks burn and I need to rub my eyes, but if I do I'll smear grease on my face, and then Mom will know I've been out "tinkering with those cars again." She tries to understand my fascination, but I always see the disappointment in her eyes. So I hide my passion from her and discuss whatever I had read in one of her fashion magazines. Mom loves fashion.

I ask so softly that if West doesn't hear my question, I'll know it means he wasn't meant to answer, "Did you ever tell a girl that you'd call, and you never did?"

The winding sound of the ratchet stops, and the heaviness of the silence cause me to look up. Uncharacteristically solemn, he stares straight at me. "What's this about?"

I refocus on the filter. "Nothing."

"No." West's sneakers squeak against the concrete floor as he walks over to me. "This is something. You've been carrying your phone around like...like a normal teenage girl would, instead of leaving it in your room like you usually do. And you've been acting off since the charity ball. Did you meet some guy? Did he not call?"

I yank hard on the wrench, but the oil on the filter created a slick surface. "Make yourself useful and grab that oil pan. Oil's going to drip when I get this loosened."

With a huff, West does what I ask and hovers over the engine next to me. "Who is it, Rach? Who's the asshole who didn't call?"

"No one." Just some really hot guy who I shared my first kiss with. I grit my teeth and put all of my strength into the wrench.

"Tell me who it is. His ass is mine." The pure malice in his tone gives me chills. West has a flash-fire temper when pushed too far, and he can kick ass when the line is crossed. But I've never believed he'd hurt a guy in my honor...until now.

"Is it Brian?" The anger within him builds like a snowball. The pan trembles in his hand. "I saw him talking to you at the party. If it is, stay away from him. The guy's a prick."

I open my mouth to tell him what type of friends he has, since they were the ones who took me to the drag race and left me to fend for myself. But then I remember that he'd crucify me if he knew that I hung out with them, participated in a drag race, ran from the police and then kissed a guy while alone in his apartment.

West moves the pan to catch the leaking oil as I remove the old filter. "There's no guy, okay? I'm curious. You date a lot of girls, and I was wondering if you call every single one of them." I wipe off the filter mount and finish the rest of what I have to say. "And what it means if you don't call."

My brother stays unusually quiet while I finish replacing the old filter with the new one and add new oil. When I motion with my head that he can pull the pan away, West finally answers, "The ones I don't like, I don't call back."

My lips turn down and an ache ripples through my chest. I toss the old filter into the garbage, snatch West's keys from the tool bench and open the driver's-side door so I can start the engine to check for leaks. I wish I were alone. "That's all I needed to know."

West begins to say something else, but I flip the keys in the ignition and apply the gas so that the loud revving noise of the engine will drown him out. West's words confirmed what I already knew from the silence: Isaiah never liked me.

I reach into my pocket and power off my phone. Why continue to wait for a call that will never come?

Isaiah

MRS. COLLINS WAITED UNTIL THURSDAY to yank me from class. While not surprised by the summons, the delay did catch me off guard. I walk into the main office and freeze when I see the person sitting in Mrs. Collins's office. My heart stalls. *The bitch called my fucking social worker.*

In midsentence, Courtney notices me and immediately yells, "Don't you dare bolt, Isaiah." Her swinging blond hair gives her that pissed-off-racehorse effect again.

I give her credit. She knows what I'm thinking. I toss my books onto the row of chairs lining the wall and head for Mrs. Collins's office. Odds are I won't need that shit anymore. A screwup like this will mean a group home. Not that I'd let it get that far. I'll run before anyone forces me to set foot into that hell.

Once inside, I lean against the wall next to the door. Mrs. Collins, a middle-aged version of Courtney, swivels back and forth in her oversize business chair. Tilting stacks of papers clutter the desk and look close to tipping. This lady has the organizational skills of a hoarder.

"Would you like to take a seat?" Mrs. Collins asks with a sweet smile.

"No." I cross my arms over my chest. The only chair available is the one that would trap me in the room. I'm only interested in easy outs.

"Isaiah, you should sit..." Courtney starts, but Echo's head-shrinker cuts her off.

"It's okay. You're free to stand."

Damn straight I am. "What do you want?"

Courtney rocks on the edge of her seat, as if contemplating joining me against the wall. She hates it when I stand and she sits. "You haven't returned any of my phone calls."

"So?"

"So? My job is to keep tabs on you. I want to make sure you're okay."

"You found me." I snap a ta-da movement with my hands. "I'm alive. Can I go?"

Courtney's a tiny thing. She shifts in her seat so that her knees are angled in my direction. "Your mom still wants to talk."

My arms fall to my sides and I push off the wall. "My mom can kiss my ass."

Mrs. Collins's chair squeaks when it rolls toward her desk. "Isaiah, Courtney is here because I requested her presence on a school matter. If you don't want to discuss your mother, then you don't have to."

"But..." Courtney shoots a confused glance at Mrs. Collins, and even I catch the subtle shake of the shrink's head.

Mrs. Collins overpronounces her next words in a sweet tone. "He doesn't."

And I won't.

"I asked Mr. Holden to join us," Mrs. Collins continues. "He should be here soon."

Trying not to show that I'm insanely curious about why Mrs. Collins is involving my automotive instructor, I retake my position against the wall.

Mrs. Collins taps a pencil against her desk. "How was your winter break, Isaiah?"

Noah warned me about this woman. When he was black-mailed into counseling last year, he said she enjoyed torturing him with questions. "Good."

"Great!" The pencil keeps knocking against the desk. "How's Noah?"

"Good."

"Fantastic. And have you seen him recently?"

And that's when it hits me—Mrs. Collins hasn't told a soul that I'm living with Noah. This entire meeting is a bluff. "Yes."

"When?"

"This morning."

Her eyes light up. "You saw Noah this early in the morning? Were you at his place?"

"No." I was at our place. "I saw Echo, too."

The pencil stops tapping. "How is Echo? Did she have anything interesting to say?"

I shrug. "Nothing really. Other than she doesn't like a snitch."

A shadow crosses her face, but damn if she doesn't make a good recovery.

Courtney slicks back her ponytail. "Why do I feel like I'm missing something here?"

The gravelly sound of a pencil sharpener from the main office fills the silence as Mrs. Collins and I stare at each other. This is too much fun. "Because you are," I answer.

Courtney shuffles her feet. She's young, new and hates being the low man on the totem pole. Mrs. Collins rests her elbows on her desk. If she had big guns, she'd be whipping them out now. "How are your foster parents?"

"Good." Haven't heard that they died, so I assume that statement's true.

"And Christmas with them was…"

"Fine." I enjoyed not seeing their faces.

"And they got you a…"

"Puppy." Now I'm just messing with her.

Her mouth twitches. Is it possible she also enjoys the game? "They got you a puppy?"

"Yep."

"What type?"

"A mutt."

"And you named it…?"

"Iwin."

Mrs. Collins brushes her fingers over her mouth. "That's a strange name for a puppy."

"Yeah. But I like the words coming out of my mouth—I win." Because I have.

Courtney clears her throat. "Your foster parents bought you a puppy?"

"Don't worry about me screwing it up," I say without looking at her. "It ran away."

"Oh, Isaiah." She places a hand over her heart. "I'm so sorry."

Christ, I hate people that obsess over animals. The world that bleeds for a malnourished dog is more than happy to fuck over people like me. "Things leave. It's the way of the world."

Mr. Holden walks in, twirling his safety glasses in his hand. "Mrs. Collins," he says as a hello. He nods at me. I nod back. Wearing his typical blue mechanic's coveralls, my favorite instructor regards Courtney as if she were a hybrid in the presence of gas guzzlers.

"Mr. Holden," says Mrs. Collins. "This is Isaiah's social worker, Courtney Blevins."

Courtney moves as if she's going to extend her hand, but withdraws it when Mr. Holden gives her a curt nod. "I'm between classes, Mrs. Collins."

She flips open a laptop and scrolls down the screen. "I appreciate you joining us, Mr. Holden. Give me a second while I access Isaiah's file."

Mr. Holden chuckles. "How's going paperless?"

"Tedious, but I like password protection. Finally...Mr. Walker. Currently living with..."

"Shirley and Dale Easum." I finish for her.

"Yes, that's what it says." She glances up from her computer. "Mr. Holden, were you able to work out what we discussed last night?"

"Never had a problem," he answers. "Isaiah's talent made it easy."

My head whirls in his direction. He's not a man to give praise lightly.

"I talked to the owner of Pro Performance." Mr. Holden speaks directly to me now. "He'll give you a shot at a full-time job when you graduate."

Mr. Holden and I have talked over this possibility several times. Pro Performance deals with high-end cars and suped-up dragsters. It's my dream job, but the business has one request that I can't grant. "What about the internship?"

To earn the full-time job, I'd have to intern with them this semester. Being an intern means no cash, and I need money.

"You can work at Pro Performance on Tuesday and Thursday afternoons when you'd typically be taking my classes. You can keep your job at Tom's shop in the evenings and complete the internship during the day. The guy at Pro Performance will give us a grade on the work you do there. Mrs. Collins is calling it an outside classroom experience."

My mind goes blank. There's no way this is happening to me. I can make money and I have a shot at my dream: working on cars that go fast—very fast. "Are you fucking with me?"

"No. The only other requirement is to become ASE certified by graduation, which should be a breeze for you."

The ASE—the Automotive Service Excellence certification. I've been studying for that exam and earning hours in the garage toward the certification for over two years.

Mrs. Collins raises her hand in the air. "Actually, there's another requirement. The business in question called me to verify Isaiah's credits and grades. They mentioned something about needing three letters of recommendation."

The back of my head hits the wall. I can come up with two letters. One from Mr. Holden. Another from my current place of employment. A third? Adults tend to avoid me. I never should have allowed hope.

Mr. Holden knows me better than most. "I'll give you one. Tom will, too," he says. "Can you think of one more?"

Mrs. Collins mutters, "Who is a responsible adult who knows what Isaiah is capable of?"

I hate that woman. I really do. How can Echo and Noah stomach her?

"I'll do it." Courtney has been so silent that I forgot about her. "One condition."

"And that is?" I rub my neck to relieve the building pressure.

"You answer my phone calls and you meet with me when I ask."

Mrs. Collins barely contains her excitement. This meeting was never a bluff. The head-shrinker held a full house the entire time.

With her hands in her lap, Courtney waits patiently for my answer. I hate being on a leash. All I want is freedom— to be out from underneath everything that holds me down. With Courtney, I won't just be on a damn leash; she'll keep me on a choke collar. But this opportunity is a once-in-a- lifetime shot. The money Pro Performance pays their mechanics is sweet. "Okay."

Courtney flashes a smile that's all teeth. "Excellent. Our first meeting will be next Thursday. Right after school."

Feeling the grip of a leash choking my neck, I grab at the collar of my T-shirt. "Fine."

Courtney stands. "Mrs. Collins, thank you for the invite. I need to run, though. Staff meeting."

"We'll talk again soon," answers Mrs. Collins as Courtney goes out the door.

Mr. Holden leaves without acknowledging anyone. The sound of the second hand ticking is the only noise in the room. Mrs. Collins relaxes back in her chair and folds her hands over her lap. "Now that we're alone, is there anything you'd like to tell me?"

"No."

"Anything about your foster parents or Noah or where you've been staying the night?"

"No."

Her eyes drift to the tricked-out compass tattooed on the inside of my right arm. "What does your tattoo mean?"

"Nothing that concerns you." She needs to steer clear of what's personal. "You think you're slick setting me up so that Courtney can keep tabs on me, don't you?"

A satisfied smile crosses her lips. "Occasionally I can be crafty. Regardless of how you see yourself, you're still a minor. The system may not be perfect, but it exists to keep you safe."

Spoken by a lady who wasn't raised in the nonperfect system since she was six. The clock ticks. She breaks the silence. "It was interesting what you said earlier."

My muscles tense. "What?"

"You said everything leaves."

Not interested in being analyzed, I switch the topic. "Can I go?"

"I can help you," she says in a soothing voice that probably puts insomniacs to sleep. "Echo trusts me and so does Noah."

CRASH INTO YOU 155

CRASH INTO YOU   155

Echo and Noah needed help. Hell, they had problems that could be fixed. "I ain't them."

"No." Her eyes bore into mine. "You're not, but that doesn't mean that I can't help."

I push off the wall. "Actually, that's exactly what it means." And I leave.

Irritated, I punch a streamer hanging from the ceiling. I'm late for sixth period. Mrs. Collins would have written me a note, but I'd rather risk detention than stay in the same room with her. I turn the corner and skid to a halt when I spot Abby on the floor next to my locker.

"About time you showed," I say. She already skipped two days this week. Her head jerks up and her wide eyes freak me out. "What's wrong?"

Abby quickly stands. "It's Eric. He found Rachel."

Rachel

WORTHINGTON PRIVATE HAS A HUGE parking lot, and because of the sheer number of students that own cars, the administration permits overflow parking near the football stadium. This is where I park every morning—a few feet from the ticket booth. My brothers, on the other hand, who drive separately because of their millions of after-school activities, park as close as they can to the front doors without a handicap sticker.

By parking here, I don't have to worry about some idiot with a driver's permit hitting my car or some overzealous door opener scratching my paint. I can also sit by myself without people gawking at the lone Young sibling who doesn't have their act together.

The last number on the clock radio changes and my mouth dries out. Today's going to be awful. I grab my backpack off the passenger seat, slide out the door and shiver against the January air. The first rays of dawn glimmer against the frost on the grass.

The pressure inside me feels like an elevator filled with

sludge slowly rising to the top floor. The doors are begging to be opened so everything can spill out.

Jack and Gavin have been relentless about me helping Mom with the charity. Dad reminded me this morning that my answer is due to him this afternoon and said he knew I'd make the right decision. The overpowering combination of my two oldest brothers' pressure and West and Ethan urging me to accept Dad's offer edges me toward insanity. All of it is a perfect recipe for a panic attack, and I can't have another one with Ethan watching me like a hawk.

"Rachel Young," says a voice behind me.

I don't know this voice. Scanning the overflow lot, I realize how alone I am. Rays of the sun peek around the school, but darkness still owns most of the sky. I slowly turn and suck in a breath when I recognize a face I never thought I would see again. It's the guy from the drag race. The one that scared me. It's Eric.

A flood of adrenaline flows through my body. For some, adrenaline makes them stronger and sharpens their reactions. The rush causes me to freeze. I consider screaming, but even if I regained control of the muscles in my throat, would anyone hear me? From the main parking lot, bass lines pound from several expensive cars with even more expensive sound systems.

It's frightening seeing Eric. At the drag race he fit in, but here, among guys who wear white shirts and ties to school, he looks...terrifying. He's tall, blond, and his body is more bones than muscle, like this skinny man I saw once in a drug prevention video. My heart quickens its pace. Why is he here? How does he know my name?

"Rachel Young," he says again. "You have something of mine."

My head shakes back and forth and then I wonder if it's my body shaking. "I don't have anything of yours."

He tips a hand to his ear. "What was that? I didn't hear you. You should speak up."

The smile on his face says he's mocking me, but I don't know why. I've done nothing to him.

Eric invades my personal space and I beg my feet to move. Instead, I become stone embedded in the ground. My breath comes out faster and I can't draw in enough air to compensate for the loss. He reaches in my direction and touches my hair. His hand is ashy, cracked in spots, and I want so badly for him to disappear.

"You're pretty," he says. My gold hair falls from his fingers like rain. "And you played the innocent act well. I bought it then, but I won't buy it now. Give me my fucking money or I'll have my boys put you in the hospital."

My voice trembles. "I don't know what you're talking about."

"Bullshit!" he snaps. His anger gives me the courage to stumble back.

He advances on me with his hand waving in the air. "The cops can't touch me. Your parents can't touch me. But I can touch you. The only thing that will stop that from happening is if you give me my money."

The world spins and all the thoughts in my head jumble together. I can't breathe. I can't. Instinctively, my arms wrap around my stomach as I sway.

Rough hands grab my face and all I see are eyes with no

soul. "Hell no. You're not going down. Give me my money or tell me where it is."

My stomach lurches and a high-pitched buzzing washes away his voice. I can't think. I can't breathe. Eric tightens his hold on my chin, creating pain, making me unable to open my mouth for air. He's going to crush my skull.

My airways no longer work. Small lights flutter in the periphery, and Eric's mouth moves as if he's yelling. I can't hear him over the loud humming in my head. I close my eyes. A hand clamps on my shoulder and shakes me as if I'm a doll. The buzzing shifts into roaring.

The pressure on my chin, on my shoulder, disappears—leaving me floating in nothing until gravity forces me to the ground. I crumple—gasping. I convulse with the dry heaves. Blood pounds at every pressure point. I retch forward and place my hands on the cold blacktop to keep my face from hitting the loose rocks.

I suck in air and the sound is a wheeze. I draw air in again, lift my head, and through disoriented tunnel vision I spot a shadow throwing Eric against my car. Someone has come for me. A savior.

He turns and I know those eyes. Isaiah. "Rachel!"

I sit back on my knees and waver when a fresh flash of dizziness disorients me.

With a fist curled into the material of Eric's coat and an arm shoved into his windpipe, Isaiah slams Eric into my car. "What the fuck did you do to her?"

Eric speaks as if he, too, is having trouble breathing. "Make your move, my brother. But if you do, you better kill me because you will not like my retaliation."

Lifetimes stretch as Isaiah stares into Eric's eyes. With a final push, Isaiah releases him. "Stay away from her."

Eric smooths out his shirt and readjusts his coat. He leans into Isaiah. "I am not your enemy. That girl—" he points at me "—stole what's mine. Stop thinking with your dick and get your head in the game. That was your money, too."

The staring continues and Eric glances away first. Isaiah rounds on me, and I fall back onto my bottom in terror. This isn't the guy who protected me in the bar and kissed me in his apartment. Like a thundercloud racing across the sky, he's massive, strong, and he's moving my way. The muscles in his arms ripple as he stalks.

My breath continues to pump in and out in shallow intervals. Isaiah crouches next to me. His eyes a gray storm; his expression cold, flat. "Rachel."

I don't remember his voice sounding gruff. I don't remember him being this frightening.

He lifts his hand and hesitates when I shudder. His lips press together in a line. "He will pay for touching you."

Several feet behind Isaiah, Eric calls out, "Whenever you're ready to discuss this situation, I'll be standing right here."

My eyes dart behind Isaiah's shoulder, but Isaiah shifts so that he fills my line of sight. "I've got you, Rachel. You need to trust me."

Trust him. His eyes soften to liquid silver, and for the first time I can inhale a lungful of air. And I smell him: his calming scent of spices. Isaiah did scare me before—when I first met him, but then he saved me, like he's doing now.

I nod and Isaiah caresses my cheek. His fingers are warm against my freezing skin.

"I need you strong, okay?" he whispers. "Eric thrives off of weakness. I need you to stand and let me handle this."

I lick my dry lips and test my voice. "He said I have his money." *He said he's going to hurt me.* "I don't understand."

Isaiah places his finger over my lips. My heart stutters. It's a calming touch, yet equally strong. "I know. I'll fix everything."

He didn't call. It's what I want to say, but for now, I accept Isaiah's offered hand and rise on trembling legs.

Isaiah partially obstructs Eric's view of me and crosses his arms over his chest. I let the fingers of my right hand rest on his left shoulder blade. Isaiah peeks at me and tilts his head to let me know that my touch is welcomed. I exhale in relief. I need this connection. I need his strength.

"You want to talk, Eric," says Isaiah. "Let's talk."

In a sloppy posture, Eric leans to the left with his hands in his jeans pockets. "Her boys fingered her yesterday. They said she was involved in the robbery and that she has my money."

I open my mouth to protest, but a glare from Isaiah instills silence. "Those weren't her boys and she wasn't involved."

"She showed with them."

"And they abandoned her when the cops came. Rachel and I had to fly through the back alleys to keep from getting caught. She stuck her neck out for me. I owe her a debt."

That obviously wasn't news Eric was prepared to hear. He scratches his jaw. "You owe her a debt?"

"Yes," says Isaiah simply.

A wan smile slants Eric's lips. "You never owe people."

Becoming a statue, Isaiah says nothing in return. My fingers relax so that my palm connects with his back. Even through his shirt, my hand soaks in his warmth and energy.

I focus on the steady movement of his breathing. In...and out. In...and out. A rhythm that shows no fear.

"They stole five thousand dollars from me," says Eric. "And I want it back. I don't care who pays for it or how. No one steals from me, and that message needs to be public."

"Send a message all you want, but leave Rachel out of it."

Eric advances on Isaiah. Isaiah never moves as Eric shoves a finger in his face. "She showed with them, and they made me look like a fool! No one makes me look like a fool!"

The finger slowly descends, but Eric stays in Isaiah's face. Isaiah's expression never changes: one long, continuous stone-cold glare. "No one looks at you as a fool. Everyone on the street has heard how you put those college boys in the hospital. No one doubts your strength."

"It's not enough," Eric snarls.

"I think tire irons and baseball bats against skin is convincing to everyone."

Eric backs away from Isaiah and glances at me. "Is she yours?"

Isaiah remains silent.

Eric slides to the side, acting as if he'll skirt around Isaiah in order to be close to me, but he halts the moment Isaiah speaks. "Go near her and you'll join those boys in the hospital."

Dangerous—both of them are. But Isaiah would scare me more if he wasn't protecting me. My eyes dart between them. The two males before me are barely civilized animals fighting for dominance and control.

Eric regards Isaiah. "She showed with them so people think she was involved. If I don't act on her then people will believe that I have a weakness. She won't go unpunished. If she gives me my money, I'll wipe her slate clean. My decision is made. Short of killing me, Isaiah, you aren't changing my mind."

"If she doesn't pay?" asks Isaiah.

Eric flashes a smile full of teeth. "She is pretty."

I swallow a dry heave and slap a hand over my mouth.

A muscle in Isaiah's jaw tics. "I'll take on her debt."

Isaiah

MY STOMACH BOTTOMS OUT WITH the last words I said: *I'll take on her debt.* Five thousand dollars or Eric will own me for life. Hell, with those words, he owns me now.

I risk breaking eye contact with Eric for a brief second to observe my surroundings. His threat to me earlier, that I either kill him or walk away, indicated he wasn't alone. Sure enough, back in the main parking lot, two of his most trusted guards watch.

Eric laughs, yet I find nothing funny. "Isn't this a strange turn of events. Isaiah Walker, the guy who owes nobody nothing, takes on a debt for a girl."

"Isaiah?"

I close my eyes at the sound of my name from Rachel's mouth. She wants reassurance, and I can't console her. Not with Eric inspecting my every movement. He already knows I care about Rachel, and that's bad for both of us. She just became a liability.

I try to repress any thoughts of Rachel: her beauty, her kindness, how frightened she was when I found her. Emotions are evil. Ice water needs to flow in my veins. "No girl should face your wrath."

"Yeah," Eric says in mock disbelief. "You're selling yourself to me so I won't hit a girl. Sell your shit someplace else."

This situation hovers between dangerous and deadly. Eric will use her against me if he realizes Rachel's more than someone I owe. He'll keep me as a dog on a chain, wielding her as a weapon. I can't do that to myself. *Dammit.* I can't do that to her. Because, God help us both, I do care. "She means nothing. I owe her a debt for saving me, and like you said yourself, I don't owe debts."

Her hand drops from my back and I hear her sharp intake of air. Eric's observant eyes catch her reaction, and he's discovered a new person to toy with. "So she was a fuck."

I've had enough of this. "When's the money due?"

"Now."

Even if Rachel did have five thousand dollars, which I doubt, she wouldn't have it in her pocket. "I need longer."

Eric rolls one shoulder as if we're debating the cost of an item at a yard sale instead of my life and her safety. "Because I've always liked you, two weeks."

"Eight."

"Six. And if she doesn't pay I take her car and I own you. Are we clear?"

Crystal. Because, for Eric and his crew, the beating is the payment. The taking of the car is for kicks. "No one touches her, Eric."

Having accomplished what he came for, Eric pulls his keys out of his pocket and strolls toward the main parking lot. "As long as someone pays. But if you don't..." He looks

over his shoulder and slides his eyes over Rachel. My fingers
curl with the thoughts of strangling him. "For you, pretty
girl, I promise there won't be baseball bats involved."

I watch him until he drives off, then examine Rachel.
She's so beautiful it hurts. Golden blond hair flows past her
shoulders. Those gorgeous violet eyes shouldn't be so wide
with fear. I've dreamed of being this close to her again. I ache
to gather her in my arms and keep her safe from the world...
to be her protector, but I can't be that man.

"You okay?" I ask.

Rachel moves her head as a yes, but the answer's no. After
being touched by Eric, how can she be fine? I run my hand
over my head. Just fuck. "Get in the car."

Rachel fidgets with the oversize buttons on her black coat,
then readjusts her skirt, drawing my attention to her bare
legs. Her warm breaths billow out into the air as white fog.
"I'm late for school."

So am I. "You and I need to skip today."

It's difficult to discern her head shaking no as her body
shudders from the cold. "My parents will kill me."

I rub my eyes with both hands. "Eric will actually kill us
both. My car—now."

Without looking at me, Rachel retrieves her backpack
and heads to the passenger side of my black Mustang. The
driver's side door hangs open and the engine still purrs.
When I cut into the overflow lot, I saw his hands on her
and my whole world went red.

She slams her door shut before I have a chance to go
around and close it for her. I don't want her to hate me. I

don't want her to fear me. But she witnessed who I really am, and now there's no avoiding reality.

I slide into my seat and put my car into First. "Can your brother cover for you at school?"

"Yeah," she barely whispers. "Maybe." Rachel pulls a phone out of her pack. The screen brightens as she powers it on, and I notice her go completely still. "You called."

A lot. Every half hour since Abby told me that Eric had found her. "You didn't answer."

"I turned my phone off." An edge of hurt creeps into her tone. I want to reassure her that we'll be okay. But I shouldn't.

Rachel types into her cell. We drive in silence as she stares at the phone, possibly waiting for a reply. It chirps and she sighs with relief. "My twin, Ethan, says he'll cover for me, but he wants to know why I'm ditching."

Tell him I'm saving your life. I shift gears as I hit the freeway heading downtown. There's only one place I can think to take her to guarantee her safety.

"Where are we going?" she asks.

I tug at my bottom loop earring. "To the police station."

Her hair flies as she whips her head to face me. "To the... Where? No!" she screeches. "No. We can't go there."

Time to be honest with her. "*We* aren't. *You* are. It's the only way."

One of her hands grips the edge of her seat. The other holds on to the door. The knuckles on both her hands fade to white. "There has to be another way. The police will call my parents."

"Better grounded than in the hospital," I mutter.

"Isaiah…"

I cut her off. "Do you have five thousand dollars?"

"No," she says quickly.

"Do you own the papers to your car?"

She shakes her head this time.

"Look." I force calm even though everything inside me writhes in rage. I want to fix this. Dammit, I want to fix us. "Go to the police. Tell them you made a mistake and street raced once. Tell them that the guy who took the bets threatened you if you don't race for him again. And for Christ's sake, don't name names. Tell them you never learned anyone's name. Tell them you were scared to death."

We breeze by a row of tractor trailers, and I press harder on the gas. We're cruising at seventy. My eyes narrow on the road. I itch to hit eighty and then ninety. I crave speed.

Her hands flutter in the air, signaling impending hysterics. "What will that accomplish, besides upsetting my parents?"

I shift down and reluctantly reduce my speed when I spot the exit. "The police have been after Eric for a year. They know who he is and what he's capable of. The moment you say *drag racing* and *threatened,* they'll put the pieces together. They'll protect you in ways I can't."

She draws in several quick breaths. "He threatened you, too. Why aren't you going to come with me?"

I flex my fingers then grip the wheel again. "Because I'm not a snitch."

Rachel straightens in her seat and the spark of attitude that I remember from the night we met flashes. "And I am?"

Off the freeway, I turn the wheel sharply to the left, coast into an abandoned parking lot and cut the engine. "You don't have to live by the rules I live by. Those streets you played in one time *are* my home. I don't get to go back to a gated community when I decide I'm done slumming. You street raced and you got burned. I'm trying to make sure you don't die from your mistakes. So what if you don't get to go to a dance because you're grounded. You'll be safe."

Her eyes brim with tears. "You don't understand. This will crush my mom. It's my job to make everything in her life all right. She can't know. This would destroy her."

"Dammit, Rachel," I yell. "You can't be this fucking dense!"

Her door opens and she darts out of the car. I slam my hand on the steering wheel and bolt after her. "Where do you think you're going?"

"School!" she shouts. With one foot in front of the other, she heads across the lot—in the wrong direction.

"Get back in the fucking car!"

"No! I'll figure this out. It's not your debt, it's mine. Leave me alone!"

I stalk after her, grab her arm and swing her around. My face lowers to her. "Do you think this is a game? Do you think that you can ignore this and it will go away? It won't, Rachel. He knows who you are and where you go to school. Eric will never stop tracking you until he gets what he wants."

"Stop swearing at me!" Her entire body trembles. Back is the terrified girl from the bar after she got pegged by the beer. Maybe her life is more complicated than I thought.

Rachel jerks her arm in a pathetic attempt at freedom,

but I hold tight. She has to understand the dangers of this situation.

"Take your hands off of me," she yells. "No, I don't live near you, but that doesn't make me stupid. He threatened me. Not you. You want me to go the police and I can't. I'll do this on my own."

On her own? She'll get herself killed, and that'll take my already-serious problems with Eric into the realm of lethal. If he hurts her, he'll die. And then his boys will hunt me like a dog and take me down. My goal is to get us the fuck out of this situation without all that Romeo and Juliet bullshit.

Both of my hands slide up to her shoulders. "Do you know what some of the gangs in town do for initiation?"

"What?" The hysteria leaves for a second as she tries to understand my question.

"They have to rape someone."

Her eyes study my face. "What does that have to do with Eric? With me?"

I hesitate, the words frozen on my tongue. *His boys could rape you, Rachel.* I brought this up on purpose—so that she'll understand the lethal reality of Eric. To push her away from me, toward the cops. But the innocence and terror in her eyes stop me. Is it possible to spook an angel to death?

I should resist, but it's like I'm physically drawn to her. I loosen my grip and allow one hand to caress her cheek. Her skin burns under my touch. "You're in danger, and without five thousand dollars, I can't protect you from my world."

Beneath me, Rachel's body crumples in defeat. She sways, and I wrap an arm around her to keep her from collapsing.

"We'll give him my car," she whispers. "It's worth three times that amount."

My thumb traces the path of her cheekbone. I've missed her. I'll miss her again when she sees I'm right about the police. "If Eric wanted your car, he would have taken your car."

"But he said..." she starts with a mixture of exhaustion and frustration.

She's searching for hope, and I have none to offer. There's no pot at the end of the rainbow. No spell that will undo what's been done. This isn't a fairy tale, but a nightmare. "He said he'd take your car if you don't pay the debt. He meant after he beats the life out of me and—" rapes "—hurts you. This isn't about the money. This is about control."

Her body presses against my arm for release, and I let her go. She stumbles back and I silently curse myself. I gave her the truth, but it's a truth a girl like her should've never heard. Her chest moves rapidly, and she claws at the material of her sweater as if she's choking. I understand. With each passing second, I feel the noose Eric placed on me tightening.

Rachel's lower lip quivers and the words tumble out. "I can't go to the police." Her eyes snap shut and the way she fights to keep tears from falling rips me in half. "My family will hate me and I'll destroy her. Making her happy is the only reason I'm alive."

Her words make no sense, but the pure agony underlying her tone tells me she means them. She yanks again at her sweater, threatening to tear it. "Why is this happening?"

It doesn't matter why. It's happening. I close the distance between us and fold her smaller body into mine. She fights me at first—her fists knock against my chest. Each swipe stings, but it's nothing like the hurt beating at me because of her pain. Eventually, she stops hitting and rests her forehead on my chest. Her body quakes with sobs.

"What am I going to do?" she whispers.

I kiss the top of her head. The early-morning sun warms her hair and I linger so I can inhale the delicious scent of jasmine mixed with salty waves. I gave her up once and touching her like this again... I refuse to abandon her again. She needs me.

"I'll fix this." I have no idea how, but I can't stomach her tears. "Give me twenty-four hours and I'll have a way to fix this."

Rachel

STANDING IN THE GARAGE AT home, I stare at Isaiah's phone number programmed into my cell. Isaiah said that he'll fix things with Eric, but what does that mean for us? For our relationship? Or our lack of a relationship? If he had given me his number last week I would have been full of joy. Now—I feel tired.

Isaiah told Eric I was a debt.

Eric called me a fuck.

I close my eyes and cringe at that last word. Was Isaiah right? He called me dense. I have to be, because I honestly believed that the kiss in his apartment meant something to him. That our moment together, that my first kiss, was more than a lead-in to...to...sex.

With a sigh, I swing my pack over my shoulder and head to the house. It's early. Not even ten yet. There's no way I can return to school, not when my mind's a turbulent mess over Eric and Isaiah and five thousand dollars. It all seems overwhelming and impossible. It probably is, but Isaiah told me not to worry. He told me to have hope. I'm torn between the two emotions.

The same words circle in my head: I'm a debt. I. Am. A. Debt.

I unlock the back door, enter the kitchen and disable the alarm. Dad's at work, West and Ethan are at school, Mom is... who knows where. My fingers brush where Isaiah stroked my cheek before we parted ways. My heart flutters and then crashes to a halt. I'm a debt. A debt.

Eric pops into my mind and my skin crawls because he touched my hair. My head starts to ache. What I need is a hot, pounding shower and a new train of thought.

I'm a debt.

"Rach? What are you doing here?"

A jolt of shock causes me to drop my backpack and turn. My oldest brother, Gavin, stands next to the pantry, a bag of chips in his hand. *It's just Gavin!* I scream in my mind, but after Eric, everything seems like a threat. Especially Gavin. My brother is huge: played football in college and was good at it, too. He's smart and opinionated and he just plain intimidates me.

"I asked what you were doing here," he demands.

My fingers twine and untwine. "I didn't feel good so I came home." The lie comes easily. Guilt follows.

His eyes lower to my pack on the floor by my feet. "You're too young to sign yourself out."

"I never made it into school. I sat in the parking lot until I felt well enough to come home." *Please believe me. Please believe me.*

"Does Mom know?"

"No." Crap. Mom. I'm not ready to face Mom. "But I'll tell her. Is she here?"

Gavin scratches the back of his head, and the chip bag crackles in his hand. I glance around the kitchen and realize that everything about this moment is wrong. "Where's the staff?"

"Mom gives them Friday mornings off," he says.

I didn't know that. "And Mom?"

"Out," he says. "You should go upstairs if you aren't feeling good."

Yeah, because Gavin always looks out for my best interests—and by always I mean never. "What are you doing here? Don't you have a job?"

The bag crackles again, and that's when I notice a gym bag full of food on the floor. And the jeans he's wearing... and T-shirt. "What's going on?"

Gavin drops the chips and steps in my direction. Remembering Eric, I stumble back. I've already been threatened by one guy today. I don't want to be threatened by another. Faster than me, because let's face it, who isn't, Gavin grabs my wrist to steady me as I ram into the fridge.

"Calm down, Rach. What's gotten into you?" He doesn't wait for my response as he continues, "I lost my job."

All of me sinks. "Oh, Gavin. I'm sorry. When?" Gavin became an energy broker after college. Mom and Dad were so proud. As Mom announced at parties: one in medical school—referencing Jack—and one moving straight to the top in business.

"A couple of weeks ago," he rushes out. "I'll find something else soon."

My head tilts as I understand. "You haven't told Mom and Dad."

"Dad knows." He omits that Mom doesn't and frees my wrist. "He wants to tell Mom after you agree to speak at the fundraisers. That way she'll be in a good place, not a bad one."

I try to rub away the worry lines forming on my forehead. Why is it always on me to fix everything? "That's not fair."

"Life's not fair," he snaps. "When are you going to grow up and accept that?"

It's too much. All of it. Eric and money and Isaiah and now Gavin. "I never asked for this."

"And I did?" Gavin says. "Do you think this is the life that Jack and I wanted? To watch our sister die? To watch Mom's soul die? But it's what we got. We all have roles to play, Rachel, and I'm tired of having to remind you of yours."

His hands go to his hips, a certain sign of an impending lecture, but at least he softens his tone. "Look, we all know you're the best of us. You're sweet, kind, possibly the only one of us who has the natural ability to stay out of trouble. So why are you being so selfish? You can make Mom happy and you're choosing not to. You're a better person than that."

I'm not. My arm brushes against the handle of the fridge as I withdraw farther from him.

My fingers massage the painful pulse that's penetrated the frontal lobe of my brain. Gavin dips his head to look me in the eye. I'm not afraid he'll see a lie. I really do feel awful. My stomach gurgles with distress.

"You're not looking good, kid," he says. "Do you want me to stick around? Watch some movies with you?"

My lips fall into a frown and tremble. Gavin loves me and all I do is lie.

"Ah, Rach. I'm sorry." He envelops me in a bone-breaking

bear hug. "I'm sorry I yelled and I'm sorry that you don't feel good. I've just got a lot on my plate right now."

I rest my head on his shoulder. Gavin loves me. He always has, just in his big-brother way. Would Eric hurt them, my family? Or would Gavin be able to scare off this threat if I told him? "Have you ever been in trouble?" I ask.

Gavin releases me. "Are you scared Mom's going to be upset that you came home from school without asking? Rach, I swear, you look like shit. She's not going to care. Well, she'll care, but in the obsessive way and not the pissed way."

And I'm reminded that once more everything is about Mom's reaction and that my brothers could never imagine me in trouble. "I'm going to go lie down."

"I'll stay if you want," he says as I pick up my pack and turn for the stairs.

"I'm okay." But I'm not. I'm not sure anything will be okay again. I'm slow on my way up the stairs. I've run this staircase a million times. Slid down the banister until Mom caught me at the age of seven. Today, my legs throb as if I'm climbing a mountain.

Five thousand dollars. How will Isaiah and I find five thousand dollars?

At the top of the stairs, I take a left, away from the four rooms that currently house West and Ethan and the two other rooms where Jack and Gavin used to live. I pass one of the guest bedrooms and a sickening nausea claws through my bloodstream at the sight of the cracked door of the room across from mine. There's only one person who goes into Colleen's room—Mom.

Leaving my backpack leaning against my door frame, I inhale slowly and peek into the room I wish would disappear. The walls are pink, Colleen's favorite color. The canopy bed is perfectly made. One doll and one stuffed bear still wait on the pillow for their owner to return.

A dollhouse-sized perfect replica of our house sits on the floor. Like always, within the dollhouse, the figure meant to represent Mom lies next to the figurine meant to represent Colleen. My brothers told me that Mom slept with Colleen during the last weeks of her life and that Mom never stopped praying for a miracle.

"Rachel?" a small voice that hardly sounds like my mother whispers from the room. Gavin must not have realized she'd come home. I swallow to calm my nerves. I hate this room, and I hate entering it even more.

I nudge the door open and the hinges squeak painfully. With her legs curled underneath her, Mom slides her hand against the soft, shaggy white throw rug lying near the doll-house. In her other hand, she clutches a baby-pink fleece blanket just the right size for a newborn. Her blue eyes are hollow as she regards me. "What are you doing home?"

The thumb of my left hand pushes against the sweating palm of my right. "I'm not feeling well."

Worry consumes her face, and I force myself to enter the room to keep her from bolting off the floor. "I'm okay," I say. "Just a headache."

She gets on her knees. "You haven't had a migraine in years." Because a migraine is typically the aftermath of a panic attack.

"No, I haven't." Bold-faced lie. I step closer to the rug and flutter my hands in a downward movement to indicate she should stay where she is. "It's a fluke. Probably my period."

The conflict of whether to overanalyze my health or to stay where she feels a connection with Colleen wages war on her face. What I dread the most happens. Mom decides she can't choose and wants both. She extends her hand to me and I notice that her long fingernails are a freshly painted pink. I kick off my shoes, accept her hand and join her on the rug. Does Mom know she still holds the blanket she brought Colleen home from the hospital in?

Mom surveys the room. Porcelain dolls perfectly dressed in ruffles and lace line several shelves. The only indication that Colleen made it anywhere near thirteen is the ancient Discman with headphones resting on the bedside table alongside of her diary and a book opened to the last page Colleen read.

"I dreamed of her last night." Mom squeezes my hand. "She was calling to me and no matter how hard I tried, I could never find her."

But I'm here. Right beside you. Look at me. See me. I exert pressure back. The gesture does nothing to rip her away from the nightmare imprisoning her mind.

"I always wonder if Colleen's death was a punishment for my past sins," she says.

My muscles tense with edginess, the same feeling as if I'm teetering on a ledge. Mom behaves like this sometimes. Her body here, but her mind far-off. She says things that make me unable to breathe. Mom's hand tightens around mine and I suddenly feel claustrophobic.

"I made mistakes," she says. "When I was younger. Before I met your father. Colleen was such a good girl. So good..."

Look at me, Mom. I'm your daughter and I'm right here. "Mom?"

She blinks and turns her head, the glow of life back in her blue eyes. I suck in a relieved breath. Mom tucks my hair over my shoulder. "You're such a good girl, too."

My eyes shut. I'm not. I defied curfew, drag raced and now owe five thousand dollars to a guy my mother would faint at the sight of. I'm in danger, I'm putting Isaiah in danger and I'm risking my mother's—my family's—happiness because I am not a good girl. I'm exactly who Gavin described: I'm selfish.

"Mom..." A lump forms in my throat. "Dad told me about the amazing opportunity to help with the Leukemia Foundation. I...I want to speak on Colleen's behalf."

My mother's face explodes into a smile. Her blue eyes glitter like light dancing on the ocean. She abandons the blanket and hugs me. Reactions like this from Mom are, in theory, what I live for, but I can't enjoy it. Being in Colleen's room, understanding what I just agreed to, it's like I've agreed to a death sentence and I've become numb.

 Isaiah

I PACE OUTSIDE THE SHOP, feeling restless, a little wild.

Eric.

Rachel.

Five thousand dollars.

I slide my hand over the tiger tattooed over my right biceps. Eric's not the first predator I've been up against.

I went to the zoo once in elementary school on a field trip. Being the smallest kid in the class, I never saw much other than the back of someone's head. The zoo had built a towering three-story glass house over the tiger's habitat. Everyone else in class ran to the top to watch the tiger cub playing with a ball in the roughage. I stayed where I knew I belonged: on the bottom.

I leaned against the glass to stare at the worn mud tracks. This was where the tiger no one was interested in would wander. A raggedy thing, his skin hung from his body, his coat was devoid of any shine, his ear half-chewed-off—he was a pathetic creature. A rescued animal, my teacher had said, that would die in the wild.

From out of nowhere, the old tiger pounced from the right,

slammed both massive paws against the glass and roared. My heart tripped out of my chest; my body shook from head to toe, but I never moved and I never stopped making eye contact. The tiger paced in front of me, its head whipping with every turn, never letting me out of his turbulent gaze.

I knew in that moment, without a doubt, that I no longer wanted to be the smallest in my class, the smallest in my group home. I yearned to be this badass tiger that no one messed with. My teacher, like all adults, was dead wrong: this tiger would have ruled the wild.

I don't rule the streets. That title can belong to someone else, but no one messes with me. Eric knows this, and he's spent years trying to place me under his thumb. I won't allow that to happen, and I won't allow him to hurt Rachel.

In order to protect her, I have a plan to set in motion. A plan that hinges on the following yes. I take a deep breath and enter the shop.

The heaters in the old garage are so jacked up that it may be warmer outside. With no car on the lift and none in the parking lot, Tom, the owner of the auto shop that employs me, is short on work and long on stories. He and the full-time auto mechanic, Mack, sit in his cramped office and laugh over a shared bottle of whiskey.

"Isaiah." Tom grabs his cane as if he's going to stand. Everything in the shop is old, out-of-date and paid off. Since he makes only enough to pay Mack and, occasionally, me, Tom's sole reason for keeping the place open is that his wife died a few years ago and he hates to be alone. "How was the first week back at school?"

"Fine." I wonder if he's aware that this is Saturday morning and that when I saw him yesterday I had told him the news. His mind drifts more in the past than it does the present. "Eastwick is going to let me intern on Tuesday and Thursdays at Pro Performance."

"You told me that," he murmurs.

Tom smooths his thinning white hair and shifts back in his seat. He pats the pocket of his red flannel shirt, no doubt searching for a pack of Marlboros and a lighter even though the doctor told him to quit over a year ago. His kind light blue eyes dart as his mind sorts through the memory and the present. Today is a good day as his face brightens with the rare retained knowledge. "You told me that. They're going to give you a job when you graduate."

"Yes, sir." My gut untwists with his words. I dread the day he does forget.

The old man and Mack have been good to me. A friend of theirs fostered me for a while. Then the one good family I had left town, the system moved me to Shirley and Dale's and these two old guys got it in their head to hire me at the raw age of thirteen.

"Good," Tom says to himself and then stares at Mack. "Isn't that good."

A thirty-years-served retired vet, Mack tips his Marine Corps baseball cap once in my direction. "Don't fuck it up."

"Not planning on it."

"Good." Mack reiterates Tom's sentiments. "That job will take you somewhere."

I glance around the sparse garage. "No work?"

Mack shakes his head. Tom may own the shop, but Mack manages it. Like Tom, Mack has no need to work. He pre-

fers the garage over his empty apartment. "I finished the
Chevelle."

"Do you mind if I work on some side business during the
day? Assuming there's nothing coming in?" I doubt Rachel
will be able to stay late.

Since I was fourteen, I've done side work for friends. They
find the parts; I do the manual labor in exchange for a fee,
parts to supe up my own Mustang, or a debt they owe me to
be paid later. The side work typically waits until the garage
is officially closed at night, but with business being slow
maybe they'll give on the timing.

Mack sips the whiskey from the bottle. "No problem.
What are you working on?"

Anything I can scavenge in order to make extra money.
"My car." I clear my throat. "And a 2005 Mustang GT."

A ghost of a smile plays on Mack's lips, creating deep crev-
ices around his mouth. "Finally save enough to supe your
car?"

No. "Calling in favors."

More like I'm calling in debts owed to me. Debts I saved
for times when I would need help—like bail. Some of those
people will pay in cash. Others who don't have a cash flow
can supply parts. I hate that I'm using my rainy-day fund,
but owing Eric could be worse than jail.

"And I'm assuming that's why I'm here?" asks Abby from
behind me.

Mack, Tom and I turn our heads. She nods at me, acknowledges Tom, and like always, ignores Mack. Mack finishes
the whiskey, throws the empty bottle into the trash and
leaves the office. He'll be MIA for the rest of the day. Abby's

never told me why the two stare at each other from opposite sides of a battlefield, and because I respect her, I never ask.

Tom pats his pocket again, still searching for his cigarettes. "Keep your politics out of my garage, Miss Abby."

Politics as in her drugs. Tom's the only person I've seen Abby cave to. "I always do."

"Good." By the way Tom's eyes glaze over I can tell we've lost him to a memory.

I head to the other side of the garage and Abby follows.

"Everyone knows about the deal you made with Eric," she says. "He means business, Isaiah, and he wants your head and Fuzzy Bunny's on a platter. Eric's threatened to retaliate against anyone who helps you raise the money."

Shit. That complicates things. I had hoped to raise half of the five thousand from collecting on debts. Now I'll have to rely solely on the parts. "I'll respect whatever decision you make as long as you make it now. What side are you playing, Abby? Are you my friend in this or my enemy?"

"I can't help," she says.

I place my hands on the tool bench and lean into it. Not what I wished to hear. "Abby..."

"I can't give you money." Her eyes flash to mine. "What I make, I need. Eric may own some of the streets, but he doesn't own me. I'll help in what ways I can, but I still have to watch my own back."

Because nobody else will. She doesn't have to say that part. Because life is like that for me, too. I straighten. It's her response and I have to accept it. "I have favors to call in, and I'd like some help doing it."

"I'm game." With a tilt of her chin, she falls into business mode. I hate that deadpan look, but that expression is the reason I'm asking for her help. The amount of work to be accomplished would normally take weeks. I don't have weeks. I'm allowing days on a job that needed to be done last night.

I snag a list from my back pocket and tell her the names of the people to visit. As she listens, her only change in expression is one eyebrow that slowly lifts and then just as slowly eases down. She shoves the list into her jeans. "You've been busy playing Boy Scout to a lot of resourceful people."

Yeah, I have. "I like knowing there's help when I need it."

"Or you could save your full house for another play and take the offer of jacking the cars. With your car knowledge you could easily steal five in a night. You'd have Eric off your back and Fuzzy Bunny on your arm by the time the church doors open tomorrow morning."

I shake my head before she finishes. "I'm doing this clean." Illegally street racing got me in this mess and I don't want to take the chance of screwing things up more.

"Clean?" Her mouth flattens into a thin line. "How do you think these people are going to supply the car parts you're asking for as payment? You honestly think they're going to waltz into a store and buy them?"

No. I don't. But I'm all for claiming denial. "Last time I'm saying it. Choose now if you're going to help."

"God, you're cranky. What does that girl see in you?"

I have no idea. "She likes my tats."

The deadpan look washes away and she laughs. "You're a crazy son of a bitch. Fine, waste a good list like this on car parts. I'll check in later." Without another word, Abby walks out of the garage.

I run a hand over my head and contemplate calling Rachel. I crave hearing her voice again, but she'll expect answers and I only have theories. After I talk to my list of people, I'll know more and then I can tell her to come.

I'm still not good enough for a girl like her, but she's back in my life and she needs someone to protect her. I'll fill the role and absorb as much of her light as I can before she leaves me behind in the darkness.

Rachel

WHEN I WAS FOUR I had an infatuation with electrical out-
lets. Dark holes that led into the wall and if I plugged something in, the machine would spring to life. Electricity! What
would electricity look like? Feel like? Submitting to temptation, I stuck my finger into the socket at the moment someone turned on the vacuum. My body jolted with the shock. I
learned two lessons that day. One: don't stick your finger into
the socket. Two: I liked the rush.

Closing the door to my Mustang, I fumble with the buttons
of my black winter coat. My blood pulses with the same buzz
of electrical energy. I'm going to see Isaiah.

He never called, I remind myself. Isaiah never called and
he looked me square in the eye at the bar and told me he
owed me a debt. The same words he said to Eric in my school's
parking lot. *Stop any silly daydreams that he cares. He doesn't. I'm
a debt to be paid. Nothing more.*

The small sickly garage appears different during the day.
Oddly enough, that night, this place became a beacon of light,
a haven. Now, with the gray clouds hovering low in the sky

and the cracks in the exterior wall, I'm reminded that I'm out of my element.

I pull on the heavy door and enter. Heat belonging to a jungle suffocates me and defrosts my cold fingers. My hair blows across my face as a surge of cold air encircles me when the door shuts. A radio plays music that is loud and angry and full of electric guitars. With no shirt on, Isaiah hovers over the open hood of his Mustang. Both of his hands deep within her body.

The flaming tail of the dragon I noticed on his biceps the night I first met him continues up his shoulder and curls around to his back. The green eyes of the wicked red creature peer at me like a sentry protecting his master. Near Isaiah's shoulder blade, fire snakes out of the dragon's mouth. With a socket in his hand, Isaiah works on the car in a fluid motion. The broad strong muscles in his back become more pronounced the faster he labors.

Isaiah shifts, getting a better grip on whatever he's working on. My mouth goes dry and alien sensations warm my body. Isaiah is absolutely beautiful.

My purse slips out of my hand and lands on the floor in an embarrassing thump. His head jerks up and he spots me gaping. A knowing smile slides across his lips, causing heat to creep along my cheeks. If only I could die.

He straightens, and I try not to stare at the liquid way he moves. I grab my purse, drop it again, then snag it back off the floor. Why am I always such a mess?

"Hey, Rachel," he says easily in that deep voice that causes my heart to skip more beats than it should. *He didn't call. He didn't call*, I repeat. *He doesn't want me. I'm a debt.*

"Hi," I respond, proud I didn't stutter the small word.

Snatching his black T-shirt off the bench, Isaiah shrugs it on and indicates that I should walk in farther. "Sorry about the heat. It's either the tropics or the arctic. Take your pick."

"Tropics," I say. "I hate the cold."

"Me, too," he agrees. So we have at least one thing in common, besides cars and the drag race and Eric....

I pause on the other side of the open hood and openly appreciate the machinery embedded in the frame. He was right on one thing: that's not the original engine of a '94 Mustang GT. "You upgraded."

"Rebuilt." Isaiah studies the car with an intensity that suggests deep thought. "Found the trashed body in a junkyard when I was fourteen then spent the past couple of years smoothing out the frame and piecing together parts until I could make her run. On paper, I should be running more torque and horsepower, but too many of the parts are past their prime."

My hands sweat, not from the heat, and I clutch the strap of my purse. I swing it a little so that it hits my knees. I miss the way the two of us acted that night. I miss the idea of him liking me. "I'm sorry," I say.

His eyes snap to mine. "For what?"

For not being someone you could really like. "For all of it." I lower my head and watch my purse smack my legs over and over again. "I know you think you owe me, but you don't. This is my problem. I'll figure it out." Though I have no idea how.

His eyes darken back into the serious charcoal I remember when he swore his promise to me. "This is our problem."

I'm a debt. He said I meant nothing. I gave Isaiah my first

kiss, he never called and I'm a debt. Eric called me a fuck and Isaiah silently agreed. I've got lots of problems, and the last thing I want is to force a guy to help me because he thinks he owes me something. Not when I have feelings for him and he has none for me. Not when seeing him will continue to crush my soul. "Isaiah..."

He cuts me off. "One thing you should learn about me—I don't argue."

The purse stops swinging. "What?"

His eyes fade into a beautiful shade of silver. "This isn't your problem. It's our problem. And I know how we're going to solve it."

"You do?" I ask a little breathlessly. Oh, those eyes are gorgeous. Too much heat curls along my body and with one finger, I tug at the collar of my coat.

His eyes follow the movement. "You should take off your coat," he says and my heart jumps in my chest at the thought of taking anything off in front of him. "It's warm in here."

Warm. The screwed-up heater. Right. Clearing my throat, I unbutton my jacket and slide it off. Isaiah takes it from me and I feel suddenly alone and naked as he crosses the room to place it on a hook on the wall. "We're going to drag race," he announces.

I snort. "Because that worked out so well the first time."

He flashes that breathtaking smile, then it disappears so quickly I'm not sure it was there to begin with. "Street racing was a mistake I don't plan on repeating, and neither will you."

Isaiah pauses as if he's waiting for me to protest. I'm not. Lesson learned: no street racing. He continues, "Have you ever heard of The Motor Yard?"

"No."

"It's a one-eighth of a mile dragway in the southwestern part of the county."

"Is it legal?"

"Yeah. And that's where I'm going to win us the money we need to pay off Eric." Standing in the middle of the garage, Isaiah radiates confidence. I envy him.

"How is racing there going to be any different from the streets?"

"Because the place is legit and family-oriented. The guys racing there are generational—dads, uncles, grandpas, great-grandpas. I'll make the money off side bets. The money per bet won't be large, but I hope to win enough to compensate."

I'm already shaking my head. It doesn't sound like much of a plan. "So the two of us are going to race and *hope* to win some side bets along the way and all of this will *hopefully* total five thousand dollars?"

"Not the two of us," he says with no apology. "I'll be racing and winning with your car."

I blink. "My car."

"Yes," he says with absolutely no hesitation. "Your car."

There's no way he can do it—make that much money in races he *hopes* to win. My lips shift to the right as I mull over what he said. He believes, but I...can't.

Isaiah focuses on my mouth. In two easy strides, he crosses the distance between us and places his fingers under my chin. His warm thumb sweeps across the edge of my lips and my heart flutters. He performs the enticing movement one more time...but slower and my mouth responds by relaxing. I quit breathing and thinking. I have so missed his touch.

"I told you not to worry," he whispers.

I choke on the sarcastic laugh and turn my head to breathe in air that's free of his scent. Worrying is all I'm good at. "I'm not."

"You are," he responds quickly. "When I say I'm going to do something, I do it."

Not true—he said he'd call and he didn't. I fiddle with a wayward thread on the cuff of my sleeve as my heart sinks. What do I do if he bails on me? What do I do if I don't work with him? Maybe I could ask West and Ethan for help. Maybe they have money.

I lift my head to find him staring at me. "I'm glad you're here, Rachel." He slides his fingers around my wrist and the brush of his skin against mine melts my muscles like hot dripping butter.

Disgust immediately weaves through me. I'm so pathetic. He never called. Isaiah never freaking called, and with a few words and a few caresses I fall right back to where I started: as a stupid naive girl.

I step away and push my bangs from my face. I can't do this. I can't let him toy with me. I've got a couple hundred dollars saved from my birthday and Christmas. I'll pawn some of my jewelry. I'll beg Eric for more time. Anything other than having my heart ripped out. "This is a mistake. I'll figure it out on my own."

As I walk past him, toward my coat, toward the door, Isaiah grabs my hand. "What's wrong." It's not a question. It's a demand.

"You said I was a one-night stand." I jerk my hand, but he

doesn't give. Anger flares through me and I jerk harder. "You said I meant nothing!"

His hand slips away. "I never said you were a one-night stand. Rachel...I could never think of you as a fuck."

I wince from the word leaving his mouth and hate how he inclines his head in pity as he notices the weakness.

"But Eric did," I say. "And you didn't argue."

"I'm sorry," he says simply as if that will wash away a week's worth of ignoring me.

My throat burns as tears threaten my eyes. I should keep my mouth shut and bolt. Instead, I stay and say the stupid words. "I waited for you to call. You said you would. You said you liked me. And then you tell Eric I meant nothing."

"I showed for you." A bit of irritation leaks into his voice. "I got into Eric's face for you."

"Because you owe me! Because I stopped my car and let you drive it until we ditched the police."

His expression becomes a brewing storm. "It's not like that."

I throw my arms out in a mock parody of not caring, but the truth is I do. I care so much about this guy that he's tearing me to shreds. "So you don't owe me?"

"Jesus Christ," he mutters as his hands fist at his sides. "I do owe you."

He wants to say more, but I can't listen to lies. "Just say it, Isaiah. Cut the crap and say that I was a game. Tell me how I was the stupid, pathetic rich girl you tried to sleep with. Just say it and then we'll figure a way out of this mess without you having to charm me into doing what you want." *Without you breaking what's left of my soul.* "Just say it!"

But before he can say anything, the door to the garage

creaks open. I turn my head reluctantly in time to catch two people who look roughly our age shuffling in. The guy is tall, looming over the girl who, if it's possible, is shorter than me. Her eyes dart between me and Isaiah and finally settle on him. "Hello, Isaiah," she says.

Her ripped blue jeans and blond hair with black streaks scream that she's fine with danger. She's beautiful, and by the way she holds herself, she's confident—strong. I wipe at my eyes and angle my body in the opposite direction of her. My chest moves with the heavy beating of my heart and a moronic, traitorous tear falls.

Isaiah lowers his head and utters a curse. I can tell by how he tries not to look at her, yet keeps doing so that this girl means something to him. Guess he just got busted for cheating on her—with me.

Isaiah

"HELLO, ISAIAH." MY NAME ON the lips of few can cause my world to stall. As if in slow motion, I turn my head and watch her sweep into my life as if she never left.

"Fuck," I mumble. Would it be so damn difficult for the universe to give me a break? Rachel flips her golden hair over her shoulder to prevent me from examining her face.

"Am I interrupting?" Beth asks as she glides farther into the garage. A million questions form, but the return of the dull ache in my body deters me from voicing any of them. She's still gorgeous: a tiny pissed-off fairy, but her hair is different. She wears it chin-length now and blond has replaced the black except for two stripes of the color I knew.

"Yes," I say with way too much anger. Beth notices and mockingly raises one brow.

A guy I don't know strolls in. I straighten and feel my muscles flex. What the hell? Has she already run through the guy she chose over me and come here to show off another? Beth glances behind her before squaring her gaze back on me. "Isaiah, this is Logan. He's a friend of mine…and Ryan's."

Dressed in a jock jacket with a big letter *B* on the front and

his name embroidered underneath it, the kid nods at me.
On the white arm of the coat, two baseball bats cross over
each other. The guy Beth fell for, Ryan, was also a baseball-
playing jock.

I roll my shoulders. I don't want to hand Beth the opportunity to rip me into pieces again. Not now. Not when everything has gone to shit. Not with Rachel in my life. "You
need to go."

"I've tried calling you," she says, ignoring me and the fact
that Rachel stands completely broken not two feet away.
"And texting."

She has. Since Thanksgiving, but I'm not ready to forgive her. "Leave."

Beth stops in front of Rachel and gives her a once-over.
"I'm Beth," she says. "Since Isaiah has lost his manners."

Rachel lifts her chin in the air. A surge of pride courses
through my blood. Damn if she'll permit Beth to get the better of her. "I'm Rachel."

"She's with me," I say, causing Rachel to meet my eyes.
*Come on, angel, I know we've got stuff to work out, but stay
with me. Beth is the one who doesn't belong here.*

Beth clears her throat. She wants my attention, but she's
not receiving it. "Logan inherited a car, and I told him you
could help him fix it. I told him you were the best."

"I only do favors for friends," I respond while holding Rachel's gaze. *That's right. Keep those gorgeous violet eyes on
me. Instinctively, you trust me. Keep on doing it.*

I need time with Rachel: time to explain why I never
called, time to explain that our one night together meant
something and time to explain why I said those words to

Eric that hurt her so badly. Time to understand why the hell
I care so much that Rachel's mad at me. Because the world
never works in my favor, I have no time.

"I used to be your best friend," Beth sneers. "Is she your
friend now?"

Clearly curious for the answer, Rachel pushes her hair
behind her ear as if to hear me better. I don't want Beth involved in my life anymore, plus I don't know what to say
about me and Rachel. I like her. She's a mystery. And I'm
seriously attracted to her. I guess we're friends, but something stops me from saying that aloud. "Shop's closed, Beth."

Rachel's eyes shut, and when she opens them, she looks
at Beth. "He owes me a favor."

Beth's shoulders visibly relax, and I wonder why she cares
who I'm spending time with. Beth left me. "So, Isaiah, what
type of favor do you owe her?"

"I need money," Rachel answers with a boldness few have
used with Beth. Anger shoots through me. That's business
strictly between me and Rachel. Not information for Beth.
"And Isaiah is going to drag race my car in order to help me
get it. So when I'm finished with him, you can have your
friend back."

The sadistic smile I remember so well from when Beth
feels threatened slides across her face. "Thanks, but I don't
need your permission."

Rachel swings her purse onto her shoulder and cocks her
head at me. "You want to race my car, fine. You can race my
car. Text me the when and where and I'll be there. And don't
worry about coming up with the full amount. I can come up
with some of it on my own."

"Rachel..." I start.

But she's already across the garage. Her coat falls off the hook when she slams the door.

Just fuck. I stalk past Beth and glance out the door's small window. The engine of her Mustang growls as it pulls out of the lot. I pick up her coat. It smells like her—like the ocean. I gently place it back on the hook. "Get out of my life, Beth."

"Beth," says jock boy. "Let's go."

"Now, that you've decided to speak up," I say to him, "take Beth and get the fuck out."

"No, Logan," Beth interjects. "Give me a few minutes with Isaiah."

The guy with dark hair releases a frustrated breath. "I promised Ryan I wouldn't let you out of my sight, so whatever you have to say or do..." He shrugs his shoulders.

I wait for Beth to tell the guy—Logan—where to shove what he said. She only crosses her arms over her chest. I let out a sarcastic chuckle. The girl's been domesticated. I head back to my Mustang, deciding it's best to ignore them both.

Beth follows and stands a foot from me. "Noah and I talk," she says.

Silence.

"You and I were friends before, and we can be friends again."

More silence.

"I miss you."

And she went too far. I turn to the jock. "What type of work are we talking?" I'm desperate for additional sources of income and maybe he can pay.

Logan moves his head in a who-knows fashion. "It runs,

but makes strange noises when it hits forty. I'd like it to not explode on the freeway and for it to run faster."

"Can you pay?"

"Yes."

Beth knew I could help. "Bring the car in sometime. Without *her.*"

He jerks his thumb behind him. "I got it out in the parking lot."

It. As if the car means nothing. I remind myself he can pay. "Slide her in."

Logan assesses Beth in a way that says he's put up with her antics before. "Can I leave you for two seconds without you starting a world war?"

"I used to like you," she says to Logan.

He leaves and Beth stays. Why did she return? To screw with me? To rub it in that she's happy? I glance at her from the corner of my eye. She touches the pink ribbons on her wrist that that asshole Ryan gave her. He makes her happy. I hate the guy.

"So are you into her?" Beth asks.

"Does your uncle know you're here?" I push the button to open the bay and then busy myself with some wrenches. Rachel is the opposite of Beth with her brilliant smile and joyous laughter. A beam of light. Even when I was into her, Beth was nothing but darkness.

"Yes," she answers immediately.

A muffled *humph* leaves my throat because I don't buy that.

"Fine. No, he doesn't. And before you ask, Ryan does."

I move onto the screwdrivers. "When did you become a dog on a leash?"

"Fuck you," she growls then sighs. "I'm not. Ryan knows I miss you and he knows I love him. He's okay with you and me being friends."

Yeah. Right. I'm sure he prefers not to be the prick who said no, so he's depending on me to tell her to go. At least the asshole called that move correctly. I turn my head to the sound of an engine rumbling and briefly smile when I see a red '57 Chevy roll into the bay.

Beth walks up beside me. "I knew you'd like her."

Her. Because Beth knows I love cars. In fact, she knows too much about me. Beth is like a bad trip. She always has been, and I don't want to be on a ride with her anymore. "Go."

"No. Not until we're friends again."

Logan cuts the engine, gets out and pops the hood. "What do you think?" he asks.

I think I could get a hard-on with a car like this. "This car was made to race."

Logan snaps to attention. "You think you could get the car to go fast?"

I pause while assessing the kid. It was there in his voice and still present in the expectant way he holds his body. Speed. He craves it. Wants it. Maybe the jock's not so bad. "Are you interested in keeping her street legal?"

"More interested in speed. Can you hook me up with a race once this is done?"

I place both of my hands on the car and lean over to inspect the engine. It's not the original, which is good; otherwise, I'd hate doing anything to her. "If you're looking for fast driving there's a dragway in the southwestern part of the county. It opens next week."

"Do you race there?" he asks.

"Yes." And I plan on spending a lot of time there over the next six weeks.

"Isaiah." Beth attempts to step in between us, but Logan angles himself so that she can't. "That's not why I brought him here."

An insane glint strikes the guy's eyes and all of a sudden, I feel a connection to him. A twitch of his lips shows he might be my kind of crazy. "How fast do the cars there go?"

"Some guys hit speeds of 120 mph in an eighth mile."

"No!" Beth stomps her foot. "No. I promised Ryan nothing crazy would happen. Logan, this is not why I brought you here."

"Have you hit those speeds?" He swats his hand at Beth as if she's a fly, earning my respect. Most guys would be terrified of having their balls ripped off and handed to them for dismissing Beth like that.

"Not driving my car, I haven't," I answer honestly. But I hope to with Rachel's car, and with mine, after a few modifications. "Speed can be bought. Just depends on how much you want to spend."

Logan offers his hand. "I'm Logan."

"Isaiah," I say as we shake.

"Shit," mumbles Beth.

Rachel

MY ROOM IS PURPLE. THE walls, the throw rug over the white carpet, my comforter, my pillows, the floor-to-ceiling curtains—purple. Lavender really, but that's just another way to say the word *purple*. I hate purple, but Mom doesn't like green.

I sit in the middle of my four-poster bed and recount the money. Five hundred dollars. That's what I have. Several pieces of jewelry rest on the pillow beside me. Those four pieces are the only ones I don't think Mom would notice missing.

If my gowns weren't in Mom's closet, I could try selling those. While my mother can't scrape up the ability to see who I am on the inside, she watches the outside like a hawk.

Someone knocks. I flip the pillow over to hide the jewelry and wad the cash. The door opens and Ethan catches sight of the money right as I slam it into my jewelry box. He strides into my room and plops on the bed. The pillow shifts and I glance over to confirm the jewelry is still hidden.

"Whatcha doing?" he asks as he stares at the box full of cash.

"Nothing."

"Buying a new part for your car?" Because in Ethan's mind, it's the only thing I would need cash for. After a lecture from my dad, Ethan knows I won't put my car parts on the credit card.

No. I'm paying off a psychopath. "Maybe."

Me and my brothers, we're spoiled. Each of us has a credit card so we can buy whatever we desire, but that financial freedom also carries a burden. Dad meets with us each month and reviews our spending. Two years ago, when I'd spent too much on parts for my car, I wondered if the women tried in Salem for witchcraft sweated as much as I had. This afternoon, for a brief thirty seconds, I considered a cash advance on the card, but West had done that once and Dad was on his case within twenty-four hours. Turns out, Dad set certain alerts.

"I need amnesty," Ethan says.

Of course he does. "Tonight?"

"Yes."

A burst of air rushes out of my mouth and moves my hair. "What if I have plans? It is Saturday night." He and West always assume the social worst of me.

Ethan's face pales. "Do you? And if so, with who?"

"Maybe I want to drive my car."

He rolls his eyes. "You can drive whenever you want."

"Fine."

Ethan swings his feet off my bed. "You're the best." He pauses at the door frame. "By the way, what would you think of extending twin amnesty?"

I pick at the lint on my bed. "To how many?"

My brother bobs his head as if he hasn't already chosen a number. "Limitless."

Dread weighs on my chest. Ethan and West sometimes can be out all night and I'm not always that creative in the lies I spin to cover for them. "I don't know."

"Sleep on it. And Rach." The way he focuses on his sneakers makes the silence uncomfortable. Something that rarely happens between us. "I'm glad you're helping Mom."

I rub the skin between my eyebrows, fighting any thoughts that could lead to anxiety. On the corner of my dresser, taunting me, is a speech I have to memorize by next week.

"Will..." He closes the door to my room and leans his back against it as if to lock everyone out or imprison me. "Will you tell Mom if you get sick?"

I clutch a pillow to my chest. "Just leave me alone, okay?"

"Maybe you should talk to Mom and Dad."

"And then what?" I fling the pillow off the bed. "Mom freaks? Dad's disappointed? You and West and Gavin and Jack get on me for being weak? No, thanks. Where was your pity when Jack laid into me the other night because I hadn't said yes yet?"

"They wouldn't have asked if they knew you still had panic attacks."

Disgust weaves into my voice. "Look me in the eye and tell me that this family isn't happier because I'm hiding what they can't handle." What I can't handle.

"Maybe I should tell them." There's an edge of seriousness to his tone that creates horror movie fear.

"You wouldn't." I search for words. "You want Mom happy, just like everyone else."

"I know, but I keep thinking of you on that damn bathroom floor puking up your guts...."

My phone vibrates, and my stupid heart stutters because there's only one person who would call or text me—Isaiah.

Ethan eyes my cell. "Who's texting you?"

I grab my phone and try not to shake when I see Isaiah's name. "West," I lie. "He's been having problems with his SUV because he forgot to change the oil again."

"Moron," Ethan mutters then looks at me again. "Think about what I said. At least about the amnesty."

"Okay." I struggle to keep my focus on my brother and not on the phone as Ethan leaves. If I don't find a way to control my crazy emotions, Isaiah will only hurt me worse in six weeks when we pay Eric.

Meet me at the dragway at 7. My phone vibrates again with directions.

I toss my cell across the bed and fall back onto my pillows with a loud huff. A demand. Not a request or even a please. A demand. Like he knows he's all hot and mysterious and how I can't stop obsessing over him. I shouldn't go. I shouldn't answer. I should stand my ground.

The phone vibrates again. With a sigh too dramatic to use without an audience, I kick the phone toward me. I read the words then smother a pillow over my face: bring your car gassed

Because I'm nothing more than a debt. Stupid, stupid me.

My headlights flash across Isaiah as I park next to his black Mustang. With his back resting against his passenger door and his arms folded across his chest, he waits in the parking lot just like his texts said he would. The gravel beneath my tires cracks, and I hate the thought of rocks kicking up and hitting the paint.

I inhale, then slowly release the air. I'm a debt. I mean nothing to him. I will not lose it. I will not yell. I will be calm and collected and everything other than the crashing emotions and anxiety brewing inside of me. He will not know that he hurt me. I may be weak, but I'm good at hiding how I really feel. Pretending he didn't break my heart should be easy.

I almost tumble out of the car when the door swings open without my assistance. Isaiah offers a hand as if I need help. Because it's a strange gesture and one that catches me off guard, I accept and then internally curse myself once his strong hand wraps around mine. Crap. I still like his hands on me.

"Hey," he says.

He closes my door, and the two of us stand there, holding hands, staring in silence. Well, almost silence; the sound of two engines simultaneously revving gains my attention. Isaiah smirks when I lean to the left to glimpse what's behind the metal bleachers.

His finger performs this swipe on the back of my hand that sends an electric shock through my body. The blaring lights from the dragway cast a shadow across Isaiah, and I shiver at how comfortable he appears in the darkness.

"It's a sweet sound," he says referring to the engines, but all I hear is his deep voice.

I shrug as if I don't care, but yeah...that sound rocks, the engines and his voice. *Take your hand back, Rach. He's playing you.* One of his fingers moves slowly against my skin again, and goose bumps rise on my arms. The annoying voice in my head repeats the warning, but I don't listen.

"I wasn't sure if you were coming." He sounds both a little hurt and relieved. Good. I can't contain the slight curve of my lips. I showed, but I also stood my ground by refusing to text back.

"You left your jacket at the garage. I've got it in the car, but it looks like you found another."

Okay, that is sweet, but I'm still standing my ground.

"Come on, Rachel," he says with a smoothness that reminds me of silk. "Talk to me."

I shrug again. Okay, I know, completely immature. I haven't even played this game with my brothers in years, but Isaiah so deserves it. We're business, he and I. I'm a debt. He wants to use my car so we can pay off Eric. Nowhere in that agreement does it indicate I have to speak.

In one swift motion, I find the courage to remove my hand and shove it into my coat pocket so Isaiah knows touching me is off-limits. It's a warm night for January, upper fifties, yet I use my jacket as a shield.

"Fine. We'll talk later." He pulls on his bottom earring. "Let me show you the place."

I fall in step with him, and my eyes widen when I see the rows of cars looping around the metal bleachers, each waiting for their turn on the dragway. Mustangs, Camaros, Chargers, Novas, Chevelles, Corvettes. Oh, holy mother of God, the list is endless. All beautiful. All painted in reds or yellows or blacks or whites or blues or oranges—a glorious rainbow. All grumbling with the sounds of fantastic fast engines.

Gathered under smaller streetlights, guys lean against their cars or stand in small groups and call out to Isaiah. He nods or says something in greeting. My world freezes when I notice the gorgeous black beauty near the front of the pack.

"That's a 2004 Mustang Cobra," I say. My head snaps to Isaiah, and I repeat what I said, emphasizing each word. "That is a 2004 Mustang Cobra."

He licks his lips in a pathetic effort to conceal his smile. Yeah, whatever, I'm talking so he won, but who cares. That's a 2004 Mustang Cobra. *That* is the car I have always dreamed of owning.

"I know the guy who owns it," he says. "Do you want a closer look?"

"Are you kidding?" I ask with a bounce that I'm sure makes me look like a five-year-old. "I sort of want to lie on the hood and hug it."

Isaiah laughs the same laugh as the night in the bar. The one that creates an energized rush. The one that messes with my head and warms my blood. My excitement fades as I remember—Isaiah doesn't want me.

Over the loudspeaker, the announcer calls the race. The groups quickly disintegrate and the drivers return to their cars.

"I'll introduce you later," Isaiah says. "Let's go watch."

We weave through the cars, past the bleachers, and stand at the fence near the starting line. I've never seen anything like it before: a flat stretch of road with concrete barricades following the eighth-mile course. Toward the end, two large electronic boards loom on both sides of the track. One set of numbers on top, another on the bottom.

The roar of an engine causes me to return my attention

to the starting line. Guys walk alongside a red Camaro. One waves his hand in the air, indicating the driver should inch closer. "What's he doing?" I ask.

Isaiah props his arms on the fence. "They spray water at the start of the track for the burnout. It's better to get your tires right on the edge of the water."

Holy freaking crap—a burnout. I've seen this hundreds of times on TV, but never in person. On cue, the back tires of the Camaro explode to life, spinning, sending heavy white smoke into the air as the driver heats his tires so he can gain better traction on the track. The sweet smoldering smell of burning rubber fills my nose. Finally, the tires catch and the car jerks forward.

The driver opens the door and fans it repeatedly to rid the interior of the smoke. Once clear, he shuts it and obeys the hand signals of his friend to move to the starting line.

"How do they know where to place their car to start the race?"

"Everything's done by lasers," Isaiah explains. "You need to hit the first laser without going too far. That guy doing all the hand motions is guiding the driver to the line. When he's at the laser, a light over there will turn on."

The competing car completes his burnout and thrusts to the line without help and without smoke infiltrating the car. "Why does the other driver need help and he doesn't?"

"Because of the speeds some of these cars go, you can't use regular seat belts. If we can get your engine to sing, we'll have to install a safety harness in your car. Sometimes the harness keeps you so pinned in you can't see the line. Sometimes the helmet keeps you from seeing it. Sometimes your friends want to help."

He lost me at installing a safety harness in my car. Panic eats at my insides. "You're going to change my car?"

Isaiah watches the cars at the line. "First they have to hit the line for prestaging. See that thing in the middle between the cars? That thing that looks like a traffic light?"

"Yes." No. Not really. I mean, I see it. For both racers, the "traffic light" tower has two rows of white lights at the top, three rows of yellow lights, a single row of green and finally a single row of red. But what I really see is Isaiah missing the point. "As in you're going to physically make a change to my car?"

"Yeah," he answers calmly, as if he didn't just announce he's going to take the one thing in my life I love and ruin it. "It's called a Christmas Tree. The white lights on top are pre-stage for the start of the race. They light up when the front of the car hits the first beam. When you hit the second beam, then the second row of lights glow to let you know that you're ready to race. When both cars are staged, you have seconds before the lights on the tree drop."

Yeah. Sure. Whatever. "What else are you planning to do to my car?" I grip the fence as a fresh wave of dizziness makes me light-headed. My car. I don't want anyone messing with my car.

Either he's ignoring me or he's seriously into the race. "The yellow lights drop in descending order in .5 second intervals. If you leave before the green light, then the red light flashes."

That snaps me out of near hysteria. "What does it mean if you get a red light?"

Isaiah glances at me. "It means you lost."

Understanding socks me in the stomach. That's why I'm not racing—I stalled at the line on the street and if I panic, I'll possibly stall again. If I get overexcited and leave before the light turns green—and let's admit it, I would—then I'll lose the race before I even hit twenty miles per hour. "You don't trust my reaction at the line."

He kicks at the bottom of the fence, and I can tell he doesn't want to answer. "We need a fast car, Rachel. Speed still means something, but out here at the dragway, whoever catches the light first is typically the winner."

The cars in front of us roar. Torque causes the front end of the Camaro to pull up into the air, and I step back, half expecting the car to flip completely backward. It doesn't. The front tires slam back down onto the asphalt. The Camaro races past the Mustang at a blinding speed. The sign at the end flashes. In an eighth mile the Camaro hits ninety-six miles per hour in 6.94 seconds.

My eyes widen and my heart beats hard in my chest. "I so want to do that."

Isaiah

WITH MY ARMS TIGHTLY CROSSED over my chest and my feet spread apart, I watch from a distance as Rachel chats animatedly with Zach, the owner of the Mustang Cobra. Her hair cascades down her back like a waterfall and her hands move gracefully in the air as she relays some story involving her Mustang on a country road.

Zach touches her arm right above her elbow and says something that incites her laughter. A muscle in my jaw jumps. I've known Zach since freshman year. We've taken every automotive course together, and I was there when he bought the Cobra for dirt cheap. If the boy keeps flirting with Rachel, he and I may not be friends by the end of the night.

"Hey, Isaiah."

I tear my eyes off of Rachel for a second to greet Logan. "S'up."

"Thought I'd check out the action," he says, following my gaze to Rachel.

In a motion I've memorized, Rachel shyly bites her bottom lip. *Don't do it. Don't look at Zach with those gorgeous eyes searching for him to be your answer like you did with me.*

The muscles in my neck relax when she brushes her hair over her shoulder and steps back, causing him to remove his hand. Distracting Zach, she points to the Cobra and moves closer to the car.

"What did you think?" I ask Logan, hoping to distract myself. Watching Rachel laugh with another guy twists knots in my gut.

"That was some insane shit." A jean jacket replaces Logan's school one, and he almost fits in with a T-shirt and jeans, but his black hair still has that straitlaced gel-style.

"Think you can handle a car going that fast, man?"

A lunatic smile crosses his face. "Yes."

Before Beth fell for Logan's friend, Ryan, she had told me stories involving this kid. She said his only fuel was adrenaline. "You're a crazy son of a bitch, aren't you?"

"Yeah," he answers immediately. "Got a problem with that?"

"No," I reply. "But I do have a problem with Beth. You want me to work on your car, then I'm fine with that, but keep her out of my garage." And out of my life.

Zach opens his car door for Rachel and she trembles with excitement as she slides into the driver's seat. Part of me loves seeing her happy. The other part yearns to shove Zach in a body bag.

"Look," says Logan. "I'm a couple of weeks away from earning enough to buy a used supercharger from a friend, and I have a feeling we'll need to replace some of the exhaust."

Several parts of his statement catch me off guard. "You already know cars, don't you?"

"What if I do?"

What if he does? When I say nothing, he continues, "Beth heard about the car and went nuts, knowing it gave her an excuse to see you. She misses you, but she's with Ryan."

Logan waits for his words to sink in. Yeah, I got it. Beth's in love with his best friend. "Ryan's got nothing to fear from me." And that's the damn truth. There's no part of me that wants Beth anymore.

She's in love with someone else and having my heart ripped out and burnt to ashes keeps me from wanting to replay the game with her.

"Beth's my friend so I played car idiot. She needed an excuse to see you, and we wanted an excuse for someone to come with her."

Because Beth is a fucking hurricane and would have blown into town regardless of what anyone else thought or desired. Yeah, I understood that, too. I may not like what happened between me and Beth, but I can respect the guy for being loyal to her.

"To be honest," says Logan. "I could use your help." He gestures at the dragway. "And nothing in Groveton can offer me that type of rush."

"Can you pay me?" I ask.

"Not if I buy the supercharger. But if you agree to help me put the charger in and help make some other modifications, then I'll give you anything I win at the dragway."

I had planned to ask Noah to help drag race my way out

of the debt, but he's been slammed with his own problems. "Have you drag raced before?"

"Illegally, on backcountry roads and with other guys' cars."

"Are you any good?"

He shrugs. I can tell by the cocky way his shoulders flex that the kid's an ace. Or at least he's won against his redneck friends. "I've won a few."

I can't believe I'm going to explain this or that I'm making the offer. No one other than me drives my car, but desperate times... "Rachel and I are in some bad shit. I'll be racing her car to win money. If you want, you can race mine."

The parts I intend to add to her car will mean speeds that will put me against better racers. Better racers translates to bigger bets.

"You owe money," Logan says—a statement, not a question.

"To the wrong people, and they won't take kindly to anyone helping us."

His smile widens, proving the kid is bat-shit crazy. "A debt, a villain, speed and bad odds. This is something I definitely want to be a part of."

Amused, I shake my head. I'm joining forces with a fucking country-jock. I extend my hand. "We got a deal."

He has a strong grip and doesn't fear eye contact. I already like the son of a bitch. Logan jerks his thumb at Rachel. "Is she your girlfriend?"

My eyes shoot to his, and he immediately holds up his hands. "Beth's my friend, and with that handshake, you are, too. I am neutral territory."

"We're friends," I answer in regards to Rachel.

She spent the first part of the evening trying to ignore me. Eventually, she broke down and talked cars, but it's obvious she meant what she said to me in the garage: that she and I would work together and nothing more.

Zach rests his hands on the roof of his car and leans down to put his head closer to Rachel's. She still sits in the driver's seat with both hands on the wheel. Because fate has taken pity on me, she's totally absorbed with the machinery and not with Zach. It's like he knows nothing about personal space.

"You look like the two of you are just friends," says Logan.

"I'm just watching her back." I promised Rachel and myself that I'd protect her—from Eric, from the world.

"So you're telling me that you're into delusional shit?"

My spine straightens. "What did you say?"

Not giving a damn that I'm two seconds away from throwing a fist into his face, Logan lazily hooks his thumbs into his pockets and slouches to the side. "I got this friend Chris, right? He fell for another friend of ours, Lacy, but he didn't want to admit it. Claimed the friend card, just like you, but for six months he looked at Lacy just like you're looking at Rachel."

"How's that?"

"Like she amputated part of you and took it with her the last time she walked away."

"Naw, you have it wrong." But as my gaze switches to Rachel again there's an ache growing in my chest. "Rachel and I are complicated."

"Does your homeboy know you're in a 'complicated' relationship with her?" asks Logan.

Since I've never brought a girl to the track before, you'd think my "homeboy" would be reserved. "Not sure."

"So you're standing thirty feet away because…"

"She wanted to see that car."

"You could have gone over to see it with her."

"Could've."

"Jealousy's a bitch," taunts Logan. "And a symptom."

"Why do you care?" I pop my neck to the side. If I look too close at the reason why I chose to keep distance between me and Zach, it's because Zach's a player and if I were any closer, I'd kick his ass and then Rachel would never see that car.

"I don't," he answers. "For some reason I've got a thing with stating the obvious. So you're into her. If this shit you're in is that bad, you might want to figure out what's going on with the two of you first. Save yourself the drama of a breakdown in the middle, you know?"

I rub my hands over my face and feel as if my knees are about to give out. Fuck me, I am jealous and that is bad news. Wanting her is one thing, kissing her once in a moment of weakness is another. But having feelings for her? This is the type of shit that almost killed me with Beth.

"The look on your face is why I'm never falling," Logan says. "I'll swing my car by this week."

I nod my goodbye and search for calm before I head over to the Cobra. The car may be named after a reptile, but its owner is the damned snake.

"Why would you mess with the original engine, though?"

Rachel slides her fingers over the steering wheel as if she's in mourning. "She was beautiful just the way she was born."

Zach finally acknowledges me when my elbow smacks against his side as I shove my way between him and Rachel. He straightens and mumbles so only I can hear, "Damn, she gives me a hard-on. Gorgeous, and she knows cars."

"I suggest you back the fuck off," I mutter.

Zach smirks. "Hey, you're the one that left her here with me."

"What are you guys talking about?" Rachel asks.

"Cars," I say. "You said you needed to be home by ten. It's nine-thirty."

She blinks as if she just woke up. "Crap. Already?"

I step aside so Rachel can exit the driver's seat. Because Rachel is every guy's fantasy, Zach begs her to stay: she should see the engine, she can ride in his car, she can drive his car. Each of his attempts to lure her to stay causes me to think of one more way to hide the body parts after I kill him. Rachel laughs him off and thankfully follows me to the parking lot.

The gravel crunches beneath our feet, and I envision a million different ways to wipe that conceited smirk off Zach's face as she describes, in detail, every inch of the Cobra. A continual pressure builds with each word out of her mouth. I remind myself I was the one who introduced her to the dick.

"...and the inside was perfect." Rachel rambles with a level of excitement I only thought possible in four-year-olds. "Like it just rolled off the lot. Well, not really, but you can tell he's done a great job trying to re-create the feel..."

She's impressed with him. Impressed with his car. Just impressed. And it's not with me. We reach our cars, and the pressure rises to the level of explosion. "Do you like him?"

"What?" She half chokes.

"Zach. He asked you out. Do you want to date him?"

Rachel grimaces. "He did not ask me out."

"Yeah. He did. He asked you to take a ride with him next weekend and you blew past the question. Did you want to say yes, but didn't because I was there?"

Her mouth opens and closes several times. "He didn't... It's me, so he wouldn't... Why do you care?"

Fuck it. "Because I do."

Adrenaline pours into my bloodstream with the words, and my eyes dart around her face hoping to see some sort of a sign that what I said mattered. That I matter.

"Give me something, Rachel." A word. A knowing glance. Anything.

Her beautiful eyes widen and because she must be the type that enjoys playing with fire her gaze falls to my lips. "Give you what?"

My heart rate increases. I'd give anything to kiss her again. Without realizing it, I step forward and Rachel retreats, backing into the car. Keeping her eyes locked with mine, I slowly reach out and cradle the slender curve of her waist, and when she says or does nothing to stop me, I step closer, letting my body slide against hers.

She sucks in air, and I love the soft sound. Her body heat reaches out and warms me and I wish I could wrap my arms fully around her. I crave to lose myself in the crook of her neck and be surrounded by her silky hair. Rachel tries to lower her head, but I reach up and touch her chin. "Don't."

I tilt her head up, engulfing her line of vision. She's going to see me and me alone. No cars, no Zach, none of the other assholes trying to win her eye during the night. The sweet scent of jasmine entwining with the salty smell of the beach rushes into my lungs. I lick my lips, wanting to kiss her, but I'm too full of energy to dare let my lips brush hers.

Beneath my fingertips, her pulse beats wildly. "I don't understand you, Isaiah."

"Then we have something in common, because I don't get you at all." Nor do I understand the edge of anger and confusion beginning to roll in my veins.

Rachel was supposed to be a memory burned into my brain. The girl that I kissed, the girl that left me wanting more. But she's delved deeper than physical, become embedded, and I don't know how to dig her out. "I shouldn't like you."

She blinks several times as her eyes get glossy, but the tears I expect never come. Instead she jerks her chin and I drop my hand. "I think that's clear. You kissed me then you never called."

"If Eric knew I care for you, he'd use that against me." Tons of people Eric know could be watching us, calling him, telling him that I'm close to the girl he felt betrayed him. It'll give him an advantage over me. It'll let him know my weaknesses, but the thought of Rachel accepting a date from another guy overpowers any logical thought.

"That sounds like a convenient excuse." She wraps her arms around her waist, but she doesn't push me away. Part of her wants me. A part she doesn't understand, probably just like the part I can't control. We're at a tipping point. Both of us teetering one way or the other. I need the right words.

"I found out that night from a friend that you were in danger. I couldn't let Eric think I liked you, not when your life was on the line. You were never going to be a fuck and I never called because I couldn't be the link that led Eric to you."

She shakes her head as I talk. "You told Eric I meant nothing!"

My voice rises to her level. What doesn't she understand? "I was protecting you!"

Rachel presses both of her hands against my chest and forces me away. "I gave you my first kiss! I deserved better than to be left hanging. I deserved better than to be treated like I was nothing! Then I deserved better than to have your girlfriend thrown in my face!"

Girlfriend? "What the hell are you talking about?"

"Beth," she says as a slur.

"Beth is not my girlfriend!" I yell and the sound of any conversation around us ceases. Both of us are breathing hard, as if we've run miles. She's right. She deserved better then and deserves better now. She blinks and I hate that I can't read her expression.

"What do you want from me?" I demand. I've tried to explain. I've tried to make nice and it's not enough. Just like with Beth, nothing I do will be enough.

Rachel turns her head away and stares out into the dark night. No response. No words. Withdrawn into her head.

Fuck this. I'm standing here bleeding, and she doesn't give a damn. "You can ignore me, Rachel, and you can try to treat me as a friend, but none of that will erase the fact that I think about kissing you every second I'm awake and dream at night of my hands on your body. And it sure as hell won't erase that I'm terrified by how much I like you."

I'm trembling, and my instincts scream at me to run. I said too much and feel things that are too dangerous. Her eyes snap to mine, but she says nothing. Does nothing. My heart drops as I realize what a fool I am. I'm just a guy who injured her pride. I mean nothing to her.

It's too much. All of it.

"Forget about it," I mutter as I wheel away and avoid eye contact.

I stalk off, unable to look back. Logan's several spots down, talking to someone, and I point to where I left Rachel. "Make sure she gets in her car and leaves."

Logan grins because I proved him right. "Sure. Where are you headed?"

"The dragway." I need speed.

Rachel

WITH A HUFF, I FLIP over in my bed again. It's Sunday night, I have hours 'til school, and I can't sleep. This does not bode well for me keeping my routine in the morning. The same thought circles my brain like one of those news tickers at the bottom of a TV screen: Isaiah.

He said he liked me. And the way he said it, the way his body was pressed against mine and how his hands held my body...that's not the I-like-you-as-a-friend kind of like. It's possibly the same like I feel for him. The type of like where I go sort of crazy when I don't see him and then go crazier when I do. The type where he consumes my thoughts and then I can't sleep.

Like now.

Isaiah said he liked me, and I didn't say a word back.

The hurt in his eyes; the way his shoulders crumpled as he turned away from me...I am an awful person. I pull the covers over my head. What is wrong with me? A really great, really hot guy tells me that he cares for me, and I freeze. And to make it worse, the courage to contact him completely eludes me.

I now understand why so many deer are hit by cars.

I emerge from the covers and reach for my phone. The screen lights up the moment I swipe at it. One in the morning. Who else in the world would be awake at one in the morning? No one. The rest of the world knows how to sleep. The rest of the world wouldn't blow the biggest moment of their lives.

I scroll through my contacts until I find Isaiah. Underneath his picture is his name and number. My mouth dries out as I ponder the possibility. I could text him.

Nerves cause my heart to beat faster. What if I text him and he doesn't text back? But what if I text him and he does text back?

Not allowing time to overanalyze the decision, I quickly type and hit Send.

Isaiah

THE STREETLIGHT SHINES THROUGH THE slats of the blinds, creating a light ladder on the wooden floor. I fell into bed an hour ago, and at one in the morning I still can't sleep.

Noah's mattress creaks as he rolls and throws his arms out as if he's searching for something. More like someone. When he comes up empty, his eyes crack open into slits. Echo's staying at the dorms tonight, and he's here because he's pulling an early shift this morning. Noah messes his hands through his hair then lets out a disgruntled sigh as he resettles.

I swing my legs off the bed and my bare feet hit the cold subfloor. I rub at my bare chest, hoping to wake the rest of me up. My body's tired, but my mind won't shut off. I want to chase after the girl, but I don't know how. Short of going to her house and scaling the walls like a punked-out Romeo, I've got no idea how to win Rachel. Besides, that Romeo shit is not my style.

Maybe a drive will clear my head.

"What's eating you?" Noah asks with his eyes closed.

"Nothing."

"Bullshit."

Except for the fact he said something, Noah appears asleep. He's been working his ass off between school, studying, seeing his brothers and Echo, then squeezing in as many hours as he can flipping burgers to keep us afloat. The most I see him is when he sleeps at night. The kid is almost a walking corpse.

"You're worried about the money for rent, aren't you?" Noah mutters.

Fuck me. I slide both hands over my face then cup my mouth and my nose. On top of owing Eric, I owe Noah money for rent. I can't believe I forgot. "I'm sorry, man."

"Don't be," he said. "I'm the one that's sorry. I don't want to fail you."

"You won't. You aren't." My shoulders roll forward like I've got a damn aircraft carrier on my back. I've thought time and time again about telling Noah the truth, but I haven't. Only because there never seems to be a good time, but now I can't tell him. I can't let him shoulder this burden. Not when he already has too much riding on him. "It'll work out."

Noah opens his eyes and examines me. "Yeah, it will, so don't do anything fucked-up over it."

Pressure builds in my neck because I already know what he's referring to. "Like what?"

"Like street racing. Seeing Beth in handcuffs gave me my fill of police stations for a lifetime. I don't need you to be joining the ranks."

My phone buzzes in the back pocket of my jeans on the

floor. I close my eyes. It's gotta be Beth. She's the only one who'd text this late.

Noah throws his arm back over his face. "Answer her, Isaiah. Beth's going nuts over your silence."

"Not interested in making her feel better."

"Here's some crazy shit—maybe I'm more interested in you feeling better. If you could find a way to let her go maybe I'd see you happy again. Like you were the night you brought Rachel home."

Anger twists in my body. Noah's talking about stuff he should stay away from. "Fuck you."

Noah raises his hand and flashes me the finger.

I grab my shirt and start to lift off the bed, but when my eyes drift to my jeans my ass hits the mattress again. To hell with this. To hell with her. Beth fell in love with Ryan. For weeks she acted like she couldn't stand him, but knowing her like I do...like I did...Beth didn't like people who made her feel.

And damn me to hell, she felt something for him.

Without thinking too much about it, I snatch the phone out of my jeans. If Beth wants to talk, we'll talk. I'll tell her everything I think about her and Ryan and her idea that we can be friends.

The phone springs to life and my heart stalls out. It wasn't Beth.

It's weird how the anger and tension recedes. What rattles me the most is the flood of anticipation and nerves. Like swaying right on the edge of being high or drunk. The message from Rachel is simple, but the olive branch extended is weighted: Hi

I stare at it like it's the answer to life after death. Shit, in my case it probably is: Hey

Can't sleep?

No. You?

I can feel my pulse at every pressure point in my body. Seconds pass, and there's a longer pause as I wait for her next message. Come on, angel. Don't leave me hanging like you did on Saturday night.

At the dragway you said you liked me.

I lower my head. She's going to make me put it in writing. I've never felt so much like a sideshow monkey as I do now: Yeah, I like you. A lot.

I pop my neck to the side. How fucking long does it take to write a response?

I like you too and I'm also scared.

I inhale air and release it like a man who's been pulled from the bottom of a lake. She likes me. I want to see you tomorrow morning.

I have school.

I'll meet you there.

You have school. Rachel texts back immediately. And your school starts before mine.

I chuckle. How have I ended up pursuing a girl as naive as her? It's called skipping. What time do you get to school?

Isaiah!

I chuckle again as I imagine those beautiful violet eyes widening and her cheeks turning red at the thought of doing something wrong. I'm skipping. You're not.

Noah turns over in bed to face me. "Did you just laugh, bro?"

"If I swing by the Malt and Burger tomorrow can you score me breakfast?"

He assesses me and the cell. "If it'll get you to shut up and go to bed."

A smile forms on my lips. "Go to hell."

"Fuck you."

"Original, man. Think I said that earlier."

"Tell Rachel I said hi." My best friend knows me.

My phone vibrates again. I can be there by 8.

I roll onto my back and hold the phone up as I text back: See you then.

Rachel

I RELEASE A SHAKY BREATH as I pull into my school's parking lot. One hour before the first bell, Worthington resembles a dystopian ghost town. I've trashed my morning routine, but it'll either be really worth it or the resulting aftermath will send me into a panic attack never before seen by man. Only time will tell, but the mere thought of meeting with Isaiah is enough to force me out of my shell.

Bypassing every open spot, I turn down the one-lane road to the overflow lot and millions of butterflies spring to life in my stomach when I spot Isaiah leaning against his black Mustang. It's seven-fifty in the morning. He's early and he's waiting for me. This is totally unreal.

I ease my car beside him and my hands tremble when I shift into Park and pull the keys out of the ignition.

Breathe. Air in. Air out.

Breathe.

Keeping the flow of air going, I fiddle with the keys in my lap. Driving here was the simple part. Simple. I wish I could make Isaiah and me simple.

I glance up, and he watches me through the windshield.

The moment our eyes meet he holds up a white bag. The door feels heavy as I open it, and the cool morning air nips at my legs. As I approach Isaiah, I smooth out a lock of my hair and flatten my hands against my coat, then my skirt. I like him. He says he likes me. For the first time in my life, I really want to look my best for someone because...well, because I want him to see me as special.

In his worn blue jeans and a black T-shirt, the early-morning sun hits Isaiah just right, highlighting him like he's a relaxed tiger bathing in the warmth. The light glints off his double rows of hoop earrings and there's a twinkle in his eyes that makes me feel like he has a secret, but not the type kept from me. No, it's the type that suggests I'm in on it, and that it involves a lack of my clothes.

And maybe some of his.

As if I spoke the thought instead of keeping it internal, Isaiah lifts his shirt to scratch at a spot right above his hip bone. Good Lord, he's pretty. I soak in the sight of the muscles in his abdomen like I'm a plant in the Sahara Desert, except it doesn't quench my thirst. It only causes my mouth to run dry.

Isaiah smiles like he knows what I'm thinking, and heat licks up my body and pools in my cheeks. What really causes my blood to curve into itself is the wicked gleam in his eye. It's a spark that says he's done very naughty things I've never even heard about.

"I brought food," he says.

My stomach growls at the words and my head falls back because he had to hear it. God, why am I always a walking disaster? "I missed breakfast." And the rest of my morning routine. "So this is awesome."

The bag crunches in his hand when he holds it out and I step close enough to take it from him. My mouth waters as the scent of bacon, toasted carbs and sausage wafts into the air. I peek inside. "That's a lot of food. Do you also eat small children as appetizers?"

"I didn't know what you liked so..." He trails off and takes a sudden interest in the nearby football field.

I brush my bangs away from my face and have to force myself not to bounce. He bought me breakfast. I bite my lip to stop the smile, but then let it go. I'm happy and I don't care if he knows. "Thanks."

"S'all good."

In the middle of the bag is a half-wrapped bagel with cream cheese oozing down the sides. It's like I died and went to heaven. I pull it out and hand the bag to Isaiah while motioning at him with the bagel. "Do you want some of this?"

"Not a bagel guy." Isaiah chooses a breakfast sandwich that's more meat than biscuit. I break off parts of the bagel and eat them while he bites into his. Everything about us is different, yet from what little I know there are some things that are the same—like how we love cars.

But that's probably the problem. I don't know him. He doesn't know me. I like what I've seen. I like most of what I've experienced with him, but is it enough? Halfway through one side of the bagel, I lick my fingers and wrap it back up. "I'm sort of a mess."

Isaiah slows down his chewing, and I watch as he swallows. "I have to say that is the first time a girl has used that as a come-on line."

I laugh without thinking then slam my hand over my

mouth because it shocks me that it popped out. "I wasn't coming on to you."

His eyes linger way too long where my uniform skirt ends above my knees. "You sure about that? Because those legs are telling me something different."

My knees rub together as I shift. I have never been as aware of my body as when I'm around Isaiah. My outside, my insides, everywhere—even places I never thought much about before. Places that sort of wake up in his presence. "I was trying to tell you something. Something important."

Isaiah tucks the rest of his sandwich in the bag and places it on the hood of the car. I still hold the bagel and it becomes that obvious thing in my hand that I don't know what to do with. Nerves have tightened my throat, making finishing it impossible, but there's no way I'm trashing it. Isaiah brought it for me.

Playing mind reader, Isaiah holds out his hand. "It'll stay warm in the bag." I hand the bagel to him and he asks, "So what are you trying to tell me?"

Why couldn't I have just been happy eating the bagel? "I'm complicated."

He shrugs like it's no big thing. "So am I."

"No." My fingers close into a fist. "My family is really, really..." Messed up. "Complicated."

"You told me that," he says. "At my apartment."

Yeah, I did.

"Are you in danger at home?" he asks.

"No," I answer immediately. "They just expect a lot...from me."

He nods like he gets it. "Will seeing me be a problem?"

While there's this overwhelming voice screaming yes in the back of my mind, there's a smile twisting on my face and I bring my hands together in front of me, feeling suddenly shy. Did he just say...? "So we're seeing each other?"

Isaiah touches an earring. "Yeah. I guess we are."

My head bobs back and forth because I so need more. "Like more than friends?"

"We can be friends if you want. But..."

"But what?" My stomach begins to plummet. Did I misread all of this?

His gray eyes bore into mine with an intensity I've never seen from anyone before. "But I want more."

"More?" I whisper.

"I want to kiss you again."

A heat wave crashes into my body and I tug at the collar of my winter coat. I could take this thing off and probably still sweat. The memories of his mouth moving against mine and how his hands pressed into my body flood my brain. I lick my lips in anticipation. I crave for him to kiss me again, but... "Are you going to call me after?"

A small grin plays on his lips. "You aren't going to cut me any slack, are you?"

It's like he's begging me to tease him, and without thought, I slide back to the braver girl at the bar. "Is that a problem?"

He shakes his head. "Not from you."

Isaiah pushes off his car and invades my personal space. His dark scent envelops me and my heart literally trips several times as it tries to continue to beat. Even though he doesn't touch me, it's like Isaiah is everywhere. Only centimeters separate us, but his warmth surrounds me like a bubble.

I have to force myself to lift my chin to look at him. His gray eyes soften, and there's this playful aura to him, accompanied by a devious tilt of his mouth.

"I feel like a mouse with you," I whisper. "The one that's already been caught by the cat."

That's when he touches me. Isaiah runs his hand through my hair, and every cell in my body vibrates with the gentle pull. "Rachel."

"Yes." It's hard to breathe.

"Kiss me."

Isaiah doesn't wait for my answer. Instead his lips meet mine and his arms wrap around my body. All the hesitancy I felt the first night we kissed evaporates like mist on the heels of a summer storm. Within seconds, our mouths open, and Isaiah slips his tongue against mine. I get lost, liking the way my body curves around his, liking the way my hands explore as if they have a mind of their own, and loving how Isaiah grips my hair while tracing my spine.

Tingles and shock waves and earthquakes and hurricanes. All of it takes place at the same time as our mouths move not nearly fast enough. Nothing seems fast enough. The closer I become, the closer Isaiah presses, and the more he presses, the more I want to crawl inside and live in this delicious world of warmth and fantastic hunger.

Isaiah hooks an arm around my waist, and I suck in a breath when he turns us and shifts me up against the door to his Mustang. My eyes widen and I stare up at him as he stares down at me. Our chests move in unison, as do our breaths. My fingers curl into the muscles of his arms, and I briefly close my eyes, loving how his body fits into mine.

As much as I love it...this is so, so new. "That was a pretty awesome second kiss."

"I agree. How about a third?"

I giggle, and that rare genuine smile spreads across his face.

"How about we try out our third kiss somewhere other than my school's parking lot?"

Isaiah rubs that sensitive spot on my shoulder right near the curve of my neck. "I think that sounds like a plan."

I glance over at the main parking lot and note that cars have begun to fill the first few rows. As much as I wish this moment could last forever, it can't. Especially when I have two brothers who would lose their minds if they caught me like this with Isaiah. "I don't know what to do about my family."

"You like me, right?"

I nod.

"That's all that matters. Let's figure this out, pay off Eric, and then we'll tackle the rest."

The blood drains from my face at the mention of Eric and I slip my hands down from his shoulders to wrap around his stomach.

As if knowing that Eric haunts me, Isaiah brings his arms around me, creating this protective blanket. I rest my head on his solid chest and listen to the sound of his heart. I could get very used to this.

After a few seconds, Isaiah kisses the top of my head. "I'll keep you safe."

"I trust you." I regretfully slide away. "You're going back to school, right?"

"Yeah." Isaiah pulls out the bagel and I take it as the need to bounce again returns. "Go on to class, Rachel. One of us shouldn't break all the rules."

"I think I'm a rule breaker," I say. "I mean, I did drag race."

Isaiah chuckles. "You're gangster for sure."

With a silly smile plastered on my face, I retrieve my backpack from the passenger side of my car and wave at Isaiah before walking away.

Midway across the student lot, my phone rings, and I have to juggle the bagel in order to reach it before the call goes to voice mail. Quickly swallowing a piece, I answer. "Hello?"

"Hey, Rachel?" Isaiah says.

I spin around and in the distance I can spot him leaning against his car again. "Yes?"

"I called."

Joy blossoms through me, from my toes up into the rest of my body to the point that I look down to see if I'm flying. "Yeah, you did."

Isaiah

I LEAN AGAINST THE FRAME of a '76 Nova and listen as the guys from class shoot the shit during the last remaining minutes of school. Today, some other guys from class and I taught the freshmen how to strip the paint. With the paint job done, they continue their jacked-up conversation about some jock from school caught juicing. Life must suck when you have parents and money to blow on steroids.

I pull out my phone and reread last night's conversation with Rachel. The two of us text. Sometimes we talk on the phone. Because of her parents and brothers, it's hard for her to get out to see me, and I don't want her taking a risk that'll raise flags when we have other days that require her being out of the house.

I try not to overanalyze what's going on with Rachel. I like her. She likes me. At some point, she'll change her mind, but for now I'll enjoy the ride.

In another world, she would have been the kind of girl I would have taken to dinner and a movie. I would have knocked on her front door, met her father, charmed her mother, brought flowers and done all that wooing shit that guys are supposed to do when trying to win the girl.

But all that crap means I would have lived another life. One with parents who gave a damn. One where I had a home and maybe a bed frame, maybe a room. In the span of one week, I've done the two things the system taught me never to do: felt too much and dreamed of a different life. Wandering thoughts and feelings lead to an impending wreck.

I shove it all away. I've had a past that promises no future so it's better to stick with the present.

Last night, my remaining favors came in. I bring up Rachel's name in a text message. It's time for me and her to meet again.

Me: where r u

The right side of my mouth tilts up with Rachel's immediate reply: intern in library 4 last period

Me: got the parts I need 4 your car. Come tomorrow.

Rachel: Thursday w Mom, remember?

She mentioned earlier in the week that she had plans with her mom that night.

Me: Friday, right after school.

Her: K

Because I don't want to let her go yet: Saturday we race.

Her: :)

"Isaiah," says Zach from the middle of the group. "You smiling?"

Yeah, guess I am. I slide my phone back into my pocket and the smile off my face. My image has kept me alive, and I play the part to perfection: badass, loyal, ready for a fight. "You staring, man?"

He raises a hand. "No offense meant. Are you taking the ASE certification next week?"

I nod and watch the second hand of the clock. Only a few more seconds until the bell.

"Some of us are worried," Zach says. "About passing."

I've failed a lot of tests in my life, but this is the one I know I can kill. The ten guys I've gone through the program with since my freshman year focus on me. For most of these guys, myself included, the ASE is our key to avoid becoming minimum-wage car-wash attendants. "Holden gave us a study guide."

"We all know you're gonna pass," says Zach. That humming sensation that informs me something's not right vibrates below my skin. Several of the guys glance cautiously at each other.

As if preparing for a fight, I widen my stance. "What's this about?"

Most look away or shuffle back. Zach also averts his gaze, but he keeps talking. "You know it's computerized, right?"

"Yeah."

"And we'll all be in the same room?"

"Yeah."

"What if we could find a way where you could offer us assistance during the test?"

The muscles in my shoulders flex, and the guys closest to me take an interest in the equipment behind them. "I've carried your ass for four years, showing you the same shit with cars over and over again. I think that's been enough assistance."

The bell rings and everyone bolts for the door—everyone

but me and Zach. Cheating on this test could cost me my certification, and I will not permit anyone to fuck up my future. His shoulders slump and I head for the exit.

"Isaiah," he says as my arm smacks into his. "I hear you're in debt to Eric."

I freeze, our arms still touching. "So."

He shrugs, but he's anything but uncaring. "Just repeating what I heard. Wouldn't want things to become worse."

I shift so that we're chest to chest and tilt my head so that I'm in his face. "Is that a threat?"

Zach wilts because the ass has always been a coward. "Not if you remember who your friends are." He slinks toward the hallway and turns at the last minute. "And if the person you were texting was Rachel, tell her I said hi."

Certain truths are always self-evident: on the streets there is no such thing as a friend. Zach could be playing odds right now, knowing I'm in debt to Eric and trying to ride the coattails of my fears, but Zach's never been the creative sort.

That sick sixth sense continues to rattle around in my brain. If Zach's become Eric's lapdog then my life and Rachel's life just entered another realm of complicated, because that means Eric has upped the stakes of the game.

Twenty buck says that while Rachel and I have been moving pawns, Eric just moved his rook.

Rachel

IN THE SMALLEST CONFERENCE ROOM in Dad's office, eleven women in various colored business suits and dresses fill the high-backed cushioned chairs. Mom sits at the head of the table, chatting gaily with the woman on her right. To Mom's left, I continue to push the catered chicken Caesar salad around on my plate so Mom will believe I ate.

Dad closed the blinds—one solace in the midst of the storm. At least the employees working won't gawk as they pass by. Mom signed me out of school for this travesty. I call it a speech. Mom calls it an introduction. Really, the few para-graphs are lies.

The women gathered around the table are the chosen few of Mom's friends invited to help with her new volunteer posi-tion of fundraising coordinator for the Leukemia Foundation. Mom explained last night that they'll start off with small teas, then lunches, and in a few weeks they'll move on to a dinner. All of which she has planned for me to attend...and speak at.

"Ladies," Mom says. "Let's take a twenty-minute break be-fore we start the meeting. That will give the caterers time to clean and us time to check on our families."

They giggle, but I'm not sure over what. Some women break off into groups of two or three and whisper private gossip. Some head into the hallway to use their cells or the restroom. I stare at a crouton in my salad.

Still sitting, Mom pats my hand. "Are you ready, sweetheart? You'll speak first."

My lungs constrict. "Yeah."

I memorized what she wants me to say, but the words have become a jumbled mess in my mind. Sort of like a crossword puzzle completed by someone with dyslexia.

"Meredith," one of Mom's friends calls from the opposite side of the room. "You have to come look at this."

Mom flashes me a smile that reminds me why I'm torturing myself and leaves. I ate two bites of salad and the lettuce and the chicken are not agreeing in my stomach. In fact, I think they've declared war.

I suck in a breath to calm myself. Only eleven people. Twenty-two eyes. My heart rate increases and I lick my suddenly dry lips. A jabbing pain hits my stomach, and I tug at the collar of my blouse as it becomes hard to breathe. It's hot in here. Too hot. Hot enough that if I stand I'll faint, hit my head and bleed all over Dad's new carpet.

And then he'll be disappointed in me.

And then Mom will be disappointed in me.

And then my brothers will find out and they'll blow a freaking head gasket.

My hands sweat and I rub my palms against my black skirt. What did Mom want me to say? I see the words. They drift in my mind, but not in order. I'm going to fail.

I stand abruptly, startling the ladies huddled in conversation behind me. Forcing a smile, I nod toward the door, hoping they understand I'm excusing myself. I half trip on the way out as my stomach cramps.

Mom's best friend touches my arm as I turn left. "Are you okay?"

"Bathroom. I mean, I'm trying to find the..." And I ran out of air.

"The bathroom is that way."

"Thanks." I have no idea why I'm thanking her and by the strained lines on her forehead, she doesn't, either. This is my father's office, and one would think I would already know where the bathroom is. I go in the direction she said, praying she doesn't mention my odd behavior to my mother. Before I hit the bathroom, I take a left through the cubicles and run for my father's office.

Please don't let him be there. Please don't let him be there. Please. Please. Please.

I almost cry when I see the light off and the empty chair. Pictures of me and my brothers rest on the table near the window. The only picture on his desk is of Mom and Colleen. It's always been about her: Colleen. Her name floats in my head as I try to breathe past the first dry heave. In one motion, I flip the switch to his private bathroom and slam the door shut.

Isaiah

BECAUSE I WAS BLACKMAILED INTO giving my word to Courtney, I force myself into the Social Services building and grimace at the sight of the messed-up people in the waiting area. Kids cry. Moms scream. Each sound a razor against my skin. It's so damn cliché my fingers twitch; there isn't a man in sight. Of course there isn't—men are notorious family leavers.

"Isaiah," Courtney says from behind the receptionist window. Her hesitant smile is too hopeful. "Come on back."

The door buzzes open, and I slink past two toddlers on the floor pulling at an already-damaged stuffed zebra. When the door shuts behind me the noise fades, but my skin still crawls.

Today Courtney wears a blue bow in her ponytail. "Thanks for coming."

"Thought it wasn't optional."

Her smile widens. "It's not, but I like to pretend that you want to be here. It makes my day go smoother. Let's go." She nods to the right and when I don't move, she heads down the hallway, looking back to make sure I follow.

I can almost feel the tug of the leash around my neck. "Do the other hostages you torture tear you apart for wearing a bow in your hair?"

She stops at a cubicle and grabs a manila file folder. "Clients, not hostages. Help, not torture. And you're my only teenager. The little ones love my bows."

"Maybe you should transfer me." To someone who doesn't give a shit and will leave me the fuck alone. "You could pick a hostage you like."

"Client." Courtney pauses outside a closed door. "I like you."

That brings me up short. "No, you don't."

"Yes," she says slowly, as if my response surprises her, "I do. Isaiah, I requested to be your social worker."

I glance behind me, half expecting a smaller child also named Isaiah to be there. "Why?"

She knocks lightly on the door. "Because." Courtney's hand rests on the knob. "You and I agreed on thirty minutes."

"You've wasted five."

"I sent the letter of recommendation in. I kept my part of the bargain, I expect you to keep yours. I call—you answer. I schedule a meeting—you come and stay for thirty minutes."

"Like rubbing it in, don't you?" But I'll show because I gave her my word.

"Good. Now that we're firm on the agreement, I should tell you that your mom is here."

I tower over Courtney. "Fuck no."

She never flinches. Instead she tilts her head, causing her ponytail to slide over her shoulder. "Are you keeping your word or not?"

The muscles in my body turn to lead. I want more than anything to run; to get behind the wheel of my car and gun the engine. The little bitch in front of me has backed me into a corner. I rub at my neck, feeling as if the collar she placed there has spikes.

Courtney opens the door and anger races like venom in my veins. I stalk into the room and slam my ass into the chair farthest from the woman already sitting at the table. "Twenty-two fucking minutes, Courtney. And if I were you, I'd get the hell out of here because you are the last person I want to see...besides that thing over there."

"Isaiah," Courtney says apologetically. "I can't leave the two of you alone with you so angry."

"It's okay," *she* says from across the room. I lower my head into my hands. The sound of the soft voice I remember as a child resurrects too many memories—too many emotions. "We'll be fine."

We'll be fine. The same three words she said to me before my entire life went to hell.

"I don't think that's wise," says Courtney. "I haven't seen him this upset before."

The chair beside me moves and I smell Courtney's faint perfume. "Your mom just wants to visit."

"She *is not* my mom." My voice trembles and a fresh wave of rage washes over me. My mother will not hurt me again. I lift my head and fight for control. "I don't have a mom."

"Then call me Melanie," she says with the same damn soothing voice that used to sing me to sleep. "We are strangers."

I glance at her and immediately look away because the

sight of her causes strangling pain. My head hits the back of the wall and I cross my arms over my chest. "How many more *fucking* minutes?"

"You look good, Isaiah," she tells me. And because I can't help it, I peer at her again. Her lips are pressed into a thin line and her forehead buckles with anxiety as she stares at me. The thoughts in her head and the words she says are not in agreement. She doesn't like what she sees: a punk.

The piercings, the tattoos, yeah, I think the shit's cool, but what I really like is how they tell people to stay the fuck away. From the way her eyes travel over my arms, "Melanie" reads the signals loud and clear.

"You look old," I say with as much menace as I can muster. She doesn't look old—just middle-aged. She had me young, barely out of high school. I never knew her age. What six-year-old would? I don't even know her birthdate.

Her dark brown hair is cut short at her shoulders. She's thin, but not drug-addict thin. Her oversize hoop earrings sway when she tucks her hair behind her ear. The blue jean jacket matches her pants and underneath the jacket I spot a gray tank. The worn brown cowboy boots on her feet make me consider a maternity test.

"How are you?" Melanie asks.

"Do you mean how have I been for the last eleven years?"

She scratches her forehead. Good, I drew blood. "Yeah. And that."

I stretch my legs out, kicking one scratched-up combat booted foot over the other. "Let's see. Years six through eight blew. Found out Santa didn't exist. I'm pretty sure foster father number two shot the Easter bunny with his sawed-off shotgun during one of his backyard hunting escapades. Foster mom one liked to slap me until I stopped crying. She'd quote Bible verses while she did it because Jesus was obviously about tough love."

Melanie shuts her eyes. Attempting to redirect my attention, Courtney nudges her chair closer to mine. "Isaiah, maybe we should take a break."

"Nah, Courtney," I say with a mock smile. "You just don't want me to tell her about the group home I lived in between eight and ten and how the bigger boys used to beat the shit out of me for kicks."

I hold my hand out to Melanie. "Don't get me wrong. They'd punish the other boys and document my bruises in their nice files. Get me a doctor. Maybe a therapist, but it never stopped the new boys from pushing around the smallest kid."

"I'm sorry," Melanie says in a tiny voice.

"Yeah," I say. "You should be. And what really fucking sucks is to find out that the woman who gave birth to you was released from prison two years ago and never cared to see what happened to her son. That..." I lean forward. "That is what really blows."

Melanie goes dead-person-white, and her hands tremble as she touches her cheeks. "I can explain."

And I don't want to hear it. I stand. "I've got to take a piss. Where's the fucking bathroom?"

"Down the hall." Courtney massages her temples. "On the left."

I tear out of the room and the door bangs against the wall.

From their safe, tidy cubicles, several people gape at me. I ram my hand against the bathroom door and slam it shut, locking it behind me.

With my palms flat against the door, I suck in deep breaths and swallow the lump in my throat. My mom. My mom. My fucking mother.

I want to go back and tell her that I still love her—so time can unwind and she can hold me like she did when I was six. I yearn for her to tell me that everything is going to be okay. But all of it is lies. My entire life is one big fucking lie. A strange wounded sound escapes my lips as my body shakes. Every part of me begs to cry and that's just too damn sad.

I open the bathroom door to find Courtney waiting on the other side. "She left."

Good. "Yeah, that's her specialty."

Courtney has lost her enthusiasm and part of me hates it. "I learned my lesson," she says. "I won't force this again. I thought...I thought..."

"That if you could throw us in the same room we'd make up and live happily-ever-after?"

She releases a loud, pathetic sigh. "Actually, no. Look, I know this is the last thing you want to hear, but you should give her another shot."

Hell... "No."

"Consider it, and if you change your mind I'll schedule another meeting."

"Are we done?"

"Yes. Next time it'll be just you and me. I'll buy ice cream."

I blink. "Do I look five?"

She shrugs and almost smiles. "Sometimes you act five."

And I almost crack my own smile. Did she just joke at my expense? "Funny." I head for the exit, and when I glance back, I see her smile has grown.

The gray clouds hang low in the sky. I heard last night that the rest of the winter will be mild. I sure as hell hope so. The track will only stay open if it's warm. As I approach my car, I spot a woman with short brown hair and a blue jean jacket. I quicken my pace.

"Isaiah," she calls out and walks toward me.

Is this lady a damn masochist? "Maybe I was too subtle in there, so I'll make it clear. Fuck off."

"Please," she says. "Please, wait."

With keys in hand, I point at her. "Even I know you don't have permission to see me without one of those crazy people inside near us. In case you don't know, because let's face it, you wouldn't, I'm seventeen and their ward. You are on parole, so step back."

I could give a fuck if she breaks rules and returns to prison, but I'll use those laws to keep her from me. She doesn't stop her advance. "I want to see you again. Promise you'll let Courtney schedule another meeting. I'll do anything for the opportunity."

With my key in the lock, I freeze. "Anything?"

Too much hope floods her face. "Anything."

"One hundred dollars in cash for each visit. Courtney never knows about the money."

Melanie blinks as the hope fades. She doesn't have it. I

know she doesn't have it. It's why I made the demand. "Why do you need the money? Are you using drugs?"

"Yeah," I say. "I'm a junkie. Are you paying or not?"

She brushes her hair from her face. "I'll pay."

Rachel

IT'S A PAINFUL PULSE BENEATH my skull and above my brain. It radiates down from my forehead to wrap around my temples, my cheeks and my nose. Light makes the pain worse. Sound nearly kills me. This is the aftermath of my panic attack.

All off at some important meeting or game or social life event, my family is missing from the house. My lights are on, and my iPod plays softly next to the closed door of my room on the off chance someone does return home before their curfew of eleven—the boys, as sexist as it is, get an hour later than me.

The goal is to appear normal so I can cover up the migraine. That leaves me lying in bed with a pillow over my head and praying for the pain to cease.

After vomiting in my father's bathroom at work, I cleaned myself up and returned to the conference room. Eleven pairs of eyes watched as I stood at the front, beside my mother, and announced how honored I was to speak on Colleen's behalf.

My phone rings and the sound echoes violently in my head, yet at the same time a rush of adrenaline hits me. Isaiah is the only person who would call. I adjust the pillow so I can check the caller ID. My lips lift at the sight of his name. "Hello?"

"Rachel?" There is major question in his voice.

"It's me." Just me, my painful migraine and my sensitivity to light and sound.

"You sound off."

I clear my throat. "I was resting."

"I can let you go."

Anxiety shoots through my bloodstream at the thought. "No. I'm glad you called."

"Yeah," he says. "I wanted to hear your voice."

I wake up when I notice the strained tone in his voice. Suddenly my head doesn't hurt so bad, and I edge the pillow onto the bed and off my face. "Are you okay?"

"Yeah." A car honks. "Tell me how the thing with your mom went."

"Good," I say, and place the pillow back over my head. Every part of me flounders. I don't want to lie to him, too. But if I tell him about my attacks then he'll view me as weak, and that'll mess up what's between us. Maybe I don't have to lie. I can leave some things out—just like Ethan does to me when he uses twin amnesty. "Actually, horrible."

I hear a car door close. "What happened?"

"Maybe we can meet someplace and talk?"

"Yeah. Tell me where."

I swing my legs off the bed to stand, but the headache hammers my head hard and fast. A sound of pain escapes my lips, and I wince because Isaiah had to hear it.

"What's going on, Rachel?" Isaiah became very serious, very fast.

"Just a headache, I swear. So I was thinking we could meet at this coffee shop—"

He cuts me off. "You're not driving if you're hurting."

I lie back down as my eyesight doubles. With a touch to my iPod, music stops playing from the speakers. I strain to listen for any sound, and all that comes back is glorious silence.

What I'm about to do is wrong. So wrong. The exact opposite of everything my parents expect from me, and for that reason alone it feels right. "Would you like to come over?"

Isaiah

THE GUARD LEANS OUT OF his little boxed-in brick house at the entrance to Rachel's neighborhood and assesses me like I'm a serial killer broken out of death row. "Who did you say you want to see?"

"Rachel Young."

His hand falls to his hip as if he's packing, but both the rent-a-cop and I know that the only thing he's carrying is thirty additional pounds of beer and nachos in his stomach. "I think you have the wrong neighborhood, son."

Not in the mood for his games, I push redial on my cell and Rachel immediately answers, "Are you here?"

"At the gate. Do you mind informing your militia that I'm not here to rape and pillage?"

She sighs. "Put Rick on."

With his mouth set into a pissed-off line he takes my cell and turns his back to me. His whispered words have an edge to them and after a few seconds he hands me the phone back. The gate lifts in front of me, but my car remains idling next to him.

I glance at him from the corner of my eye. "Don't tell her parents."

"Or what?" he asks.

"Or what is right." I place my foot on the clutch and shift into gear. It's not a threat I'll carry out, but it's an empty one worth issuing to keep Rachel safe and happy.

Following the directions she texted, I wind my way past mansions the size of miniature castles with far more land between them than needed for a single family.

At the end of its very own road, Rachel's house sits entirely illuminated against the night sky. It has white columns and white marble steps and what the fuck is she doing with me?

I drive around the front loop and kill the engine. Therapists, social workers, teachers...they've spent years looking down their noses at me, but they were hard-pressed to make me feel smaller than shit. Being here in front of Rachel's, that's accomplished what very few have been able to do.

I force myself out of the car, up the steps, and before I can ring the bell, the door swings open and Rachel greets me with a smile. "Hi."

She's in sweatpants, a T-shirt, and her hair's pulled up on top of her head with loose pieces falling around her face. Not an ounce of makeup covers her face and she's barefoot. Each toe painted a mild form of red. Except for the dark circles under her eyes, I've never seen something so gorgeous in my life. "Hey."

Rachel sweeps her hand for me to enter, and I shove my hands into the pockets of my jeans when I step in. People have a fancy-ass name for this type of area of the house and because I'm not fancy-ass, I don't know it. It's a hallway that's a room but is bigger than some of the foster homes I've lived in.

"I don't think anyone will be home before eleven, but if you don't mind, I think I'd like you to only stay an hour just in case."

"Going gangster with boundaries. I like it." The tease is there in my voice, but I can't stop the sweep of the place. Huge-ass winding stairs. A skylight above me. Several double-doored rooms off to the sides and probably a whole other wing down that hallway straight in front of us.

Rachel tries to smooth out her hair, but the pieces only fall back to her shoulders. "Sorry about this. I know I should have tried to change, but..."

That's when I notice how pale she is, how sick she looks, and a warning sensation crawls along my spine. Something's wrong. "You're beautiful."

Rachel lowers her head, but I can tell she liked the compliment. "We can watch a movie or listen to music or—" She closes her eyes and goes from pale to drained of blood. Her forehead scrunches like she's in pain, and I reach out to snatch her as she leans to the left.

"That's no fucking headache," I growl.

She sucks in air through her nose. "Migraine. I get them occasionally, but I'll be okay."

Fuck this. I bend my knees and have Rachel up in my arms before she can protest. "Where's your bedroom?"

Her mouth falls completely open.

"You need sleep. I can come with you or I can put you down and I'll leave. Your choice."

"Isaiah," she protests.

"Rachel." I use the same tone back.

"Fine. Upstairs on the left." Giving in, she weaves her arms around my neck and rests her head on my shoulder. I can't help but note that she fits perfectly.

Taking two steps at a time, I climb the stairs, cut to the left and pause when I come to two open doors. One room is painted pink. The other purple. Both look very girly and very perfect. The pink room looks younger, but neither fit my image of Rachel. "Which one?"

She points to the purple room. "That's mine."

I do a double take at the pink room before entering Rachel's and gently place her on the mattress of the four-poster bed. The sheets and blanket are twisted in ways that suggest a restless sleep. Five pillows lie on the floor and three remain on the bed. Rachel eases over and pats the empty space beside her. "Do you mind?"

The question is, does she mind? I look over my shoulder, half expecting her father or the cops to show and when I spot nothing, I sit on the bed beside her, leaving my booted feet hanging off. If I keep my shoes on, I'll remember not to go too far with a girl I've only kissed twice and who's in pain with a migraine.

Rachel messes with her fingernail and steals glances at me every few seconds. Girls are normally forward with me. The type that mess with me know what they want, what I'll give, and they're prepared to act so they can get it. This change of pace makes me almost as nervous as her.

I stretch my arm so that it goes around her back, but leave my hand extended so that she knows if she wants me to hold her, she's going to have to move in my direction. Rachel immediately slides over, places her head on my chest and wraps herself around me. I tuck her closer and nuzzle the top of her head.

Everything inside of me relaxes, and I didn't even know I was tense. Remembering she has a headache, my hand drifts up and I begin to rub her temple. I don't like the idea of her being in pain.

"I didn't know you had a younger sister," I say softly.

"I don't. That's Colleen's room. She died before I was born."

My fingers freeze. "I'm sorry."

"Don't be. I know it's going to sound like an awful thing, but it doesn't bother me. I mean, it does, because my parents and my oldest brothers are seriously torn up about it, but I didn't know her. Mom wants me to miss her, but I can't. Especially not when Mom's shoving her in my face every five minutes."

There's an edge in Rachel's tone I've never heard before. "What happened with your mom today?"

Rachel picks lint off my T-shirt and the small pinches of her nails nip my stomach. I close my eyes and slightly shift to keep from thinking about the fact that she's touching my stomach, even though it's through a thin piece of material.

After she's found every fuzz ball of avoidance, Rachel finally answers, "My sister died of cancer so my mom raises money for the Leukemia Foundation."

"Admirable." Though I feel an impending derailment to the good deed. I've seen that shit plenty of times with rich people. They sweep in, do their one good deed for the year to cleanse their soul of all the fucked-up things they do the other three hundred and sixty-four days. And most of the time, they jack up that one day, as well. "But you still haven't told me what happened with your mom today."

Rachel releases a strangled "Humph."

I begin to massage her head again, except this time I give in to temptation and run my hand through her hair between rubs. Rachel's shoulders relax and she melts further against me. The sweet scent of jasmine reaches my nose, and I only want to lie like this forever.

"Waiting, Rachel."

"My mom has me make speeches on Colleen's behalf."

Rachel gets uncomfortable if I stare at her longer than ten seconds. I can't imagine her in front of a crowd. "Do you want to?"

Her head rocks a no against my chest.

"They why do you?"

"Because I want to make her happy."

Not having had a mom to want to make happy since I was six, I'm at a loss over what to say so instead I run my hand up and down her spine. I may not understand, but I care.

"Can I tell you a secret?" she whispers.

"Yeah."

A weighted silence builds between us, and I begin to count the unspoken beats. One. Two. Three. Four.

"Sometimes I hate Colleen," she whispers like she's in a confessional. "Does that make me an awful person?"

I think of seeing my mom today and of the anger still festering deep inside. If someone had told me she died four years ago when she was in prison, would I have honestly missed her? If someone told me the dad I never knew croaked, I could guarantee there wouldn't be any tears. If Rachel's an awful person then I must be related to Satan. "No, it doesn't."

Rachel pulls her head off my chest, and her violet eyes have a glaze that shows the extent of her headache. "Are you just saying that?"

I brush my fingers under the dark circles of her eyes, wishing my touch could make her better. "I saw my mom today."

She blinks and an ache fills my chest. When I opened my mouth, that wasn't what I thought I would say.

"Do you see her often?"

"It's the first time I've seen her since I was six."

"Oh, Isaiah." Rachel grips the fingers of my right hand and rests our joined hands on my stomach. "Are you okay?"

I start to say yes, but then think about Rachel telling me about her mom and Colleen. "No."

She squeezes my hand and I squeeze back, grateful that she doesn't say a thing. There are no words for what happened today. For neither me nor Rachel. Being born into the world is the greatest crapshoot there is. Some are born lucky, others aren't. For the first time, I see that this rule transcends money.

"I wish I could make you feel better." Rachel places her chin back on my chest and flutters her eyelids like it's a struggle to keep them open. She's in pain, and she wants to take on mine.

Not sure how to handle her statement, I rub her temple again while gently guiding her head so that she rests her cheek against me once more. "This makes me better."

Rachel shifts her mouth to the side, clearly not buying it.

"How are you?" I ask to deflect.

"Tired," she mumbles.

So am I, but when I'm with her, the weight of my problems

doesn't feel as draining. "Go to sleep. I promise I'll be gone before anyone knows I was here. Remember, be at the garage tomorrow after school."

"After school," she repeats.

Rachel snuggles close, and I tighten my hold. I have a feeling tonight I'll roll over in bed searching for Rachel, because this moment right here is the closest I've come to having peace in a long time.

Rachel

THE ENGINE SWITCHES FROM A growl to a purr as I shift down and ease into the bay of Isaiah's garage. My heart does that nauseating skip, squeeze, beat once combination the moment I spot Isaiah. His eyes go right to mine, and the slight slant of his mouth gives me flutters.

Unable to hold his gaze, I stare at the console as I place her in Park. Oh, God, he *is* happy to see me. At least I think he is. My insides explode at the sight of him striding over. Last night, I fell asleep in his arms and woke up this morning to find my cell on the pillow beside me with the message Tomorrow typed into an open window.

I thought school was never going to end.

Isaiah opens my car door and his warm silver eyes smile at me. "Hey."

I sweep my bangs from my eyes. "Hi."

He offers his hand and I accept. His fingers wrap around mine and heat surges up my arm, flushes my neck and settles into a blush on my face. He tugs gently and I slip out. I'm not sure if my body vibrates from the rumbling of the garage door closing or from the blood pounding in my veins.

Our fingers lace together, and his other hand smoothly cups my hip. I suck in a breath, surprised that someone touches me so easily and with such care.

"You look nice," he says.

"I'm in my school uniform." White button-down blouse, maroon-and-black plaid skirt, and a pair of white Keds. Nothing spectacular.

"I know." The seductive slide in his voice causes the back of my neck to tickle.

"Hi!"

We snap our heads to the right, and if it weren't for Isaiah's hold, I would have stumbled back. Practically on top of us is a girl with long brown hair, a black hoodie and the tightest jeans I have ever seen. I automatically hate her because those jeans make her look good.

Isaiah sighs loudly. "Rachel, this is my *friend*, Abby. Abby this is my *girlfriend*, Rachel."

I have to restrain from dancing. He called me his girlfriend. "It's nice to meet you."

"What's your favorite color?" asks Abby.

"Green?" That is a beyond odd question—I mean it's normal, yet not.

"Tacos or spaghetti?"

"Tacos."

"Disney World or Disneyland?"

"Neither."

"Rolling Stones or Beatles?"

"Beatles."

She squishes her lips to the left. "Oh, so close, but I can let the last one go." Abby regards Isaiah with the same familiarity I have with my brothers. "We should keep her, but we may have to set up a visitation schedule. You know, control issues and all."

My eyebrows rise. "Keep me?" Abby's words crash in my mind. "Control issues?"

She pokes a finger at her chest. "My issues. Not his. You and I are going to be friends, and I don't do friendships. Well, I obviously do," she adds as her finger lazily points to Isaiah. "But he doesn't count. See, we met inside of a Dumpster when we were ten."

My eyes widen to the point I start to wonder if I'll ever blink again.

"Abby," says Isaiah, interrupting her before she can continue. "Shut the fuck up."

"Okay." The Rolling Stones' "Miss You" plays from her phone. "Shit," she says. "Hold on a sec." She answers and heads outside.

"Wow." It's the only response I can think of.

"That's one way to describe her. Look, if you don't want to deal with her..."

"No," I interrupt. "She's your friend..."

And he interrupts me. "But if she makes you uncomfortable..."

My turn. "I like her." From the moment she said that we'd be friends, I liked her.

I walk away from Isaiah and stand near the open hood of his car. Holy hell, he's been busy. "You installed a cold air intake." That will help increase the horsepower in his car.

Isaiah runs a hand over his freshly buzzed dark brown hair.

He kept the shadowed stubble on his jaw. If it's possible, the combination makes him so much sexier and more dangerous.

"I'm serious about Abby. She's different. I put up with her because I've known her longer than anyone else. That type of stuff is important to me, but if Abby bothers you, then I'll make sure she keeps her distance."

I touch the curved piece he added to the engine. "Did you really meet her inside a Dumpster?"

When he doesn't answer immediately, I sneak a peek out of the corner of my eye. His hands are on his hips as he stares at the floor. "Yeah. We were both looking for food."

I close my eyes as my heart aches. I can't imagine what his life has been like.

"I don't want your pity," he says with a mix of hurt and pride.

"I'm not offering you pity." Understanding hopefully, not pity. It's not much, and it's not nearly on the same level, but it still causes me enough pain that I can't face him. "I don't have friends. I have my brothers, and there are some girls at school that I can sit with at lunch if I want to, but they don't get bent out of shape if I don't show. I'm...I'm weird."

His boots tap against the floor as he moves in my direction. "No, you're not."

I stiffen, irritated and tired of everyone telling me what I am. "How many girls do you know who work on cars, like speed and can happily tell you what a cold air intake looks like?"

Isaiah places his fingers underneath my chin and tilts my head in his direction. "Only one, and she's my type of girl."

A flurry of rose petals swirls in my chest. I swallow and

remind myself to breathe. He lowers his head as I lick my lips. His warm breath mingles with mine and right as our lips come close to connecting, the garage door squeaks open.

I flinch as if jolted with electricity and immediately slide a foot away from Isaiah. He softly chuckles. An audience obviously wouldn't bother him. I toss him a dirty look that only makes him chuckle more.

"You've got company," says Abby. Right behind her is the guy that showed with that girl Beth. My hand goes to my stomach as it cramps. Isaiah and the guy share a short shake. "Logan, remember Rachel?"

He nods at me. "What's up?"

"Nothing." My eyes flicker from him to the door as I keep waiting for *her* to show. A strange uneasiness curls between my skin and bones. Beautiful, confident, mysterious Beth: the antithesis of me and everything a guy like Isaiah should want.

This week, Isaiah explained how Logan will race his car while Isaiah drives my car at the dragway. The better parts will go into my car since it's in better condition.

Isaiah never mentioned anything about Beth helping, and I never asked. After Isaiah announced that she wasn't his girlfriend, I thought I could let her go, but the uncertainty of what his relationship was with her before I crashed into his life gnaws at my soul.

Isaiah claps his hands then rubs them together. "We've got a turbocharger, a cold air intake, an exhaust cutout to install and a girl with a curfew. Let's move."

With anxiety coiled and poised to spring on a moment's notice, I digress to a bad habit: nibbling on my nails. I used to bite, but then my mother would have an aneurysm when she'd see what I'd done to my manicure.

I should be right beside Isaiah and Logan as they work on my car, but I can't. Being in the same room is bad enough. How can anyone watch surgery being performed on a loved one, much less hold the scalpel? Isaiah pushes a button and the lift's ear-crushing whine accompanies the sight of my car floating into the air. The turbocharger is in. Now he's installing the cutout to the muffler. Once this is done, my baby will never sound the same again.

"So," says Abby. "What do best friends do?"

Kind of like a cartoon character, I whip my head back and forth from Abby to the lift. She's been next to me during the whole ordeal, sharing strange broken conversations about nothing. "What do you mean?" *By best friends?*

"I've never been to the mall."

And she gained my full attention. "Never?"

Abby twirls the string attached to her hoodie. "Well, yeah, I've gone for work, but never to hang. Are you one of those girls? The ones that go to the mall? I think I could do it. Wander the mall for no reason."

"Why haven't you?" I don't feel like answering that I don't hang at malls. Most of the girls I know think my hatred of all things retail is weird.

She wraps the string tightly around her finger three times. "Malls are expensive, and as I said before, I don't do friendships."

"Besides Isaiah," I say.

"Besides him," she agrees. "And you."

"Why me?" It's a bold question to ask, but everything about this girl is bold.

"Because," she answers. When neither one of us say anything for a while she finally continues, "Because you like Isaiah. If you like him, then maybe you can like me. Besides, I like bunnies."

I try not to smile. A strange answer, yet normal for her. We watch as the two guys tinker with the underside of my car. Actually, Abby observes, I avoid looking. "Where do you work?"

Abby pulls hard on her string, causing it to become uneven. "What?"

"At the mall," I prompt.

She scratches her mouth as if attempting to hide the uneven smirk. "I don't work at the mall."

I mull over what she said earlier. No, she said...

"I make deliveries to people at the mall."

"Oh." She must sell cosmetics or something like that. "So you have a home business?"

"Who's the guy with Isaiah? Is he a friend of yours? He's hot."

"No. He's Beth's friend." A twinge of jealousy rattles my bones. Abby's sneakers squeak when she kicks at a nonexistent spot on the floor. While I've never asked Isaiah about Beth, Isaiah's also never offered information. Maybe Abby can fill me in on Beth since Isaiah is closemouthed. "Do you know Beth?"

"Yes," she says.

Not helpful. "Were you friends with her?"

"Hell no. She twisted Isaiah so damn tight even I couldn't breathe."

The overhead heater clicks three times as we all groan. Isaiah turned it off earlier, but we all began to freeze. Cold fingers aren't good for my baby so he powered it back on. Isaiah swears as he yanks off his T-shirt.

My heart trips. Last night, I dreamed of touching his body. "He has a lot of tattoos," I say, hoping Abby doesn't notice how I stare at Isaiah.

"Yeah," she replies. "He got his first one, the tiger, when we were fourteen."

Huh. "Does it mean something?"

"Don't know. Isaiah won't discuss his tattoos. He gets them and moves on." "Paint It Black" plays from her cell. Abby presses a hand to her forehead. "I've gotta split." And she disappears, leaving me alone with my thoughts.

She had Isaiah twisted so damn tight even I couldn't breathe. Abby's words circle in my mind. What was an attempt to make me feel better has progressed to nausea tearing at my throat.

A whistle draws my attention. Isaiah flashes the craziest smile I've ever seen. "Almost done, angel. You're going to love how she'll sing for you."

This time when I smile, I have to force the muscles to comply. How can I compete with Beth—the girl who kept, possibly still keeps, him twisted?

Isaiah

THE GODS ARE ON OUR side. The weather's warm—
upper fifties—with clear skies predicted for this Saturday
night. With my hip cocked against Rachel's car, I assess the
Camaro pulling beside me in the waiting lane behind the
grandstand. The big-ass dragsters are having their turn in
the lanes. Next will be the street cars.

Rachel stands near the hood petting her car like the pony
it is. "Promise you won't wreck."

"I'll take care of your car."

"Isaiah, I'm worried about *you*."

About me? My heart stalls in my chest. Rachel, Logan and
I checked out a few races before we signed in and unfortunately, we witnessed a wreck. No one hurt, but it totaled the
cars. Rachel's face faded into an unnatural shade of white
when an older guy mumbled how the rules enforced at the
track were written by the blood of other generations. Since
then, when Rachel's watched the races, I think all she sees
are ghosts.

I meet her violet eyes. "I'll be okay, Rachel."

She lowers her head, raises it, then lets it fall back. I can't read her very well and I wish I could. "What's going on in your head?" I ask.

Rachel sucks in a breath to answer right as the driver of the Camaro slides out. Doing what I asked of her earlier when a possible bet came into the picture, she walks straight for the grandstands. Her long hair swings forward, hiding her face. My legs twitch with the desire to follow her, kiss her and ask what's wrong.

When Rachel arrived at the garage yesterday, she was one hundred percent with me, but by the time I finished her car, she became distant again. I'll dig for the issues tonight. Now I need to focus and win us money.

I glance behind me at Logan. He's already deep in conversation with his competition: a Dodge Charger. That'll be a nice race for Logan. That driver always jumps the green light.

The Camaro driver appreciates Rachel's car. "When did you upgrade?"

He may not know my name, but he recognizes me by my old car. I'm the same with him. "This week."

"Still think you can take me?" he asks.

"Easily."

He nods to his car. "I've made some updates, too."

"Not concerned."

Just as I hoped, he produces a wad of cash from his pocket. "Then you won't mind putting money on the table."

No. I wouldn't.

Rachel

MY FINGERS KNOT AROUND THE cold metal fence as I watch Isaiah drive my car to the burnout area. The accident we saw occurred a second after the race began. A tire blew, causing the driver to lose control and ram into the side of a Chevy Comet.

It scared the crap out of me—especially when a burst of flame shot out one of the cars. Men scrambled over the barricades, hauling the drivers to safety, spraying fire extinguishers at the hood. Isaiah went to launch himself over the fence to help, but my grip on his arm stopped him.

I looked up at him. He looked down at me. And when my body began to tremble, he placed an arm around me.

Isaiah drives past the waterline, jerking me back to the present, and he immediately heads to the staging area. The unexpected move paralyzes the anxiety spiders crawling in my stomach. "Why isn't he doing a burnout?" I whisper.

"Because the car doesn't have slicks," says Zach as he approaches me and leans an arm on the fence. His blond hair shags over his face. "Street cars typically avoid burnouts."

Right. Slicks are a type of tire that sticks better to the tracks. Zach was nice last weekend, but he reminds me of the guys from my school—how he speaks, knows everyone, and how he has plenty of the girls vying for him. So, in other words, he puts me on edge, and I slip back into Rachel mode. I step away from him when he invades my personal space.

The driver competing against Isaiah spins his tires at the waterline, creating a haze of white smoke. Because the Camaro has slicks, will it have an advantage? Isaiah bet everything he had against this guy: fifty dollars. If we don't win, we go home.

"I haven't seen you race," I say to Zach when I think of something coherent.

"The Cobra sounded funny so I'm sitting her out."

I nod to let him know that I heard him, but keep my eyes on Isaiah. *Please, please, please God, take care of Isaiah.*

"That's your car, isn't it?" he asks.

"Yes." I wish he'd be silent. If he talks then I can't concentrate, and if I can't concentrate then God will stop listening to my prayers.

"Why aren't you driving?" he asks.

Isaiah's competition hits the second staging line. The yellow lights flash down and right; as the light turns green, my car lurches with a power I never believed possible, lifting the front wheels. Isaiah rushes forward, with the Camaro following less than a second behind. Both cars fly by me, with Isaiah easily in the lead.

Come on, come on, come on... Yes! Isaiah crosses the finish line first. I lower my head and suck in a breath. Thank You, God, for keeping him safe.

"Did you hear me?" asks Zach.

"Um..." This is awkward. "No. Sorry."

"I said that I want to race against you."

The red lights of my car glow in the distance as Isaiah leaves the track. My body automatically angles toward the exit, as if a gravitational pull exists between Isaiah and me. "I'll tell Isaiah."

"No, Rachel." Zach places a hand on my arm and his unwanted touch feels foreign against my skin. "I want to race you when you drive your car."

I move my arm, pretending to itch my shoulder. "I won't be racing."

"Why?"

"Because..." I don't know how to explain in a way that doesn't make me appear weak.

"Because Isaiah's one of those guys that doesn't think that a girl should be behind a wheel."

I huff. "No, he's not."

"I've got money." Zach smirks. "And I hear he needs it. Tell him I'll race, but only against you. He knows my stakes."

Something deep inside of me shifts, and it's not the good type of stirring.

"And Rachel?" Zach begins to slowly walk backward. "If you were my girl, I'd let you race."

"He's not like that," I say, but Zach already turned his back to me and is too far away to hear.

"He's not," I repeat. At least I don't think he is.

Isaiah permitted Logan to drive his car without seeing how

he would do behind the wheel. Yes, I messed up once, but why hasn't Isaiah granted me another chance?

Maybe because he's discovered my secret. Maybe he already knows that I'm weak.

Isaiah

HITTING EIGHTY-NINE, I SHIFT DOWN and slam my hand onto the steering wheel. "That's what I'm fucking talking about!"

The surge of adrenaline rushing through my veins makes me feel like I'm flying high without the loss of control that drugs or alcohol brings. This is the only time I feel truly alive. I turn left at the end of the drag strip and pause for my competition to catch up: a Nova with sweet upgrades.

This is my last race for the night and damn, I feel good. My competition, a guy ten years older than me, shakes his head as he gets out of the car with a hundred in his hand. "I should have smoked you, kid. What's under my hood is ten times what you've got."

He's right. His upgrades should have kicked my ass. I take the money and resist the urge to kiss it. "Good race, man."

"Your reaction time at the light is insane," he says. "I want a rematch Friday night."

My luck must be changing. "Bring cash and I'll race you all night."

We share a short nod, and I drive Rachel's car to where

Logan and Rachel wait for me. I've won every race tonight. After getting his feet wet, Logan won more than he lost, bringing money to the table.

In the darkness, Rachel shines as bright as the sun. Her hair a halo framing her face, her eyes stars. "That was awesome!"

In two easy strides, I reach her, weave my arms around her waist and lift her feet off the ground. My angel is so light she practically floats. "Isaiah! You're crazy!"

"Insane," I answer.

She rests her forehead against mine and braids her hands tightly on my neck. "That was close. He almost got you in the end."

I love the sensation of her body against mine. Tonight, I'm going to kiss her again and, if she'll let me, I'll explore a little further. "Were you doubting me?"

She smiles when she notices the lightness in my voice. "Never."

That's right, angel. I'll never let you down.

Rachel wiggles in my hold. "You're strong."

My lips twitch. "Pure steel." *Strong enough to protect you.*

"Hate to break in here," says Logan, "but I've got a game tomorrow and a full pocket."

I set Rachel on her feet while keeping her tucked beneath my shoulder. "Then let's go."

Though I consider The Motor Yard safe, it's still not a good idea to flash money—especially the type of money Logan and I banked tonight. Logan follows me back to my apartment, where we had left his car.

Logan hands me his wad of cash. "Have you ever thought of adding a nitro system? Those cars were flying."

I shake my head. "That'll put us against a different class of cars, and in order to compete in that we'll have to go bracket racing. Plus, nitro's some crazy-ass shit. A lot can go wrong."

Logan flashes his not-guilty-by-reason-of-insanity grin. "All the more reason to do it. What's bracket racing?"

Leaning against her car, Rachel tunnels her hands into the sleeves of her black coat. She's cold, and I crave to make her warm. "I'll explain it later."

Logan's eyes shift to Rachel. "Got it. See you."

He drives away and I head over to my angel. "Want to see how much we made?"

"Definitely."

Rachel allows me to open the door for her in the entrance and to my apartment. Once inside, she slides off her coat and rests it on the kitchen table. In a nervous gesture, she laces her fingers together and glances around the room. "Is your roommate home?"

"No," I say. "He's staying with Echo tonight. You sure your brother will cover curfew?"

She stares at her fingers. "I covered for him last night so he agreed to tonight."

Giving her space, I sit at the card table and begin counting cash. She sinks into the other folding chair and counts the other pile. For a brief few seconds, the only sound in the room is the scratching of dollars moving against each other, and thanks to the crazy bat downstairs, we get to listen to Elvis singing about shoes.

"Six hundred," she says in awe. That would be my winnings.

"Four hundred and forty," I tell her, holding Logan's stash.

Rachel slumps in her seat as if in shock. "Off of your fifty and Logan's twenty we made one thousand and forty dollars." She pauses. "That's not possible."

"It is." Has it not hit her that in *one* race on the streets the pot was five thousand dollars? And that was a slow night.

She leaves the table and begins to pace. "We're going to do this, aren't we? We're going to pay Eric off and be free of him, and my parents will never know what I did. I mean, we have over two-thousand dollars already."

My mind clears with that info. "How are you coming up with two thousand?"

Rachel repeats the endless loop she's created from one corner of the couch to another. "I have a thousand. A little over five hundred in birthday and Christmas money. I pawned some jewelry for another five hundred. Oh, Isaiah." Her face flushes. "We're close to halfway there. We could pay Eric back before the six weeks."

She's a mixture of anxious and excited, and those feelings become contagious. Knots form in my stomach and I think of the million ways I want to touch her and kiss her and let her know that she's the only one in my life.

What I should tell her is that tonight will be our only money rush. Now that people know how Logan and I race, they'll either avoid us or not wager as much. I have no doubt we'll raise the amount we need, but it could still be a struggle.

I also decide to keep it to myself that Eric has eyes on us and that he'll be unhappy we're making money.

Rachel finally stops the frantic path she's wearing onto the subflooring. Her face beams. She's light in a world full of darkness. Rachel is happy and that's all I desire.

"We could be together, Isaiah. With no worrying over Eric or debts or anything. We could be happy."

Electricity shoots into my veins and shocks me as if I've never been alive. I stand abruptly, knocking over the folding chair. My heart races and this surge is something unknown. Something I don't understand. Something that fosters confusion, panic.

Her eyes glimmer with too much adoration; with too much of an emotion I've only seen people give to anyone *other* than me. I see love in her eyes and it scares the hell out of me.

"You need to go," I say. My voice is deeper than normal and a tremor courses through my body. My eyes burn as a shadow crosses her face, snuffing out all the light. Damn me to hell. I'm the one who created that sorrow. If I stay with her, she'll never know light and happiness.

"Isaiah," she says carefully. "I don't understand."

"Go home." I swipe the money off the table and stalk into the bedroom. With three steps, I circle the room and perform the act again. My thinking is messed up, as if I'm high or took a severe blow to the head. My thoughts detach from my mind, away from my body.

"Will you tell me what's wrong?" comes a soft voice from behind me.

Why hasn't she left? "Nothing. I'm looking for a place to

hide the money. This is a shitty place, Rachel, and awful things happen here."

"Like people breaking in," she says.

That's exactly what can happen. "Just go."

Rachel looks small and defenseless as she rests her temple against the door frame. The dim light of the kitchen silhouettes her frame. Obscured by blackness, I can't see her face.

"You could give the money to me." Her voice is so soothing that part of me clings to the sound. "Where I live is safe."

My thoughts collide into one another. The back of my legs hit the bed and I sink onto it. My entire life is one long thick rope full of knots and kinks where people have twisted me inside and out. Nothing about me is solid or sturdy. I'm frayed and tattered. "I'm no good, Rachel."

I stare at the cash in my hands. My fingers clench and the money crackles. I won't lead Rachel further into the abyss. This ends here. It ends tonight. "You need to leave and never come back. I'll race my car. I'll pay off the debt. Leave and know I'll always keep you safe."

Silence. Nothing from her. Nothing from me. I close my eyes, cursing the scorching wetness behind my lids. I don't want to feel anymore. Feelings hurt too damn much.

Quiet footsteps shuffle in my direction and the cash crackles again in my fist. "Go, Rachel." My voice is so raw it's nothing more than a rasp.

The bed moves and sinks to my left. A touch so light I almost believe I'm imagining it presses on my shoulder. "I think I'm falling for you, Isaiah."

My head dips. *I think I'm falling for you, too, and it terrifies me.*

The pressure remains on my shoulder as the fingers of her other hand trace the compass tattooed on my forearm. "I don't know what love is or how it should feel, but I know that when I'm with you I like who I am, and that's never happened to me before."

I like who I am when I'm with her. The music below us is soft, lyrical with a steady beat. Elvis's deep voice sings about suspicious minds.

"I like who you are, Isaiah, and I like how you look at me. But what I really like is the rush that hits me when you're in the room."

Because Rachel has always been magic, she gives words to the emotion tearing at my soul. "People don't attach themselves to me, Rachel."

She kisses my shoulder, and a shudder runs through my body, igniting every cell. "Then maybe they don't know you like I do."

The finger tracing the tattoo slides down to my hands. "Give me the money, Isaiah. Trust me to keep it safe."

I clutch the money tighter, but as her hands weave around mine, my grip loosens. "Do you understand the trouble, the danger, you're taking on?"

With her fingers holding on to the cash she whispers, "Yes."

I place my hand over hers. "Put it down."

"But, Isaiah..."

I lift my head. "If you say you're going to keep it safe, I believe you, but right now, I want you to put it on the floor."

She half smirks with a twinkle in her eye. "You're bossy."

"Yes," I admit. *Hear what I'm saying, Rachel. Listen to what a controlling mess you're falling for.* "I am."

The money hits the floor, and my hands immediately frame her face. She has skin so soft that I worry about damaging her with a gentle touch. Her breathing hitches as my lips come close to hers. I'm going to kiss her. "Tell me I'm who you want." So I know there are no mistakes.

Her nose slides against mine as she slowly nods. "I don't want anyone else."

God help us both for her allowing the devil permission.

Rachel

THE KISS COMES HOTTER AND faster than before. Our lips move quickly, a hunger grows between us that can't seem to be quenched. There's a rhythm, a dance, and somehow, I know the steps. An instinct tells me to follow his lead, to explore even further, to touch.

My hands drift down his back and when I feel scorching skin near the hem of his shirt, I gasp for air. Isaiah moans, and his lips leave mine to travel along my throat. My heart picks up speed as my entire body becomes one live electrical current.

His tongue swirls against the sensitive skin right where my jaw meets my neck. I shiver and press my body closer to his. When he meets my lips again, Isaiah loops his arm around my waist and pulls me farther onto the bed. On our sides, his body heat penetrates past my clothes, past my skin, creating an inferno in my blood.

A sudden coldness causes my eyes to flash open. Kneeling beside me, Isaiah's hands go behind his head and he yanks off his shirt, tossing it to the floor. A flutter of excitement and nerves trembles in my stomach. I swallow and stare at the golden tiger rippling with the muscle in his arm. Biting my lip, I dig deep for courage. My hand reaches out. Stops. And I curl my fingers in.

"It's okay, Rachel. Go ahead." He angles so that the tiger is closer to me.

I outline the tattoo, enjoying its beauty. "I love this one."

In the beams of street light scattered into the dark bedroom by the slatted blinds, I watch as Isaiah's eyes melt into silver. "It's my favorite," he says. "One day I'll get a tattoo for you."

Warmth explodes in my chest, in awe that he would mark himself for me. "You don't have to."

"I will." His fingers trace my cheek and chills of pleasure run down my spine. "It's what I do. Each tattoo represents the only happy memories I've had. And you, Rachel, you're the happiest."

My lips move up, and his fingers brush them in response.

"I dream of your smile." He follows the curve as if he's an artist. "I've thought about you every night since the first night we met."

There's a power I only feel when I'm with Isaiah. A boldness I've never possessed in my life. Never in a million years would I have imagined I'd be the girl who'd say she was falling fast for a boy before he did. Never in a million years did I think I'd be lying in bed with a totally ripped guy that has his shirt off. But Isaiah has this effect on me. He makes me feel stronger than I really am.

There's a pulse in my body, vibrating every pressure point. "I like kissing you."

His hand lowers to my waist. "I could kiss you forever."

I lazily glance at him from under my eyelashes. "Just kissing." Because I think I'll combust if we do more.

The right side of his mouth quirks. "Just kissing. And some touching." To prove his point Isaiah's hands caress my back, weave into my hair and slide against the dip of my waist.

Yes, definitely some touching. I inhale deeply, reminding myself that breathing is still a requirement. "I agree. Some touching. No new clothes off."

Because I'd probably pass out at the thought of his jeans off. They already hang low on his hips. Too low. Very low. Low enough that I start to imagine what more there is to him.

Isaiah wraps his hand around the back of my neck and performs this deep massage that makes my eyes roll into my head in ecstasy. "I'll put my shirt back on if you want."

"No," I breathe out. "I'm fine with it off." More than fine.

I lick my lips as his teeth nibble on my earlobe. Between my muscles melting under his touch, my blood tingling with the teasing of my ear and the way my foot rubs against his calf, my thoughts become hazy.

My shirt rides up and Isaiah rubs his thumb in small circles on the bare skin of my stomach. The sensation causes me to arch my back and Isaiah groans as I kiss his neck. I like these feelings. Actually, I more than like them. They're addicting, and I love how every little thing I do causes Isaiah to kiss and touch me more.

He rolls and I move with him. Our tangled legs become unraveled as my thighs fall open, accepting his weight. Isaiah's body over mine is heavier than I would have imagined, but it's a weight I craved without knowing it.

Isaiah kisses up my neck and when his lips meet mine

again, he rocks his hips. Suddenly very aware parts of him are touching very aware parts of me, and my head falls to the side as a new sensation spikes through my body. One I've never felt before. One I want to feel again. One that...

My hands slip to Isaiah's chest and I push. "Isaiah."

Isaiah rolls us again, except this time his back is against the mattress and he slides me next to his side. His chest moves up and down at a rapid pace, and that's when I notice that my breaths match his.

"You okay?" he asks.

I nod, unable to think of anything coherent to explain why I did what I did. It was just new and fast and glorious and...

Isaiah places his fingers under my chin and has me look into his eyes. "It's okay to stop."

"I know," I whisper, but to be honest, I don't know if it is. I'm seventeen. Everyone else I know has done more...some way more...some into territories beyond way and into lands I don't think I'll ever visit.

Isaiah has to be more experienced than me. Has probably been with the girls who have no fear of pushing every boundary. Is it really okay for me to be... "I'm sorry I'm slow."

He brushes my hair over my shoulder. "You're not slow."

I raise an eyebrow.

"I'm serious." When he sees I'm unconvinced, he rubs at his stubble and starts again. "I don't want you to give any more than you want. What makes this special is that you're into it. The moment you aren't, that's where I become a bastard for asking for more. I'm telling you, I've got no problem taking it slow."

I sigh. It's the right words, but—

"Stop with the analyzing. Rachel, I've listened to the same movie bullshit you have about guys wanting to find the right girl and then wanting to take it slow because they believe the girl is worth the wait. I'll admit, I never believed it, but meeting you...it's not bullshit anymore."

The right side of my mouth curves up. I'm worth waiting for.

Isaiah

THE CLOCK ON THE SCREEN flashes as it hits the one-minute mark. I finished the test fifteen minutes ago, but I review my answers repeatedly. This is my future, and there is no room for mistakes. In less than sixty seconds, I'll have earned my ASE certification.

The computer freezes—time's up. What had been a silent room becomes noisy as the other guys from class who took the "field trip" to the testing center relax back in their seats and talk to one another.

"Isaiah," Zach calls. "How'd you do?"

"Okay." I kicked ass.

"Good." He leaves his buddies and rests his hip against the half cubicle wall meant to dissuade cheating. "Did Rachel tell you about my proposal?"

"I don't think you need to be proposing anything to *my* girl." The area between my skin and muscles vibrates. Rachel didn't tell me crap, but I won't let Zach know that. I plaster a deadpan look on my face, stretch out my legs so that Zach has to move and angle my arms so that he sees my tats.

Zach takes a wise step away. "Just trying to help. Heard you need money and you know I'll match any wager."

"If you want to race me, you come to me. Not to Rachel."

He becomes a cocky prick when he smiles. "I don't want to race you. I want to race her."

My legs fold in as I lean forward. Zach nearly trips over himself as he stumbles back. "She's not racing." An eerie silence hangs in the room as everyone watches the showdown.

After a few seconds of me staring and Zach saying nothing, the room returns to normal.

"Money is money," mutters Zach. "Who cares who drives?"

I whisper so only he can hear, "I'm not racing for ten bucks. I've made serious money so I'm betting serious money."

He glances around to verify everyone else has returned to their business. "I'm making serious money now. I'll match whatever you got."

I stare straight at him and, like always, Zach averts his eyes. Zach comes from a broken home, and they've always lived on the edge of government assistance. There's no way this asshole fell into money this fast without playing with the devil. "Tell me you haven't become Eric's bitch."

Zach nervously laughs, but before he can try to deny it, I hook a foot around the chair next to me and shove it into his legs. "Sit."

He looks around, trying to save face, but sits anyway. Once upon a time, he and I could have been considered friends and because of that, I give him this break. "You and I both know that Eric's bad shit. If you've fallen in, maybe I can help you out."

Zach bows his head as he pulls his legs under the chair. "He just wants Rachel to race me. That's it."

Fuck me. My fingers tighten into fists. "He wants Rachel and me to fail."

His head snaps up. "You're seeing this all wrong. Eric wants to help us. He said if the two of us work for him then he can pay us cash. Real cash. Not the minimum wage we're going to end up with after we graduate. We'll be kings, Isaiah. Not the trash we are now."

I kick the wall between us and the keyboard falls to the floor. "Eric owns you now."

"Not own. He's helping me, just like he wants to help you."

Before I can ask how the hell he's become so delusional he believes any of that shit, Mr. Holden enters the room. "Test results are in. I'll call you out one at a time to go over the results. Isaiah, let's go."

My heart thrashes and I stand, trying to control the anger. I lean down and whisper the threat. "Stay the fuck away from Rachel."

"You can't touch me," Zach replies.

Since he's under Eric, maybe not, but Eric's underestimating what I would do to keep Rachel safe.

Rachel

WITH MY HAND LINGERING OVER the equation, my pencil rocks back and forth. Third-period Physics is torture. Both of my brothers are in here, along with over half of their friends, and the remaining people in the class love to gossip about me. We were supposed to separate into groups of four, but let's be honest, I don't like groups.

The sun filters through the windows and bathes me in warmth. I could probably focus better if I could stop daydreaming about Isaiah. Each time I think of how he rolled us in bed and how his body covered mine, I smile.

"Have you figured it out yet, Rach?" West whispers.

That snaps me out of the daydream. Ethan and West, of course, are in a group together, with two of their buddies. Because the room is uneven, I avoided a group, but I can't ditch my brothers. They hover next to me.

"There are four of you and one of me. I'd say your odds are better than mine," I answer. The pencil moves faster in my hand.

"But you're good at this shit," says West.

With a screech of metal against the linoleum floor, Ethan

slides his desk closer to mine. "She's got an answer. Give it here."

Before I can protest, West grabs my sheet and places it in the middle of his friends. "Thank you, baby sister."

"I'm not done yet," I whisper severely. "That's only half the equation."

"Better than a blank sheet," mutters Ethan.

"Besides." West winks as he flicks my paper back at me. "It's all about family."

"Mr. Young." Our Physics teacher looms over the group.

"Which one?" asks West. "There are two of us and a Miss."

Our physics teacher doesn't like West. He's a smart-ass. Which means she's not a big fan of me and Ethan by default. "I don't remember Rachel being included in your original group."

I press my face into my hand and tilt it so that I'm looking out the window and not at the class watching the power trip.

"She's our sister. Of course she's included in our group."

Paper crinkles, and I peek to see her examining everyone's sheets. "It's the same answer, but half done."

West relaxes in his seat, totally unaffected by her accusation of copying. "We're a group. I think that's expected."

"Then explain it," she says. "Explain how you solved half the answer."

West's mouth pops open, then he shuts it. "Rachel was in the process of explaining it to us. See, we were a little lost, and we didn't want to hold her back so she went ahead with the work and stopped halfway so she could teach us."

Our physics teacher's eyes settle on me. So do West's and

Ethan's. So do the eyes of their friends and of everyone else who has made fun of me since middle school.

"Well then, Rachel." In an overdramatic swooping motion, our teacher gestures me toward the front of the room. "Since you're so generous, why don't you go to the board and teach the rest of the class how to complete the first half of the equation?"

Blood and heat rush to my face. Besides the fact this is one of my worst nightmares, I'm not even sure if I have the equation right. What if I'm wrong? What if I fall apart? At least with the speeches I can prepare for the impending meltdown.

This...this is out of nowhere. Begging for a way out, I frantically glance at West and Ethan. West locks his eyes on the floor while his fingers drum against his desk in an angry rhythm. "That *is* not necessary."

"I think it is," says Mrs. Patterson. "Unless you want to explain the work, but keep in mind, what goes on that board is your group's grade."

West jerks in his seat. Ethan leans over and whispers, "He's going to blow."

West is one detention away from suspension, a fact Ethan and I have helped hide from Mom, and Ethan's grades have dropped this semester. He can't risk a bad score. "I'll do it."

West's head shakes back and forth, heat from his anger creating small red circles on his cheeks. Ethan kicks at our brother from underneath the desks. The two share a look, and both immediately focus on the floor.

When I reach the board, my body trembles as I grab the dry erase marker. I clear my throat twice and perspiration forms along my hairline. A couple of girls in the corner giggle.

My voice breaks as I incoherently explain how I solved half the equation. Due to my quaking hand, the numbers barely resemble squiggles. I clear my throat again, this time tasting bile. I inhale, only for the air to stop before reaching my lungs. My palms sweat, and the marker slips from my grasp. It taps the floor twice before rolling under the teacher's desk. The world becomes a tunnel. Around me, laughter erupts.

"Rachel." Mrs. Patterson sounds distant, almost like an echo. "I was wrong. As the teacher, I should be showing the class."

My breathing is short, shallow, and my head has that floating feeling like when I'm sick with a fever. A buzzing noise fills my ears. Everyone stands and gathers their things. I try to suck in air, but my lungs won't expand. If I can't breathe, I'll die.

Ethan appears in my line of vision. "She's fine, Mrs. Patterson. Aren't you, Rachel?"

I nod. No, I'm not fine. Ethan wraps an arm around me and ushers me into the hall. Cold metal supports my back. A hanging lock digs into my kidney.

West appears in the tunnel. "What the hell, Ethan? I thought she was over this shit."

"Break into her locker and get her stuff," he says. "We need to get her to a bathroom."

Lunch is me, West, Ethan and a bottle of Sprite. Because West plays every sport imaginable, he was able to sneak us into the guy's changing room. Sitting on an old jersey that had been stuffed into the abyss of West's locker, I glance at the toilet bowl containing the remnants of breakfast.

Confident I'm going to survive, I flush the toilet and peek at my two brothers, who have hovered over me since the end of third period. "See," I say with a raspy voice. "No blood."

But my throat is raw and sore. If I continue to vomit with the attacks, it won't be long until the blood vessels in my throat crack.

Holding on to the stall door, West's knuckles turn white. "How long?"

I drink slowly, buying myself not nearly enough time. West's fingers tap a death march. He isn't going to let this go. "It never stopped," I answer.

His head whips to Ethan. "And you've been in on this?"

Ethan won't stop staring at the toilet. "For a few weeks."

I wince when West slams the door against the neighboring stall. "She was in the hospital over this shit. Do you want to watch her body waste away again?"

Tears threaten my eyes, and I rub at my nose. "Just stop."

"Stop!" West shouts. "Why should I stop? You've been lying!"

"Whatever," Ethan spits at West. "You pretended not to see it. So did I. Look me in the eye...no, look Rachel in the eye and tell her that you haven't suspected the truth the entire time. She lied to make Mom happy, to make us happy and you're pissed the dream is over."

West takes two steps and stands nose to nose with Ethan. The anger in the air between them is so thick I could gag. They're the same height, both over six feet. Ethan with dark hair and dark eyes. West with blond hair and blue eyes. Brothers less than a year apart.

West shoves his finger in Ethan's chest. "You should have told me."

"Now you know."

After a few more tense seconds, West eases away. "What now?"

"We keep the secret," says Ethan. "Mom's happy. Jack's working on Gavin."

West becomes a statue. "She knows about Gavin?"

"Yes. She knows he's out of work." Something in the way Ethan overpronounces the words makes me question their meaning, but West is finally calming down and I don't want to risk another eruption.

West's shoulders visibly relax. "And the speeches?"

"We help her. One of us should go with her to the speeches and deflect Mom if she has an attack. And Rachel will tell us if her panic attacks escalate to blood."

West picks up the bag I keep in my gym locker with extra clothes. "I got this for you. You've got ten minutes to take a shower and make it to fourth period."

Both of my brothers stare at me, and I draw my knees to my chest. I hated this feeling back in middle school, and I hate this feeling now. No matter what I do in my life, the two of them will always view me as someone to be controlled.

By the time sixth period rolls around, the school salivates with the news: recluse Rachel Young is weird again. When I enter the library for my internship, I'm greeted by the sound of giggles. The words whispered between ponytail tosses are not lost on me. "I told you she was strange..." Chuckles and lower whispers. "...completely freaked out in physics."

Unable to face anyone, I duck into one of the stacks. I suck in a breath, not for an attack, but to stop the tears. Why? Why am I like this?

At the back wall, I sink to the ground and my phone vibrates. I pull it out and see the one person who doesn't treat me as weird or as incompetent. Isaiah: Look out the window.

My forehead furrows. I grab my pack and walk to the windows overlooking the student parking lot. In the back, Isaiah leans against his black Mustang. My smile automatically appears.

Me: See you.

Isaiah: Skip with me.

Skip. Besides that day with Eric, I've never ditched before. But that day was covered with a sick note from Mom. Leaving today would be different. It would be scandalous. It would be...everything I need.

Isaiah

I EASE MY CAR TO the curb, and Rachel dashes out of school like a robber running out of a convenience store, her blond hair trailing behind her in the wind. I chuckle and reach over to open the passenger side. She falls into the car with her cheeks red from the cold. "Let's go!"

Weaving her hand in mine, I kiss her knuckles and place her palm over the stick shift with my hand securely covering hers. I step on the clutch and apply pressure to her hand so that she'll shift into First. "You're letting me drive your car?" she asks.

"Shift," I correct. "But I've never let a girl shift my car before. Feel honored."

"I do." Rachel leans over and kisses my cheek. The sweet scent of jasmine and the ocean washes over me. On the open road, the rpms build, and like a perfectly synced machine, I step on the clutch right as Rachel shifts to Second.

The excitement is hard to contain, but it's weird. I've never been eager to share news with anyone, and I want her to be excited along with me. The engine begins to strain, and in effortless coordination, she shifts to Third while I press the clutch.

A stirring in my heart overcomes the excitement for a second. Rachel is perfect for me. She never needs words because she understands my rhythm.

"I passed the ASE certification test," I say, as if I'm telling her it's Thursday.

Rachel doesn't disappoint as she gasps. "Oh, Isaiah! That is amazing. No, fantastic. No...the best news ever. I knew you'd pass. We have to do something to celebrate! What, though? I don't know. What do you want to do? Whatever it is, it has to be special."

Out of the corner of my eye, I glance at her. "I'm doing it."

A grimace stains her face. "What? Driving? You always drive."

How can she not see it? "I'm spending time with you."

Silence. Except for the purring of my engine. The floorboard barely vibrates beneath me, and I wonder if she also notices the sensation. I scratch the thought. I don't have to wonder. Someone like her relishes the feel of a car's every movement—just like me.

"I'm proud of you," she says as simply as when I announced that I passed. My chest hurts as if she punched through a wall. Taking her hand off the stick shift, I kiss her knuckles again and keep her fingers pressed against my face until I have to place her hand back so she can shift down.

These feelings inside of me, I don't understand them, but I do understand Rachel and I know she understands me. I want her in my life in a way no one else has ever been.

When I can talk without my voice breaking, I say to her, "I'd like you to come somewhere with me. It's not special, but I'd like you there."

Rachel

AFTER SCHOOL ENDED, ISAIAH DROVE me back to the lot to get my car and then I followed him to the garage to leave it there. Once again in his car he circles a small park east of Tom's garage. It's not quite far east enough to hit my area of town, but far enough away from his area that I'm not terri-fied. Because of the cold, gray day, the park is relatively empty.

Empty except for the woman with blond hair standing next to a car several spots down from ours. From the moment we pulled in, she's stared at Isaiah and me. Also in the park is a middle-aged woman with short, dark brown hair. From the bench nearest the swings, she subtly watches us. Isaiah fell into a heavy silence the moment he placed the car into Park.

"I don't like being stared at," I say quietly. Isaiah glances at me then to the two women.

"She's my mom," he says with a short gruffness. "The one next to the car is my social worker." His fingers tighten into fists as he rests the back of his head against his seat. "I asked to meet with my mom, but now I'm not sure I can."

"You'll see her when you're ready." Wrapping my fingers over his, he grasps my hand like I'm a life raft. I shouldn't revel in this moment, but I do. He's searching for strength, and I'm more than happy to provide it. In fact, doing so makes me feel stronger. "Do you want me to go with you?"

Isaiah shakes his head. "No. But thanks...for being here." In a swift movement, Isaiah leans over and kisses me. His mouth barely opens so he can tease my bottom lip. A move that causes my heart to stumble.

Before I can kiss him back, Isaiah breaks away. "Stay here."

Isaiah

WITH HER LONG TAN COAT slapping against her knees, Courtney intercepts me before I step onto the grass. "I have a million questions, Isaiah."

I shove my hands into my jeans pockets. "I don't know, I don't care or none of your business."

"What?"

"Every possible answer to your millions of questions."

She smirks. "Very funny."

I wasn't joking.

Courtney glances at my car with a smug expression. "Who's that?"

"Answer number three."

My social worker ignores me and continues to evaluate Rachel like she's a lab rat. "She's pretty. Does she go to your school?"

"She is and no." If I don't give her something she'll keep digging. "She goes to Worthington Private."

Courtney blinks rapidly. "Wow. No kidding. That's... impressive."

I jerk my chin in Melanie's direction. "I got things to do."

She sighs. "Are you sure about this?"

No. "I'm here and she's there."

Courtney waves me on, and I can feel the heat of her stare burning into my back. Not believing I had a change of heart, she questioned my motivations when I asked her to schedule this meeting. Gotta give Courtney credit...the girl knows her shit.

Huddled in a jean jacket, Melanie slides from the middle of the bench to create room for me. I perch on the edge farthest from her. Once again, she wears cowboy boots and big hoop earrings. "You listen to country music, don't you?" I say.

"Yes," she answers. "Garth Brooks used to be your favorite."

I rub my forehead, not wanting to hear anything she has to say in regards to me.

"Do you remember?" she asks.

"No." Yes. "Did you bring the money?"

"Yes. I'll give it to you when we're done."

In the distance, a crow caws. How long do the two of us have to sit here to satisfy Courtney's curiosity over my visitation request? Five minutes? Fifteen? In my head, thirty seconds has been long enough.

"Is she your girlfriend?" Melanie asks.

I narrow my eyes at the ground, confused as to why I answer, "Yes."

I hate myself for wanting to tell her, but what I hate more is the realization that I brought Rachel to show her off to Mom, even at a distance. To prove to her that I didn't need her for the past eleven years and that I don't need her now.

"She's pretty."

"There's more to Rachel than that."

"I'm sure there is."

Occasional tufts of green sprout from the dried-up yellow-and-white grass. A large box of brown dirt lines the swing sets. It's early spring and all I smell is cold and earth.

"Why I went to prison...I did it for you," she says. "To protect you."

A dangerous pulse beats through my veins. "You don't get to talk about this."

Melanie angles her body toward me and lowers her voice. "You want your money, then listen. This has to be said."

"No." The imaginary collar around my neck tightens, and I tug at my shirt. "It doesn't and the deal was that I show. Not listen."

She continues as if I never spoke. "Life isn't made-for-television movies or books with happy-ever-afters. Sometimes the choices we're presented with are bad or worse."

"You don't think I know that? For one year of my life, I had the shit beat out of me by other kids because I was the smallest. Don't you dare talk to me about choices. You had one and you blew it."

Melanie holds her hands out, pleading. I begged those boys to stop. They never did.

"I had nowhere to go," she says. "I had no help. It was me and you, Isaiah. We were out of money, and I thought it was the safest way. You were hungry and I lost my job and we were late on rent and they were going to throw us out. The shelter scared you. You were so small for so long. I was the only one around to defend you, so I made the decision...."

Her words begin to weave past my skin, and I refuse to let her twist and demean me. I stand. "You don't get to make yourself feel better. Give me the money."

Melanie places her hands over her lips to hide their trembling. I resist the deep-rooted urge to feel sorry for her. "The fucking money, Melanie."

She stands and unexpectedly hugs me. I stiffen, holding my arms at my sides. Pressure at my back pocket tells me she's giving me the cash. "Twenty-three forty-five Elmont Way. 2345, Isaiah. That's where I live. You want the money, I'll keep paying. Courtney can schedule the visitation. But if you need someone, find me. 2345 Elmont."

I step away from her and head back to Rachel, knowing I will never need Melanie.

I pull into the parking lot of Tom's garage, ease my car next to Rachel's and cut the engine. Rachel granted me silence and for that I'm grateful. I would have thought spending eleven years without my mother would make me immune to her, but it doesn't. It just makes old hurts ache more.

As if sensing the blood oozing from my internal wounds, Rachel places her hand over mine. "Are you okay?"

No. "My mother went to prison when I was six. She was released two years ago and for some reason, she wants back in my life."

I can't look at Rachel, so I stare out the driver's-side window. New gang graffiti painted in red marks the warehouse across the street. An old man wearing a knitted cap, Tom's old overalls and pink mittens pushes a shopping cart loaded down with blankets and clothes. Rachel doesn't belong here, and she shouldn't be with me.

Her hand squeezes mine. "I'm sorry."

"I loved her." And everything inside of me burns in pain. Terrified I'll hurt Rachel, I remove my hand from hers and grip the steering wheel. My hold so tight I'm convinced the leather will buckle. "I defended her for years because I always thought she'd come back for me."

I close my eyes and try to erase the unwanted memories of the group home: how the boys would taunt me over my size and my faith in my mother; the crushing blow to my face and soul when the oldest broke my nose while yelling at me that I was no different from any of them, that I was there because she was never coming back. By the time I left the home, I no longer believed in my mother or love.

"Everything I've known has always been twisted," I say. "I don't want to twist you. I don't want you to slip into my world and leave everything that's good about you behind."

"Isaiah, look at me."

I do. If only because there's a power in her voice I haven't heard since she told me to back off her car the first night we met. "The only way you'd twist me is if you left. You're a great guy, and someday, I'm going to make you see it."

Rachel has hit too close, and I lean away and flip the keys in my hand. "Do you need to go home before the races tonight?"

She fiddles with the cuff of her coat, not meeting my eyes. It bothers me that I hurt her by pulling away.

"No. Dad's traveling. Mom's with the foundation, and

West and Ethan have plans, but they said they'd cover for me if I wanted to drive tonight."

"We'll celebrate tonight when we win." I force the cheer, hoping it'll bring that spark back in her eye. "I'll take you someplace special." Someplace I've never invited a girl before.

She scrunches her face. "You're always sure of yourself."

"Yeah, I am. When I say I'm going to do something I do it." My word is the only thing I truly own.

"So...where's your special place?"

"Patience," I tell her as I open the door. "You need some patience."

Rachel

WE WON AGAIN TONIGHT, MORE than we lost, and because of that, Isaiah is taking me to his special place to celebrate. Logan and Isaiah didn't win as much as the weekend before, but Isaiah promised we'd have enough time to make the money needed to pay off the debt.

The debt. Eric. A shudder runs along my spine and I repress any thought of my nightmares.

It's been a long day: skipping, Isaiah meeting his mom, spending the evening at the dragway and now this. According to Isaiah's radio, it's 12:01 which means today is Saturday. I'm pressing my luck being gone so late, but Ethan said he'd cover for me, so he will.

I watch in the side mirror as Isaiah heaves an aging wooden barricade back over the abandoned road. The forest is thick around us, and I can only see a few feet into the black night. Goose bumps form on my arms, and I run my hands along them in order to ease the chill the shadows create.

The interior light springs on when Isaiah slips back into the car then fades just as quickly as he shuts the door.

"You okay?" he asks.

I nod, but wonder if he misses it in the darkness. Fear of the unknown pushes me to a make-believe edge in my mind and I have to breathe in deeply several times to keep from falling off the ledge. Each time I inhale, Isaiah's scent fills my nose and I'm reminded that whatever happens, wherever he's taking me, I'm safe.

Isaiah would never let anything happen to me.

The engine growls as Isaiah presses on the gas. It's an upward path, curving continually higher. Through sporadic breaks in the trees, I can spot lights below us, and because of Isaiah's speed, they appear like fireflies dancing in the night.

It's only then when I realize where we are and what we're doing. "This is Lovers' Leap."

Isaiah's only answer is the minuscule tilt of his lips. I sit up and my hands press against the dashboard of the car as I try to catch a glimpse of the rocky cliff that has become urban legend from the front windshield. I've seen this place safely on the ground as I've passed it by on the freeway. My eyes, like everyone else's, driven to the sky to ogle the place where people years ago drove off a cliff in a drag race and died.

There's just something magnetic and curious about the morbid.

But as Isaiah races around the bends of the road, I lose the sense of somber and replace it with curiosity. "Is it scary?"

"No."

The fir trees and climbing oaks grow so close together and near the road they appear to smother each other until a clearing appears. Isaiah shifts down and eases to a stop. With a flick of his wrist, he turns off the ignition and has the keys in his hands. "Come on."

Isaiah's out of the car and around the front to my side before I can slide from the seat. In a slick movement, he closes my door, links our hands together and nudges me ahead. I glance over my shoulder at the thick forest behind me and shiver at what lies in wait there, but Isaiah has no interest in what we've already seen. His eyes and body are pointed forward.

"What do you think?" he asks.

My breath catches in my throat when I see the splendor panning before me. Thousands of tiny lights twinkle all around the ground below and in the middle of the panoramic view the skyscrapers of Louisville soar into the air. "It's gorgeous."

"Yeah." But he's not looking at the view, but at me. I bite my lip and look away.

"So, am I the really the first one you've brought here?"

"Abby's been here, but I didn't bring her. She follows." Isaiah lets go of my hand and jumps onto the only thing separating the two of us from a drop of death—a crumbling stone wall.

My heart smashes past my rib cage. "Be careful!"

"It's safe." Isaiah holds his hand out to me. "I won't let you fall."

My eyes drift to the dark hole on the other side of the wall. From the ground, the drop looked staggering, but Isaiah said he wouldn't let me fall and from the sincerity leaking from his face, he means it more than he means anything else.

As if in a tunnel, I outstretch my arm, and just as my fingers hover over his, my cell pings. Isaiah's eyebrows draw together and my blood flow halts. We both know it has to be Ethan.

Isaiah jumps down and I pull the cell out of my pocket. With one touch, the phone lights up.

Ethan: you need to come home.

My pulse quickens. Have I been busted? why?

Isaiah shifts beside me, but remains patient. He knows my twin typically leaves me alone and that a text from him can mean problems. The seconds stretch into an eternity: come home

Me: what's the problem?

Ethan: I think you're lying to me. I don't think you're driving.

The entire world sways to the right, then to the left, before refocusing. What does Ethan know? From behind me, Isaiah wraps his arms around my waist, engulfing me in the warmth and strength of his body. "What's wrong, angel?"

"I don't know."

Me: you're paranoid

Ethan: r u with the guy you skipped school with?

Adrenaline shoots down my arms and into my fingers as I break out of Isaiah's embrace and press buttons on the phone.

"Rachel?" Isaiah's eyes become storm clouds as he watches me raise my cell to my ear. "What's wrong?"

"I don't know." I glance at the beautiful skyline. Isaiah brought me here to celebrate his and Logan's wins tonight at the dragway and to celebrate his passing of the ASE. This glorious overlook is Isaiah's special place, a place he's never brought anyone else. This moment was huge and Ethan is ruining it.

Ethan answers on the first ring. "Come home, Rachel."

Fire rages inside of me as the voice sinks in. It's not Ethan— it's West. "Give the phone to Ethan."

"No," says West. "You two have that screwed-up twin thing, and he'll cover for you."

Yes, he will. "This is between me and Ethan. Not me and you. He covers for me. I cover for him. And in case you never noticed, both of us have been covering for you for years."

I hear shifting, a button hit wrong on the phone, then static. "Rachel," says Ethan. My head drops. They put me on speaker. "Come home."

"We had a deal!" I kick at a rock and it skips into the brush. "Twin amnesty, remember? How can you sell me out?"

"We had amnesty when I thought you were going for a drive." There's an unfamiliar edge to Ethan's voice. The same tone Dad used on West when West was caught fighting at school. "Guess what we just heard about at a party? Something about you skipping school with some punk in a black Mustang. I told them they were crazy and then they showed me the damned picture on their cell phone. I'm going to say this one more time. Get home, Rachel, and get home now."

I could crush brick with the amount of anger seething in me. "Both of you are such hypocrites!"

"Don't want to hear it," says Ethan. "It's like we don't even know who you are anymore. Running around with some punk, ditching school, lying to us about the panic attacks...."

Something cracks inside of me. A dam I had created over the years to hold in every emotion unwanted by my family. "You want me to lie about the panic attacks, remember? Anything to keep Mom happy!"

On their side, the phone rattles as if someone grabbed it. West lets loose a string of profanities. "Rachel!" he shouts. "Here's the truth, *baby sister,* you need someone to take care of you. You always have. It's our job to keep you from making bad decisions and the one you're making right now is colossal. Your track record proves you need Ethan and me making these decisions for you."

I end the call, throw the phone across the crumbled blacktop and shriek at the top of my lungs. West's words roll in my mind. *You need someone to take care of you. You always have.*

"It's not true!" I yell out into the night. "It's not." Tears burn my eyes.

The warm touch first slides against my hip, followed by a brush on my cheek. My bones become weary, almost too heavy for my skin. Isaiah heard the conversation. He heard me admit my weakness. I said out loud, in front of him, that I suffer from panic attacks.

"Are you in trouble at home?" The urgency in his tone is clear.

I nod, then shake my head. "With my brothers."

"Are they going to rat?"

I tremble at the malice in his tone. "I don't think so. Somebody saw me skip with you. This is bad. So bad. Without them covering for me, I can't make it out. And if I can't make it out then you can't drive my car."

And I can't see you.

It's like I've been sucked into a tornado and I'm a rag doll being torn apart. My thoughts all twist and my body begins to feel cold and warm all at the same time. "And if you can't drive my car then you can't race and we can't make money if you don't race and then there's Eric—"

"It's okay." Isaiah cups my head and guides me into his

chest. His lips graze my forehead as he whispers, "It's okay. Calm down. It's okay. I promise."

I don't know what to say, and as hard as I try to keep from crying, more tears fill my eyes. I suck in air and each inhale shakes. I sniff and I sniff, but none of my efforts keeps the chaos on the inside from trying to break free to the outside. "I don't know how to make my family like you."

"I don't care if they like me. I only care about you." Isaiah soothingly rubs my spine and hair.

A winter wind blows, freezing my cheeks, but a single traitorous hot tear escapes from my eyes and I hold tighter to Isaiah, terrified of becoming unglued. "But they cover for me. This is how I see you! What if I can't see you?"

"We'll make it work." His words are all low-pitched, all gentle, but the twirling tornado inside of me picks up speed, becomes a monster all its own.

"It won't work." The strangled words emerge between a sob, and I hold my breath to keep any more from bursting free. I can feel my brain tearing away from my sane mind, the sadness and anger spiraling into panicked hysteria. "I don't want to be without you. I like who I am with you, and I don't want to go back to who I was before."

"I love you, Rachel. So this will work. No matter what or who stands in our way."

My body rocks as if Isaiah used a defibrillator on my chest. He loves me.

His words gain traction in my head...he loves me. My heart patters faster and faster. Not because of anxiety but because of hope. Gathering air into my lungs, I rest my head against his shirt, which is wet with my tears. His heart has a slow, steady beat. One that never panics. One that is always strong. "You love me?"

Isaiah

I BUNCH RACHEL'S HAIR IN my fist. The silky strands rub the spot between my fingers and I press my lips to her head. My heart hurts and soars and hurts again, all at the same time. I said I love her. Love her. Each repeat of the words confirms something I didn't know or want to know and I scramble to figure out if I want to embrace it.

Love her.

Rachel.

Love has always been a dirty word. My mother said she did what she did because she loved me. Beth took the words I said to her and twisted them into saying it was only friend-ship. She broke my heart. My mother broke my heart. If I love Rachel she'll have more power than both of them combined because this overwhelming pulse in my body...this over-whelming need to protect her and hold her close...

I nuzzle into her hair and close my eyes, inhaling the sweet scent of jasmine. I should let her go, let her go, just let her go. Walk away now. Hang on to what's left of my sanity.

But as Rachel presses tighter to me, I know I'm too far

gone to stand a chance alone. I'm in love, fucking in love, and I pray to the God that abandoned me years ago that He doesn't use this to destroy me. "I love you."

Rachel

ISAIAH TRAPS ME CLOSE TO his body and I press against his arms as I try to raise my head off his chest. He said he loved me. Me. The shy girl. The awkward girl. The one born to re-place the girl everyone really wanted. The more I think about it, the harder I press back against his hold. This doesn't make sense. Any sense. Why would he want to love me?

"Isaiah," I whisper and push again. When he doesn't react, I place both of my hands against his chest. "Isaiah!"

His arms give and I meet his eyes. "I know you heard what I said."

He searches my face. "What?"

"The panic attacks." I grab on to his forearms. "I have panic attacks. Often. You say you love me, but can you? Not when you don't see me for who I am!"

"See you for who you are?" His forehead wrinkles. "I see exactly who you are."

I'm shaking my head. "You don't. It's a fake. A mirage. What you think you see is a lie!"

"Rachel..." Isaiah's chest rises as he inhales. "Come on."

Taking my hand, he grabs a frayed blanket out of the backseat of his car and walks over to an area where the deteriorating wall ends and the ground slopes into nothing. A few feet away from the edge, he releases me, spreads out the blanket and sits with his bent legs spread apart.

I wipe my still-moist eyes and brush my bangs away, a bit unsure what to do.

"Sit with me," Isaiah says. As I move to rest next to him, he stops me. "Not there. Here." He motions to the spot between his legs.

Awkwardly, I settle in front of him. Isaiah, the king of secure, waves off any distance between us as he gathers me into the safe shelter of his body. The blood pulses faster in my veins. I like being this close to him. Maybe a little too much.

"You're beautiful." His breath tickles the skin behind my ear, and the small hairs stand on end with the joyous sensation. "You're smart and funny. I love how your eyes shine when you laugh."

He glides his fingers against my skin causing an addictive tingling. "I love how you lace your fingers and brush your hair from your face when you're nervous. I love how you offer yourself so completely to me—no fear. You're loyal and strong."

"I'm not strong." I cut him off. The panic attacks confirm that. Unable to be near him anymore, I attempt to untangle myself from him, but Isaiah becomes a solid wall around me and I jerk in his arms in protest.

His tender hold tightens, and the words feel like poetry because of the deep, soothing way he speaks. "You're wrong. I see you exactly as you are."

The anger loses its stronghold as his lips tease the sensitive curve of my ear. I swallow, thinking about the night in his room. Of how his body felt heavy over mine and how I loved feeling smaller under his touch. "You're just repeating what I said to you."

"What's that?" he says in a breath that was barely words.

I shiver with pleasure. My thoughts become fragments, and I struggle to retain composure. "I told you that you don't see yourself as you really are. You're manipulating my words." Words not meant for me.

He tucks his head next to mine. The rough stubble on his jaw seductively scratches my cheek, heightening my senses. I don't want this feeling to go away: being completely immersed in Isaiah's strength, his body, his love.

"When I'm with you, even my past seems like a bad dream," he says. "I've sat on this hill a hundred times, and all I used to see were lights that represented places where I wasn't wanted, where I never belonged. Now, when you aren't with me, I look east and know that one of those lights represents you, and I don't feel alone anymore."

I stare out onto the east side of town. The sparkling lights in that area are more spread out than on the south side. "Where is your light, Isaiah?"

Isaiah shifts as his hand goes into his pocket and extracts a lighter. In one smooth motion, he flicks the wheel against the flint and a single flame bursts into the darkness. The small wild flame licks against the night and fights to stay alive as the wind blows over the top of the hill. Like a moth, my hand slides over the flame—craving the warmth, daring to be burned.

Maybe this is what happens when you fall in love. On the outside a lighter is nothing amazing, but it holds all the ingredients that can create something wonderful. With a few pushes in the right direction, you can inspire something so brilliant that it pushes back the darkness.

As Isaiah holds the light close enough to warm me, but far enough away to keep me safe, I wonder if this is the reason why I've always been drawn to a flame. I've been hoping to be burned. I've been hoping to be loved.

I turn my head toward Isaiah. His silver eyes glow as he stares at me with the same intensity as the first night in his apartment. That night, his gaze frightened me. Tonight, I know that it means love.

"You're the first person to ever see me," whispers Isaiah as he releases the lighter. He flips the top back on and in a swift motion he presses the still-warm metal into my hand. "I want you to keep it."

My mouth drops open. He's protective of that lighter. I've seen how he holds it, how he looks at it, and now understanding what it means, it would be like me giving him my car. "Isaiah..."

"I want to know I'm with you. It's all I've got to give, so please, take it."

I touch the double row of silver hoop earrings hanging from his left ear, trail along his jawline, his neck, down his shoulder, to the flaming tail of the dragon on his arm. He leans into the caress, and my own body feels on fire with the continued way his eyes gaze upon me. The first moment I saw him, the night people clamored over each other to step out of his way, I was frightened. The guy with earrings and tattoos and an energy radiating danger. Now—inside and out—all I see is beauty.

"Isaiah...I love you, too."

Isaiah

A NORTHERN GUST HEAVY WITH moisture sweeps across the hill, and Rachel shivers. Cold water droplets hit my bare skin. There's a chance we could lose our mild winter tonight to snow.

I stand, snatch the blanket off the ground and love how Rachel automatically accepts my offered hand as I guide her to my car. She hesitates as I open the passenger-side door. "I don't want to go home yet."

There's innocence in her eyes, an innocence I lost years ago, so I know there's no underlying meaning in her statement. I move the seat and Rachel slides into the back. Freezing rain pelts like bullets as I follow. I shut the door and rain patters against the car.

"Did you get wet?" I ask her.

Rachel shakes her head as she grabs for the blanket. I lean into the front, turn the engine over, crank the heat and click on the parking lights to illuminate the console. I slip back beside Rachel and wonder how the two of us ended up like this. "I've never had a girl in the backseat of my car."

The wrinkles in her forehead scream disbelief. "I'm not stupid, Isaiah. I know I'm not your first kiss or...you know."

No, she's not. "Sounds awful, but I respected my car too much to bring girls..." I'm right. It does sound awful.

Rachel grows quiet. The rain drives harder against the windshield and even with the heater running, the temperature plummets. "Honestly, do you not want me in your car?"

"Rachel, you're the only girl I've wanted in this car."

Her body trembles as if she's having a seizure. "Ar-re y-you s-sure?"

I wedge my hands beneath her legs and lift her onto my lap. Rachel relaxes her head into the crook of my neck as I bundle us in the blanket. "Never been more sure of anything."

Resting my cheek against her, I inhale her sweet scent. "You remind me of the ocean."

"It's my perfume." I hear the smile in her voice. Her hand peeks out of the blanket and I knot my fingers with hers.

"My mom took me to the ocean once," I tell her. "I think her parents lived in Florida, and she went there for help."

I don't remember much other than the visit was short, there was a lot of yelling, and the wallpaper in the entryway curled near the floorboards. "We left and spent the day at the ocean before we drove back to Kentucky."

Rachel squeezes my fingers. I like that she doesn't feel the need to make me better with words when I tell her something from my past. She understands that all I need is the strength in her touch. "I've always wondered if Mom's parents didn't welcome her because of me. They refused to take me in when my mom went to prison."

"What did your mom go to jail for?"

Noah and Beth were the only people I'd told about where my mom was, and I never discussed the why. "Armed robbery." Plus child endangerment.

Her thumb moves against my wrist as a silent acknowledgment of how much it cost me to tell her the truth and that she's done asking questions. I kiss her forehead, a thank-you for not pushing me to places I can't visit.

Rachel shifts forward on my lap, unbuttons her coat and slides it off. "Little warm."

I take the lighter she still grasps in her hand and place it in the cup holder. When I go to move the blanket she stops me by cuddling back into my body. "I chose the blanket over my coat."

Tonight has been a constant give-and-take between us, and I'd like her to give a little more. "Do you see a therapist about your panic attacks?"

When I'm greeted with the sound of the rain tapping the top of the car, I switch tactics. "Noah's girlfriend, Echo— she's had some issues and she sees someone. It helps her."

"I used to. In middle school and a little in my freshman year, but then I stopped." Rachel's pause highlights her struggle for words. "My mom worried. Constantly. It wasn't normal. She wouldn't let me out of her sight. My older brothers said that she was just as manic as when Colleen had cancer. And then I had several panic attacks in high school."

Her breath catches as if the memory causes her physical pain.

"I had a couple of harsh attacks in a short period of time and ended up in the hospital. I...I..." It's as if the words are programmed not to leave her body. "I hated it. I hated how Mom hovered. I hated how my oldest two brothers would compare me to Colleen. I hated how West and Ethan would look at me as if I was dying.

"So...when I got out of the hospital...I found a way to hide the attacks...the anxiety...and eventually my family believed I defeated the panic and for the first time in my life they didn't see me as weak."

Weak. I hate the word, especially from her. "If you still suffer from this, you should get help. Screw your family."

"There's no way for me to get help without them knowing. Isaiah, I can't..."

"I see you, you see me, remember? You're going to have to trust me on this. If you have these attacks then we'll fix them. I only care about you. Not your family."

"You are bossy."

"Protective," I counter, and run my hand along the length of her leg.

Rachel lets out a contented sigh. "I wish we could be like this forever."

"We will be." I break a cardinal rule and dream of the future. Rachel is a future kind of girl, and I'm going to have to work hard to give her a world worth living in. "With this certification and internship, I'll have the best jobs. I can't give you the world, Rachel, but I'll give you all I got."

Her soft lips kiss my jaw and my body temperature spikes. Holding on to Rachel is like holding on to a flame. It's a soothing burn and an addictive burn. Her kiss is pure fire.

"Being with you is enough." She adjusts so that she can

look at me, and I love how the spark has returned to her eyes. "We could open our own shop."

I curl her silky hair around my finger and tug lightly. "You and me alone in the garage with you bent over the hood of a powerful engine. I think I can handle that."

She blushes at my words, but keeps the banter alive. "We'll only take fast cars or clients who want faster cars. The faster the better."

I like how she thinks. "If you're touching cars in our shop, then you'll have to get your certification."

"Will you tutor me?"

I shouldn't, but I can't resist. Cradling her face in my hands, I brush my lips against hers. "I'll teach you everything you need to know."

She rests her forehead on mine. My hand stays against her cheek, and my thumb glides over her soft skin. Rachel's chest moves faster, almost matching my pace. Energy rushes into my veins and the heat between us teeters on the edge of flames.

"My brothers are going to try to keep us apart," she whispers, then presses her mouth against my bottom lip. My grip on her waist tightens in response. "What are we going to do?"

I don't know, but the way she curls in my arms makes me feel like I'm the hero. I like being her hero. I like the way her eyes shine at me, the way her body melts when I touch her, her soft lips on mine. I love her warmth and every curve.

I love her.

My fingers draw up her back and tangle into her hair. "They'll never separate us."

"Never," she repeats.

Our lips crush together, our bodies pressed tight. An inferno of lips and hands and movements that continues to grow in heat. The blanket falls away as Rachel slides her legs so that she straddles me. On the verge of burning up completely, I groan and cling to her small frame. Her hands drift under my shirt, leaving a singeing trail.

We've become a wildfire. Almost unstoppable. I kiss her neck and the beautiful sounds escaping her mouth encourage me further. My hands skim under her shirt, up her back, linger for seconds near her bra, and I gently nip her ear when I feel lace.

Images pour into my mind of what she'd look like with her shirt off, then her jeans. My fist traps strands of her hair. "I want you, Rachel."

And because I do, I kiss her fully on the mouth—nothing left to the imagination. Every fantasy becomes a reality with that one embrace. Then, summoning more willpower than I possess, I end the kiss, cupping her head to my chest.

We both breathe hard. Blood pulses in my temples, throughout my entire body. Need screams for me to bring her back into my arms. But I love Rachel, and the physical between us has to go slow.

"Can we stay here?" Rachel asks. "For a little longer?"

We can stay here for life. "Yes."

Rachel

MY BROTHERS FOLLOW ME TO class. Every class. I ditch one brother when class starts and pick up another when class ends. I tried losing them at lunch by seeking refuge in the library, but one or both still trailed behind me. I'm furious with my unwanted bodyguards.

The bell rings. The collective sigh of it's-Friday relief from the English class visiting the library is tangible. Books snap shut and zippers on backpacks close into place. I shelve the remaining books, grab my stuff and head into the hallway. My skin feels as if it's going to peel off my bones. I haven't seen Isaiah since Saturday and I miss him—desperately.

Against the wall of lockers, Ethan waits with his hands stuffed in the pockets of his dress khakis. "You've never gone this long without talking to me."

For the first time in a week, Ethan and I look at each other without glaring. I attempt to ignore the hurt swimming in his dark eyes, but I can't. Ethan is my twin—my best friend. "You started this."

"Tell me you aren't seeing the punk and it'll end."

My grip tightens on my pack. "He is not a punk."

"West and I are trying to protect you. That's all." Ethan reaches out as if he's going to take my hand, a reaction to his hurt and mine. A comforting touch we've shared since toddlerhood. "We saw the picture. Tattoos. Earrings. The guy looks like a damn serial killer."

"He's not."

Ethan's arm falls to his side. My hand twitches, not used to feeling empty.

I step toward him, pleading. "I know he looks tough, but he's an amazing guy on the inside. If you and West would try to get to know him..."

"Then bring him home to meet Mom and Dad. To meet us."

"I can't." I shift from my left to right foot. "Not yet."

Because if Mom and Dad discover I'm dating Isaiah they'll become grime caked on an axle, and I'll never be allowed out of the house. Isaiah and I agreed that we need to pay off Eric before we drop the dating bomb on my parents.

Ethan and West want me to dump Isaiah, and they'd prefer for me to do it without anyone, meaning my parents and our older brothers, finding out that he existed. I'm gambling that their need to protect Mom and Dad, coupled with the fact that Gavin and Jack will kick their asses for letting me get close to a guy, will keep them from ratting me out. So far, I've been right. This weekend, I may have to be home by ten, since Ethan won't cover for me anymore, but at least I can make it to the races.

Ethan pushes off the lockers. "You won't introduce him to Mom and Dad because he's bad news and you know it."

I roll my eyes and walk alongside Ethan. My heart aches. I miss my best friend. I miss not being able to tell him everything in my life. He can blame Isaiah for our strained relationship, but that's not the case. Our relationship started to deteriorate years ago when I began to lie about the attacks.

My head tilts when the words he said to West in the locker room last week haunt me. "You told West that you knew that I'd been lying about my panic attacks."

Ethan dips his head, as if he's counting the floor tiles. "I know you better than anyone else. At least I thought I did. I know when you're in pain. I know when you hurt."

Neither one of us say anything as we pass a group of seniors cutting up. Both of us scan the crowd for West. In the middle, dark blue eyes that mirror mine peer at me. West's smile falters, but he's quick to hide the concern. My chest hurts. Both of them love me.

"If the two of you suspected, then why didn't you say anything?"

"Because..." He takes a deep breath. "Because we're selfish assholes who wanted Mom for a few seconds. She was always so obsessed with you and your attacks that we got nothing. When you claimed to be better, she was still up your butt, but at least we got something."

"I never asked for this," I say as we go down the stairs. "Any of it. For the panic attacks. To be Colleen's replacement."

"I know," he says. "And to be honest, that's why West and I pity you instead of hate you."

How on earth has my family become so dysfunctional? We walk outside, and Ethan places a hand on my shoulder to stop me. My stomach cramps as if I've been sucker punched when he immediately removes his arm. We're so distant we can't even touch.

"Talk to us—me and West. Tell us the whole truth about the attacks. We'll find a way to make everything work between you and Mom and the speeches. And dump the punk. It's not like you're going to see him anyway. I won't cover you anymore, and if I don't cover you, Mom will start asking questions about where you're going. There's no way you'll be able to think of a good enough excuse as to why you suddenly have a life."

Ethan is right, and I start to wonder how I'll make it to the dragway without his help. If I tell Ethan the truth about Eric, he'll go ballistic and he'll possibly snitch on me to my parents. Movement near where I parked my car causes me to shift so I can look past my brother.

Holy hell. I brush past Ethan and try to think of something coherent to say other than, "What are you doing here, Abby?"

In a white button-down shirt remarkably like mine, and a blue-and-green plaid uniform skirt, Abby leans against my car. "Do you like it? Isaiah and I skipped this afternoon and went to Goodwill. Don't you think it's ironic that Goodwill has clothes for a private school? If you have money to go to a private school, you probably wouldn't shop at Goodwill."

My mouth pops open with a million questions, but before I can ask any of them, Ethan appears by my side. "Who are you?"

"Abby," she says. "And you are?"

"Ethan," I answer. "He's my twin."

Her eyes dart between us. "You don't look anything alike."

"I'm a boy. She's a girl. I sure as hell hope we don't," says Ethan.

Abby flashes a daring smile. "I like you."

Ethan ignores her statement. "How do you know Rachel?"

"We're friends," she answers. "I go to that other rich school."

My eyes widen as I understand. Blue-and-green uniform. Abby's faking that she belongs in my world by pretending she goes to a school that is acceptable to my family. "Mason Academy."

"Yeah," she says. "That one. I'm new to town and met Rachel at the mall."

I clear my throat as Ethan automatically doesn't buy anything that involves me and malls.

"Parking lot," adds Abby. "Mall parking lot. I had a flat. She helped. It was all serendipitous. I like bunnies. She likes bunnies. We totally clicked."

Ethan's eyebrows furrow together as he assesses me. "You like bunnies?"

"My brother dropped me off," Abby continues, "because our school gets out before your school and you promised we could do girl stuff at your house."

"Abby," I interrupt before she says anything else. "Let's go."

"I'll meet you at home, Rach." Ethan continues to eye Abby.

With Ethan safely in his car behind us and Abby in the passenger side, I let the questions flow. "What are you doing? How did you get here? What is going on?"

"Did you snort crack? Don't answer. Isaiah said you lost your way out of the house past curfew. We bought these clothes, he dropped me off here, and ta-da...I'm your new best friend—private school–going, new in town, rich Abby."

I glance in my rearview mirror. Ethan is hot on my tail. "I don't get it. How is this supposed to help?"

"Introduce me to your parents tonight and then I'll invite you for a sleepover tomorrow."

My entire body feels lighter. Isaiah thinks of everything. "Serendipitous?"

"Do you like it?" She waggles her eyebrows. "I learned it for today."

Isaiah

LOGAN HOVERS OVER THE ENGINE as I slide myself underneath. I'm changing the oil in my car, again. The engine's been acting funny, and my gut tells me she's close to overheating. The continued drag racing is aging my baby.

"I'm not feeling the cash flow tonight," says Logan.

"Me, either." The types of people we race do it for shits and giggles. Side bets are for those who feel cocky. Logan and I have kicked ass for two weekends straight. Tonight, we'll have plenty of people who will race against us for bragging rights, but few will put up money.

"Explain bracket racing," he says.

My hands hesitate as I work. Bracket racing. The thought has circled in my head. "They do it on Sundays. If you think you can hit an eighth mile in 10 seconds then you race against other cars that can do the same. Same rules apply at the line. You can't go before the green, but they will give you a handicap. If the competition is a second faster than you, then you'll get to leave a second faster. Whoever crosses the line first without breaking the green wins."

"Sounds fair enough," says Logan.

I roll out from underneath my car. "But if you say you can hit an eighth in 10 seconds and you take the finish line at 9.9 seconds, then you lose. You have to stay above 10 seconds."

"What?"

"You pick your target, man. It's like a game show. You pick the number you think you can take the finish line in without going over. If you go over that number, you lose."

Logan scratches the back of his head. "That means we have to have an insane reaction time at the line and watch that we don't go too fast, but fast enough to beat whoever we're against all in a matter of seconds."

I nod.

"And the world got complicated."

"Always does."

"What's the draw?" says Logan.

"There's a pot for the first three finishers. The pot for a street car like mine isn't worth the investment, but if we add a nitro system, then we could compete in a class where the money may be worth it."

Logan gets that crazy glint in his eye anytime we discuss something that involves the cars going faster. "Then we should add a nitro system. I can't think of anything holding you back."

Both of us turn our heads to the sweet sound of Rachel's Mustang pulling in. Sitting on the rolling board, I rest my arms on my bent knees and watch as my angel glides into the garage.

Logan glances at her then me. "Think I discovered your issue."

"Yeah." Nitro can be dangerous, and I don't want the system in her car.

In the used designer jeans and soft blue sweater we bought at the Goodwill, Abby looks like a completely different person.

"Her brothers are hot. Annoying, but hot," announces Abby. "Just saying."

I stand, and Rachel weaves her arms around my neck. I kiss her lips. "Hey, angel."

"Hi." Red touches her cheeks. Either because she hasn't seen me in a week or because she's staying the night with me.

"You look nice," says Logan. Rachel and I turn to see Logan checking Abby out.

"Did I mention her brothers aren't nearly as hot as you?" Abby flashes a sexy grin. She doesn't release that smile often and flags shoot straight into the air.

I roll my eyes. Logan and Abby hooking up is not a good idea. She destroys guys and...I like Logan. "Logan, I forgot my seed money. Wanna come back with me to pick it up?"

"Sure."

I kiss Rachel's lips again. "Be back in a sec."

Rachel

FIDDLING WITH A WRENCH, I listen to Abby gush about my family. How insanely nice my parents are and how crazy it is that all of my brothers are good-looking. I'll admit, I'm blessed. I have so much more than others, and on the outside my family is absolutely perfect.

"Hello, Rachel."

My head snaps up and Abby falls silent. My heart drums, and a cold sweat breaks out over my body, onto my palms. I swipe my hands against my jeans the moment I see the face that haunts my nightmares. "Eric."

He strides into the garage as if he owns the place. His green army jacket engulfs his bony body. "Making new friends, Abby?"

Abby straightens beside me, and gone is the girl that I've come to know over the past couple of weeks. All emotion drains from her face and leaves a hardness that frightens me. "This isn't your block, Eric. It belongs to me."

"No, it belongs to the person you pay off to keep you and your family safe." Eric makes a show of glancing over both of his shoulders before leaning into Abby. His nose nearly touches hers. "And I don't see him here."

She doesn't flinch. A creepy smile eases onto her face as she tosses her hair so she can stare him straight in the eye. "One phone call, Eric, and it'll be raining fire and brimstone."

If I didn't know better, I would have thought fear flashed in his eyes. "You'd let Isaiah be caught in the crosshairs? I don't think so." Eric switches his sights to me. "How's it going with my money?"

"Fine." I rub my arms. The skin crawls as he invades my personal space. He's so close that I smell his breath.

"Word on the street is that you might make deadline," he breathes out as his eyes linger near my chest.

I cross my arms, trying to hide what he's focusing on. Adrenaline begins to leak into my bloodstream, and I silently pray for Isaiah to stride back into the door. Isaiah can fix this. He knows how to make me feel safe.

"Don't let him get to you," Abby says. "He's like those damn annoying dogs always starved for attention and begging for scraps at the table. It's best to pretend he doesn't exist."

"Watch your mouth," he mutters.

"You're pathetic and transparent. Isaiah won't fall for your intimidation shit, which is why I'm guessing you're here."

Eric tears his eyes away from Abby and this time stares at my lips. "How close are you really to paying me off? We could make a deal. You do something for me and I'll provide a discount for you."

Abby appears at my side. "Step back, Eric."

He smirks. "Or what, Abby? You gonna jack up the prices on the drugs you sell? I'm aware of the service charge reserved only for me. You need to start rethinking your business practices."

My head jerks and Abby falters. Our eyes meet and her calm, cold facade cracks.

Eric laughs. "She didn't know that you're a drug dealer, did she?"

When Abby says nothing, Eric inches closer. I inch to the side, but Eric follows. Without thinking, I trapped myself against a wall. I don't like how Eric looks at me. The panic begins to claw at my chest and I swallow. I need to stay in control.

"Did you know that Isaiah is an addict? Uses like the rest of us street rats." His eyes wander up, then down. "What kind of currency are you paying Isaiah to take on this debt? Not cash, I'm guessing."

Eric raises his hand and all the air squeezes out of my lungs. I gasp right as he moves to touch my skin. He can't touch me. I won't let him. My hands thrust out and I push at his chest.

Anger explodes in his dark, soulless eyes. He grabs my wrist, slamming it over my head into the concrete wall. I scream.

Abby screams.

And with my free hand I'm hitting and kicking and so is Abby and suddenly...

He's gone.

The world spins, and I can't find my bearings. There's more yelling and more voices. Gravity overtakes me as I can't inhale. Abby appears in front of me—dark eyes and hair. "Rachel!"

Abby is free of Eric. We both are. I grab her, still struggling for air, and drag both of us as I stumble into the office. I need to make sure we're safe—me and Abby. She's my friend and I can't leave her behind.

She says things, things I don't understand, and she strokes my hair while she talks. I can't breathe. I can't.

She disappears and in her place are gray storm clouds. "Breathe, angel. Come on."

Isaiah. I wrap my arms around him, and he holds me—tightly. I listen to his heart: the steady beat, the steady pace, and within a few seconds I start to match his breathing. I inhale deeply one more time. "Isaiah."

He cups my face and forces me to meet his eyes. "Are you okay?"

I nod. "Eric?"

"Is gone," says Logan from the doorway of the office.

Isaiah helps me walk back into the garage. Logan's right. It's only the four of us. With her shoulders hunched, Abby stands beside Logan. She lifts her head only to share a wary glance with him, then Isaiah, but not me.

"What's wrong?" I ask. Because I can feel it. A heaviness that wasn't here before.

Isaiah swears under his breath. "I'm sorry."

I hate the prickling in my stomach, a sensation foretelling doom. "For what?"

"I hit him. Eric. I came in and saw the two of you fighting him off, and I hit him. Hard."

"Good." I mean it. If I could have socked him in the jaw and caused the bastard to bleed then I would have, but I'm not that strong.

"You don't hit Eric." Abby nudges her foot at the concrete. "Not without repercussions."

My stomach cramps. "Is he going to hurt you?" No, please no. My hands flutter near Isaiah's face, terrified of Eric hurting him. "I'll apologize. I'll...I'll..." I have no idea what to do.

Isaiah takes my hands. "He moved up the due date. We have to pay him in one week."

My head becomes light and I sway. Isaiah places his hands on my waist to steady me.

"It's unexpected," he says. "But not impossible. We're close to the total. Let's race tonight, count our winnings and see where we stand."

Okay. He's right. Plus Isaiah would never lie. "All right."

"Abby!" Logan calls out. "Where're you going?"

With her hands in her pockets, Abby walks away from the garage. Isaiah holds on when I move to go after her. "I'm okay," I tell him. "I need to talk to her."

Isaiah releases me, but keeps his arm near my elbow in case I drop. "Abby!"

She continues to walk away and I quicken my pace. "Abby!"

Abby stops on the sidewalk and doesn't turn around. I slow as I approach and think of Eric's words and Abby's description of her job. She's a drug dealer.

A drug dealer. My first real girlfriend is a drug dealer. My entire world feels upside down and sideways; yanked inside out then pulled back out again. With new eyes, I look at Abby. She's exactly the same as before: black hoodie, braver-than-I-could-ever-be jeans and long brown hair. She's a beautiful girl—a mystery to me, and bold, but what I've never seen is how seventeen she appears. How...young, like me.

She's what I should hate in the world, yet she's come to be someone I love.

"Thanks," I say.

She flips her hair over her shoulder. "For what?"

"For helping me with Eric."

"He's an asshole."

"Yes. He is." I hesitate. Eric called Isaiah an addict. He called her a drug dealer. Drug dealers are bad and Abby isn't. She's good. "Why?"

She shrugs, not even pretending she doesn't know what I mean. "I inherited a mess, and someday, I'm not going to do this anymore. But right now, there are problems with my family and I'm the only one who can fix them."

I understand inheriting a mess. My birthright is to make up for Colleen's death and as for family problems, I understand those, too. "Can you come with us tonight? It gets lonely sitting in the stands by myself."

Abby stares at me blankly, as if she never heard me speak. "I don't use the drugs. I swear to God I'm clean. And I never bring them around you."

"I believe you."

She narrows her eyes. "Why?"

Because she stands by me. Because I think she loves me like I love her. "Because we're friends."

Abby smiles. "I knew there was a reason I chose you to be my best friend."

Is it strange that that just made me incredibly happy? "Me, too."

Abby and I both take interest in anything else but each other. I think this whole friend thing is completely new to both of us. From the open bay of the garage, Isaiah watches us with his hands shoved in his pockets. Logan stands right behind him. They're a strange combo, but so are Abby and I.

There's so much I thought I understood, but that's not the truth. I avoid issues more than I try to understand. "Abby?" Deep breath. "Does Isaiah use drugs?"

She tucks her hair behind her ear again. "I think you should talk to him."

It's as if my soul became too heavy for my heart. That's a conversation I don't want to have.

Isaiah

RACHEL'S LIGHT FOOTFALLS CAUSE THE wooden stairs to groan. "Seven hundred dollars. If you asked me two weeks ago if we could make seven hundred dollars in one week, I would have said yes, but after tonight...I don't know."

As predicted, we found plenty of guys willing to race us, but not as many who were willing to place bets. I carry her overnight bag in one hand and hold her fingers with the other. "Logan and I knew that this could be a problem. But I think we can make seven hundred in the next week. It'll be tight, but it will happen."

She continues to stare at the floor as we walk to my apartment. "I could hock more of my jewelry, but Mom figured out I got rid of one of the pieces. I told her I lost it. I'm not sure if she'll continue to buy the excuse if I 'lose' any more."

I let go of her hand, unlock the door and push it open. She enters first, flipping on the light as she goes. I love how she feels comfortable here.

"It feels hopeless," she says. "Like we get two steps forward and take a trillion back."

I can't help but smile. Rachel does this sometimes—

wallows, but I don't mind. It never lasts long, and she's usually repentant when she's done.

"Do you trust me?" I ask as I close the door and lock the dead bolt.

Rachel blinks and the crimson on her cheeks tells me she snapped out of wallowing. "Yes."

"Then you know that when I say I'm going to fix something, I do. On my life, Rachel, Eric will be paid back in a week."

She fidgets with the ends of her hair. "I'm sorry. It's just that everything seems so big all the time and..."

And here comes the repentance. I wrap my arms around her waist. "I want you to forget about it. At least for tonight."

She bites her bottom lip and glances up from below heavy eyelashes. "Okay."

Nerves are written all over her face. I kiss the top of her head and give her the room she needs by going into the kitchen and cocking a hip against the counter. Rachel's never stayed the night with a girlfriend, much less a boyfriend.

She leans against the back of the couch. "If I ask you something, will you be honest?"

"Always."

"Did you know that Abby is a drug dealer?"

Damn, straight to the point. I pull at my bottom earring. Abby warned me at the dragway about this conversation. I had no idea Rachel would yank out the guns this early. "Yes."

"Why didn't you tell me?" She inspects her nails like this is casual for her, but I know better.

"Because it's Abby's story to tell, not mine. She promised

to keep her business away from you, and when Abby gives her word, she means it. If I thought you'd be in danger, I'd be in the middle of this."

She scoffs like I told a joke. "You can't get in the middle of anything."

I say nothing because I don't argue. Rachel's safety and happiness is my priority. "What you did for Abby tonight was nice." *Nice* is an understatement. For the first time since I've known Abby, someone gave her love.

"She's my friend," she says softly.

Rachel laces her hands together, unlaces and repeats. Something's digging at her and I want her inner thoughts. "What's bothering you?"

She lets her hands fall to her sides. "Zach offered to race against me. Since we need money, I should accept."

The guy is becoming a switchblade in my thigh. "Did he say something to you tonight?"

"Yes, but he first brought it up weeks ago..."

"I know." And I told him to stay clear of her. It's too coincidental, Eric showing at the garage this evening then Zach approaching her at the dragway tonight, and I don't believe in chance. Zach's trying to pull Rachel into a race, but I can't see the benefit of it. I can't see how that would help Eric win.

"I want to help." There's hurt in her eyes, and it dawns on me that there's more to her and Zach's conversations than cars.

"What's he saying to you?"

Rachel pauses as she chooses her words. She doesn't do that often and my gut twists. "Do you trust me?" she asks.

A combination of dread and anger pummels my insides

as the answer slams into my head. Zach is trying to create doubt. They're trying to place a wedge between us.

"I trust you." And she needs to trust me back. "I'll take care of the money, Rachel. All right?" I'm not asking permission, but I am asking her to drop it. "And stay away from Zach."

"Why? I know he can come on a little strong, but he really doesn't bother me."

My neck tightens as I contemplate telling Rachel my theory on Zach and Eric. But then I wonder if that would scare her. She already mentioned a few minutes ago how she feels overwhelmed by it all. "Can you just trust me?"

"Okay." She glances around the empty apartment, reminiscent of her first night here. "Do you mind if I take a shower? I smell like burnt rubber."

"Sure." If she does, then I must reek like I bathed in it. "I'll take one after."

The subflooring is cold beneath my feet, and after the heat from the misty bathroom my body shudders against the temperature of the apartment. I change to a fresh pair of jeans and walk into the dark bedroom for a shirt.

In a tank top and pair of cotton drawstring pants, Rachel sits in the middle of my bed with her knees drawn to her chest. Her hair is blown dry and angles around her face. Light from the street highlights her perfectly, casting a heavenly glow.

I'm reaching into the laundry basket next to the bed for a T-shirt when delicate fingers touch my wrist. "Can I look at your tattoos?"

My mouth dries out when I meet her eyes. There's no seduction there, but honest curiosity. My heart beats faster when I nod and join her on the bed. Rachel traces the dragon. Playing with fire again, her tickling caress strikes a match and creates a slow burn.

"Did it hurt?" she asks. "The tattoos?"

"Some areas more than others."

"What was it like?"

As her fingernails slide down my arm to the knot tattooed on my forearm, shivers run through my blood. "Like someone with sharp nails scratching a sunburn."

"Why do you do it?"

It's a simple question, but a complex answer. "So I'll always remember."

Rachel traces the twists and turns of the Brothers of Arrow Knot, granting me silence. It's my decision whether or not to continue the conversation. My angel does this—she opens the door and allows me the freedom to decide whether or not I want to step through. It's strange, my entire life I've had doors closed on me and now that one's open, I'm not sure how to enter.

I suck in air, guessing one way is headfirst. "That one's for Noah."

Rachel's eyes flash to mine, and I take comfort in the happiness I created there.

"It's a Celtic knot—it means warriors bonded as brothers through battle."

The right side of her mouth tips. "Does that mean you and Noah have been on the same side of several fistfights?"

I chuckle, remembering a few we probably shouldn't have

taken on. "Yeah. But it's more than that. Noah accepts people as they are. Doesn't ask. Doesn't judge. He's family."

Though lately he's been inching away by following his dreams. Someday, he'll graduate from college, get a real job and marry Echo. Then they'll be a family without me.

Rachel moves to kneel in front of me. Everything about her is softness and curves. Too innocent. Too beautiful. She admires her favorite tattoo—the tiger.

I sweep the bangs from her eyes. "I used to be weak when I was younger. The smallest kid in the class and the group home. I kept waiting for someone to save me." Like how that old tiger must have waited for someone to release him from his cage. "One day I decided to save myself, and I stopped being weak."

She touches the tiger. "So you got the tattoo."

I shrug. Such honesty makes me uncomfortable. "Earrings first. Then I started hanging out with the type of people most avoided. Got in fights just to prove I'd never run. Then, when I scraped up enough money, I got the tattoo."

Rachel withdraws her hand and prepares for the other question Abby warned would be coming. "Do you do drugs?"

"I have." I won't lie. Not to her. "I do drink. But I don't like the feeling of being high or being drunk. Losing control isn't my style. I make people believe I do drugs. It's better if people are scared of me."

"Why?"

I jerk my chin toward the window. "Life is different out there. I've survived because of what I make people think. No one messes with me, and that same reputation has kept you safe because no one would mess with anything that's mine."

She wipes at her forehead, but her bangs were already swept to the side. "Eric messed with me."

"Because he knows we're close to paying him off. He wanted to push my buttons and I fell for it. He wants us to fail. Eric wants more than money. He wants power, and it would be a strong message to a lot of people if he held power over me."

Rachel picks at the lint on the blanket with her eyes cast down. My iron wall, the one she expertly maneuvered around, becomes cold underneath my skin. I've bared my soul and she has to be second-guessing being with me.

"This is who I am, Rachel. Accept it or not. The tattoos won't wash off. The earrings will never change. I am who I am and nothing more. I'm loyal to a chosen few, I always keep my word and I'll protect you with my life.

"I scare the hell out of most people, but you will never have anything to fear from me. Choose. Love me or don't. But tell me now." Because I can't leave my heart open for her to rip out later. If I belong to her, then I do, and nothing will stand in our way.

She sits up on her knees and inches closer to me. Giving me my answer, she lets her warm, smooth fingers caress my cheek. "What's the dragon for?"

I tunnel my hand through her hair, enjoying the silky rain, and I take a deep breath. She's chosen me. Rachel's decided to love me beyond the sharp edges. I have no idea what I've done to deserve her. "The dragon's for the only good foster father I had. He's the one who taught me everything about cars. He used to call me a dragon."

Her forehead furrows. "Why?"

I smirk and the memory lightens my mood. "Because he said I was either breathing fire and destroying everything or I took the fire inside of me and created life."

"Created life?"

"Fire can destroy, but it can also create—provide warmth, protection." I still remember him explaining when I asked the same question. "He told me until I chose my path, I would always be capable of life and destruction."

"Did you choose?" She weaves her arms around my neck.

My hands melt into the indentation of her waist as I wonder how far we should go tonight. Rachel takes my bottom lip between hers, and the kindling bursts into flames.

"I don't think it's up to me," I answer. "My path chooses me."

"You've chosen, Isaiah." She kisses the side of my neck. "You're life."

"I'm still destruction."

"Not to me," she whispers.

"How far?" I ask while I still have a voice. Cupping her face, I reclaim her lips and gently guide her body next to mine on the bed. Rachel's tank rides up and my fingers explore the satin skin of her belly. There are so many places I long to go, so many places I crave to take her.

"I want to go further," she whispers. When I skim the waistband of her pants, her breathing hitches.

Further. Damn, my entire body responds. I don't miss the way her hand fidgets with the hem of her shirt. Scared I'll spook her, I don't push her too far, but I'm all for reading body language. I place my hand over hers and her smile appears.

"You sure?" I ask.

She nods and her hand falls away. I lower my head as I slowly edge the material of her tank off her stomach. Jesus, her stomach is gorgeous. Flat and smooth. As my lips press the spot above her belly button I confirm how undeniably sweet Rachel is.

I kiss each and every centimeter of her exposed skin as I move up her tank. I linger over the material of her bra and Rachel fists the sheet with both hands. She's so damn hot I'm about to forget slow and go for fast.

But I ignore those urges and guide the material up and over her head. I don't know what the hell I did to have such a beautiful creature in my bed, but she's here and I'm going to spend tonight worshipping this gift in front of me.

I roll my body over Rachel's, and her legs tangle with mine. Elvis's deep voice drifts from the apartment below. He sings about wise men and fools who rush in. I know as I hold Rachel in my arms that I, too, had no choice in falling in love.

We become lost in kisses, warm bare skin and touches. I move, and this time Rachel moves along with me. There's a building, a sweet pressure. It's as if we're not even two separate people anymore, but one.

Hands are everywhere. Kisses on the lips, the neck and shoulders. I move faster and Rachel keeps the pace as her thighs press against my hips, bringing me closer.

Right as my world is about to be pushed over the edge, Rachel grasps on to my body and calls out my name. I wrap my arms around her, holding on as if I'm saving myself from dying. My body jerks, and behind my closed lids there are bright colors. I inhale, and it's the scent of jasmine and when I open my eyes, I see an angel.

"I love you," Rachel whispers, and her eyelids flutter with the delicious exhaustion.

I slip to the side and gather her into my arms. I want Rachel here every night for the rest of my life. It's what feels right, what feels natural. "I love you."

"I'm tired," she yawns.

"Sleep, angel." I rub my hand up her spine and revel in the feel of her body pressed tight to me. "Sleep."

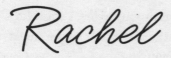

Rachel

MY EYES POP OPEN AND a nervous adrenaline beats through my system. A nightmare. Just a nightmare. One of my mom and my father and of speeches...

I'm in the same position as when I fell asleep: one leg draped over Isaiah's and my head resting against his bare chest. His heart has the same steady rhythm that I've come to depend upon. Slants of light filter into the room from the streetlamp. Time lost all meaning hours ago. With one hand wrapped around me, keeping me tucked close to his body, Isaiah dozes.

Tonight, Isaiah took me places I've never been, and the memory almost drives away all the fear from the nightmare....

The nightmare. Isaiah was in it, too. His words became a mantra: *I've survived because of what I make people believe.*

I swallow and cringe. My throat is raw from vomiting with the panic attacks. I'm exhausted, unable to sleep for long periods of time, and my body is wearing out further every day.

My mother wants me to give a twenty-minute speech at a dinner party for hundreds of guests. I'm not sure how much more my body can take, but I risk too much if I tell my parents the truth. If I can hold on until we pay off the debt, then I can introduce Isaiah to my family, and if I give this speech, then my mother will be proud.

Proud of me like she was always proud of Colleen.

While Isaiah creates an outside that pushes everyone away, I've created an outside in order to draw in my family. No, I've done it to win my mother's love.

My body is breaking down because of what I make people believe.

I snuggle closer to Isaiah, and he locks his other arm around me. I ignore the voices in my head and focus on the one person who loves what no one else can: the real me.

My mind separates from itself as I scan my bedroom. I said goodbye to Isaiah an hour ago, and now my world is in tattered pieces. I did this damage in my search. My purple comforter is ripped off the bed. The pillows strewn across the floor. Every possible container opened and the contents poured out. Last night's meager winnings crunch in my hand as I close my fist.

My body trembles as I circle the room again. The money... it's gone.

Maybe I missed it. Maybe I got so panicked that it was right in front of me and I didn't see it. I reach for my jewelry box again, and this time toss the contents as I come across them. As I dig to the bottom, I do see something new: a note. Before I can read the entire thing, I scramble across the floor to my bathroom and discover that my panic has entered a new stage: vomiting blood.

★ ★ ★

The door to West's room bounces against his wall as I throw it open. Ethan and West drop their video game controllers and jump to their feet when they see what I can only assume is pure anger radiating from my face. My body shakes and I sway slightly to the side. My strength is gone. Damn them for doing this to me.

Ethan grabs my arm. "Jesus Christ, Rach. You're dead on your feet."

I smack him off, choosing to be supported by the wall instead. "You took my money."

Ethan and West share a knowing glance, and for some reason they both appear relieved as their shoulders lose their tension. West readjusts the baseball cap on his head. "Yeah. That. Did you bother reading the note? We said we'd pay you back."

Over months. It said they would pay me back over months. "That was my money!"

Ethan's eyes flicker over me and his head falls back. "You had a panic attack over the money, didn't you? Shit, West, I told you we should have taped the note to the outside of the box. You didn't see the note, and I bet you freaked out when you found the money gone."

West flops back into his chair. "A little overdramatic, don't you think, Rach? I mean, who else is going to take your money? We said we'd pay you back, and we will."

"That was my money!" I scream. "Give it back! Now!"

Like always, the two continue their conversation as if I don't matter. Ethan turns to West. "You'd flip if someone took over four thousand dollars from your room. By the way, Rach, what type of part were you planning on buying? You had to be saving for a while."

"Can you two even try to pretend that you feel bad for stealing?"

West turns his back to me, preparing to rejoin his game. "We said we'd pay you back. Chill the fuck out."

Screw it. I walk over to West's desk and begin pulling on drawers, tossing papers and pens and books and crap onto the floor. If they won't give it to me, then I'll find it. My brothers shout as I rummage through the room. When they figure out yelling won't stop me, one of them restrains me from behind. His hands become iron bands around my arms.

I'm done being weak. I'm done being controlled. I kick and I scream and I only snap out of it when Ethan gets in my face. "Rachel!"

My twin's dark eyes bore into mine. When we were children, those eyes used to be right there when I fell asleep at night and there when I'd wake in the morning. Even when our parents forced us into our own rooms, we'd sneak away to be with each other. For years, we fought to be together and now, we seem forever apart.

"You stole from me."

West holds my arms at my sides. "I stole from you. Ethan objected. Blame me."

I stare at Ethan. He's been keeping something from me, and like he did with me over the panic attacks, I never asked. Maybe because I never wanted to know. "Why?"

Ethan presses his lips into a fine line. "Gavin has a gambling addiction."

West releases my arms. "Ethan!"

Ethan throws out his arms. "What? We took over four thousand dollars from her, West. That's not money you take because you need gas."

The two of them argue as I stumble across the items I had tossed on the floor. Gavin, my oldest brother, the head of all of us, the strongest, the leader, has a problem. I sit on the bed and clear my throat, ignoring the raw pain. "How bad?"

West shoves his hands in his pockets with such force that his boxers stick out. "Bad. None of us ever meant for it to happen. You know those nights you'd cover for Ethan, we figured out it worked for me, too, so the four of us started hanging."

Of course they did. Leaving me out would be the thing to do. I rub my forehead as the migraine from the panic attack sets in.

"We wanted to have fun," says Ethan. "Away from Mom and Dad. It's hard on Gavin and Jack. They hate being a part of this family. They look down the hall and they see Colleen's room. They look at how Mom treated you and they felt like they were reliving the cancer. They saw you and..."

They saw her.

"So one night we went to the riverboat." West continues Ethan's story, no doubt hoping I wouldn't make the connection. "I'd scored me and Ethan some fake IDs. Gavin got hooked and we tried to help, but..."

"He found other ways to gamble when we stopped him from going to the boat," finishes Ethan. "He owed some bad people money. Thank God you had enough to pay them off."

I lower my head into my hands. Isaiah and I are screwed. "You have no idea what you've done," I whisper.

The bed shifts, and I peek to find Ethan sitting beside me

and West standing in front of me. Both of them hold their shoulders slouched forward.

"We're not enabling him." West clearly believes that what I said means something completely different. "Gavin tried going to Dad, but Dad was too busy to listen, so Gavin came to me. He agreed to get help if I helped him pay the debt. And he's going to get help. Gavin just didn't want Dad to know how bad it was, and he never wants Mom to know."

"Rach," says Ethan. "Gavin's going to rehab after the charity dinner. Dad wants Mom to have one perfect night before Gavin goes and then Dad will tell Mom everything."

I massage my temples, wishing the throb would disappear. This entire family is one big mess. When I think my legs won't give out, I stand. Ethan joins me, and West braces his arms as if I'm going to fall. I push past them and go for the door.

"Where are you going?" asks Ethan.

I pause and choke back the automatic lie. What would this family have been like if Colleen had never died? "I'm going to see Isaiah, and you aren't going to stop me."

Isaiah

I ROLL A GLASS JAR full of nuts against the tool bench at the garage. Completely broken, Rachel sits a few feet from me in the chair Abby dragged out of the office for her when her sobs became too intense for her to stand. Logan leans against the office window with the back of his head resting against the glass. This isn't his problem, but he treats it like it is. For that, I have respect.

Abby crouches in front of Rachel, doing what I should be doing, consoling. Saying the words I should be saying, that's it's not her fault and it'll be okay. Abby's right. It's not her fault. She did nothing wrong by protecting our money in her room. Her brothers on the other hand...

I grab the jar and throw it across the room. Glass shatters against the wall. My chest moves rapidly. We have seven hundred dollars. Four-thousand three hundred dollars short of what we need.

"Feel better?" asks Logan with absolutely no inflection.

My head falls back. "Some." At least the anger is under control. That is, until I get my hands on her brothers. "The nitro system goes in my car."

"Isaiah," Logan says again. "Rachel's car is the better one. Add the system to hers. We'll have a better shot at winning."

I cross my arms over my chest, unmoved and unconvinced. Movies and television make nitro look like child's play, but it's not. The systems are tricky and too many things can go wrong. Even though she won't be the person drag racing with it, I don't want her in a car with that type of danger. "Not your call."

Rachel wipes her eyes and stands. "Then it's mine. I don't understand why you're fighting us on this. We have a better chance to win with the system in my car."

"No."

Her hair moves with her frustrated breath. "If you won't put the system in my car, then let me race against Zach."

Tension cramps my neck and I pop it to the right. Drag racing is dangerous. Nitro is dangerous. If Zach is working with Eric, then Zach is lethal. Rachel is the one thing in my life I can't lose. Why can't she see how much I love her? That I need to protect her?

Logan pushes off the wall. "The way I see it, you're out-voted. It's her car. If she wants the system in it, install it. Besides, you'll be the one firing the tanks, not her."

Because I don't argue, I stay silent, but let my arms drop. Rachel misreads me and wraps herself around me. Last night, I spent a few hours in heaven by holding my angel tight. Rachel went home, and we were both sent to hell. I kiss the top of her head. I promised I'd take care of her, and I'll do anything to keep that promise.

It's Monday morning and because Pro Performance in-sists on a high school diploma along with the certification,

I have to ignore my problems and go to school. The moment I walk into the building, Abby joins my side.

"You're actually going today?" I ask.

She shrugs. "Might as well. Occasionally I like to throw people off. By the way, I got my hands on a nitro system."

"How much?"

Abby matches my strides up the stairs. "Consider it a gift."

I freeze on the landing. "I thought you had to stay financially out."

Reaching the second floor, Abby walks backward. "You aren't the only one who had people owing them favors." She enters the second room on the right and I smirk. I never knew she took honors math.

Mr. Holden calls me from the steps below and waits as I head back down. I jack my thumb in the other direction. "I don't want to be late."

"I'll give you a slip," he says, as if he ran to catch me. "We need to talk."

I nod and follow him. Instead of going to the school's auto shop, he chooses an empty classroom and closes the door. "What's going on?" I ask.

Mr. Holden fiddles with his safety glasses. "There were some irregularities with the certification testing."

I say nothing, having no idea how this involves me. I knew everything on that test.

"Several of the guys you tested with had the same scores, missing the same questions. They reviewed the tapes and caught them cheating."

"I didn't cheat."

"I know," says Mr. Holden. "But this scandal has the testing facility questioning everything from that day. They're zeroing in on you because of your score. They have adults who don't score as well as you did, so it makes them wonder if you had outside help."

I slam my books on the desk beside me. "I studied for years for this test."

"I know," says Mr. Holden.

"I didn't cheat."

He runs a hand over his salt-and-pepper hair. "I talked to the facility's manager. Told him you're a good kid so he agreed to let you retake the test."

My teeth click together. Retake the test. For once in my life, I followed proper society's rules, and all I got was a kick in the nuts. "What happens when I ace that one? Are they going to accuse me of cheating again? Because there is no way a street punk foster kid can have a fucking brain?"

I hold my hand up, not wanting to hear the answer, and back away. The bell rings. Class has started for everyone else but I don't see the point of attending anymore.

Out in the hallway, I catch Zach staring at me from a few doors down. Without a word, he slinks into a classroom. There's no doubt in my mind now that the boy is working for Eric, because the guy I know would have never done something as low as this. Good thing for him that he's on Eric's payroll. Otherwise, he'd be dead.

Rachel

BESIDES THE TINKLING OF SILVERWARE against plates, dinner is unusually silent. The presence of Gavin and Jack at the dinner table every Monday usually means plenty of banter between my brothers, but each of them appears lost in their own thoughts.

The long cherry table is made for eight people. Mom and Dad sit at either end. Gavin and Jack are seated closest to Dad. Ethan and West share the middle seats. My chair is next to Mom, and I stare at the only empty seat: the one meant for Colleen.

"Everyone's quiet tonight," says Mom. Her blue eyes jump to each of our faces.

My brothers throw out excuses: work, school or tired. I say nothing.

I shove at the enchilada on my plate. The last thing I want touching my raw throat is anything spicy.

"Rachel," Mom says. "Are you feeling okay? You've got circles under your eyes."

Every single person gawks at me, including my father. "I'm fine."

No one drops their gaze. In fact, no one eats. Dad leans his elbows on the white tablecloth as he studies me closer. "Your mom is right. You don't have your typical bounce."

No, I don't. I'm exhausted and worn and on the verge of collapsing. I'm mad at my brothers, I'm pretty sure they're angry with me, and my boyfriend and I are going to get our butts kicked by Eric when we can't pay him five thousand dollars.

"She's been overpreparing for that speech on Saturday, right, Rach?" Gavin shoves a forkful of rice into his mouth.

"I want to make everyone proud," I say. At the word *proud*, Gavin glances away.

With the mere mention of her event, Mom fills everyone in on the details. How every seat is sold and how there is a waiting list and how five hundred people will be attending. My stomach cramps. Eric may not be an issue after all since this speech will possibly kill me first.

I escaped after dessert, asking Dad in front of everyone for permission to go to Abby's. Understanding that I probably wasn't going to hang with my new "rich" friend and was instead going to hang with Isaiah, Ethan and West slammed their silverware. My mother raised an eyebrow at their behavior, but said nothing. Once Dad confirmed I had finished homework, he told me to be home by ten.

Isaiah texted earlier today that he had work to do in the garage this evening. Needing to be someplace calm, I park next to the auto shop. I scan the lot and wonder if he went home when I don't see his car. The puzzle is solved when I walk into the garage. In the bay, the hood to his Mustang is open and so are the doors. "Isaiah?"

I'm greeted by the buzzing of the overhead heaters. Isaiah mentioned that he was concerned about his engine over-heating. I look to see what he's done, and I rub my eyes. No.

A weariness overtakes me. A weariness that sleep could never solve.

I hit my hand against the open passenger door in my haste to peer inside the vehicle. In the backseat are two tanks of nitro. The door to the garage squeaks open. Isaiah's eyes meet mine, and I swear I hear my heart ripping in two when I spot guilt.

"What are you doing here?" Isaiah asks.

I say nothing. We both know how bad this is—how this bor-ders on a betrayal that is unspeakable.

Isaiah tugs at his bottom earring—a sure sign of inner tur-moil. The silence builds between us and I'm the first to crack. "Did Abby get two systems?"

"No," he says.

Red-hot tears of anger well in my eyes. "I thought we agreed..."

He cuts me off. "We didn't agree. You and Logan wanted the system in your car, and I didn't. End of story."

Isaiah doesn't argue. How many times has he told me that? "So what? I don't get a vote? You aren't the only one on the line here. Eric is coming after me, too."

A string of curses leaves his mouth as he stalks over to me. "Every second of my day is consumed with the knowledge that you're under him. I'm doing this to protect you."

"By lying to me?"

Isaiah seems taken aback. "I didn't lie."

The first stupid tear breaks through and I quickly wipe it

away. "You knew I expected you to put the system in my car. Regardless that you never said the words, it's a lie." My mind reels with the implications of what's happened. "It's worse than a lie. This is major. You made a decision without me."

"That's bull. You, Logan, Abby and I discussed the options."

"But you decided our fate without me." My hand pounds at my chest. "I thought we were a team. I thought we were partners."

Isaiah places his hands on my shoulders. His gray eyes are waves crashing between anger and fear. "I don't have much, Rachel, and I refuse to lose you."

"I told you, I won't ever touch the system. It'll only be used on the dragway. We'll take it out after we pay the debt."

"These systems are dangerous. If someone hits you or the system malfunctions or you accidently set something off..." Isaiah runs through the impossible scenarios. His eyes dart as he talks, as if he's searching for a way to fix all of the problems. My energy fades as I realize that's exactly what he is doing. He's trying to fix one more thing.

"The risks are small. You can't control everything."

"You're wrong." His hands move to my face warm, strong, and I notice they tremble. "Let this go, Rachel. The decision is made. I'm doing this to protect you."

To protect me. Because I'm not capable of making my own decisions. My hands shoot up and smack his arms off me. "I am not weak."

His eyes widen. "I never said you were."

I pull a hand through my hair and tug at the strands, hoping that I'm wrong. But I'm not. "You're just like my brothers.

You see me as fragile and stupid and as someone who can't make her own decisions."

Isaiah reaches out. "No, it's not like that. I love you. You know this."

I step away from him. "Yeah, that's what they say, too."

Isaiah

THE PHONE RINGS THREE TIMES and Rachel's sweet voice answers again, "Hi, this is Rachel Young. Leave a message after the beep."

Like the other ten times, the beep happens, and I sit with my head hanging down listening to static. I should say I'm sorry, but I'm not. I should tell her I'm wrong and that we'll install the system in her car, but that would be a lie. What I want is for her to walk through the door of the garage and tell me that she understands my need to protect her, my need to fix things.

From cars to situations to myself. Because if I didn't take care of me, no one else would. This is me doing what no one ever did on my behalf—I'm protecting her because that's what you do when you love someone. It's what I always wanted someone to do for me.

"Call me."

It's Tuesday afternoon. The day's dragged as I've waited for Rachel to contact me, and the seconds continue to stretch now that I know she's out of school. The door to the garage squeaks open, and my heart speeds up in anticipation. I stand, wiping my hands against my jeans. I'll tell her I love her. I'll tell her that there's nothing I won't do to make her happy. I'll tell her...

Logan strolls in and I silently curse. I forgot I asked him to spot me when I tested the nitro system. If I weren't so damned screwed in the head, I'd laugh at his jock baseball uniform. "Nice getup."

"Came straight from an exposition game. Spring season starts soon."

I close the hood of my car. "Baseball seems tame for you. I would have pegged you for football."

"Naw," says Logan. "Catcher is a crazy position. Bats flying near your head, a guy that hurls one-hundred-mile-per-hour fastballs at you and a runner going at full speed trying to take you out as you stand over home plate. That's an adrenaline rush."

Speaking of adrenaline rushes. "Follow me in your car. We're going to head out past Fox Lane and test the system."

The sky turns pink as the sun prepares to set. Logan and I stand in front of my car, staring at the mile stretch of new blacktop that will someday shepherd people to a crapload of new homes. Currently, it leads to construction vehicles and woods.

I motion toward the side. "Wait over there."

"No way," says Logan. "I want in on this action."

I shake my head. "I haven't driven with nitro before. If it weren't for Eric breathing down our necks, I wouldn't even be dealing with the shit. And if I did decide to play with it, I'd be testing this car on the drag strip during Test and Tune. But I'm short on time."

Logan pats my shoulder. "Let's live a little."

He opens the door to the passenger side and closes it. The space between my skin and bones begins to vibrate; the dread that something nuclear is on the verge of exploding. I'm out of time, and something worse is going to happen if I don't make money. I slide into my car.

My eyes flutter open and my vision blurs. I blink and it doesn't help. I shut my eyes and press my thumb and forefinger against them, hoping to rub away the issue. Pain shoots through my body and when I open my mouth I taste blood.

The car spun. It kept spinning. I lost control.

"Logan." My voice doesn't sound like my own.

Silence. My eyes stay closed and everything floats on a haze—like a dream. Maybe I am dreaming. No. We crashed. My eyes won't open again so I throw my hand out toward the passenger side. It claws through the air and smacks the empty seat.

"Logan, answer me, man," I call out louder. Something trickles down my nose and my mind drifts. Maybe this was only a dream.

Rachel

I IGNORE ISAIAH'S MESSAGES. I'M in love with a guy who thinks I'm as weak as my brothers say I am. The sad part is, I almost believed I was strong.

Three knocks on the door and I know it's Mom. "Come in."

With her blond hair slicked back into a ponytail at the nape of her neck, Mom pops her head in with a glowing smile. "Abby's here."

"Abby?" I sit up. Mom fell in love with private school–going, rich Abby. Not that Abby wowed them with her personality as much as Mom is wowed I have a friend. I wonder how much she'll love her if she discovers my new best friend deals drugs.

Mom widens the door to reveal Abby dressed in her typical black hoodie and painted-on jeans. I start to smile until I notice she won't meet my gaze. She's only avoided me once, and that was when Eric revealed her real job.

I slide off the bed and dismiss my mother with one word. "Thanks."

"Do you girls want anything?" Mom asks as she stands between us. "Food or drinks?"

Abby enters my room and handles a picture of me and my brothers. Her behavior is seriously freaking me out.

"No, thanks," I say. "But we'll let you know if we change our minds."

Mom claps her hands against her legs. "All right then. Oh." Her eyes brighten. "Abby, would you like to come to a charity event I'm throwing for the Leukemia Foundation on Saturday? It'll be at The Lakes Country Club. Rachel will be speaking."

"Sure," says Abby.

"Great!" Mom rattles out a few details neither Abby nor I catch before excusing herself.

When the door clicks shut, Abby puts the picture down. "Think of a good lie to leave, and think of it fast. Isaiah and Logan are in the hospital."

Isaiah

MY HEAD THROBS. A PULSE that originates from the twelve stitches on my forehead and vibrates my skull. If it weren't for my head, I'd probably feel the rest of my body. The doctor called me lucky. Lots of bruises. No broken bones. No internal injuries.

I'd feel luckier if someone would tell me about Logan. The bastard...my friend...a lump forms in my throat...I saw blood.

I raise my hand to my head. The tubing of the IV line rubs against my forearm.

"You shouldn't touch it."

With the sight of her, my stomach twists to the point that the doctor may have to rethink internal injuries. "I'm not in the fucking mood, Beth."

A chair scrapes against the floor, causing the pounding in my head to increase. "We could be twins," she says. "I've got a nice-size scar over my eye, too."

I drop my arm and stare at the girl I had thought I loved since I was fourteen. When I met her, she had straight black hair and an attitude that scared the shit out of bikers. The prickly disposition Beth used to carry as a physical shield no longer drapes her aura. There's a peacefulness that surrounds her that I never noticed in all our years together.

"You got your scar because you wouldn't listen," I say.

Beth flashes her patented sarcastic grin. "Twenty dollars I'll find out the same thing about you."

Back in October, I stood in this same hospital waiting to hear if she was alive. Her mother's boyfriend tried to kill Beth. Her boyfriend, Ryan, saved her. Once I heard she was fine, I left. Beth obviously doesn't live by the same policy.

"How did you know I was here?"

"Shirley and Dale."

My foster parents—her aunt and uncle. They stopped in a half hour ago. They were part pissed I interrupted their long weekend at the lake, part pissed that my social worker is now up their ass and even more pissed I hurt myself. Who knew the two of them gave a slight shit.

"How's Logan?" I ask.

The peacefulness fades from her face. "We don't know. They took his dad straight back and he hasn't been out since. No one will tell us a thing. Ryan's going nuts."

I place a fist to my forehead. "I've fucked it all up. If something's wrong with him..."

I could never forgive myself.

Beth places a hand over mine and squeezes. "He's an adrenaline junkie. We all know it. If it wasn't with you, it would have been with someone else at some other time. At least you were there. At least you could call the police. You can't fix everything."

"You don't know how deep I'm in."

"No, I don't. Because we're not friends anymore."

"Not the time."

"I love you, Isaiah. I always have, but I've never been *in* love with you. Both of us were so damn fucked in the head that neither of us understood the difference between friendship and love. We're friends. We always have been. I know you know what I mean because Logan's told me about Rachel."

My eyes snap to hers and Beth waves me off. "He never betrayed you. I annoyed the hell out of him until he told me, and all he would say was that you look at Rachel like Ryan looks at me. In all the years we knew each other, you never looked at me like that."

Beth opens her mouth to continue, but I cut her off. "I know."

"You do?"

I return Beth's grip. "You let me take care of you."

She raises an eyebrow, highlighting the scar above her eye. "So?"

"Rachel doesn't. She always wants to take care of herself. Drives me crazy."

Beth laughs. "Then it must be love. I drive Ryan insane."

There's an ache that goes deeper than the physical wounds of my skin. "I really did care for you." Beth's right—I didn't love her, at least not in the way I love Rachel, but it doesn't negate the fact that I had feelings, even if she didn't return them.

"I know." She repeats the answer I gave her. "I also know you love her, but is there room for me? Just as what we were good at? As friends?"

Friends with Beth. I assess the small devilish pixie, and

it's one of the first times in my life I've seen her desperate for an answer. I rub my hand over my head. This could be really good, or the worst mistake ever. But because Beth's right again, I nod. She and I were always at our best as friends. "Friends."

A female clears her throat at the doorway, and Courtney walks into the room. Beth stands. "Noah and Echo are on their way," Beth says. "And I dropped Abby off at Rachel's. They should be here soon."

"Thanks." Noah's going to blow a gasket, and I'm not sure Rachel will want to show.

Courtney slips into the seat Beth abandoned. "How are you?"

I motion toward my arm with the IV. "I'll be better when they spring me."

"Isaiah..." She inhales deeply and exhales. "What the hell were you doing?"

"How's Logan?"

Courtney shakes her head so sadly that her ponytail slumps. "I don't know. I'll be honest...the longer his dad stays back there, the more anxious I become. He's got a lot of friends out there, and you'd think his father would want to give them good news."

I shut my eyes, not allowing Courtney to see the fear there...the weakness.

"The police believe your story, Isaiah. That you tested a nitrous system on an abandoned road and it failed."

"It's not a story," I say. "It's the truth. Something went wrong and I lost control."

"Regardless of what happens with Logan, the police won't

press charges. Logan's father waived away the option of holding you responsible."

"Yay for fucking me. At least I won't be in prison like my mom, right?"

My vision blurs for the second time today. This time it's because of tears. For years, I've been fine. But now, emotions are everywhere and I can't control a damn thing.

"Do you know why I asked to be your social worker?" Courtney asks.

I peer at the blood pressure machine, wishing I could stop feeling. "Why?"

"Because I grew up in foster care, too."

The heart rate monitor increases speed, and Courtney pretends she doesn't notice that her bombshell affects me. "Entered at six, just like you. I had the good homes, the bad ones and the group homes. I even have a tattoo from my pissed-off years."

My chest moves faster as my emotions threaten to consume me. I reach for anger, because it feels better than hurt. "Is that what you think I am? Pissed-off?"

"Oh, Isaiah." Courtney stares straight into my eyes. "Pissed-off is the easy emotion. Having been in the same *exact* position you're in..." She flutters her hand at the hospital bed and then grows still. Her mouth attempts to quirk up, but her lower lip trembles. "I'd bet, right now, you're feeling very alone."

Alone.

Logan's got a dad beside him. Me? I've got a social worker. I shake my head, fighting the hurt. "What's wrong with me that nobody wants to keep me?"

Why no one wanted to love me. Right now, I don't feel bad-ass. I feel seventeen and crave for someone to tell me that my friend will be okay.

Her fingers find mine and I don't draw away. "Nothing," she says firmly. "There is *nothing* wrong with you."

I suck in air, close my eyes and exhale out the emotions. Courtney withdraws her hand, and I'm grateful she doesn't push me further.

"Can you find out about Logan?" I ask.

"Yes," she says. "I'll be back."

Rachel

ABBY GRIPS THE PASSENGER DOOR. "I'm going to be sick."

"Throw up in my car, and that will be the last thing you ever do." Spotting the exit for the hospital, I cut over two lanes and shift down. Isaiah's been teaching me some tricks after school. Never in a million years would I have thought I'd be using those skills to race to the hospital to see if he's alive.

"You were doing ninety and switching lanes like we were being chased by the police."

"Are you sure he's here?" Because I'd prefer for Isaiah to be at any of the other hospitals in the county over University. This is where they bring the awful trauma cases.

"Yes." Abby loosens her hold on the door as we approach the stoplight at the end of the ramp. "Echo told me."

Isaiah called me and I never called back. My last words to him were in anger. What if he thinks I don't love him? My fingers beat against the steering wheel, counting how long it takes for the cross light to turn yellow. "Are you sure she said University?"

"Yes."

"That's where they take the worst trauma patients." I admit my fear out loud.

Abby releases a heavy sigh. "It's also where they take people with no insurance. He's a foster kid, Rachel, and a line item on the government's budget. That is where they'd take him. Not the fancy-ass hospital with the flat-screen televisions."

Like Isaiah taught me, my foot hovers over the gas while my other presses on the clutch. My fingers grasp the gear-shift. A solid wall with no windows, a practical fortress, University Hospital looms over us two blocks ahead. I watch the cross light turn yellow, and my eyes flick to my light, waiting for the green.

In one instantaneous movement, I lay off the clutch, step on the gas and shift into gear the second the light flips. Next to me, Abby curses.

Abby and I run past the sliding glass doors of the hospital and hesitate. The bland waiting room with beige-painted cinder block walls is cramped with people. Wet coughing hacks, crying babies and the sound of someone vomiting makes me turn my head. In the corner, wearing too many layers of clothes that haven't been washed, a man hunches over and talks to himself.

Abby nudges my elbow. "Over there."

My heart soars out of my body when I spot Isaiah. He's hugging his roommate, Noah. Strong arms wrapped around each other in a brief embrace. They separate, and I cover my mouth when I see the wound on his head, the bruises forming on his face, the blood dried on his clothing.

Stepping forward out of the shadows and touching Isaiah's arm is one of my many nightmares: Beth. She smiles up at him, and when he smiles back my heart shatters.

WITH NO CLUE ABOUT LOGAN'S condition, I walk into the waiting room. Hearing that Noah was on his way, Shirley and Dale left, but told me I could crash in their basement if I needed. After all, the state still pays them for me.

I see red hair and curls first. Echo chokes me. It's nice to have a sister. "Are you okay?"

"I'm good." I glance at Noah from over her head. With his hair hiding his eyes and hands on his hips, I can't read my best friend. "How's Noah?" I mutter.

"Scared," she whispers. "Mad."

I nod at Noah. "S'up, man." He embraces me—a strong crush of arms and muscles. We hold it for a second, keep it tight and then let go. The two of us are brothers.

"Give me a reason why I shouldn't kick your ass," says Noah. "What were you thinking?"

"Damn, Noah," says Beth from behind me. "He already has stitches."

Beth and I used to gang up against Noah all the time. She's right about us. We were friends first. Always friends. Not understanding a relationship that close, it got muddled.

She flashes a genuine smile and I smile back. Yeah, Beth and I, we can do friends. A few feet behind her and hanging with what I assume is Logan's entire baseball team, Beth's guy, Ryan, watches us with his arms folded over his chest. I tip my chin at him to let him know I'm good, and he tilts his head in acceptance. That'll probably be the longest conversation the two of us ever have.

Noah leans into us so that we form our own circle. "Do you know what he's been doing?"

Beth shrugs. "He's always liked to drive fast. Stupidity caught up."

"Stupidity did catch up, but not in that way." Noah's dark eyes snap to mine and he rolls his shoulders back. He's looking for a fight and my body reacts. My head continues to throb like a bad bass line, but if Noah wants to have it out, we will.

"Say what you gotta say, Noah."

"Whoa." Beth places an arm between us. "He just got out of the hospital. This is the first time I've been with the two of you in months. You are not ruining this for me by fighting."

Noah and I stand toe to toe and neither one of us flinch. "Do you want to tell her, Isaiah?"

"Naw, man. It sounds like you've got all the answers."

Keeping his eyes locked on me, Noah drops the bomb. "He owes money to Eric."

The silence between the three of us builds pressure in my neck.

"How much," asks Beth in a low tone.

"Enough," I answer. Too much.

"Why?" she demands. "Why did you street race?"

Noah finally looks away. "Because I told him I was moving into the dorms."

"Noah!" Beth grabs hold of the arm of his jacket. "What
the hell? You promised both of us a year ago that you would
never leave us behind."

"Why are you here?" Noah asks Beth. "You promised you'd
stay away from Louisville."

Beth's head tilts in her familiar pissed-off way. "Logan's
my friend. So is Isaiah. Explain why you're bailing on us?
You break a promise to him, you break it to me."

"I kept my promise to you," says Noah. "Who do you think
told Shirley to call your uncle when you got arrested last
fall? Do you think the lush figured it out on her own? I reminded her that your Uncle Scott had money and would be
able to help with bail. As for Isaiah, I can't help him if he
owes people like Eric."

Beth pales. "You...you did that to me?"

Noah lowers himself to stare into her eyes. "Don't stand
there acting like I ratted you out. You're better off and you
know it. You're happy. You've told me that yourself."

Beth clenches her hands together. "But it should have been
my choice."

"Beth...you never saw your choices." And his eyes flash
to me. "And neither do you."

I gesture with palms open. "Show me my rich uncle, Noah,
and I'm game. Wait...my bad...out of the three of us, I'm the
only trash here."

Noah shoves a finger into my chest, daring me into a physical confrontation. "You're so bent on believing what you
want people to see that you forget that you're more. Keep

saying it. Keep saying you're trash and take the fucking swing at me, but if you do, know I'm hitting back."

My head is so close to Noah's that I feel the heat of his anger, or maybe it's mine.

"You want to fight, man?" I ask. "Is that what you want?"

"No, bro. But I do want to kick some sense into your head."

Around us, several guys leap to their feet, calling at us to back down. Most of them wear jock jackets like Logan's. One has the balls to touch me. Ryan, Beth's guy, has the balls to touch Noah. "Bring it down a notch."

Beth smacks Ryan's arm. "Let him go, Ryan." She turns to the one with his arm on me. "You, too, Chris. This is how the two of them communicate."

Ryan yanks on the bill of his baseball cap. "This is a fight, Beth."

She rolls her eyes. "It's a family reunion. A fucked-up one, but how else would we do it."

Noah cracks his crazy-ass grin with her words and chuckles. I pop the tension out of my neck, and Noah flexes his shoulders to relax. "You should have told me you had problems."

I shrug. "I got problems."

Noah pats my back. "Then we'll figure it out."

For the first time in a while, the pressure inside of me dips. "Thanks, man."

The door to the emergency room opens. On crutches, Logan hobbles out of the E.R. with a man who must be his dad by his side. Some of the guys near us clap or yell out Logan's name.

For the first time since waking up from the crash, I feel

like I can take a lungful of air. Logan acknowledges his friends as he and his two poles maneuver through the mass of people. There's no mistake that he's making his way to me, Beth, Chris and Ryan.

Chris is the first to speak. "You're a moron, Junior."

Logan pops that insane grin. "But it was a hell of a rush." He nods at me. "You okay?"

"Stitches."

"Same with me." He kicks out his right leg. "Twenty-four stitches on my thigh. Nothing broken." Logan loses the spark. "I'm out for a bit." He's referring to helping with the money.

"It's good," I say. "Thanks, man."

"Don't thank me. You still have to fix my '57 Chevy."

Logan turns to Ryan and the pair embrace. Beth told me they'd been friends since elementary school. I can only imagine their bond. Beth wraps her arms around me. "Thanks for being my friend again."

I hug her back. "No problem."

"Hey, Isaiah," says Logan. "Wasn't that Rachel?"

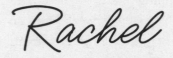

Rachel

ISAIAH HUGGED BETH.

Beth—the strong girl, the beautiful girl, the girl who twisted Isaiah in knots. He smiled at her. He hugged her. And they looked perfect together.

I've watched Abby and Isaiah for weeks, and never once has he touched her, much less *hugged* her. And Isaiah doesn't smile easily. It's a rare gift and he gave it to *her*. Our fight must have opened his eyes. The crash must have revealed his true feelings.

And his feelings aren't for me.

I yank my keys out of my purse. They fall through my fingers and clank on the blacktop. Abby, I should go back for Abby, but I can't stay. She went to pester a nurse for news on Logan and never returned. Isaiah can drive her home. Or Noah can. Or *Beth*.

All people who belong together. I don't belong in their world. I'm weak. They're strong.

Beth is strong.

I snatch the keys off the ground, and they clink together in my hands. I'm shaking, and it's not because of the chill in the evening air. The guy I fell in love with never loved me. Never.

"Rachel!" Isaiah calls out.

I glance over my shoulder, gripping the keys tighter in my hand. My breathing hitches. I can't do it. I can't hear him say the words. Not with the memory of him holding her so fresh. Not with her probably observing through the glass door. A girl like her would enjoy watching me break.

My thoughts become a distorted mess, and my stomach hollows out as if I've been pushed over a ravine. I feel the sickening weightlessness like I'm falling, my arms flailing to stop.

I should run, but I'm paralyzed by the sight of him. Even moving slowly, Isaiah possesses the prowess of a panther. His muscles pronounced in the easy way he strides. The set, determined gaze on me as his prey. This only proves how weak I am. Like the animal on the verge of being devoured in the wild, I stand here stunned by his dangerous beauty.

Isaiah touches me. His warm palm to my face. A soft slide of his thumb. My body has memorized the motion. I lean into his hand and close my eyes. I'll miss this. I'll miss everything about him. A tear escapes and creates a wet trail down my face.

Isaiah has always been gentle, and he is again as he wipes it away. "Why did you leave?"

Hundreds of pounds of weight stack on top of my chest, restricting air. I open my eyes, not daring to meet his stare. "Are you okay?"

"Some stitches and bruises, but yeah, I'm fine."

"And Logan?" I ask with as much strength as I can muster.

I fight the tingling in my blood, a reaction to the shortage of oxygen. I have seconds before I lose control. Breathe.

"Stitches, too. But fine. Rachel, look at me."

Because his hand on my cheek prods me to face him, because I've hardly ever been able to defy him when he speaks to me in such a deep, soothing voice...my eyes rise to meet his. Confusion and hurt swirl in a murky storm in his gray eyes. I'd do anything if that pain was for me, but it's not. It can't be.

I don't want to hear his words, not yet, so I ask, "Your car?"

His head drops as he presses his hands to his face. "Totaled."

Pain for him, pain for me, rips at my heart. Another tear escapes. The car was his—a part of his soul. The sorrow he must feel—there has to be a better word than *mourning*.

Yearning to touch him, longing to comfort him, my fingers instinctively brush against his temple. Isaiah takes my hand and knots our fingers together, squeezing a little too tight. "*This* is why I didn't want the system in your car."

We're back to this—so easily. His words are a sandblaster against my soul, decimating my insides, crushing my bones, leaving me as a completely empty shell. "Because your car, your life, is worth less?"

"Yes," he answers with stubborn resolve.

The hospital doors open, and Beth steps onto the sidewalk. My throat thickens, and the warning contortion of my stomach tells me my time is up. I yank my hand from his. "She's waiting for you."

He glances over his shoulder, and I take advantage by fleeing. Quickly. Turning into the maze of cars. Hoping to disappear. Words fly in my head—all related, yet not; all tangible, yet slipping through my fingers: Eric and debt and Isaiah and love and Beth and strength and weakness...

And my mother and my brothers and my father and Colleen...

All of us dominoes on a board where one event results in chaos. One tip of a piece and everything scatters. There's no control. Like everyone else, I'm a piece to be overturned. I will never control my destiny.

My hand grabs at my coat, jerking it off as heat consumes me and chokes my neck. At the intersection of four parked cars, I fall to my knees and convulse with the first dry heave. Searing pain cuts through my throat and I become lightheaded.

"Rachel!" Isaiah lifts me upright, wiping my hair from my face.

"No hospital." They can't know...they can't know...they can't... "Promise they won't know...."

My stomach cramps, and I roll away from him with the blast of heat rushing through my body.

"Jesus!" Isaiah scrambles beside me. "There's blood."

Isaiah

PROMISE THEY WON'T KNOW...

Craving a physical connection, I slide my finger along the back of Rachel's hand. She's asleep. Has been for a while. Curled in the fetal position in the middle of my bed, Rachel wears the mask of a ravaged person. Somehow, I missed the signs: dark circles under her eyes, the clothes that once fit perfectly now hang, her skin so pale it's translucent.

Rachel told me she had attacks, that she ended up in the hospital once, and that she hides them from her family. I never thought to ask if she was concealing them from me.

Her eyes press tightly in her sleep, and she flinches as she swallows. I wish she'd sleep deeply, but she doesn't. Staying restless, Rachel turns her head. I tuck the blanket back around her, whispering for her to rest.

"Isaiah," Abby says softly from the doorway. "Everyone's here."

I nod and Abby slips behind the door. Everyone being here would be Noah's doing, not mine. He found us—me cradling a broken Rachel in my arms—and drove us home. Took everything I had not to rush Rachel into the E.R., but she made me promise not to. I've never considered going back on my word as much as I do right now.

The world is stacked against Rachel and me. The money is due this weekend. We're down a car and we aren't even close to the amount. Rachel's body is worn, her spirit drowning. If we don't pay off this debt, a nightmare will visit us both. Eric will come after me and he'll hurt her. My fingers ball into a fist. I'll die before I let that happen.

A rustle of sheets, then soft fingers glide against mine. I glance at Rachel and meet glazed-over blue eyes. The spark is gone, taking the violet hue along with it.

"How are you?" I ask, and focus on not demanding why the hell she's kept all this from me. We'll have the conversation, but not in this moment.

"Okay," she says in a hoarse, cracked voice. "I'm sorry."

I shake my head, not wanting her apology. "Me, too." I lace my fingers with hers. "Why did you run from me?"

"I saw you hug Beth," she croaks.

"I love you. Not anyone else."

"I know. I'm sorry. My head got messed up. I was worried about you and we had a fight and I didn't know if you were alive and when I saw you two together..." Rachel lets the words trail off. "Beth's strong."

"So are you," I say.

"You don't think that."

"Fuck that," I snap, then close my eyes to rein in my temper. I suck in a breath before reopening them. "I do think that. Most girls I know would be lying under a bed in the fetal position after living a day with Eric on their backs. You've stood strong the entire time."

"Except now."

I'm shaking my head again. "Everyone has a breaking point, and I'd lay odds this isn't Eric." But I won't go near a conversation about her family. "Your body may need a break, but your spirit is still strong."

"I bet this wouldn't happen to Beth."

"No, it wouldn't, because Beth always ran."

Rachel blinks.

"Beth was always a runner. She may have stood in place, but she always hid behind the wall she built, and if that didn't work, she ran to a guy, to drugs, to anywhere other than where she should have been, to forget. You and Beth— you're night and day."

"If you really think that then let me race Zach." Her voice breaks, leaving her only able to whisper. "Let me bet the seven hundred and race him. I'd do it without you, but he already said that he won't race me without your permission because he doesn't want to mess with you."

The muscles in my jaw contract. "Is that all he said?"

She winces. "He'd also race me if I broke up with you. But ignore that. Isaiah, we're already in trouble. If I win, then we try to double the fourteen hundred, and then we try to double again. Let me help dig us out of this hole."

Rachel's so pale I can see the veins beneath her skin. She could win. Rachel's been practicing. Stolen moments between us in abandoned parking lots. All she lacked was experience and confidence. My angel has both now. Even with her body defying her, she's a force of nature.

But what if the race Zach's offering isn't innocent? What

if his association with Eric drags her in deeper? Not able to see the angle he's playing, I can't take the risk.

"Everyone's waiting on me," I say as a cop-out. "Let me talk to them."

She casts her eyes down. "We won't work if you never trust me to be strong enough."

I kiss her forehead. "It has nothing to do with trust or strength." But with keeping her safe. "Rest. You can't do anything if you don't sleep."

I close the door to the bedroom behind me and freeze when I assess the room. All eyes fall on me. Echo and Abby lean against the kitchen counter. Noah stands near the couch. Ryan and Beth sit next to Logan, who has his bum leg propped on the old coffee table.

"I thought you were out," I say to Logan. "And you were with your dad."

"Dad works third shift," he replies. "He asked Ryan to take me home. I'm out of driving. Doesn't mean my mind stopped working."

Ryan snorts. "That's up for debate." I throw him a questioning glare, and he earns a little respect when he doesn't look away.

"Beth and Logan see something in you," he says. "But know if you hurt either one of them again, I'll kick your ass."

Fair enough. "Noted. But good luck with that."

"Now that the pissing contest is over," says Abby, "how's Rachel?"

I shrug. Rachel wouldn't want her business discussed.

"Abby and I told them everything," Logan says, unrepentant. "In detail."

"Wasn't your place." Embarrassment thinly disguised as anger seeps into my tone.

"Wasn't, but I did it anyhow."

"I borrowed two thousand dollars from my brothers' parents." Noah jumps in, possibly to stop my anger at Logan from accelerating. Noah's a proud guy, and that type of gesture had to kill his soul. "To cover rent for the semester. I hoped to buy us enough time until you got a job where you could support yourself. The money is yours."

An understanding passes between us. If I accept the money, Noah moves into the dorms and I return to foster care. "It's not enough."

"More than half," says Logan. "We still have that seven hundred."

"Fine, twenty-seven hundred, but we're still short."

"I've got five hundred saved to buy a car," says Beth. She winks at Ryan. "You'll have to drive me around longer."

Before I can tell her no Logan says, "Thirty-two hundred."

Noah stretches his arms out to his sides. "And we race for the rest."

We've entered the land of fantasy. "With what? Your piece of shit couldn't beat a Yugo."

Echo crosses the room and curls around Noah. "No, but I bet a '65 'Vette could."

"No, Echo." The Corvette belonged to her brother. It's the only memory she has left of him. "The car is vintage and worth more than my sorry ass. Racing it could burn out the engine."

"Could," she says. "But Noah would win first. We can always fix the car. You've done it before."

No. I shift my gaze to Noah. "Eric will find out that you helped. He'll mark both you and Echo."

A dangerous shadow crosses Noah's face as he holds Echo tighter. "I can take care of what's mine. Besides, Eric will back off once he's paid."

He may not be wary of Eric, but I am. I'm not sure I can allow the target on his back. I glance at the clock on the microwave. "I've got to get Rachel home in time for curfew. I'll drive her car, but I need someone to follow to bring me home."

"I'll do it," says Abby.

"You don't have a car," I say.

"I told Tom about the accident. He's going to let you use one of his cars until you get your Mustang working again. I'll get it, then meet you at Rachel's."

"Fine."

Abby leaves and a second later I follow. She stalls near the front entrance, waiting for me to join her. "I know what you're thinking, Isaiah, and I think you're wrong."

I place my hand over the door handle, keeping her there. "What exactly am I thinking?"

"The same thing I think when I look in the mirror every morning—that's the face of someone living in pissed-off desperation."

"A few weeks ago you wanted me to steal. A thousand dollars a car. I could make the money in one night and have Rachel on my arm by morning, remember?"

Abby rubs her hands over her face. "That was before."

"Before what?"

"Before I met Rachel. Before she became my friend. Before I saw how happy she made you. Before I saw that you could be like Noah and get out of this part of town. You got your certification, a job waiting after graduation and a girl who loves you. If you steal those cars..." She stares at her feet. "It'll change you. Once you go down that road, there's no going back."

Abby hates selling drugs, but she's stuck. Her family has seen to that. So has her employer. "I'll be in and then right back out," I say.

"Yeah, keep telling yourself that. You'll be owned. Not as bad as if Eric owns you, but they'll always hold what you've done over your head. You'll never be free."

I'm not free. The future I once dreamed of has crumbled into dust. "I don't care about my freedom anymore. This is about Rachel."

The door upstairs opens and closes. Rachel appears at the top of the stairs. I've got thirty-two hundred in seed money and only one night to race. If I take everyone up on their offer, I'll go back to foster care and Noah and Echo will have targets painted on their backs. I would be wreaking all this damage in the hope I can win at the dragway.

Rachel holds tightly to the banister. Yeah, Abby's employer will own me, but Rachel will be safe. "Make the deal, Abby."

Rachel

ISAIAH PARKS MY CAR A block from the security gate of my neighborhood. Headlights flash behind us as Abby follows his lead. Her lights turn off, indicating that she's granting us time.

We've been silent—Isaiah and I. Not that silence is unusual between us, but it's never been so heavy. We're both angry, hurt. I'll admit to being scared. "We're not going to make the money, are we?"

"Eric will be paid off this weekend," he says. "What happened tonight, the panic attack, that's been going on for a while, hasn't it?"

The unspoken accusation that I've lied to him slices like a knife. I rest my head on the back of the seat. "How are we coming up with the money?"

"You vomited blood," he says, ignoring me. "I'm not talking about anything until we discuss this."

"Isaiah—"

"You vomited blood," he repeats.

"I know."

"Rachel...you need help."

I laugh and it's the same bitter laugh I remember him giving when we met so many weeks ago. "So do you."

"I love you." Isaiah says it so simply that my heart soars and sinks at the same time.

"I love you," I whisper. "Did you ever think that loving someone could hurt so bad?"

Isaiah shakes his head and stares out the window.

"What's going to happen to us?" I ask. Because I don't know how the two of us can continue forward. Isaiah refuses to let me in. It's sort of cruel. He's brought me close with his stories of his childhood and with his words of love, but he can't relinquish control. I refuse to be with someone who won't treat me as an equal.

Isaiah clears his throat. "I failed the ASE."

Dread washes over me. "You said you passed...."

"They accused me of cheating so they failed me. Once Pro Performance finds out, I'll lose the internship and the job. I have nothing left to offer you."

I grow numb as my mind races to understand. "Why would they think you cheated? I mean, there's no way you would, so why would anyone else think it?"

"Doesn't matter. It's over."

"It's not. You can retake it. Prove to them that you know everything about cars."

His hands hover over the wheel as if he wants to hit it, but he doesn't. Instead he slowly lowers his palms to the leather covering. "It's over. The certification. The job. The hope we could pay Eric off by racing."

"I'm going to race Zach." It's the only way. "And I don't need your permission to do it."

Isaiah slams his hand against the steering wheel and I flinch. "With what, Rachel? Our seven hundred? Let's say you win, we're still down over three thousand dollars. We tried and we failed. Playing by the rules is no longer an option."

"Then we'll take on more races. I'll race Zach more than once. He said money wasn't a problem—"

"Because he's betting Eric's money."

My face whips as if I've been smacked. "What did you say?"

"Zach's working for Eric."

There's a disorientation like I'm having an out-of-body experience. He's known this and he hasn't told me.

"I'm going to steal cars to make the money to pay Eric." There's no mistaking the determination in his voice or the set of his jaw. He's made his decision, and *nothing* I can say will change his mind. I open the door to the car.

"Rachel," Isaiah pleads.

I pause, long enough to give him the opportunity to apologize for keeping the secret. To tell me that I misheard about stealing the cars.

"Even if it wasn't the case, we'd need to race Friday and Saturday night. Are you going to walk away from your mom's charity event to race? Just give me time to fix this and then—"

"Then what?" I snap. When Isaiah says nothing, I point at his door. "Get out of my car."

With a click of the handle he does, and he meets me in front of the hood. Without looking at him, I reach into my coat, extract his lighter and hold it out to him.

Isaiah's forehead wrinkles as he looks away. "Don't do this, Rachel."

"I'm not the one doing this." I hold my palm out, waiting

for my keys. Isaiah's hand covers mine. The keys feel frozen against my skin and the lighter is gone.

"I'm doing it to protect you," he says.

"No, you're not," I whisper to the ground. "You're doing it to protect yourself. You never really let me in, did you?"

His hand falls away and I slide behind the wheel. Isaiah stands off to the side and I drive home without looking back. Isaiah says he's protecting me. My brothers and father say the same thing about my mom. For the first time in my life, I wonder if my mother wants to be protected.

It's supposed to be used as a windowless conference room, but Mom fashioned it into her command center. The ballroom across the hall is decorated with thousands of mini pink roses and shimmering crystals. Dressed in their best gowns and tuxes, hundreds of people nibble on hors d'oeuvres. There will be a salad, followed by a choice of fish or steak, and during the cheesecake dessert, I'll stand and tell everyone how much I loved Colleen. Then there will be dancing.

I'll excuse myself, with grace I hope, and spend the rest of the evening in the bathroom—dying.

Taped to the mirror my mother brought in so the two of us could fix our hair and makeup is a picture of Colleen. Mom's right. Everyone's right. I resemble her. Long blond hair. Dark blue eyes. Even the smile. Except everything about me looks better on her.

I hate Colleen. Hate her. I've never met her and I despise her.

How dare she be perfect and beautiful and everything everyone could have ever dreamed of in a sister and daughter.

How dare she get sick and die and leave this entire family in shambles. How dare she haunt me from her grave, taunting me with how I will never be good enough.

I glance at my cell resting on the table. Like the first few days after I met Isaiah, I carry it around, hoping for a call or a text. I've received neither. Abby and I talk. She says he's miserable, a bear to be around, and that he's stealing the cars tonight.

The deadline to pay Eric is midnight.

I don't want Isaiah to become a criminal. My heart thuds faster when I pick up the phone. The worst that will happen is that he doesn't respond. I've already proved once that I can live through that. Me: :(

The door opens, and the sound of laughter and conversation drifts in with my mother. She's radiant in red, and she's complete happiness and smiles. My mother lost Colleen, but she's content living with the replacement who fakes every moment.

"The party is going beautifully. You should come out, Rachel. There are several nice-looking young men from school in attendance. Is Abby here yet?"

Abby. I forgot. She told Mom she'd come. "No."

"Do you like your new phone?"

I stare at the device in my hands. After I tossed my old phone at the top of the hill and left it in the rain while Isaiah and I sought shelter in his car, it stopped working. I told my parents I dropped it in the toilet. Dad purchased me something ostentatious. Too many bells. Too many whistles. "It's fine."

My fingers brush over the screen, praying for his response. From out of the corner of my eye, I peer at my mother as she reapplies her lipstick. A sinking desperation claws at me. Isaiah's off becoming a criminal to save me when he was right. Too terrified of losing my mother's love and approval, I wouldn't have walked away from this event to race.

Mom slides her finger along the bottom of her lip to wipe off the excess makeup. She's perfection to a T, but she's never seen me. What type of love is that? Better, is that a love worth having? "If I needed money, would you give it to me?"

The words fall out as if I'm on autopilot, and maybe I am. *I need five thousand dollars, Mom. I need to save the guy I love.* Beside me, Mom pushes her hair into place. "Of course. What do you need?"

As I open my mouth, preparing to ask, the door opens, and the country club's manager steps in. "Mrs. Young, your presence is requested in the kitchen."

Mom pats my shoulder. "We'll talk after dinner."

After my speech. After Isaiah becomes a criminal. Before I can ask her to stay, she leaves. My phone vibrates and my finger trembles as I awaken the screen.

Isaiah: Don't b. I love u.

Me: Please don't do it.

Isaiah: I have no choice.

The clock ticks time away and each second that passes feels like a step toward death row. Outside of that door looms either West or Ethan. Neither of them will permit me to leave. I have two choices. Give the speech and have the attack or tell the truth and disappoint my family.

Isaiah said I need help. Maybe he's right. Maybe I do.

Me: I'll get help if you do. I'll let my family in on my nightmare if you let me help you. You have to decide. Now.

I will my phone to ring; pray for it to vibrate. Too much time passes and there's a knock on the door.

"Rachel," Ethan says with sad eyes. "Mom said that it's time for us to be seated for dinner."

And after the dinner will be the speech. I rest the phone on the table and gather the skirt of my dress. Ethan places a hand on my back as I walk past him. "It'll be okay, Rach. I swear. Just breathe through the speech, and West and I will get you out unnoticed. We'll protect you."

I say nothing. I'm tired of being protected.

Isaiah

PEOPLE BELIEVE THAT CARS ARE stolen in the dead of night, while the entire world sleeps. While that may be true, there are simpler ways. Later tonight, if it comes down to it, I'll become the cliché. Otherwise, I'm opting for easy.

I stand in the shadows of the alley outside a liquor store waiting for the moron who hates cold weather yet yearns for a drink. Someone will abandon their car with it still running. Since it's early in the evening, I have the time to wait.

Rachel's text weighs on me. *I'll get help if you do. I'll let my family in on my nightmare if you let me help you. You have to decide. Now.*

For four days, Rachel and I have ignored each other, and when she breaks the silence she offers an ultimatum that cracks open my heart. Help her or protect her. Rachel needs help or she'll end up in the hospital. But I have to steal the cars to protect her. She doesn't understand.

Rachel's wrong on this. She said I never let her in. My head falls back against the cold brick of the building. I told her things I never told anyone. Yet her words have become a mantra in my mind...*you never let me in.*

I inhale, trying to erase the thoughts. I've got a job to do and distractions can cause danger. A Saturn pulls into the lot right as a pizza delivery guy walks out of the store. The Saturn owner emerges from his car and my heart pumps strongly. The motor still runs as he closes the door to his empty car.

The delivery guy asks, "Do you know Elmont?"

My head jerks back—that's my mom's street.

"Yeah," says the driver. "It's the side street to the right."

They say a few more things and the delivery guy takes off and the other man enters the store. My eyes trail after the delivery guy.

Protection—Mom used the same word with me.

"She's my mom," I told Rachel.

"You'll see her when you're ready."

For some reason, I'm ready now.

If it is at all possible, the house is smaller than Shirley and Dale's. It's a shotgun house, meaning it shoots straight back. The living room is first, the next room is typically the bedroom, followed by a makeshift bathroom and kitchen.

On an uneven sidewalk, I assess the house with my thumbs hitched in my pocket. Behind a bedraggled lace curtain, a dim light shines and the flashing of a blue screen indicates a television. The crumbling front stoop shelves an old mason jar full of cigarette butts and a small green ceramic frog. Mom liked frogs.

The metal screen door rattles as I knock. The floor creaks on the other side. There's hesitation for what I assume is a glance through the peephole, and the door swings open.

Mom's eyes are wide and color touches her cheeks. She's dressed in jeans and a T-shirt. The same big hoop earrings move when she tucks her short dark hair behind her ears. "Isaiah. Come on in."

Her living room consists of a couch, end tables, a recliner and a television. She's been out for two years so she's had time to collect. "Can you come out?"

"Sure." She steps into the cool night with bare feet, leaving the wooden door open. From the living room, the final round of *Jeopardy* begins.

Mom retrieves the pack of Marlboro Lights and a lighter from behind the glass jar. "Do you mind?"

I shake my head, and Mom sits on the step of the stoop. She pulls out a cigarette and flicks the flint of the lighter three times, curses and jiggles the lighter before trying again. Growing impatient, I yank my lighter out of my pocket and light the cigarette for her.

"Thanks," she mumbles. After a long draw and even longer exhale she says, "I don't have money to give you. I live on a tight budget, but I'll have something next week."

Jesus Christ. The weight of what I've done forces me to sit next to her. "I'm not interested in your money." Not anymore.

She taps the ashes to the ground. "I named you after a person in the Bible. Isaiah—a prophet of God. Did you know that?"

"No."

"Your grandpa, my dad, was a reverend." She inhales a long draw from the cigarette, leaving a path of red ashes. "He died three years ago." Mom dangles the cigarette. "Lung cancer. My mom died a few months later. Probably from a broken heart."

"Sorry," I say. It feels weird to hear I had family. "They didn't want me."

"I told them not to take you."

I raise an eyebrow. "They agreed."

"Yeah," she says. "They did, but it killed them. Me, Momma and Daddy were prideful to the point it hurt." She sucks away the rest of the cigarette and smashes it against the concrete. "Why are you here?"

"You had something you needed to say, and I think I'm ready for you to say it."

She slides the broken lighter in her hands. "Funny. I seemed hell-bent on saying it until now." Mom has a soft Southern accent. Not normal for someone raised in Florida.

"Did you grow up in Florida?" I ask.

She tilts her head as she looks at me and almost smiles. "You remember?"

I shrug and lie. "I remember the beach."

"I was raised a few counties south of here in a town with one stoplight. When I was sixteen Daddy took a new job in Florida and I ran away to be with the guy I loved."

"My dad?" I ask before I can stop myself.

She stares at her painted toenails. "Sorry. No. Good thing, too. Turned out the bastard was married to a crack whore."

Taking another cigarette out, she gestures for my lighter. I refuse to give it to her, but I do light the cigarette for her again.

"You're real protective of that," she says.

"I had a good home once." I return the lighter to my

pocket. "The guy gave it and a compass to me before he and his family moved to California." The same guy who called me a dragon. The compass was for me to find my way. Both tattoos are for him.

She sighs. "For ten years, I thought about how I would explain this to you. I made up lie after lie, and when I got out, I couldn't face you. So I spent two more years trying to think of something else to tell you, and now that you're here I realize it's still not good enough."

"Try the truth."

She laughs. "I'm not sure I know what it is anymore." Ashes drift into the breeze. "I slept with a couple guys, Isaiah. Not knowing for sure who your dad was, I decided to raise you myself. Me and you did okay for a while. I had a job, but then I lost it."

The smoke from her mouth billows into a ball. "I went home and asked for help. Daddy wanted me to repent in front of his congregation—to tell them how I was a sinner. I thought that made you look like a sin, so I refused. I ripped you out of that house so fast that I had burn marks on my hands. I said I was protecting you. Daddy said I was stubborn.

"We came back here. We needed food. Money. So..." She shrugs. "Do you remember?"

I do. "I liked the houses that had cable." Mom broke into houses during the day with me by her side. Images of walking up long driveways and heading into backyards fills my mind. The sound of a window being slid open and the feel of the cool central air hitting my face as she pushed me in.

My heart would hammer as I walked through the silent

house to open the back door for my mother. As she rum-
maged through the house, she'd let me watch TV and eat
whatever cookies she found in the kitchen. I thought it was
great...until she got caught.

Mom stares at the night sky, searching for something. "I
often wondered what would have happened if I stayed and
did as Daddy asked or if I had agreed to let them take you or
if I let that one couple adopt you when you were ten."

My head jerks to glare at her. "They wanted me?"

"Yeah." She draws on the cigarette again. "They wanted
you, but I didn't know how to let you go. Plus, I was worried if
I made the wrong choice, again, you'd end up in a bad home.
I thought the state would protect you." Mom rubs her eyes.
"I thought I was protecting you."

Faint memories emerge of my then social worker asking
me if I'd like to stay with that family. At the time, I hadn't
known she meant for good. "I told the state I wanted to stay
with them."

"I know," she says. "He told me. Maybe they could have
taken you without my consent. I don't know, but that guy
wanted my blessing. How could I be sure you were making
the right choice?"

"I knew what I wanted." I wanted to be with that family.
With the man who called me a dragon. A man who believed
I was more life than destruction. My mother ruined my shot
at happiness because she couldn't let go. Because she had to
control everything, even from prison.

Just like my need to control.

As if a lightning bolt ripped out of the sky and struck me,

I jump off the stoop. Mom stands, anxious over my sudden movement. "Are you okay?"

I tear my cell phone out of my pocket and text Rachel: don't do the speech.

Seconds go by, maybe minutes. Nothing in return. "I've gotta go."

Rachel

OUR ENTIRE FAMILY SITS AT a large round table. The waiters remove the remains of dinner and replace it with beautifully decorated pieces of cheesecake. Everyone claps as the
last eloquent speaker, a doctor who specializes in leukemia,
finishes his speech. Mom flashes me a smile as she slides out
of her chair so she can introduce me.

I draw in air and release it, a continual action. I try not to
obsess over how this is the longest speech I've ever given in
public or how this is the largest crowd I've ever spoken to or
how people will stare or how they'll laugh when they hear
my trembling voice.

I try not to think about Isaiah stealing cars or Eric appearing on my doorstep tomorrow morning or how Gavin is antsy
and how the news of his gambling addiction will affect our
mother. I try to ignore the heat crawling up my neck and the
way my stomach cramps. I try not to think about vomiting
in public.

My hands ball in my lap and from under the table, Ethan
grabs them. "Don't do it."

My eyes hold his. "What?"

"This is wrong. You can't do this to yourself, and I shouldn't let you."

"We're doing this for Mom," I whisper, as Mom starts to introduce me by explaining who Colleen was, because let's face it, my entire life is defined by her oldest daughter.

"But who's looking out for you?" he asks.

"...my youngest daughter, Rachel Young."

People applaud at my name. I stand, and Ethan still clutches my hand. We stare at each other as he also straightens. He wraps his arms around me and I allow the embrace.

"I forgot I was supposed to be your best friend," he says.

I hug him tightly. "So did I."

The applause continues and I leave my twin for the podium. Typically this time of year, Mom's so low, she can barely get out of bed, but this year, it's different. Her eyes shine as she kisses my cheek and the pride and love radiating from her creates a blanket of guilt over my skin. Who does that pride and love even belong to? It can't be for me.

On the podium, the speech Mom prepared is laid out—typed and double-spaced. I brush the hair from my face and ignore my shaking hand as I lower the microphone. Silence spreads across the room. Occasionally someone coughs or there is a clink of a fork against china.

I concentrate on the words on the paper, not on the eyes on me. "Colleen was barely a teenager when she discovered she had leukemia..."

My stomach aches and I shift my footing. I sip water and a man clears his throat. The crowd grows uncomfortable. I refocus on the speech and freeze on the next words...*my sister.*

Somewhere deep inside of me, this horrible emptiness folds in like a black hole.

My sister. I search the crowd…looking for Ethan. I have a brother—a twin—and I have older brothers, but I've never known a sister.

People begin to whisper, and Ethan stands. He thinks I'm on the verge of an attack. West joins him. I take a deep breath, and for the first time in my life in front of a crowd, I'm able to breathe. "I never met Colleen."

I cover the speech with my hands and focus instead on my two lifelines: Ethan and West. "I have brothers. Lots of them." And people laugh, and that makes me almost smile.

"But I don't know what it's like to have a sister. For weeks, I've talked about how great Colleen was and about her beauty and strength, and the entire time I talk all I can think is how I sort of hate her because I can never be as awesome as her."

I swallow as my throat tightens. "If she didn't die then maybe she could have taught me all those things that I lack that she possessed—like grace and compassion and how to be an extrovert. Maybe if she didn't die, then my parents and my oldest brothers wouldn't have spent so much of their lives living in the past. I used to think I hated Colleen, but I don't. I do hate cancer." I stop as my lips quiver. I hate cancer. So much.

"I hate how it took someone wonderful and destroyed her. I hate how cancer ripped apart a family. I hate…I hate…that I would have never been born without her death. Cancer wasn't fair to Colleen. It wasn't fair to Mom and Dad. It wasn't fair to Gavin and Jack."

A tear escapes from the corner of my eye as I stare straight at my parents. "And it sure wasn't fair to West, Ethan or me."

My mother places a hand over her mouth, and a sickening pain strangles my gut when I realize I spoke every thought I've had since I can remember. My body shakes and I run a hand through my hair. What have I done?

A million eyes gawk at me. The back door to the room opens and I almost weep with relief: Isaiah.

 Isaiah

THE ENTIRE ROOM TURNS AND stares. There's no doubt what they see—ripped jeans, a black T-shirt, tattoos and earrings. I don't care what *they* see. All I care about is what *she* sees: a person unwelcomed or the guy she loves.

A tear flows down her face, and the hand wrapped at her waist tells me she's paralyzed. In a long gold ball gown that's more skirt than dress, Rachel is truly the angel I believe her to be. A man in a tuxedo stands. "Son, I think you have the wrong room."

"No. I don't." I stride between the tables, keeping my eyes locked with hers. The closer I get, the more she straightens. Her hand falls from her stomach, and the tear clears from her face. Rachel gazes at me as if I'm a dream. I extend my hand, palm out. "I need help."

Her blue eyes lose their glaze, and the hue of violet I love so much returns. "So do I."

My fingers tighten around hers and I gesture to the parking lot. "Is your car here?"

She nods. "Good," I say. "Because Zach will only race you in your Mustang."

The smile she flashed to me the first night we met brightens her face. "Then let's go."

Rachel

WITH MY HAND IN HIS, Isaiah sets a blinding speed and I match it. People stand, unsure what to do. Confused and rapid conversation erupts around us. I should be freaked by the way they stare at me, but instead, I get hit with an adrenaline rush and I feel—alive.

In the hallway, I'm desperate to keep pace, hoping to leave my family behind. I kick the heels off my feet, and Isaiah flashes a crazy grin. "Blacktop's cold."

"I can't drive in heels. Besides, you can carry me."

I love how he laughs.

"I'll need clothes," I say.

"Zach would pay double for you to race him in that."

"I'm serious."

"We'll call Abby and Echo once we get in the car. They'll find something."

"Rachel!" my father yells from down the hallway and I stop cold. The blood drains from my body.

Isaiah rounds on me, concern clouding his eyes. "What's wrong?"

"I need my keys."

He yanks a key out of his pocket. "Had one made. In case you lost yours."

"Rachel!" My father slows and warily eyes us as Isaiah moves in front of me.

"My father won't hurt me," I whisper to him.

"It's not him," he mutters. "It's your asshole brothers I've got a problem with."

Taking his hand, I step by his side. Isaiah shoots me an unsaid warning.

"Dad," I say with a mixture of complete fear and courage. "This is Isaiah."

Isaiah nods. My father gapes. Overall, the first introduction could have gone worse. One by one, my brothers join my father. Each one of them a different level of angry.

"What's going on?" Dad asks.

I turn my back to my family. "Go get the car," I whisper to him.

Isaiah glares at my brothers. "I won't leave you here."

"I'm going with you. Just do as I ask."

As if it physically hurts him, Isaiah walks out the door. I inhale deeply, hoping I made the right decision as I confront my family. With wide eyes and a hand on her dress, Mom slowly joins my father. "Who was that, Rachel?"

"My boyfriend," I say. "His name is Isaiah."

My father's skin becomes a strange shade of purple as he loosens his tie. "What you've done tonight...with that boy... and that speech..."

I cut him off. "I only did what you and Mom asked. You wanted me to talk about Colleen, and I did."

His anger grows, as does the level of his voice. "That was an embarrassment!"

"It was the truth!" I scream.

My father blinks and my mother tilts her head. She peers at me as if looking at someone she's never seen before. Maybe she is, because the person in front of them *is* me: the Rachel I've hidden for years. I grab Mom's hands, squeezing, begging for her to see. "Look at me."

"I am," she says softly.

"Look at me!" I scream. "I'm not Colleen. I'm not even a bad replica. I'm Rachel. I hate purple and I hate malls and I hate shopping and I hate being a disappointment."

"But you said you learned to like..." And she closes her mouth.

"Because you wanted to believe." I snatch my hands away and point at my brothers. "At least look at them. Two of them want nothing more than for you to love them, and the other two spend their entire lives trying to be perfect. Meanwhile all of us are screwed-up."

"Rachel." My father's tone drops to a mixture of sad and tired. "Not now."

"Why not now?" My skirt swirls as I face him. "Have you ever thought that you created this? If you had given Mom an ounce of respect and treated her as an equal instead of like a child, that she would have found a way to get over her grief?"

Mom's eyes flit between me and Dad. "What is she talking about?"

I glare at Gavin, waiting for him to confess. Instead he lowers his head and leans his back against the wall. Disgusted, I stare at Mom. "They do the same thing to me that they do to you—protect. But I don't need their protection. I'm strong and I have a feeling you're strong, too."

"She still has panic attacks," says West. "I know you think you're strong on your own, Rach, but you need us."

My heart hurts as West and I stare at each other. Lines worry his forehead and the hurt that I see—is it possible that all his concern, his worry, his overprotection...could it be that he really just needs me to need him?

Mom's face becomes blank and pale as if she's going to pass out. "Why would you lie about being over them?"

"Because," I say with way too much anger and then force myself to calm down. "Because the real me made you sad, and when I changed you became happy. You wanted me to like shopping, so I did. You didn't want me to like cars, so I hid it. My panic attacks made you cry, so I lied."

The rumbling sound of my Mustang echoes behind me. I slowly back away from them and toward the door. "I'm done making this family happy."

West and Jack begin to move in my direction and I realize I won't make it.

"Rach!" Ethan yells, waving them off. They give him space as he grabs my arm. I jerk, but he subtly shakes his head. Ethan shoves my small purse into my hand and abruptly opens the door. "You owe me."

Isaiah

AT THE DRAGWAY, I PARK Rachel's Mustang next to Echo's '65 Corvette and smile when I hear the sharp intake of air from Rachel.

"She's beautiful." Either forgetting or not caring she has no shoes, Rachel plops out of the car in full ball gown and heads for the 'Vette. "Are those the original fenders?"

Standing next to each other, Echo and Noah laugh. Echo answers, "I don't know."

Completely floored the owner of such a classic doesn't know the answer, Rachel turns to me. I sweep her up into my arms, hating that she's barefoot on gravel, and she squeals when I do it. "The car belonged to Echo's brother."

"Oh," she says, remembering how I explained that he died.

"I'm rethinking that double date," says Noah. "One car freak is enough."

"Tough," I tell him. I nuzzle the top of Rachel's head, inhaling her sweet ocean scent. Part of me is higher than I've ever felt in my life. She chose me and I chose her. Nothing will stop us. "Echo, do you have clothes?"

"Yep." She shows a pair of jeans and a T-shirt. "They're mine so they'll be a bit too long."

"And I brought shoes." Abby magically appears beside Echo. She gives Rachel the pair Abby most often wears, and I set Rachel down. With a quick peck to my lips, Rachel goes off to change.

"Do you have the money?" I ask Noah.

He hands me an envelope and it feels heavy. This is how much it cost me to be free from the system. "You really did have my back," I say to him.

Noah shifts so that his hair hides his eyes. "I would do anything for you or Beth."

"Sorry, man. I've been a dick."

"Yeah, you have." He smiles and so do I.

"We've got two hours until this place closes." I take the rest of our money and slip it into the envelope. Thumbing through the cash, I realize there's more here than there should be, even with the money Beth put up. "I thought you said you only borrowed two thousand."

"I did," says Noah. "Abby said she chose a side. We need to win nine hundred."

The girls come out of the bathroom. Rachel drags the dress along with her. "We could use this thing as a parachute."

I stare at Abby as she walks by, and my never-ending gaze makes her squirm.

"What's your problem?" she asks.

"Thanks," I say.

"Pissing Eric off is fun. Besides, it was your money to begin with."

No, she did it because she and I are friends.

"I got us races." Noah leans on the driver's-side door of the Corvette. "Since you were taking your time winning the girl."

Over the loudspeaker, the announcer calls the next set of races. I look at Noah and nod with my chin. "Mount up."

Rachel

THE DRAGSTERS' ENGINES SCREAM INTO the night. From the top row of the bleachers, Eric looks down on me, waiting. Our money is due to him by midnight. We're twenty minutes away and five hundred short.

Standing next to the bleachers, I watch from a distance as Echo and Abby wait for Noah and Isaiah to bring her Corvette back around to the side. The engine burned at the line, costing Noah the race and Echo her car.

I suck in my bottom lip as I glance at Echo again. It was her brother's car. The only piece she has left of her best friend that died in Afghanistan. I think of Gavin, Jack, Ethan and West. Right now, I'm mad at them and they're mad at me, but it would kill me if they died.

And I cost Echo his car.

Loose rocks roll on the blacktop and Zach appears at my side. "I hear you're finally taking the race against me."

I nod. Isaiah didn't have to tell me that we're down to desperate. "What happens if I lose?"

Zach's eyes shoot up behind me, and I don't have to follow his gaze to know that he's looking at Eric. Shoving his hands in his pockets, Zach steps closer to me and whispers, "Don't take this race."

Ironic how Isaiah had tried to warn me away from racing on that first night we met, but I don't regret a single decision. Because I stuck around, I fell in love with him. "I don't have a choice. Now tell me what happens if I lose."

"You do have a choice," he pleads. "I thought I did, too, but I don't now. I have to win and I will. I've seen you race before. You don't have it in you to win."

"If I lose, Zach."

"He'll own you. He'll own Isaiah. Details don't matter at that point."

I suck in air and slowly release it. "I'll see you at the line."

Noah and Isaiah push the Corvette into a vacant spot and when they pop the hood they both curse as smoke billows out. I wander to stand beside Echo and Abby. Echo's finger taps anxiously against her arm.

"I'm sorry," I tell her. To see something that means so much to her fall apart is heart-wrenching. Knowing that Isaiah and I are responsible is devastating.

"So am I," she says. "Noah lost two hundred because the 'Vette broke down at the line."

"Echo..." How do I say this so she doesn't deck me, because she obviously doesn't know. "Fixing the engine on a '65 Corvette is going to cost a lot more than two hundred dollars."

Echo rips her gaze from the car. "We have forever to fix the car. We've got twenty minutes to come up with five hundred. You and Isaiah are more important than any car."

Abby elbows me. "Shocking, isn't it?"

"What I don't get is how this guy knows we're here." Echo

looks over at Eric, who seems all too happy with the turn of events.

"Because he's Satan," says Abby.

With his shoulders hunched over, as if preparing to tell a loved one the news of a death, Isaiah slowly strides over. "I'm sorry, Echo. I swear to you, I'll fix it."

"It's okay, Isaiah. I knew what I was getting into."

His heavy storm-cloud eyes glance at me. "We're short." Isaiah draws me into him. "This scares the shit out of me, angel."

I place a slow kiss against his cheek and a longer one against his lips. "I won't lose."

At least I pray I won't. The confidence I'm exuding on the outside doesn't exist on the inside. Isaiah worked hard to prohibit this race, but in the end, couldn't stop it. It's on me to save the two of us.

The loss of control, the fact he can't protect me in this moment, wages war on his face. "If you lose this race, you don't stop the car. You keep driving. This time you go to the police. You tell them everything. You get someone to protect you."

"I won't leave you."

His hands weave into my hair. "Please, Rachel. I'm trying here."

"Echo will get Rachel out," says Noah. "Rachel, I'll stay by his side."

I go to protest, but the grumble of Zach's engine interrupts. Isaiah places an arm around my waist to tuck me close. Zach yells over his engine, "What's the bet?"

"Five hundred," answers Isaiah. "Abby's holding."

"And I think I'll watch Abby." In his half strut, Eric slinks over with a few guys from the night I street raced with him.

"Pole dancers are down the street," says Abby in a bored voice. "And if I let you watch, I'd cost more."

Without waiting for his retort, Abby walks over and shows Zach our five hundred. He motions to Eric, and Eric produces a wad of cash that he holds between the slits of his fingers.

"I'll take that," she says.

"You're not neutral," Eric replies.

"And you're a jackass. Public place, Eric, and think about whose territory you're standing in. I believe at the moment I outrank you."

Eric bends his elbow to hand her the cash. She collects and counts. Once she nods to Isaiah, he crushes his lips to mine. It's a fast kiss, yet intense. Hands warm on my face, on my back. His lips moving rapidly, with such desire that when I go to catch my breath he pulls away. "I love you."

Isaiah opens the door to my Mustang, finds his helmet, flips my hair behind my ear and straps the helmet on my head. Behind me, Noah edges the fire-retardant jacket onto my arms.

Isaiah speaks at such a fast pace I can barely keep up. "If the car makes any funny sounds, does anything strange, you brake, do you understand me? Don't try to win the race. Don't floor the gas. That's when the wrecks happen. Listen to your instincts. Anything weird, you hit the brake."

I've watched Isaiah put the jacket and helmet on dozens of times, and each time my heart ached with the thought of what would happen if the car wrecked. My eyes widen as I see the sweat breaking out on his forehead. "The fire extinguisher is under the passenger seat. If the car crashes, you get out. If you can't, you grab the extinguisher, and I swear I'll be there."

"There isn't a nitrous system in the car," I remind him blankly.

His fingers pause on the zipper. "Even without it, this is dangerous." A pause. "It's okay to back out. I swear to God I'll protect you."

"I'm doing this."

"Tell her about the torque," says Noah as Isaiah zips up my jacket.

"I know what torque is," I whisper.

"Not this, angel." Isaiah secures the straps to the jacket and double-checks the helmet. "You've played with the car in parking lots, learning how to go for the light, but I've put enough torque and horsepower in your pony that she's going to kick up on you. Nothing like those bad boys with the million-dollar engines, but she'll ride up. It's a good thing. She'll come back down. Don't fight her, Rachel. Just let her run."

In the driver's seat, I numbly reach for the seat belt until Isaiah leans in. His hands quickly maneuver around the five-point harness he installed for racing. "Can you see?"

One hand grips the steering wheel, the other the stick shift. The harness has me locked tight to the chair. "Yeah." And then I start to think. "I'm not sure I'll be able to see the lines."

Isaiah squeezes my hand. "I'll walk you through it."

He closes the door and I start my pony. I rev the engine a couple of times because I need the calmness associated with her singing. Taking a deep breath, I shift into First and follow Isaiah to the starting line.

My entire life I tried to be all girl with bows and painted

nails, but feeling my baby purr beneath me, knowing that I'm about to push her—I feel very alive.

Curling his fingers as a sign to continue or using his palm as a stop, Isaiah guides me around the water to avoid a burn-out and slowly edges me to the staging area. I hit the first light and Isaiah throws his hand to a stop. My heart pounds in my chest. I'm going to drag race.

The smell of rubber hangs in the air as Zach completes his burnout. The roar of his engine grows as his car joins mine. Isaiah nods at me as he walks away. This is it. This is me on my own. Zach creeps forward, his second staging light hit. Once I hit the second line, I'll have seconds before the race starts.

I inhale deeply and tap on the gas. My second light flashes on. In rapid succession, the yellow lights count down...three...two...one...

My foot falls off the clutch as the other rams on the gas, a perfect coordination of shifting and moving. The engine roars as my body presses into the seat. Adrenaline shoots through my veins as the front wheels pop up and slam back onto the dragway. The same gravitational forces that pulled me back push me forward.

Becoming one with the car, I shift with her sounds, letting her rip, letting her run. And in seconds, I pass the finish line, laughing, soaring like a bird in flight.

I just won.

Isaiah

RACHEL BARELY PARKS HER MUSTANG when I open the door and undo the harness. She yanks the helmet off and shakes her blond hair into a mess that only makes me want to touch her more. I slip her out of the car.

She laughs as she knots her arms around my neck. Both of my arms are steel bands on her waist as I lift her feet off the ground. From this angle, she's higher than me and I have to tilt my head up to meet her lips.

Rachel sends hot shivers down my spine as her hands caress my neck and cheek. Her lips move smoothly against mine. She's drawing me in by conjuring up images of being alone with her, and forcing me to forget that we have an audience. Until Noah coughs.

Her eyes have a contagious gleam. "I want to do that again."

"You're going to make scaring the shit out of me a habit, aren't you?"

Her lips whisper against mine as she speaks. "And you won't do a thing to stop it."

"No." As much as it kills me. "I won't." I reluctantly set

Rachel on the ground. Abby extends the thousand dollars to me and I put it in the envelope.

"Mind taking a walk with me, Noah?" I ask.

"Let's end this," he says.

Eric leans against the fence line on the other side of the lot. His boys loiter a few feet down, and they keep their eyes on us.

Echo places her hand on Rachel's arm. "Should you really leave your car here?"

Rachel's violet eyes stay trained on me. "No. But it'll be okay."

"Rachel." Echo gently nudges. "Let's move your car."

"It's all right, angel. We won this one."

With reluctance, Rachel slides back into the driver's seat of her car, and Echo slips into the other side. Rachel drives off, and Abby starts off after them on foot.

"Take care of her," I call out.

"I will," Abby says without looking back.

The envelope feels heavy in my hand. Not long ago, I went to Eric so I could stay out of foster care. Now I'm handing him five thousand dollars, and I'm still losing my home.

"Think he'll keep his word?" I mutter to Noah.

"No," he answers. "It's not his style to lose."

It's not. "I've told Abby to get Rachel and Echo the hell out of here the moment the first punch is thrown."

"Thanks," he says. "This is killing Echo, but she knows what to do and will help Abby get Rachel out."

"You don't have to do this."

Noah flashes the same jackass-crazy grin as the day he

moved into Shirley and Dale's. "Yeah, bro, I do. This is what brothers do for each other."

Brother. Years without a mom. Years without a dad. Knowing that no other blood relative existed on the face of the planet for me. But within two years, water becomes thicker than blood.

I hold my hand out to Noah and when he has a firm grip, I pull him in for a fast hug. We both clap each other's back.

"We're family," he whispers.

"Family," I repeat.

I let him go and we start off for the fence line. Eric watches us approach. He says nothing so I offer him the envelope. "Count it if you want."

The skinny asshole doesn't bother opening it, but instead shoves it in the inside pocket of his coat. "You say you have it, you have it."

A pair of cars roar down the dragway, silencing the conversation between us. When the noise dies down, Eric continues, "I don't understand why you want to race here. There's no money to be made."

"You didn't have to involve Zach," I say.

"I like insurance policies, and Zach was one that didn't pay out...at least for tonight. As with any policy, the interest builds with time."

I assess the area and notice Zach's car missing. He's caused me problems over the past several weeks, but once he was a friend. No one should be underneath Eric, and what I hate is there's nothing I can do about it. Zach made his choice and I've made mine. This is how forks in roads are created.

"Come back to the streets, Isaiah." Eric pushes off the fence. "That's your home."

If Eric keeps living this life, someone will steal from him again, and one day, they may take his life in the process. Mistakes I refuse to make. "Naw, Eric. I'm done."

"Never say never, my brother." Eric gives that sly grin. "You'll find me when you're short on money again. That's when we'll stop this bullshit and you work for me. You're not the first foster kid to age out of the system."

My chin rises as he speaks my fears. "What makes you think I'll come crawling to you?"

"Because I'm letting you and your girl go home injury-free. You'll remember how I've given you grace and realize that I'm not your enemy. Now if you'll excuse me, I've got other business to attend to tonight."

Noah smacks my shoulder and the two of us leave, both occasionally glancing back. But we don't need to. Eric's moved on and so have we.

"That won't happen," says Noah. "You'll make it after you age out."

"I know." I don't, but I shove the doubt away. I can only handle one battle at a time.

Laughter representing our futures guides us to a streetlight. For Noah, the future includes a redhead, and mine includes a blonde.

When Rachel sees me, she runs right into my arms. "Are we free?"

"Free."

"We should celebrate."

"I know this place," I say real slow. "On a hill."

She blushes. "Think I've heard of it before."

"Have you?" I ask too innocently.

"Yeah. From this really hot guy. You'd like him. He has a couple of tattoos and some earrings."

I lace my hand with hers, but the smile on my face fades with the sound of one voice.

Rachel

"RACHEL."

My head snaps in the direction of my father's voice. "What are you doing here?"

With his black tie off and the top couple of buttons of his wrinkled dress shirt undone, my father appears worn. The circles under his eyes indicate exhaustion. "Let's go home."

There's no way...none... "How did you find me?"

"Your new phone. It has a GPS tracking device." My own thoughts haunt me—*too many bells, too many whistles.*

Isaiah squeezes my hand. He subtly moves one shoulder in front of me, and I realize he senses danger. My eyes search for what alarms Isaiah and my mouth goes dry. A police officer strolls up to my father.

"What are you doing, Dad?"

He places his hands on his hips. "I want you to come home."

The police officer talks into his shoulder unit and gestures to Isaiah. "Sir, we need you to step away from the young lady."

I hold tight on to Isaiah. "Why did you bring the police?"

Dad's lip pulls back. "He abducted you."

Abducted? "I *left* with him."

"Running away is just as bad. You created chaos and left your mother and me wondering if we'd ever see you again! How can you do this to her?" Dad turns his head to the police officer. "She's seventeen. He either took my daughter or this is a runaway situation. I have an entire ballroom of people who can testify to that."

"We weren't running away!" Dad is twisting everything, and no matter what I say, no one will believe us.

"Arrest him," Dad snaps. "Let's go, Rachel. We're going home before your mother sinks too low because she thinks she's losing another daughter."

What I feared from my brothers is now happening with my father. He's separating me and Isaiah. "Please. We haven't done anything wrong."

Not true. We've done lots of things wrong, but for the first time in weeks, we have the chance to do something right.

"Sir," says the police officer with more force. His hand moves to his belt and my heart trips in my chest. "Step away from the girl."

"No," says Isaiah in a voice so cold I shiver.

"She's a minor," Dad reminds Isaiah. "And has no business being here or with you."

Noah approaches from the side with his hands in the air to show he's peaceful. "Sir, Isaiah's only seventeen. Officer, if you're arresting him, I'd like to know the charge."

The officer glances at my father. "Is that true?"

Agitation leaks into my father's tone, and his jaw jumps. "I don't know how old he is. He came into a party and took my daughter."

"I left with him," I hiss. "He didn't kidnap me and we weren't running away. I was coming home."

"Let's see some ID," says the officer. "Then we'll start to sort this out, but you should go home with your father."

"Isaiah," Noah interjects in an overly calm voice. "Show the man your ID. Now."

"Step away from the girl first." The officer's hand twitches on his belt. "And slowly take out your ID. Everyone can go home if we do this right."

Still grasping me, Isaiah slowly removes his wallet and tosses it in the direction of the police officer. "And no. I don't have a record."

The way they both stare at him, I know what they see: the tattoos and earrings and every worst nightmare. But Isaiah is nothing like that. He's gentle and kind and strong... My body starts to quake and it's not a panic attack. It's my heart—breaking and ripping into shreds. "Isaiah."

Isaiah's silver eyes have turned to ice. "It'll be okay, Rachel. Won't it?" He nods at my father.

Dad all but sneers. If I had introduced them properly, would my father have given him a chance? "You either come with me peacefully or I have this police officer physically put you in the car. Your choice, but this entire fiasco you've created is done."

"I don't give a fuck who you are," says Isaiah in a low tone that indicates the threat is very real. "No one touches her."

Off to the side, Noah lets loose a string of profanities. "Go with them, Rachel. Otherwise Isaiah *will* give them a reason to put him in jail. We'll work it out."

"Not if you're afraid of them," Isaiah whispers. "I won't let you go if you're afraid of them."

I glance at my father—years older than he was this afternoon. The way he rubs his eyes shows the worry mixed with the anger.

"I'm not scared of him." I edge so that I stand beside Isaiah. "I'm scared of losing you."

"Say goodbye to him." Dad barely keeps his voice low as he glares at Isaiah. "Do not come looking for my daughter again. Contacting her in any way is out of the question."

My arms go around Isaiah's waist and my eyes immediately flash to his, searching for a solution. Isaiah always has a way to fix things, and too panicked to think, I'm desperate for help. "Isaiah?"

Isaiah touches my face. The same warm, loving caress he's tenderly given me since I first met him. "We'll be okay."

My hand covers his. "Promise me." Because Isaiah always keeps his word. He'll move hell if he has to. Isaiah never breaks a promise.

"I swear it."

The trembling turns to shaking. I can't lose Isaiah. We just found the place where the world could be good. "I love you."

"Don't say it like that." Isaiah lowers his head so that his mouth is near mine. "Don't say it like goodbye."

"Rachel!" my father snaps.

My lips touch his and I try so hard to memorize how they feel: warm and a bit sweet. I don't want to forget this, ever. When I force myself to step back, my eyesight is so blurry that I can barely see in front of me. Isaiah shoves his hands in his pockets and shifts. Knowing he has to let me go—

commanding his body to comply. "It's okay. I promise. It'll be okay."

It'll be okay. I repeat the words over and over again. *He promised. Isaiah never breaks his promise.*

As I get closer to my father, he extends his hands. "Give me your keys."

"You can't drive a stick," I choke out.

"I'll figure it out," he snaps. "I don't trust you anymore."

Staring at Isaiah, I suddenly wish I had taken more pictures of us. I only have two. One of him I took for my phone. Another of us being silly next to my car. Two pictures. It doesn't feel like nearly enough.

Feeling the loss, I snap a mental picture of Isaiah. His dark hair shaved close to his scalp, the stubble on his chin, the muscles of his arms, the kind tilt of his lips, even though his gorgeous eyes tell me that he's in pain.

I reach into my pocket and hand my father my keys. The policeman offers Isaiah his wallet back and mumbles something to him. Isaiah locks his eyes on me, never once responding to the officer.

"Get in the car," Dad says as he opens the passenger-side door to my Mustang.

I do, wondering if I'll ever see Isaiah again. Not so long ago, I asked Isaiah if he ever thought love could hurt so bad. Little did I know, at the time, I had no idea what I was asking or how awful saying goodbye would really feel.

I slip inside, and the passenger side feels off and unnatural. Dad slams his door and thrusts the keys into the ignition. "I have never been so disappointed in anyone in my life."

His cell phone begins to ring, and Dad yanks it from his

pocket. With one glance, he drops it into the drink holder. It's a familiar number—a work number. One he typically picks up immediately. I never thought I'd see the day when his anger would surpass the love he has for his job.

"I'm sorry," I whisper, and wipe my eyes. "It's not what you think."

"Then what is it?" he bites out, so forcefully that I shake.

My hand slams over my mouth to stop the sob. My throat begins to close as I desperately search for a way to explain. "You don't understand. I love him."

His cell ceases ringing and seconds later begins again. The same number, but this time it feels louder in the small confines of the car.

"You're too young to understand what love is! He's a thug. A user. Look where you are! Look at what you've done to your mother! What the hell are you even doing here?"

Dad presses the clutch and the gas while trying to shift and the engine completely stalls out. "Dad...you need to—"

"I can do it," he yells, and the pure fury shooting from his eyes shuts me up. Again the cells stops then starts all over again.

In the rearview mirror I watch as Abby eases toward Isaiah. I'm losing the two people I love the most. Dad tries again and the engine roars to life. He successfully shifts the car into First, and I close my eyes as he grinds the gears.

"Just let me drive. I'll take us home, I swear." No matter how I try to stop them, the hot tears in my eyes overflow down my cheeks. "You can't drive a stick!"

"You ruined today." Dad ignores me completely. "You've made your mother sick. This isn't what I expect from you."

The cell stops and when it begins again, Dad reaches for it. "Goddammit!"

The light at the entrance of the dragway begins to change, and my eyes dart between the cell against his ear, the light and my father's inexperienced hand off the gearshift. "Dad, I don't think you should—"

I suck in a breath at the sound of the horn, and all I see is the grill of a semi. "Dad!"

Isaiah

I SLIP MY WALLET INTO my back pocket and watch as her father murders the clutch. The ache in my chest is enough to kill me, but I hold on to the words I said to her: I swear we'll be together. Rachel knows I'll never break my word. This love between us—it will never stop.

Noah places a hand on my shoulder. "I'm sorry."

"I love her," I say. "And she loves me. She'll be eighteen in less than a year. Graduate in less than a year and a half." Then no one can keep us apart.

"And you have me." Abby appears on my other side. "Maybe my cover will work, and I can keep you connected. You never know." But she doesn't say it like she believes it.

Abby stares after Rachel as if she lost her best friend. I place an arm around her. That's because she did. "We'll get her back." I don't know if I'm trying to convince her or me.

She wipes at her eyes. "This is why I don't do relationships."

At the intersection leading out of the dragway, the police officer turns right. The brake lights release as the Mustang rolls forward on a yellow and a tightness overwhelms my throat. The sensation that I dread, the tingling between my skin and muscles, crawls over me. I release Abby and take several steps. Terrified that if I lose sight of Rachel, I'll lose her forever.

The light switches to red and the Mustang stalls in the middle of the intersection. I hear the attempt to turn over the engine, and my feet move faster as I watch the tractor trailer move into the intersection—speeding. My world goes into slow motion as my legs pump hard to reach the car, to protect Rachel.

There's a sickening crunch and the white pony flips onto its side and rolls again and again. Like a ball hurling down a hill. From the other direction another car hits, and I scream out Rachel's name. Brakes screech, glass shatters, more cars collide. The carnage lies in front of me as her car comes to a rest. The entire body smashed beyond recognition.

Buzzing fills my head as I continue to scream her name. I push my body harder, faster, but I can't reach her. A few wisps of smoke puff from the hood.

And then fire.

I jump onto the hood of a sandwiched Civic. "Rachel!"

People are crying. Others screaming. Glass falls to the pavement. "Rachel! Answer me!"

The windshield of her car is a spiderweb, allowing me no visual access. Noah joins me on the hood of the Civic, and both of us use our arms as shields when a burst of flame shoots in our direction. Heat warms my arms. My eyes flicker, hunting for her exit. She's wedged in. Both doors blocked by other vehicles. "Rachel!"

"We gotta move this car," Noah shouts.

Her car is on fire. The thought races in my head. We slide off the hood and run to the back end of the Honda Civic. "Pick it up."

The driver of the Civic joins us. Blood stains his cheek. "It happened so fast."

Noah and I say nothing to him as we raise the back end with our bare hands. We both yell as the end lifts. My fingers scream in agony, but we keep going until we create a space. The Civic slams back on the ground. The gap isn't much, but enough to wedge through. I cough as I inhale smoke and open the driver's-side door. Blood soaks her father's white shirt, but his eyes are open and he blinks. Beyond him, Rachel lies completely broken.

"Get her out," her father coughs. "She's not responding."

Panicked adrenaline surges through my body. She can't be dead. She can't. "Noah!"

"Pull him out!" Noah says on top of the Civic. "Hand him to me."

I squat down, in order to get a better grip. "Can you stand?"

He tries to move and groans instead. "Get her out!"

Smoke rises from the dashboard, and my heart rate increases. Using my shoulder, I lean into her father and yank him out of the car. He yells in pain and screams again when Noah pulls him up. The second his body is off me, I dash into the car.

"Rachel." I say her name calmly, hoping she'll answer. "Angel, I need you to open your eyes. Come on. Talk to me."

I place my arm behind her back and the other beneath her legs. She flops like a rag doll. "You're not fucking doing this, Rachel. I made a promise, and that means you made a promise to me. We're going to be together. Do you hear me?"

I tug and Rachel's body jerks back toward her seat in response. Readjusting my grip, I yank harder, and her body resists. My lungs burn from the smoke, and I wave at the air, trying to see the problem.

My hand reaches to the floorboard, exploring, and the world halts. I swear. No, no, no, no. The floorboard collapsed up and the side smashed in, metal twists around her legs. I cradle her sweet face in my hands and talk to her as if she can hear me. My voice breaks. "Your legs are stuck, angel. Your legs are stuck."

I'm going to lose her. Please no, I'm going to lose her.

"Isaiah!" yells Noah. "You've got to get out! Get out, get out, get out!"

Isaiah

May

I SPENT A GOOD PORTION of my life trying to figure out where I would get my next meal or how to avoid physical pain. In other words—how to survive. I never had a reason to contemplate death—too busy worrying about living.

Standing in this cemetery, it's hard not to think about the end of life. Noah told me that his parents are buried in the section across from here. Echo's brother's final resting place is on the other side of the massive graveyard. No one is immune to mortality.

A light misty rain makes the warm spring day humid, causing my shirt to stick to my skin. I stay motionless, staring at the plot. There's a heaviness inside of me that could produce tears. But I push it away. I've got too many emotions running rampant.

"Are you sure?" I ask.

My mother squats and touches the tombstone. "Yes. I knew he was your father the moment you walked into that visitation room. You look exactly like him, Isaiah." She glances at me with a weak smile and glassy eyes. "He was handsome, too."

My father. Unable to stand anymore, I sit on the wet grass. James McKinley. "I'm Irish?"

She laughs. "I guess. We never discussed family trees. He was a good guy. Decent. He died before I knew I was pregnant. So I crossed him off the list of possible fathers. Once again, a stupid mistake on my part."

We're not close—me and Mom. She wants to bond. I'm okay with knowing she's alive. She pressures me for more, but I tell her she should be happy that the anger I feel for her is receding. Too much time passed between six and seventeen. Too many hurts. Sometimes it's best to forgive someone and keep them at arm's length.

"James had a big family. A little odd, but great people. I wish I had known then that you belonged to him. They would have taken us both in." She goes silent. "Or at least you. You should find them."

I scratch the back of my head. Somewhere in Kentucky, I have a big family. "I'm not sure I'd want to go through a paternity test." And be proved wrong.

"I can't say they wouldn't ask for one, but one look at you and they'd know. You're all him. Right down to the earrings and tattoos."

The thought makes me smile. "No shit?"

She laughs again. "He would have said that, too. James was good to me. We were friends, and I got stupid and took advantage of him. I never forgave myself for hurting him, and I feel awful that he never knew you existed."

"How'd he die?"

"Car accident." She stares at the tombstone as if he'd appear if she focused hard enough.

"Will you tell me about him?"

Mom relaxes back on her bottom. The rain mats her dark hair against her face. "I don't know much, but I'll tell you everything I do know. James loved motorcycles..."

At the McDonald's across the street from the cemetery, I wait in a corner booth. Courtney slips me a container of vanilla ice cream before sitting across from me with her own. She opens her purse and produces a bottle of multicolored sprinkles. She shakes some on hers and pours a whole shitload on mine.

"What are you doing?" I ask.

"Buying you ice cream." Courtney drops the bottle into her purse and digs into her soft serve. "Don't tell me that at eight you didn't wish someone would have bought you ice cream with sprinkles."

Courtney can do this now. Extract a memory buried within me with scary ease. There are times I think she's a mind reader, then I remember she's not. She was a foster kid, raised by the system, just like me. A pang in my chest makes me think of being eight and watching families buy ice cream. Courtney smiles when I take a bite.

"Do you feel like you ratted by becoming a social worker?" I ask.

She's silent as her forehead furrows. "I choose to think about how I can help other kids in ways no one helped me."

Fair enough.

"You and your mom talked a lot today." Courtney observed us from her dry car.

"Met my dad." So to speak.

"Sort of figured. How are things going with her?"

I shovel the ice cream in my mouth so I don't have to answer. My eyes narrow at the way the sweet sprinkles roll on my tongue. Courtney giggles. "By the way, gummy worms on ice cream are way overrated."

"Noted." I mix the ice cream. "I can't give her what she wants."

"You don't have to," she says. "I never said a relationship with her is healthy, just that you should talk to her. From experience, you eventually would have had an ache to see your mom. I thought it would be better to deal with her while you've got me to buy you ice cream afterward."

"You should have told me when we first met you were system-produced."

She squishes her lips together. "I was once pissed-off-seventeen. You weren't ready to listen."

True.

"Congrats, by the way. Heard you aced the exam."

"Thanks." I passed my ASE...again. My internship and job secured. I nudge the ice cream away and relax back in my seat. Lately, I feel like I've been drifting. I'm back in foster care at Shirley and Dale's. Noah lives in the dorms. We still talk, but not nearly as often. There are times I feel...alone.

"I know people who have families," I say. "They graduate from high school and they get a job or go to college and if they fuck it all up they go back home." I pause, tapping my finger on the table. "What do I do if..." I fuck it all up. I clear my throat and my eyebrows move closer together. "Where do I go?"

Courtney shoves her ice cream away, too. "Foster care sucks, but so does aging out. It's weird. You spend the entire first part of your life fighting to get out and then one day... you are out. Then you want to scream at the closed door that you're still a kid, but everyone is pretty damned insistent you're an adult. I cried a lot when I first aged out."

My lips quirk. "I don't think I'll be crying."

Courtney snorts. "Or whatever boys do."

I swallow and find the courage to say the words. "I don't want to be homeless."

"You won't be." She waggles her eyebrows and pulls a folder out of her bag. "I have a plan. You don't turn eighteen until this summer, so we have a couple more months before you age out. I can teach you how to budget and help you find a place to live and all sorts of fun adult things. And here's the cool part. I'll still be around when you turn eighteen. I may not be mandatory, but I don't disappear."

The alarm on my phone rings, and Courtney smiles, knowing why I'm ready to bolt. "We'll start this next week."

I stand. "Thanks. For everything."

"No problem. And next week we're getting hot fudge."

Rachel

I DREAM A LOT. FOR the past three months, I've been sleeping more than I'm awake. Between surgeries, hospital stays, pain meds and rehab, I always seem tired.

I see Isaiah in my dreams. Giving that rare smile. Laughing that deep chuckle. Every now and then, I dream of his kiss. Those are my favorites.

Someone whispers and I open my eyes. The specialist appointment wore me out physically. My therapy appointment with my counselor knocked me out mentally. I stretch my arms on the bed and hear crinkling to the side. I turn my head and see a Mustang magazine with a note:

Tell me which one you want. I love you—Dad.

My fingers brush the note before I toss the magazine onto my bedside table. I don't want to think about cars, not yet.

"Told you she wasn't ready," whispers a deep voice from across the room.

Propping up on my elbows, I lift my upper body. West and Ethan sit on the floor, both with controllers in their hands.

Their eyes locked on the video game they play with no sound on my flat screen. The two of them practically moved in here when I came home from the hospital. Most of the time, I don't mind the company.

Ethan glances over his shoulder at me. "Finally." He tosses the controller on the floor, and West follows his lead.

"Field trip, baby sis," says West. He flips his hat so that it's backward.

I flop back on the bed. "I've got rehab in two hours."

"That's why we're going now," Ethan says. "You'll be too tired later. How do you want to do this?"

It's a question I'm used to, and one they've learned to ask. It's been weird between my family and me. My entire life I never wanted to be the family weakling, and now there's absolutely no doubt that I'm the physically weakest one under the roof. The casts are off, but both of my legs are in a full brace.

While it's apparent to anyone that I can't run as far as my brothers or dance like my mom, what can't be seen by the naked eye is the real miracle. It was hard to ask for help at first. I made everything a million times harder by my need to do it all myself, and it was a zillion times harder for my family not to do things for me. But I learned to ask. And they learned not to jump in. And so my weakness has made me stronger.

"Let me swing my legs off the bed."

My brothers both take two steps back and watch as I use my upper-body strength to readjust myself so that my legs are near the edge. My face goes red and my teeth clench, but inch by fought-after inch, both of my legs hover over the side.

I release enough air to move the hair hanging in my face. The small smile tugs at my lips. I did it. "Your turn."

"Grab her wheelchair," says Ethan as he slips his arms around me and lifts me into the air. West goes out the door of my bedroom first, and Ethan follows. The workmen in what used to be Colleen's room stare at me, then at my legs, before returning to installing the custom-made shelves and desk. Mom is being paid to fundraise now and announced she deserved an office.

At the bottom of the stairs, West sets up my chair, and Ethan settles me in the seat. They gesture for me to follow and I do. Down the hall, through the kitchen, down the ramp, and I pause when they head to the unconnected garage. "I don't have time to go anyplace."

West walks backward. "Come on, slowpoke. You got wheels, use them."

"You're such an ass."

West smacks Ethan's arm. "She called me an ass."

"You are an ass." Ethan opens the garage door.

"Yeah, but *she* called me an ass."

I blink when I roll into the garage. There's a contraption with a plank of wood covered by a cushion. "What is that?"

"It's for you." West stands next to it and shoves his hands into his pockets with straight arms. "It'll help you navigate the car."

I raise a questioning eyebrow, and West holds out his arms. "Can I?"

I nod, and West lifts me from the chair and places me on the cushion. He motions to two cranks and begins to turn one. "This one moves you up."

Surprised by the momentum into the air, I flinch and grab

the sides. He continues to turn the crank until I'm level with the open hood of his SUV. "And this one will bring you closer."

The plank extends forward and for the first time in three months, I can touch the inside of a car. As if it's a dream, I sweep my fingers across the engine. Even from this position, I won't be able to do much, but it's better than doing nothing.

Feeling a little speechless, I pop open my mouth and say the mundane. "Thanks."

"West built it for you," says Ethan.

West sheepishly raises a shoulder. "Ethan helped. Besides, who else is going to change my oil?"

A wetness invades my eyes. I'm touched that they would invest time and energy into something for me...not just anything...they created something to help me return to what I love.

"Dad wants to get you a new car," says Ethan.

"I know." But that part is more complicated. I won't lie. It hurts that I won't be able to drive—for a very long time.

"All right," says West. "Wasn't joking on the oil change. Tell me what to do and me and Moron will do it."

An adrenaline rush tickles my bloodstream. "Get me that rolling board and help me down. I'm going under the car."

Gloriously covered in grease and oil, I sit on the top of West's contraption and hover over West as he tries to figure out the oil filter. "This isn't rocket science."

"Says the car genius," he mumbles.

A clearing of a throat grabs our attention and we all pause when we see Mom in the garage door frame.

West and Ethan share a guilty glance. "Mom," Ethan says. "We were just about to bring her back to the house."

"Will you boys give Rachel and me a second?"

West wiggles his grimy hands in front of my face and wipes one particularly greasy finger across my cheek. Ethan squeezes my wrist before he leaves. I readjust myself and lean over to inspect West's work. Not too bad.

"What are you working on?" Mom asks.

I shrug. "Nothing."

Mom's dressed in a pair of gray dress pants and a blue sweater. Dad took me to my appointments this morning while Mom visited Gavin in rehab. Because of the accident, my father's original plan for Gavin and rehab tanked. But a few weeks ago, Gavin finally entered treatment. "How's Gavin?"

"Good. He's worried about you." Mom peers into the hood. "Your father said your appointments went well."

"Yup." It feels odd being here with Mom after lying about my love of cars for so long.

Mom looks at me. She does this now—actually stares at me with her blue eyes and sees me. Not being used to it, I always glance away. Mom tucks a wayward strand of hair over my shoulder. "Gavin and I had a group-therapy appointment today. He promised to not keep secrets like his addiction from me anymore. I thought about it on the way home. I think I want a promise like that from all of you. Secrets have come too close to ruining this family."

I pick at my flaking thumbnail. "I'm sorry I didn't tell you about Gavin."

Mom shifts her weight. "I care that you didn't tell me about you."

Confrontation has never been a strong suit for either of us, and I wonder if the silence is killing her like it's killing me. "You didn't want to hear it. You wanted me to be Colleen."

"Rachel—"

Preferring not to hear her deny it, I stare straight into her eyes. "I spent a good portion of my life overhearing you tell people that you dreamed of me becoming like Colleen. It's true, so please don't pretend it isn't."

Mom touches her wedding ring and turns the band. "I wish I could tell you that you weren't the replacement, but we'd both know that would be a lie. Regardless of what you think, I have always loved you."

I fidget with the tools my brothers left on the board. Over the past three months, Mom and I have danced around this issue. "You loved her more."

"Not true," says Mom. "But I do miss her. Too much. I've thought about it and think there's some truth to what you said that night. I loved you, but I don't think I ever saw you. For that I'm sorry."

"It's okay." And it is.

"In my defense, you never gave me the chance to *know* you."

I open my mouth to protest, and she waves it away. "Rachel, the problem in this family is that no one gave me credit. Instead of changing to make me happy, do you ever wonder what would have happened if you had told me what I was missing?"

And I snap my mouth shut. Part of me thinks I could have screamed until I was blue in the face, but there's another part that wonders what would have happened if I had truly tried.

"So what's going on here?" Mom leans over the engine like it might bite her and I realize that *she's* trying.

"I was teaching West how to change his oil filter."

"Is it hard?"

"I could teach you."

Her mouth contorts. "How about you explain and I'll listen."

It's a start. "Deal."

Isaiah

THE FRONT DOOR OPENS, AND I come face-to-face with Rachel's father. Strands of gray highlight the area near his ears. He looks older than that night at the dragway, but in truth, I probably look older, too. Sleeping in hospital waiting room chairs does that to a person. He and I got to know each other real well during those periods that Rachel had surgery or slept.

Her father refused to leave her side when he wasn't at work. The same was said for me when I wasn't at work or at school. Turns out we have the same business hours.

"Come on in, Isaiah."

I step into the massive front hall and, like always, I'm still amazed that people live like this. "How's she doing?"

"Nervous," he says, and from the way he rubs his head I can tell he is, too. Rachel relearns how to walk today.

Mr. Young's eyes flicker to the spot a few centimeters below the tiger tattooed on my biceps. I carry a burn mark from when I saved him and his daughter three months before. If it weren't for the fact that the dragway required me to carry a fire extinguisher during a race, Rachel may have died. And me along with her—because I never would have left that car without her.

"I've discussed what you proposed with Rachel's mother, and we both agree it would be good for Rachel to get out. But we're going to start slow. An hour and a half."

An hour and a half—alone—with Rachel. I feel like a man stepping out into daylight after years of incarceration. "I swear I won't be a minute late."

Her father wears a knowing smile. "No, you won't be, or it'll be another few months before you step out of this house with her again." Mr. Young accepts me with the condition that I follow their rules. For Rachel, I'd shovel coal into the furnace in hell.

"Isaiah," her mom calls from the living room. "She won't start without you."

Her mother turned their massive once-formal living room into their personal rehab clinic. My heart stutters when I see Rachel perched in her wheelchair. Her golden hair is pulled back into a ponytail and she wears a T-shirt and a pair of shorts. Gone are the casts on her legs, and in their place are large, full-length, black braces.

Her face brightens when she sees me. "Isaiah!"

Every time I enter this house she has the same reaction. I don't know why. I've held her hand in the hospital, sat with her after the multiple surgeries and have supported her during every rehab session. I made a promise to Rachel, and I'm never breaking it.

As I walk over to her, her physical therapist, an ex-football player and one hell of a big son of a bitch, steps in front of me. "Naw, you don't get to be beside her today."

Big or not, I'll take on any asshole keeping her from me. "Want to rethink that?"

"Isaiah," Rachel says. "This is my decision."

"But you're learning to walk today," I say, as if she doesn't understand.

"I know." The casual way she replies causes my hands to twitch.

"But you could fall."

Rachel narrows her eyes. "I know, and *you* need to be okay with that."

I release a long stream of air. Right. It all goes back to the same conversation—I've got to let Rachel make her own way, even if it means watching her stumble.

"I need you here, son." Her therapist indicates for me to stand at the end of two wooden parallel bars. "Rachel, if you want to see your boy, then you're going to have to work for it."

Footsteps and rustling by the door catches my attention. One by one, except for Gavin, her brothers walk in, followed by her parents. Rachel doesn't look at them. Those gorgeous violet eyes stay on me. Without help, Rachel uses the bars to lift herself out of the chair.

At my end, I grip the bars in a mirroring position, as if I could send her my strength. It took her weeks to grow strong enough to stand. It'll take her weeks, if not longer, to walk again. Her physical therapist stays behind her in case she should lose her balance. "Okay, Rachel. You see what you want. Go get it."

The right side of Rachel's mouth tips up as a blush touches

her cheeks. My heart pounds as I pray she doesn't fall with her first try. I force a smile. "I'm waiting, angel."

Because she's always been a miracle, Rachel lifts her leg and takes her first step.

Rachel

WITH A HIP COCKED AGAINST the door frame of my bathroom, Abby watches as I wrap one last strand of my hair around the curling iron. She showed halfway through my therapy appointment. As always, she just walked in, not announcing herself to anyone, and stayed in the shadows until I saw her lurking.

It's weird, but it's Abby.

"I don't know why you're doing all this. You could show up in a garbage bag, and Isaiah would still think you're pretty."

I release the strand from the iron and a hot curl bounces on my neck. "It's our first official date. As in Dad knows and Mom knows and everyone's okay with it."

Pretty much okay with it. Mom and Dad are still a little hesitant about Isaiah, but they understand him better. He's been shockingly open with them about his past, his present and his intentions with me. While I was in the hospital, he told them everything about Eric and the debt.

I don't think what swayed them was his honesty as much as his devotion to me. Besides school and work, and he even skipped that some, Isaiah never left my side.

"Will your mom take pictures since it's your first official date even though they know you've stayed the night with him?"

I cringe. Isaiah was a little too honest with them. "Why?"

"Can I be in the pictures?"

"Sure." I move my wheelchair to the left so that I can get a better glimpse of myself in the full-length mirror behind me. *Mascara. I need mascara.* As if hearing my thoughts, Abby hands me the mascara from my cosmetic bag.

"Can we take one of just me and you?"

I meet Abby's eyes and she looks away. That was very un-Abby to do. "Yeah. I think I'd like that."

Abby glances over her shoulder into my room. "Ethan alert."

"Heard that, freak." Ethan leans past Abby to poke his head in to see me. "There's only so much small talk Tattoo Boy and I are capable of, so get moving."

I sigh as I finish stroking on the mascara. While West and Isaiah have come to a surprising compromise, Ethan's not entirely sold on my relationship with Isaiah. I have faith that will change with time.

Abby examines my brother in a very not-best-friend way. "Hello."

"Uh...hi." Ethan blinks as if he's a fish that just realized he was hooked on a line. "How are you?"

"Better now that you're here."

I stifle the giggle when Ethan's cheeks turn red. "Ah...Mom asked if you're staying for dinner."

"What are you having?"

"Steaks?"

"Count me in." Mom's oddly adopted Abby. No one's asked outright, but they all seem to understand that she's not private-school Abby, and while they observe her as if she's a science experiment about to explode, they generally seem to like her.

"I'm not going to be here," I remind her.

She flashes a smile that promises all sorts of trouble at my brother. "But Ethan will be."

Ethan clears his throat. "Seriously, are you done?"

"Yep," I say quickly to save him from Abby. My best friend loves to make guys squirm. God help any man that falls for her, because they're going to need all the help they can get to keep up with her.

"Then let's go." Ethan swings me up and carries me down to Isaiah.

IN THE BACKSEAT OF AN '89 Mustang I bought off of Craigslist for two hundred dollars, Rachel gasps for air, and my lips trail down her neck. We both breathe hard, and our hands are everywhere we can possibly touch. Her legs rest across the bench seat as I cradle her in my lap. We were given an hour and a half and we've spent forty minutes of it kissing.

"I'm supposed to be getting you food," I whisper in her ear.

Her hand squeezes my neck, bringing my lips to hers. "I can always eat."

For three months, I've dreamed of having her in my arms again. Rachel is the kind of girl that requires a wait, and she is definitely worth waiting for. My cell chimes, and Rachel moans as she snuggles her head in the crook of my neck. "It can't be time to go home yet."

"No, but it's getting close." Hand-holding and the occasional quick, chaste kiss is all I'm allowed to do under Rachel's family's ever-present gaze. Recently, we've been promoted to a hug. I hold her tighter, my hands sliding up and down her back. "I was thinking that we could buy some land and build our shop and home there. That way we're never apart."

"I like that," she says. "But don't you think business will be better in the city?"

I smile. "We'll be so good that people will flock to us just from our reputation."

Rachel kisses my jaw, sending shivers along my spine. She cuddles into me. "I love you."

My heartbeats become lighter and happier. She's alive and loves me. "I love you."

She sighs, showing some heaviness. "I miss driving."

"I know." I wish I could tell her when she'll be able to do it again. I sit up straighter as the thought washes over me. "Come on."

I gently help her back into the passenger side and jump into the driver's seat. I start the car, and we both cringe at the sorry state of the engine. I press the clutch, take her hand and place it on the stick shift. "I can't give you the complete feeling of being behind the wheel, but I can give you control. This car ain't moving without you."

That brilliant smile lights up her face. "How fast are you wanting to go?"

I shrug. "Your choice, but I don't have problems with speed."

Keeping our eyes locked on each other, Rachel shoves the car into First. I lift off the clutch as I step on the gas.

★ ★ ★ ★ ★

ACKNOWLEDGEMENTS

To God: 1 Corinthians 13: 11–13

For Dave—For all those nights you took me to the top of the hill and we watched the lights shining below and for letting me know at all times exactly where I belonged.

Especially for A, N and P—I hope the three of you always love each other as West, Ethan and Rachel did.

Thank you to…

Kevan Lyon—You always bring a sense of calm and a smile to my face. This journey would be impossible without you.

Margo Lipschultz—Thank you seems too small of a phrase for all the support, care and love that you show me and my characters. You continually go above and beyond what's called for and I want you to know that I appreciate everything you do. You are truly amazing, Margo.

Everyone who touched my books at Mira Ink, especially Natashya Wilson. I'm so honored to work with such amazing people who have the ability to make me smile!

Drew Tarr (Street & Strip Performance), Terry Huff (Ohio Valley Dragway), Tommy Blincoe, Jason "Jayrod" Clark, Frank "Frankie" Morris and Anthony "Red" Morris—I appreciate your taking the time to answer my questions while I was plotting this book and for helping a non-car-person understand not only cars, but drag racing.

Especially for the people I met at Ohio Valley: Your love for the sport, Ohio Valley Dragway and the people who race there was evident every time we talked. You can expect to see me in the stands.

A special thank-you to Jennifer L. Brown for being brave enough to teach me how to drive a stick shift and for allowing me to learn in her car!

Mike Ballard—Thank you for sharing your incredible wife with me every other Wednesday and for taking the time to introduce me to your friends at Ohio Valley.

Colette Ballard—For loving Noah, Ryan and Isaiah, and being that ear when I needed someone to listen, and for talking when I felt like being silent.

Angela Annalaro-Murphy—You have no idea how much I appreciate our friendship. Thanks for the years of laughter, tears, prayers and more laughter.

Kristen Simmons—Because you loved Isaiah and Rachel just as much as I did. Meeting you has been one of the best parts of this entire experience!

To my continued support system of my crit group/ Wednesday-night family—Kelly Creagh, Bethany Griffin, Kurt Hampe and Bill Wolfe—and the Louisville Romance Writers. Also, to Shannon Michael for the continued friendship and support. I love you guys!

Again, to my parents, my sister, my Mt. Washington family and my in-laws… I love you.

TAKE ME ON

Look for West's story,
coming soon from
Katie McGarry

Turn the page for an
exclusive two-chapter
sneak preview...

WEST

"JESUS FUCKING CHRIST!" I SLAM on the breaks and practically push the pedal through the floor as I will my SUV to stop. My tires squeal, my body whiplashes and the car jerks to a halt. The headlights spotlight a girl. Her arms protect her face, and I try to process that she's still standing.

Standing. As in not on the ground.

Not dead.

One thing went right today.

The relief flooding through my body is quickly chased by a strong helping of anger. She jumped out in front of me. Not taking one look. Jumped.

She lowers her arms, and I'm met by the sight of wide dark eyes. Her wild mane of light brown hair whips across her face as the wind picks up. She blinks and so do I.

She glances over her shoulder and I follow her line of sight into the shadows. Panic sweeps over her face and she stumbles, acting disoriented. Shit on it all damn day, what if I did hit her?

I throw the SUV in Park and, as I open the door, she points at me. "Watch it!"

Watch it? She's the one who stepped out in front of me then froze like a damn deer. I launch out of the car. "Sidewalks, chick. That's where you stop. Not in the middle of a street!"

With a shake of her head, she tosses her hair over her shoulder and actually steps into me. If it was anyone else, such a movement would send rage from the tip of my toes to my fists, but instead I smirk and cross my arms over my chest. She may be tall, but compared to me she's a tiny thing, and for the first time today, I find amusement. I've seen that type of fire burning in people's eyes a million times in my life. Just never from a girl, and never in eyes so hauntingly gorgeous.

"You were the one not paying attention!" the girl shouts. "And besides, this is a parking lot, you moron. Not a dragway. You were going, what? Fifty?"

The word *moron* slips underneath my skin and my muscles tighten. But she has me. I was speeding. "Are you hurt?" I ask.

"What?"

"Did my car hit you?"

The fire within her wavers, and she peers into the dark again. "No."

I follow her gaze. Two huddled forms skulk near the back of the building. I refocus on the walking, talking inferno in front of me and despite my Calc teacher's opinion of my intelligence, I'm able to do the math. "Is that trouble for you?"

Her eyes shoot to mine and in them is a blaring yes, but because girls make no sense she answers, "No."

A crackling sound draws my attention. The edges of a

small white paper bag poke from a plastic bag. It's a prescription. I give her the once-over then turn to the guys hiding by the building. Dammit. Even the book geeks at my school who've never seen the outside of their PlayStation basement shrines are aware of the urban legends surrounding this neighborhood. She can deny it all she wants, but she has problems. "Get in my car."

The fire returns. "Hell no." She inspects the bruises forming along my jawline then surveys my scraped and swollen knuckles.

"Look, it's me or them." I motion toward the thugs with my chin. "And I'm telling you, I'm not the bad guy in this scenario."

She laughs. And if it wasn't such a beautiful sound, I'd be insulted.

"Because a guy driving an Escalade in this neighborhood is the equivalent of a Boy Scout."

The right side of my mouth tips up. Did she call me a drug dealer?

"From the looks of you—" She glances at my knuckles again. "Well, let's just say you must have your own baggage, and I'm not a baggage claim type of girl."

"No, you're the type who runs into traffic."

She smiles and I like it. The anger that raced through me moments before vanishes. I rub my jaw then lean my hand against my open car door. Long light brown hair with waves, dark eyes that sure as hell suck me in as they sparkle, a tight body and a kick-ass attitude. Truth be told, I like more than her smile. Too bad I almost killed her by running her over. It'll make asking her out awkward.

"Get into my car and I'll drive you home." I hold up both my palms. "I swear. No drive-by's on the way."

The smile fades when I say the word *home*, and her eyes lose the sparkle. Something deep within me hollows out.

She slides close, very close—as in her clothes brush mine. She angles herself so that she's between me and my car door. The heat of her body rolls onto me, and my fingers itch to touch. I suck in air, and I'm overwhelmed by the sweet scent of wildflowers.

She lifts her face to look at me and whispers, "Getting into that car with you is as big a risk as walking down that viaduct. If you're bent on helping me, do me a favor."

"What?" I breathe out.

"Stand here and act like you're talking to me. Convincingly enough that it'll buy me time."

And before I can process a word, she cuts past me, crouches against the Escalade, ducks behind the vehicle and escapes into the night. "Hey!"

The shadows emerge from behind the building. Two guys bolt into the beams of my headlights and in the direction of the neighborhood. Their feet pound the concrete.

In the distance, instead of two dark forms running into the night, there are three and the first one doesn't have a decent head start. I jump into my Escalade and tear off after them.

Haley

MY LUNGS BURN AND MY arms and legs pump quickly. The graffiti on the concrete walls of the freeway viaduct blend into a colored blur. I'm out of shape. Six months ago, I could have outrun them, but not now. Not today. My feet smack against the blacktop and the sound echoes in the tunnel. The stench of mold and decay fills my nose.

There's a splash as someone stomps into a puddle, followed by the sound of more shoes against the street. My breath comes out in gasps, and I will my muscles to move faster.

Heat rises off my body and into the cold night and my nose begins to run. I don't want them to hurt me, and the thought of a man's hand colliding with my body causes my heart to clench. My fist tightens around Dad's medication. I don't want to lose it. The answer is to be faster but, if they catch me, I'll be left with no other choice than to fight.

Their footsteps ring closer in my ears, and my old training floods into my brain. I need to turn, face them and form a defensive stance. I can't be dragged to the ground by my hair.

Lights from behind create a beacon of hope. My pursuers' footfalls continue in their hunt, but fall off near the walls of the tunnel, out of sight of the approaching car. I put on a burst of speed. Two more blocks and I'll be inside. Safe from this.

Brakes squeal and a door snaps open. Voices. Shouting. The sound of a fist smacking into flesh. Continuing, I peek over my shoulder and air slams out of me when I notice the Escalade.

No.

Please, God, no.

My body rocks forward as my feet become concrete. It's the guy from the shopping plaza. He's fighting them. Three shadows spar against the headlights; a hellish dogfight of arms, fists, legs, grunts and growls. They're all the same height, but I know which one's him. He's thicker. More muscular. He's a scrapper, but he's going to lose.

Two against one.

My chest rises and falls, and I glance down the street, toward my uncle's house, toward relative safety. I'm minutes away from curfew, I've got my father's prescription in my grasp, but leaving a guy behind—it's not how I was raised.

Knowing this has the potential to end extremely badly for me, I switch directions to join the fight.

PLAYLIST

Songs for Theme:
"If I Die Young" by The Band Perry
"Lighters" by Bad Meets Evil featuring Bruno Mars
"Barefoot Blue Jean Night" by Jake Owen
"Kryptonite" by 3 Doors Down

Isaiah:
"Beverly Hills" by Weezer
"Speed" by Montgomery Gentry
"Shimmer" by Fuel
"Santa Monica" by Everclear

Rachel:
"Mean" by Taylor Swift
"Little Miss" by Sugarland
"Fallen Angel" by Poison

Songs for specific scenes:
The first time Rachel sees Isaiah: "Animal" by Def Leppard
When Isaiah decides he likes Rachel in the bar/apartment:
"Possum Kingdom" by Toadies

Isaiah and Rachel's first kiss: "Just a Kiss" by Lady Antebellum
Isaiah's New Year's Eve: "You and Tequila" by Kenny Chesney featuring Grace Potter

Songs that represent Isaiah and Rachel's future:
"Ours" by Taylor Swift
"Fast Cars and Freedom" by Rascal Flatts

Q&A with Katie McGarry

Q: What type of research did you have to do to write *Crash Into You*?

A: When it became clear that Isaiah was going to have his own book, I slightly panicked. I didn't know anything about cars, and Isaiah was in love with them. Then when I realized that Isaiah was going to be involved in drag racing, I practically hyperventilated.

Thankfully I came across several people who were gracious enough to talk to me about cars and drag racing. Finding Ohio Valley Dragway, a legal dragway in the southwestern part of the county I live in, was amazing. There I met fabulous people who showed me their passion for cars and drag racing.

The best part? After signing my life away, I got to be a passenger of a car at a legal dragway that went 96.97 mph and did an eighth of a mile in 6.94 seconds. Of course, I did this with a helmet on my head and a fire suit, while strapped in by a five-point harness. This was a special onetime experience with professionals. In other words, don't try this at home.

Q: One of Isaiah's most pressing concerns in the story is figuring out how to support himself, because when he turns eighteen he won't be able to continue living with his foster parents. Is aging out of the foster care system something teens actually face?

A: Absolutely. One of my goals in writing *Crash Into You* was to bring attention to this very real issue. One night while I was writing Isaiah and Rachel, this story came on my local news. If you'd like additional information, please visit this link: www.wave3.com/story/16975220/18-and-out-of-foster-care

Q: Part of Rachel's narrative arc is learning how to face and no longer hide her panic attacks and their debilitating aftermath. You wrote about her symptoms and emotions in great detail. Have you ever had a panic attack?

A: Yes. I've had a few in my life and they were terrifying. Anyone who has read any of my books can tell that I am a huge advocate of therapy. Rachel suffers from extreme panic attacks, and I'm glad that by the end of the story, she stops worrying about what everyone around her thinks and begins to take care of herself.

Q: *Crash Into You* just might have more teen boy characters than anything you've written before! How did you keep the boys' personalities distinct as you wrote?

A: Noah, Isaiah, Ryan, Chris, Logan, West, Ethan...oh, my, that's enough to make a girl faint, isn't it? Gavin and Jack aren't technically teenagers, but they're close enough that they'd undoubtedly make any female friend of Rachel's swoon. Lord knows I'm fanning myself.

It was easy for me to keep these characters distinct because I think of them as very different people. I'm happy to share this cheat sheet that, until now, I kept locked away in my head:

Noah—the bad boy in a black leather jacket with a big heart reserved for his younger brothers and for Echo, the girl he loves.

Isaiah—tattooed, pierced, someone the world is terrified of, but who's so loyal that he would die to protect the people he loves.

Ryan—a star athlete with the heart of a poet and the ability to love people for who they are, not what others see.

Chris—a generational farm boy, with a knack for playing baseball, who fell in love with his best friend at an early age.

And then there are my bachelors:

Logan—the boy genius who loves to live life on the edge.

Ethan—devoted brother and friend. Has a habit of putting everyone else first and himself last.

West—with his signature backward baseball cap, West is the ultimate big brother and ultimate player of the field.

They say be a good girl, get good grades, be popular. They know nothing about me

I can't remember the night that changed my life. The night I went from the top of the pyramid to loner freak.

They said therapy was supposed to help.

They didn't expect Noah.

Noah is the dangerous boy my parents warned me about.

Every kiss, every promise, every touch is forbidden.

But he's the only one who'll help me find the truth.

'I dare you...'

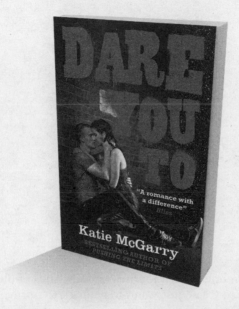

Beth's the bad girl that no one wanted, not even her parents.

Ryan's the high-school hero that everyone wants a piece of—even if no one knows the real him.

Their paths should never have crossed—now they're each other's only lifeline.

www.mirainkco.uk

M326_DYT

IN THE REAL WORLD, WHEN YOU VANISH INTO THIN AIR FOR A WEEK, PEOPLE TEND TO NOTICE

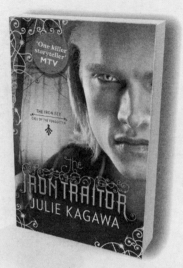

After his unexpected journey into the lands of the fey, Ethan Chase just wants to get back to normal. Well, as 'normal' as you can be when you see faeries every day of your life. Suddenly the former loner with the bad reputation has someone to try for—his girlfriend, Kenzie. Never mind that he's forbidden to see her again.

But when your name is Ethan Chase and your sister is one of the most powerful faeries in the Nevernever, 'normal' simply isn't to be.

www.miraink.co.uk

Chelsea Knot can't keep a secret...until now

The last secret Chelsea told nearly got someone killed—and made her a social outcast. So Chelsea takes a vow of silence. If she keeps her mouth shut, at least things can't get any worse, right?

Her parents don't understand and the rest of the school is punishing her. But Chelsea's finding friends in unexpected places, Sam Weston, in particular.

And for the first time, Chelsea is discovering who she really is...and who she wants to be.

www.miraink.co.uk

'I've left some clues for you. If you want them, turn the page. If you don't, put the book back on the shelf, please.'

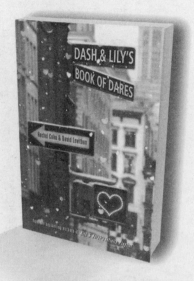

Lily has left a red notebook full of challenges on a favourite bookstore shelf, waiting for just the right guy to come along and accept its dares. But is Dash that right guy? Or are Dash and Lily only destined to trade dares, dreams, and desires in the notebook they pass back and forth at locations across New York? Could their in-person selves possibly connect as well as their notebook versions? Or will they be a comic mismatch of disastrous proportions?

www.miraink.co.uk

Rose Zarelli, self-proclaimed word geek and angry girl, has some CONFESSIONS to make...

No.1: I'm livid all the time. Why? My dad died. My mum barely talks. My brother abandoned us.

No.2: I make people furious regularly. Want an example? I kissed gorgeous Jamie Forta, boyfriend of the coolest cheerleader in the school. Now she's out for blood. Mine.

No.3: But, most of all, high school might as well be Mars. My best friend has been replaced by an alien...and now it's a case of survival of the coolest.

www.miraink.co.uk

Read Me. Love Me. Share Me.

Did you love this book? Want to read other amazing teen books for free online and have your voice heard as a reviewer, trend-spotter and all-round expert?

Then join us at **facebook.com/MIRAink** and chat with authors, watch trailers, WIN books, share reviews and help us to create the kind of books that you'll want to carry on reading forever!

Romance. Horror. Paranormal. Dystopia. Fantasy.

Whatever you're in the mood for, we've got it covered.

Don't miss a single word

 twitter.com/MIRAink

let's be friends

 facebook.com/MIRAink

Scan me with your smart phone

 to go straight to our facebook page